JUMPING IN COWPATS

By Chris Bicheno

Visit us online at www.authorsonline.co.uk

An AuthorsOnLine Book

Copyright © 2003 Authors OnLine Ltd
Text Copyright © 2003 Chris Bicheno
Cover photograph © 2003 Chris Bicheno

The moral right of the author has been asserted

All rights reserved. No part of this publication may be reproduced, stored in a retrieval system, or transmitted in any form or by any means, electronic, mechanical, photocopy, recording or otherwise, without prior written permission of the copyright owner. Nor can it be circulated in any form of binding or cover other than that in which it is published and without similar condition including this condition being imposed on a subsequent purchaser

Paperback ISBN 0-7552-0097-7

Authors OnLine Ltd
40 Castle Street
Hertford SG14 1HR
England

This book is also available in e-book format from
www.authorsonline.co.uk

Dedication

This book is dedicated to my wife Madge and our children Stephen, Emma, Richard, Michael, Alan and Marie, together with the grandchildren, and not forgetting the dogs Monty, Tasha and Daisy, without all of whom it would be largely full of blank pages.

Acknowledgements

I would like to express my sincere thanks and gratitude to the following:

My wife Madge for putting up with me while I laboured over this book.

Madge again and her friends Josephine and Jennifer for leading the lives they do, thereby giving me so much humorous material.

My father Percy and his brothers Jim, Bill, Ron, sister Brenda and cousin Bill, and my sister Margaret, for all the family history and photographs they provided me with.

Jean Nelson and Eileen Webster, for their kind permission to use information and photographs from their 'Bicheno' book, regarding my ancestors.

CONTENTS

		Page
Introduction		ix
Chapter 1:	The Origins of Prejudice	1
Chapter 2:	Chris's Family Background	4
	2.1 Ancestors	4
	2.2 Recent Family	14
	2.3 Chris and his upbringing	45
Chapter 3:	Meeting up	57
Chapter 4:	Starting Out Together	66
Chapter 5:	Madge's Family Background	83
	5.1 Ancestors	83
	5.2 Recent Family	93
	5.3 Madge and her upbringing	105
	5.4 Madge Quiz	112
Picture Gallery – 1		117
Chapter 6:	Our Life Together	133
Chapter 7:	Careers	173
	7.1 Chris's Career	173
	7.2 Madge's Career	208
Picture Gallery – 2		216
Chapter 8:	Offspring	232
	8.1 The Children	234
	8.2 The Grandchildren	249
Chapter 9:	Pets	256
Chapter 10:	Dogs	269
	10.1 Monty, Tasha and Daisy	269
	10.2 A Day in the Life	298
	10.3 Looking after Dogs	304
	10.4 Mixed Dog Breed Quiz	312
	10.5 Canine Conclusions	313
Chapter 11:	Vehicles	316
	11.1 Motorcycles and Scooters	317
	11.2 Cars	323
	11.3 Caravans	337
Epilogue		345
Timeline		346
Index		349

Introduction

So how did this book ever come to be? Well, my wife Madge had been urging me to help her discover information about her ancestors. Her mum and dad had said little to her or her brothers about them, other than to fend off any enquiries. Then, with the passing of both of her parents, she became intensely curious to learn about her family roots.

After perusing library records and census surveys, I eventually sat in a chair with a piece of paper in each hand. In my left was a copy of the birth certificate for Frederick Arthur Lenton, my wife's grandfather. In my right hand was a copy of his death certificate. I gazed from one document to the other. A whole lifetime was sandwiched between the two but we knew scarcely anything at all about him.

If he was anything like the rest of us, his life would have been crammed with memories of ecstatic highs and desperate lows; of children and laughter; of problems and tears. And judging by what was listed under 'cause of death' perhaps a few closet skeletons. Now he was just a name with a few entries on a couple of pieces of paper. Nothing existed to explain the real person or the life he led.

His immediate family would have known about him, of course, but now they were also gone and left no record behind. Even the few photographs that had existed had been destroyed along the way as time had crunched inexorably onwards. Now my wife, his descendant, his blood, his genes, was trying in vain to find out about him. If only he had passed some messages across the years. If only he had written down his experiences.

You can see what's coming. I didn't want to end up like that. I didn't want to be a few brief lines on a couple of pieces of paper so my descendants might ask in vain. 'Who was this chap?' and 'What's his story then?' There and then I resolved to provide the answers up front by writing a book. Hopefully not to create more questions than answers but to tell a tale of how it really was or at least how things appeared, as I perceived them to be.

I had for some time before the above defining moment contemplated putting pen to paper. My original intention had been to write a book about our dogs and how my initial prejudices against the species were overcome by their unconditional affection and personalities. However, this now changed as I recognised the need to put that story into the wider context of our whole family and their lives together. To develop it into the tale of the family itself (including the canine members) and the key events and incidents occurring over the years.

The sad passing of relatives also made me acutely aware the knowledge they possessed, regarding their life and times, was also being lost. Although I couldn't take on the huge task of writing a set of family biographies, I resolved to include anything from a few sentences to several pages about each one I had the opportunity of talking to. Just to draw some comparisons between their lives and with my own upbringing and also that of my children.

So now the book encompasses the background and story of how we ('we' being my wife, family and I) came to be and lived our lives. All this intertwined with the stresses and disharmonious interactions of a home full of humans (2 parents and 6 children) and a menagerie of lesser(?) species, struggling to put up with each other in and around the city of Portsmouth on the south coast of England.

Unfortunately, this book can only reflect our lives up to the time of writing. As such it can never be complete, as every event occurring afterwards will be missing. Therefore I apologise to the children, wives, husbands, friends and relatives who are yet to come, or are around now and who I have somehow omitted or dealt with in an incomplete manner. Perhaps one of them will take up the baton from me and produce another volume describing their own life and times?

I've tried to make the story of my family light hearted where I could. Putting the 'fun' into 'dysfunctional' you might say. I have selected anecdotes that were either humorous or dramatic to add a little spice.

You may also wonder about the presentation style of the book. Some say books these days don't have numbered subsections or are organised in this particular way, unless they are school textbooks or extreme flights of fancy. Well I'm afraid, as a trained computer person, my brain only works in a highly methodical way. I am only able to put words together if it's in an organised manner. If I didn't put numbered sections in and set it out this way, then this book would be just incoherent ramblings, instead of structured incoherent ramblings.

The style also changes from being factual and formal in places and downright frivolous in others, to give an overall 'pot-pourri' of selected individuals, their life and times. Certain Chapters when looked at side by side just don't belong together in the same book from the style viewpoint. However the big advantage of writing just for oneself and a family audience, with no pretensions as to the work becoming a best seller or the basis of a film script, is you can do just about anything you want to and that's exactly what I have done and I make no apology for it.

Just one more thing. Madge's dyslexia, that leads to her tendency to get mixed up between left and right and getting other things similarly confused, simply adds to the general impression of 'dottiness' she gives out and makes her personality appealing; thus inspiring my protective instincts towards her. It is therefore with nothing short of the deepest love and affection I make the overtly rude comments about her I do in several (oh alright, lots of) places in this book.

So, warts and all, here is my poor but well-intentioned effort to describe my life and those most closely connected with it. Please read on ....

Chapter 1

The Origins of Prejudice

The earliest recollection I have stored away, from sometime around the age of 5, was when my family was on holiday and visiting relatives near the town of Adrigole in Ireland. I was smartly dressed in blue trousers and a pristine white shirt and was standing on a low, stone wall. The wall surrounded a field populated by a herd of cows which, it seemed, had particularly loose bowels.

The other children around me were playing games, running about and having a long jump competition. I decided to have a go myself and scrambled onto the top of the wall in order to maximise the distance and impact of my effort. Due to miscalculation, or an overestimation of my prowess as a new Jesse Owens, my miniscule leap ended slap bang in the centre of a large, deep and very fresh cowpat.

The resultant furore among those present has stuck in my mind, although unhappily that was not the only thing sticking to me. I was covered from head to toe with something that doesn't bear thinking about. My ex-smart short trousers and shirt had borne the brunt, although every part of my exposed limbs got a jolly good coating of 'do-do.'

Immediately after the event my mother whipped all of my clothing off and scraped away the worst of the foul smelling deposit. The clothes were written off. I was then re-dressed in a minimal collection of articles borrowed from my elder sister and my parents. I must have looked like someone who had fallen victim to an alien's ray gun and been shrunk down while their clothing remained at the original size.

An hour or so later, upon our return to our lodgings, I recall being the object of a great deal of scrubbing by my mother, as I stood upright in a small tin bath and I learned a few new words from her accompanying commentary as she chipped away at the rapidly drying deposit.

Retrospectively, the incident set the tone for my entire life to come; when I have often seemed to be in the s**t, only the depth of the stuff and number of people trying to push me further into it has varied from time to time.

The experience of jumping into the cowpat has affected my outlook and led me always to expect the worst to happen. Although she didn't experience a similar encounter with a cowpat, my wife also has the same jaundiced view of life, always expecting things to go wrong. It's an extension to Murphy's Law. 'If anything can go wrong then it will … especially if your name is Bicheno.'

As such, we've both been jumping in cowpats metaphorically all of our lives, both as individuals and together as a couple, thus we have become just a teeny bit prejudiced against life in general. If the reader has the patience, then this book will go on to illustrate and justify this assertion.

*   *   *

The second oldest recollection I have is that I did not like dogs. My elder sister Margaret had been bitten on the lip by one when she was a small girl and thereafter, in my mind, all dogs were labelled as dangerous and to be avoided. This feeling was reinforced during my formative years by the occasional visit to friends or relatives' houses where dogs lived and the response to my knocking on the front door was a tempest of barking.

'It's all right, he doesn't bite' was scarcely an assurance from the human members of the dog's own pack, as a growling mass of fur and muscle threatened.

'He might not be inclined to have a go at you chum' I would think 'but I'm a stranger as far as he's concerned.' In other words 'fair game.' Friendships seemed to wither under this sort of pressure but relatives stayed the course. Blood is thicker than water, but I didn't want it to be my blood, even if it was their carpet it would stain.

Sometimes people would considerately shut the dog up in a back room but it seemed to merely be delaying the inevitable. Judging by the level of barking and thudding noise of the dog hurling itself against the door and working itself into a frenzy, it appeared to be only a matter of time before the monster broke free and fastened its jaws around my jugular. As a visiting child to a 'dog house' I perpetually lived in fear of someone either accidentally, or deliberately, opening the door, thus releasing the savage beast to put an end to my misery.

Such feelings lasted for years and although the physical threat receded as I grew up through adolescence to full adulthood, it never fully disappeared. I just couldn't relax in the presence of a canine.

Instead of the physical danger a different kind of threat manifested itself to fill the fear gap. This is best explained by describing an incident when I'd been invited to tea with people who I did not know particularly well and with whom I wanted to create a good impression.

I was sitting in a chair and been given a cup of tea in one hand and a plate of sandwiches and cake in the other. The arms of the chair were not well disposed to acting as mini tables so I was wrestling with the conundrum of how I could eat and/or drink without either emptying something onto their expensive looking carpet or doing a balancing act good enough to qualify for a circus performance. With both hands full and no way to release their contents, I was effectively paralysed.

At this point a dog entered the room. It was of medium size and of a breed I could not easily distinguish (not that I had made a study of dog breeds). They all seemed to consist of smelly coats and big teeth. It made a beeline for me. 'It's OK she's not at all aggressive' came the usual assurance. This time they seemed to be right as the dog made no threatening move.

However, after pausing for a moment, it moved forward and pushed it's muzzle deep into my crotch. And stayed there. Without hands and being unable to move for fear of spillages I just had to squirm, smile and vocally dissuade the dog without upsetting the owner, worse still upsetting the dog (who had already started making a throaty growl) or giving the impression I was actually enjoying this encounter.

We remained like that for what must have been a couple of minutes but for me, felt like an eternity. Trying to make polite and amusing conversation with a relaxed smile on your face, while a deep, threatening, rumbling sound is coming from your groin would tax the wit of Oscar Wilde. I made a mental note to look out my cricket box should I ever visit the same people again.

For the record, the owner eventually seemed to realise my predicament and called the dog away. Judging by his grin I think he delayed his intervention to enjoy my discomfort and embarrassment. I learned, for a variety of reasons, I certainly could not be at ease with a dog about and I wasn't too sure about some humans either.

So, having started to establish I am a bigot in certain key respects (reinforced later in the book when I get onto the subject of women drivers), I would now like to explore if I got this tendency genetically. We need to go through the mists of time to trace my family back as far as I am able and look at the type of people and individuals that have made my double helix (i.e. DNA) what it is.

Chapter 2

Chris's Family Background

2.1. Ancestors

It is said we are the product of our roots. Mind you, it's also said a dog is a man's best friend and I had already built a strong case against that particular saying. However, with the unusual surname of 'Bicheno', I thought it worth recording here the directly relevant family history in case some future Bicheno thinks, just as I had deluded myself over the years, we are descended from an Italian nobleman of blue blood.

Sorry to disillusion you my friend. Having said that, I could mention here I am, in fact, 'Count Christopher Bicheno' and not just plain Mr Christopher Bicheno but to understand that you'll have to dig much further into this book.

The family roots have been traced in considerable detail to around 1520, to a village named 'Over' near Cambridge. Incidentally 'Over' means 'on the banks of a river,' which in this instance is the river Ouse. There are spasmodic references to similar names before that date, back as far as the 13th century but with no proven, contiguous line to the present day.

Jean Nelson and Eileen Webster, both Bicheno's by birth, researched the family history extensively and produced 3 informal binders of historical information and a composite book, copies of which several family members, including myself, have in their possession. I have used these booklets as a key source in tracing my own personal line.

The spelling of the surname was a bit variable in the sixteenth century but 'Beechenow' was a fairly typical example. In those days surnames meant something, often representing the person's characteristics, lineage or trade. Such as 'Strong,' 'Johnson' or 'Smith.'

Nowadays, new surnames might be 'Anorexic,' 'Bastard' or 'Unemployed.' (Knowing my luck there's probably a firm of solicitors out there called Messrs Anorexic, Bastard and Unemployed who will write to me about this).

The meaning of Beechenow was 'beech tree on a bend of a river.' What happened up or under said beech tree is anybody's guess and speculation on it could possibly be the basis of a family party game at Christmas (adults only for the more inventive suggestions).

Alternative spellings were several, including Beecheno, Bechinoe, Bricheno and Brichener. According to a book by Harry Long published in 1883 entitled 'Personal and Family Names,' the origin of the name is 'Byccenho or Birchenhoe and means a haugh (alluvial land by a river) of beech trees.' Boring, I prefer the party game. Mind you the term 'alluvial' means things deposited there by a flowing river, so I expect a few cowpats are included.

The very earliest mention of the name is in 1220 (as Birchenhoe) regarding property in the Royal Forest of Whittlewood, Northamptonshire. It was a medieval hunting forest. Today, the forest consists of a core of ancient woodlands and stone built villages to the west of Silverstone and scattered remnants across to Milton Keynes. Both Birchenhoe and Byccenho are referenced in the Northamptonshire place name volume as a name in Syresham parish, which was close to Biddlesden Abbey. As a timeline, 1220 is around the time of Genghis Khan and Francis of Assisi. (You won't find many books with those two names mentioned in the same sentence).

Moving forward, there is a William Byrchenor who died in 1558 in the village of Over who is definitely related and William Brichener who died in 1601 and left land to a relative whose name was spelled 'Bricheno.' There are plenty of other references in the second half of the 16th century but little of the modern spelling or incontrovertible facts that can show a guaranteed contiguous lineage for our part of the Bicheno family between this and the earlier period.

In those days there was a tendency for people to spell their surnames in more than one way and the earliest reference to someone having a version spelt 'Bicheno' was Richard Brichener (also spelled 'Bicheno') who was born around 1550 and died in 1605 (see below).

The modern spelling firmed up over time onto 'Bicheno,' that was somewhat unusual and Italian sounding. So now it terms of identifying my ancestors, let's start getting a bit more specific.

*   *   *

Let me first make a few comments regarding the social conditions existing prior to the 20th century. Families tended to be numerically large, partially because 'family planning' methods were very limited but also as mortality rates were high, especially among babies and young children, and it was very important for a man to leave an heir. A further consideration was that a woman was needed to look after these large families and should a mother die prematurely, for whatever reason, there was pressure on the widower to re-marry quickly to secure his children's well-being.

The keeping of parish records was first ordered by Henry VIII in 1538 but not enforced until the reign of Elizabeth I. We can however trace our branch of the family back with a high degree of confidence to John Brichener (also called Byccenho and Brychener) who was one of two brothers (the other being William). John was a yeoman (i.e. a farmer) and born around 1525 and there is a record of his death on 23rd May 1587. He was buried in Over churchyard.

To put the earliest date of 1525 in perspective, it's just before King Henry VIII started lopping off his wives heads and about the time when an Italian explorer Giovanni da Verrazzano landed in the new world and found a nice little spot which he described as 'a very pleasant little place situated among hills and with a stream of water running to the sea.' This pleasant little area eventually became New York City. I believe it's not quite as tranquil these days.

John had been a landowner and he left his estate to his son Richard Brichener who was also known as Bichenoe and for the first time 'Bicheno'. Although we know of his father, Richard is the first official 'Bicheno' by name and all those of our surname we know of can be traced back to him and his family. Richard appears to have been born around 1550 and there is a record of him being named 'Brichener alias Bicheno' in the Over parish paper of 1602. He was one of a number of people that took part in a religious 'perambulation'. (Apparently the walk was inspired by a drought that had left land exposed and accessible to walk over, that was not normally accessible).

Richard was married to lady called Ann about 1573 and had 2 daughters, followed by 4 sons, (William, Robert, Edward and John) then 2 more daughters. Our interest lies with third son Edward who was born about 1582.

Edward was left land by his grandfather John but it was administered by his father Richard until his death in 1605. This would have been shortly after the English and Scottish thrones were united and the year when Shakespeare put his play Macbeth on at The Globe for the first time. We know Edward moved from Over to Cambridge prior to 1616 and was married but have no record of his wife's name. We only know of 2 children from the marriage, John born in 1596 and Edward who was born on 4th June 1616. Edward (the father) died in May 1631.

The son Edward (also known as Edmond) became a bookseller / stationer and also proved to be a bit of a rabbit. He was actually married 3 times. To Edith Baynes in 1641 and then, when Edith died following childbirth in 1648, only 4 months later to Dorothy Blackley (the daughter of a mayor of Cambridge) and on her death to Elizabeth Tilman in 1656.

There were 4 children from the first marriage, 3 from the second and 9 from the third. Edward finally died in 1689 at the age of 73, presumably through exhaustion. Our line continues via his second marriage (to Dorothy Blackley) and their first child James, born in 1650. This was about the year tea is believed to have been drunk in England for the first time (initially only by the royalty and aristocracy as it was very expensive then) and also when the first coffee house opened, in Oxford, by a Turkish Jew named Jacob. Note that a 'coffee house' in those days was more like a 'Gentlemen's Club' today, being a 'men only' establishment serving a wide variety of beverages and alcohol.

James was initially a printer by trade, later becoming a farmer. He married twice, the first time to Elinor Flower in Bottisham, a town east of Cambridge, in 1673. After 1693 James returned with his family to Over, where his wife died in 1703. He was then married for a second time to Elizabeth Hanley in Over on 21st August 1704. However we are mainly interested in his first marriage, resulting in a son also named James, who was born on 23rd November 1693, which is around the time the Bank of England was formed.

James, the father, was fairly well heeled and eventually bequeathed quite a bit of land around Over, in addition to money, in his will. It may have been the fact James the son inherited a substantial legacy helped him attract a wife and he was married in 1717 to Sarah Wilkinson (also spelled Wilceson). Ironically, both James the father and James the son died in the same year of 1725. By then, the younger James had fathered

3 children; Elizabeth, Ann and William. The last named providing us with the way forward.

*   *   *

If you're not already giddy then reach for the paracetamol and join me as we now progress through time, continuing from William and leading up to the present day.

So the line continues through James and Sarah's third child, called William (1723-1806). William moved to Haddenham (a town geographically about 10 miles to the north-east of Over, near to Ely) and by 1744 had served his apprenticeship and become a 'Glover'. The first in what appears to have been a significant association of the family with this trade. He had 14 children, 8 of whom were from his first marriage in 1746 to Elizabeth.

He returned his family to Over about 1750 where his wife died in 1761. Not hanging about, William married Sarah Adams (so we **do** have an 'Adam's family' connection!) on the 8th July 1762. Sarah bore him 6 more children, the last of whom was named Joseph and it was he who was destined to carry our line forward.

By 1779 the family had a workshop in Over in what was originally called 'Meeting House Lane' but became known as Glover Street. Incidentally, this was the year Captain Cook (the discoverer of Australia and New Zealand) died. William himself finally passed away in 1806 and was buried with his first wife. Despite the attendant pressures and hardships of raising two large families William had lived to a ripe old age.

As a child he would have learned of the exploits and hanging of the highwayman Dick Turpin; his adult years would have seen both the massive series of wars between Britain and France which effectively made North America an English speaking continent and also the upheavals of the Industrial Revolution; while his twilight years saw Napoleon Bonaparte sweep across Europe.

William's second wife Sarah, despite bringing up a very large family in arduous conditions, lived to the age of 89. She must have been a person of some significance because she had an obituary notice published in the Cambridge Chronicle on 15th October 1830.

*   *   *

Before we carry on the main line that is through William and Sarah's last child, Joseph, it's worth taking a step back and mentioning the second child of William and his first wife, Elizabeth, who was James (1752-1831) and led quite an eventful life and also his son James Ebenezer who is probably the most famous 'Bicheno' of all.

William and Elizabeth's son James initially worked in the Glover's workshop in Over and was baptised into the church at the age of 16, only to be thrown out the next year, reportedly because of a 'fling' with a young woman. He went to London where he met the infamous Mr Crispe who actually features in the Goldsmith book 'The Vicar of Wakefield.'

In 1772 James was deceived into making a trip to America, where upon his arrival in Virginia he was promptly taken into slavery and sold to a Colonel who happened to be a member of the State Council. (So it appears slaves were not just of a coloured persuasion but anyone who was 'different' to the residents and could not effectively defend himself).

However, because of his education, James was soon employed as the family tutor and he was eventually bought out of slavery and returned to England in 1774, just before the American War of Independence broke out. He seemed to attract adversity and in 1778 was shipwrecked off the Isle-of-Wight.

Then, he was not only reconciled with the church but actually became a vicar in 1780. Based in Newbury he wrote a number of historical and religious works and for that writing was given a Master's degree from Brown University in America in 1796.

During this time James married Ann Hazell in 1783 and their first child was James Ebenezer Bicheno (1785-1851) of whom more below. There are old letters in my branch of the family that claim that a Rev James Bicheno from Newbury, while taking an evening stroll, was cordially invited to join the Royal Navy in the post of Ship's Chaplain by a press gang and woke up on board a fighting ship. It is further claimed that he saw action at the Battle of Trafalgar in 1805 before finally returning home. This however does not tie in with the evidence provided by Jean Nelson and Eileen Webster's family research, placing James in the Newbury parish continuously from 1780 to 1807. Pity, it's a good story.

It was the son mentioned above, James Ebenezer, who was a member of several august bodies and wrote a number of books around the subjects of economics, botany and natural history. Some of his work can today be found in Swansea Museum. He joined the Baptist Church as a minister in 1814 and was married to Elizabeth Lloyd in 1821 but the poor girl died in childbirth within a year.

James Ebenezer was a partner in a Glamorgan Ironworks from 1832 to 1842. He was then appointed Colonial Secretary of Van Diemen's Land (now known as Tasmania) in 1842. (For those who haven't heard of Tasmania, it's not an Eastern European country; Tasmania is to Australia as the Isle of Wight is to Britain, but heavily scaled up in size. Although I'm not quite sure what that makes the IOW equivalent of the aborigines).

He was extremely popular within the island and famous for his enormous girth. James Ebenezer was president of the committee that arranged the very first public exhibition of paintings in Australia in 1844. He died in his home in Davey Street, Hobart on 25th February 1851 and his grave can be found beneath a memorial and crest in the grounds of Parliament House, Hobart. He bequeathed his extensive collection of some 2,500 books to the Tasmanian Public Library.

In his memory and for his work on ornithology an Australian species of Finch was named after him. Also the whaling village of 'Waubs Boat Harbour' in Tasmania had its name changed to 'Bicheno' and is thriving as a fishing village to this day. Finally, in Tasmania there is an item of clothing called 'The Bicheno'. It's a sleeveless vest or jumper made from a blend of Australian wools.

My grandfather's brother Alf visited the town of Bicheno during his 'round the world' tour in 1968 and Albert Bicheno (a connected descendant of Hemington (see later) from Canada) did likewise in 1961.

I said above, James Ebenezer was a member of the Baptist Church, as were many of the family over the years but some were members of other branches of Christianity. A long list of Church Wardens at the village Church of St Mary's in Over shows quite a few Bicheno's, tracing them from 1606 to 1840.

If parish records are to be believed, not all Bicheno's were quite so saintly and there are a couple of stories from the notes of 1843 that perhaps we should leave untold in this account.

*   *   *

Back to William and Sarah's child, Joseph, (1782-1865). He married Ann Hemington in 1806 and had 11 children (9 consecutive boys before 2 girls were born). The Hemington family, like the Bicheno's were an old, established family from Over and many gravestones bearing the surnames can be seen in the Over churchyards today. Joseph farmed over 50 acres of land but through his wife's inheritance (and buying out his wife's sisters' interests) they also held copyhold ownership (from the Manor of Over) of a house, homestead and orchard, together with freehold ownership of adjacent pastures and over 6 acres of allotments.

Despite this apparent wealth, Joseph left relatively little in his will, in part because a major fire destroyed his thatched home, stables and barns off Over High Street (and reported in the Cambridge Chronicle of 6th September 1856). Our line continues through Joseph and Ann's sixth child, appropriately named Hemington Bicheno (nicknamed 'Hemp') after his mother's maiden name.

Hemington (1819-1912) was married twice but all his 8 children (6 boys and 2 girls) were born to his first wife, Alice Hills. Hemington and Alice were married in 1838 and Hemington became a publican at the 'Sow and Pigs' in Over. By all accounts he was his own best customer and it seems the pub was burnt down in 1855 after a mysterious drinking session. When the pub was reconstructed, Hemington's brother took over the business.

Hemington then became a butcher and left for London where his family settled in the north-east area of Stratford. His wife died in 1867 at the age of 48 and Hemington returned to Cambridgeshire, settling in the town of March, where he met and married Susan Stimpson in 1876. She was 38, and he 60 years of age. It must have agreed with him because he went on to live to 93. Hemington is the first 'Bicheno' in my direct line for whom I am aware there is a photographic record. A picture of Hemington exists in the Bicheno binders, along with many others of indirect family members. A small number of these photographs are reproduced in this book.

Of Hemington's 8 children, apart from our direct ancestor Warren, only 2 others are relevant to this account. The fifth child, Alice had 16 children and is the grandmother of Jean Nelson, co-author with Eileen Webster of the Bicheno binders that are the source of much of the pre-1900 historical information contained within this book. Another worth mentioning in out story is Alfred, the sixth child, born in 1850. He emigrated to Nova Scotia in Canada and settled in an area known as

'Marble Mountain'. The Canadian branch of the family is derived from him.

Our line continues with Hemington's seventh child 'Warren' and it's with him our story fully enters the modern era. Up to and including Warren the family basically lived in and around Over. They were of practicing Christian religions and what you might call 'middle class.' Some members owned land and others ran shops. Today in Over can be found 'Glover Street' which is named after the (work)shop our family ran in the late 18th century.

Also in the two cemeteries of Over can be found numerous graves and headstones with generations of Bicheno names on them. The number of children in each family was quite high, often in double figures (they had no television in those days) but the rate of infant mortality and number of unmarried males combined to restrict the overall size of the Bicheno clan, and therefore, the number of males who could pass on the unusual surname.

*   *   *

The link to myself from 'Over' is through my great grandfather 'Warren' (1852-1934) mentioned above. He was born in Over where he grew up and joined the Royal Artillery in 1870. He was posted from Britain to Nova Scotia in 1873 and after a brief posting to Bermuda in 1878 went on to Gibraltar. Jersey followed in 1884 where he met and married Clara Adams in June 1885. Clara hailed from the London outskirts of Virginia Water and is believed to have come from a well-to-do family.

The couple were immediately posted back to Gibraltar where he was finally discharged in 1891 after 21 years service. He actually achieved the rank of sergeant in 1885 but was busted back down to Corporal after going AWOL, the detailed circumstances of which have not been researched.

After Warren left the service he made a brief stay in Andover before the family finally moved to Portsmouth where the modern family became firmly established. Photographs of the time show Warren to be a tall, distinguished man who carried himself with a ramrod back. My dad's brother Jim recalls Warren in his later years as being a very strict gentleman with a mass of white hair and moustache. Links must have been maintained with cousins still in London as when Warren died his son Charlie is known to have written to them, advising of the loss.

* * *

After a period in 1901 at 96 Hertford Street, Portsmouth (no longer in existence but it was off Church Street) Warren set up home in rented accommodation in Cottage Grove, Portsmouth that was and still is, near Elm Grove. Only a short distance from where Sir Arthur Conan Doyle wrote his first Sherlock Holmes story – 'A Study in Scarlet'. He could not have been too pleased when his landlord sold the property he was living in for redevelopment into one of the new fangled garages, following the introduction of the automobile the early 1900s.

It is slightly ironic over time the garage was demolished and replaced by domestic dwellings. By 1913, when their son Percy (my grandfather) left home and married, they were living at 17 Stone Street. The family moved to Hereford Street, which was just off Arundel Street but this house was destroyed by bombing during the Second World War. Fortunately, nobody was injured and they relocated to Union Street close by, in a house still standing today. Warren died in 1934 and Clara passed away in 1941.

Of Warren and Clara's 10 children, the first 4 had been born in Gibraltar and the remainder in England. For those readers interested if there are any 'twins' in the family, the only instance I know about is the third and fourth children, Mary and Arthur, born in 1889, although the latter did not survive very long.

For us, the most significant child was Percy, the fifth to be born and it is his story that forms the basis of the next section in this book.

2.2 Recent Family

My paternal grandfather was Warren and Clara Bicheno's fifth child and was christened 'Percy' (1891-1975), hereinafter known in this book as 'Poppy.' He married Nellie Rosie Foster (my paternal grandmother, who I knew as 'Nanny') in 1913. Before we follow his line, let's take a quick look at Poppy's brothers and sisters.

There were but three girls, Annie (the eldest) was born in 1888 but died as a baby. Mary (a twin with her brother Arthur) born in 1889 and Mabel born a few years later. Mary married William Youngs who was a musician in the Royal Marines. He was based on the Royal Yacht and often played for the King and Royal Family. He was proficient in several instruments including the harp, which he kept in his home for many years. Mabel married a Dockyard worker named Percy Fryer and had two boys, Dennis and Gordon.

The eldest child of Warren and Clara was James. Born in 1886 he died in 1933. He worked as a stable lad in the Druids Lodge horse racing stables run by trainer Tom Lewis on Salisbury Plain and acted as Head Lad when they were travelling. His claim to fame is he led one of their horses 'Aboyeur' with his jockey named Piper, into the winners' enclosure after the Epsom Derby in 1913.

It was to be the only race Aboyeur won that season and he had been victorious in only 1 race in the previous season. It had been an extraordinary Derby. Firstly Emily Davidson, a 'suffragette' campaigner, had stood in the path of the kings horse Anmer at Tattenham corner. The horse collided with her but was unhurt, but she later died of her injuries. Then the hot favourite Craganour actually won the race by a head but was disqualified for not running straight. This promoted Aboyeur, who was a starting 100-1 shot, to be the winner. Along with Signorinetta (1908) and Jeddah (1898), this is the longest odds for a winner in the history of the race.

Allegedly, there might have been something a bit 'iffy' regarding the decision. Apparently there had been no objection from any of the race participants but it turned out the owner of the horse first past the post was the younger brother of a VIP who had escaped from the doomed liner Titanic ahead of women and children a few months earlier, and feelings were still running high.

The horse apparently ended his days in Russia, at a time just before the revolution broke out.

The next son Charles (or Charlie) was born in 1894. He joined the army as a boy in 1909 when just 16 years of age and rose to the rank of Colour Sergeant. On leaving the army in 1930 he went into the naval Dockyard for the remainder of his working life. He lived to the age of 79, dying in 1973. I met him on a number of occasions and he seemed to me to be a very pleasant gentleman.

One small family claim to fame is Charlie was a member of the 3-man artillery battery in WWI that was the very first to shoot down a Zeppelin airship (id L15) sent over from Germany to bomb London, on the night of March 31st 1916. The Lord Mayor of London had a medal struck especially to commemorate the event and presented it to him and the other two men. After Charlie's death, his brother Alf passed the medal on in 1975 to the Regiment of Artillery Museum (Accession No 2054).

The next boy was Walter (or Wally), a very tall man. He fought in the First World War as did most of the brothers but Wally was wounded and badly shell shocked. He didn't really recover from the ordeal and his left hand was unusable for the remainder of his life.

The penultimate son Alfred (or Alf) for me is probably the most significant of the brothers, other than Poppy himself. He was born in 1901 and married Ellen Williamson in 1928. A child was born, a son (Bill) who today remains a bachelor and still lives in Cosham. Bill worked for G.A.Day for 43 years, finally retiring in 1995.

Alf also commissioned some work to research the family Coat-of-Arms. I am a little cautious about some of these organisations that seem to come up with a design for just about anybody, whatever the surname. They claimed to have discovered the meaning of 'Bicheno' as being 'Dweller on the Hill', although we suspect from the information in the Bicheno booklets this is incorrect.

The Coat-of Arms this company came up with being –
    Arms: Vaire Argent (White) and Guiles (Red) on a Canton of the Second A Garb Or (Yellow). (Whatever that means).
    Crest: Three Ostrich Feathers Proper.

The design was made up into a shield and Alf's son Bill has it in his possession.

Alf travelled the world throughout his life. For years he was in the army and very unusually rose through the lowest ranks to become a Major and by the time he retired was performing the role of Lieutenant

Colonel. When Alf retired he went to live in Newport, Wales and I met him a couple of times when he came back to Portsmouth on visits. He went on a trip around the world in 1968 and visited family members in Australasia, Canada and South Africa.

The last son was William (or Bill) was born in 1905 and died in 1980. He was a plumber by trade working at the Eldridge Pope brewery. Although the circulated family tree doesn't show this, he was actually married and had one child, a daughter called Mary. The family lived in Cosham, above off-license premises. Mary grew up and married John Scutt who at the time of writing is still living in Cosham.

*   *   *

The story now starts to focus in on my direct family line, as Percy (Poppy) was the only male to carry the family name forward from Warren down to my generation. Percy Bicheno was born in 1891 and married Nellie (Nanny) Rosie Foster in 1913. Poppy was resident at 17, Stone Street, Southsea at the time but they rented their own home at 103 Landguard Road, which was opposite Nanny's parents home (No 104) and still stands today.

Nanny had been born at home, 13 Norland Road, Southsea in 1893 to Amos and Ellen Foster (nee Welch), and had spent her early years at 41 Nancy Road, Fratton, before moving on. Houses in Landguard Road cost just £100 to buy when they were new but even so, most people could only afford to rent them.

One innovation at the time was electric light. Nanny saved up and paid to have electricity installed and she used to ask the neighbours round so she could proudly show off her electric lighting. She would invite them to turn the light switch on and off and marvel at the new invention.

This might seem surprising but even in the late 1920s most homes in Landguard Road and many others besides, still had gas lighting. Such lights were of course potentially dangerous both from naked flames and gas fumes. Also the 'mantles' (the parts actually lit) were very delicate and could easily be broken, necessitating a costly visit to the local shop for a replacement.

Nanny and Poppy's house was a 3 bedroom terraced dwelling they initially shared with Nanny's brother Amos (called 'Amie') and his wife May, who Poppy sub-let rooms to. Things didn't work out too well. The women used to share the oven for cooking with Nanny getting the top half and her sister-in-law the bottom. You can imagine what happened when they both wanted to cook at the same time but needed different temperatures to be set. It was on ongoing battle with somebody's dinner getting ruined on a regular basis. Eventually Poppy evicted his 'in-laws'.

Poppy's brothers had all been in the army but Poppy himself had a reserved occupation which meant he did not serve in the armed forces during the First World War. He worked in Southampton Docks, then in the munitions factory nearby.

After WWI Poppy was given a job by Nanny's father, Amos Foster. As one of many ventures, Amos had a 'brick stand' located at the end of Dover Road in the Milton area of Portsmouth. Here he manufactured bricks out of clay and Poppy assisted with this task. Nanny used to make a 5 mile round trip on foot every lunchtime just to take them something to eat (she couldn't even afford a bicycle then).

Amos also worked at Portsmouth Power Station, which was located close to where the Gunwharf development stands today. This was one of the very first power generating stations in the country and was given such priority because it served the nearby Royal Naval Dockyard.

As the size of Nanny's family grew, space soon became a problem in the Landguard Road house. Astonishingly all of Nanny and Poppy's 13 children were born there. The 3 bedrooms were split between Nanny and Poppy with the latest infant, a room for the girls and a room for the boys. The kids used to sleep anything up to 4 to a bed with 2 at each end. The arrangement was far from ideal with so many in the house and Nanny was always pressing Poppy to relocate. As Poppy did not enjoy change at the best of times, he refused to move.

Eventually, Nanny had enough and with the assistance of daughter Mabel, took things into her own hands. She moved the family out one day to accommodation at 51 Hatfield Road, Southsea (just around the corner) where some of the family remain to this day. Poppy was not aware of, or involved with, the arrangements and was not well pleased when he eventually found out. Also, nobody thought to tell son Bill who was away on army duties. When he returned home on his first leave from the Royal Engineers he found an empty house. He had to ask the neighbours where his mum and family had moved. (Funny really, Madge has often talked about she and I moving house and not telling any of the kids).

The Hatfield Road house was a step up because it was located on a street corner and had not only a front door but a side access as well. This meant items such as bicycles with wet and muddy tyres didn't have to be wheeled via the living rooms through to the back.

Another thing currently taken for granted in this day and age is the NHS. In Nanny and Poppy's day you had to pay the Doctor to visit you and it cost one shilling (that's 5p kids) to have the midwife come and deliver your baby. And of course there was no 'Family Allowance' in those days to provide some kind of financial safety net. Life for the Bicheno family then was a constant struggle, met by sheer hard graft.

Poppy then joined Portsmouth Corporation Roads and Works department as a stoker in the 'Destructor' (what we now call 'Incinerator') plant, located between the Eastern Road, close to the end of Tangier Road where Portsmouth College stands today and extending almost all the way to Baffins Pond.

The city's refuse lorries would gather there and large cranes grab the contents and drop them into one of six huge furnaces. Poppy's job was to clear the 'clinker' residue after the firing. These were the bits that could not be incinerated further and were utilised as the hardcore foundations of local roads. It was a job not without penalty. The intense heat from the furnaces caused his legs to ulcerate and he was to suffer greatly in later life with pains in his legs and joints.

Like many people, Poppy took on an evening job during WWII. He was a mortuary warden and his duties included the removal of bodies following an air raid. On one particular occasion a bomb shelter with many school children in it received a direct hit from a bomb and he had to carry out the children's bodies. Being a doting father of many kids himself he was deeply affected by the experience and never quite got over it.

Nanny and Poppy had 13 children, some of whom tragically did not live beyond childhood. Rita was first born in 1913. Her life was not made any easier by an eye injury, possible caused by the midwife when she was newly born, became infected and eventually resulted in her having her eye removed. From the age of 13 Rita spent increasingly lengthy periods of time away, eventually moving out and staying with friends in other houses, although they were still close by so Nanny could watch out for her.

Rita married comparatively late in life to Archie Coleman at a spectacular ceremony held at the old church in Portchester Castle. They set up home in Cherry Tree Avenue, Cowplain, just north of Portsmouth. She remained there after Archie's death and although her health started to fail as she approached her 90s and she suffered a series of strokes, she largely retains to this day her mental faculties and is not one to be trifled with.

My father Percy was next to be born in 1915 and was the eldest boy and I'll be saying much more about him later.

Charles and Alfred followed in quick succession but the former died when only a baby. Alfie was a quiet and very sweet natured little boy and was Percy's sidekick, going around with him a lot of the time. It was another tragedy when he died from peritonitis at the age of 11. Especially tragic when it would have been easily preventable in this day and age.

Then came James (Jim) born in 1921. Jim went to school at Reginald Road School as did all of Nanny's children but he still had to do his share of household chores, one of which was particularly unpleasant. Their house was only a short distance from a rag and bone scrap yard. When the yard was demolished, the resident rats vacated their dens and some sought sanctuary in the houses around the surrounding area. Jim would bait 'humane' traps to capture any rats live overnight and then the next morning he would take them out and drown them in buckets of water. He would catch one or two a week this way. Any mice seen scuttling about would just get a boot hurled at them, with a fair degree of accuracy. Horrible yes, but remember there were young babies living in the house who had to be protected from vermin.

At the age of 12 Jim took on small jobs like newspaper delivery for two separate newsagents. He also used to take a trolley up a back alley to the rear entrance of the greengrocer where his elder brother Percy (my dad) worked. At the end of the day, Percy would take any 'leftover' potatoes and cabbage out back and load Jim's cart to take the goodies off home. Perks of the job, of course.

Another little job was helping a local haulage contractor who still used horses as well as lorries. The big attraction was taking a string of big carthorses down to Eastney beach for exercising in the water.

Jim went into full time work at a butchers in the Strand, as a 'roundsman' and also helped in their local slaughterhouse where they used to prepare cows, pigs, sheep, calves and poultry. The family benefited here from some more 'perks of the job.' Like other members of staff, Jim used to take home 'danglers'. These were appropriated cuts of beef, mutton or lamb secured onto his person and hidden under his coat when he left work at the end of the day. He followed up by working in a wet fish shop located just opposite in the Strand. He finally joined 'Evans' in 1938, which was a local manufacturing firm located in Goldsmith Avenue.

During WWII the Evans Company was very much involved in the war effort and produced such things as bomb cases, Navy mine cases, gun mountings and the undercarriage for Halifax bombers. The factory then relocated to Frome in Somerset to avoid collateral damage from enemy attacks on the Dockyard. Jim's job was a progress chaser, which today might be termed a 'Project Manager.' He scheduled and monitored all the work going through the dozens of interlinked processing steps on the shop floor.

Jim also joined a detachment of 'Home Guard' set up by the Evans Company. They had no weapons or ammunition for some time after they were formed and made do with farm implements. The 'Dads Army' series on TV held many truths of what went on then. They actually did have a small radar set; the problem was it needed a battery that had to be re-charged every night or it wouldn't work.

After the war Jim had a long career with Plessey Aerospace and was even brought out of retirement to set up a further operation near Bournemouth. One of his placements with Plessey was in Liverpool and Jim lived in the up-market area of Woolton, very close to George Harrison when 'Beatlemania' was breaking out and frequently saw small armies of kids besieging his residence.

After the sad loss of his first wife Lillian, Jim married the charming Liz Hardman in 1980 and he finally retired to Ringwood near the New Forest. Even then Jim remained active, working both in Adult Teaching and as a mini-bus driver for local organisations.

Jim has two daughters, Sue who at the time of writing is about to take up a deputy headship at a private school in Kent and Christine who is a senior accountant at Epsom and Ewell Council.

Brother William (Bill) was born in February 1923. He followed the pattern of the elder boys as to his household contribution and schooling. Schools were very different then. For a start there were coal fires in classrooms during the winter months and corporal punishment was a daily occurrence. Bill wasn't the best-behaved pupil and didn't like school anyway, so he was rather prone to getting into trouble as well as playing truant. Clips around the ear were commonplace and he recalls having the cane across his hand so badly he suffered cuts and his fingers swelled up to an extent that he was unable to pick up a pencil or even feel anything.

Nanny used to do her shopping at a local food store where her purchases were logged in a book and she settled the outstanding account weekly. Bill, then a very young lad, saw Nanny acquiring the goods, apparently without handing money over and assumed they were 'free'. So he went in the shop and 'bought' a hunk of cheese, sitting down outside to devour it. At the end of the week a war broke out with the shopkeeper when Nanny checked her bill, until Bill owned up to his indiscretion.

Bill used to run errands for neighbours for a farthing a time (that's one quarter of an old penny, kids). Things like fetching a jug of beer from the off licence. A farthing could buy a good deal in those days for a child, like an 'everlasting strip of toffee', about a foot long.

When he left school at the age of 14, Bill got a job in a newsagent, then at Dorset Dairies where elder brother Percy worked. Bill was a 'yard boy' and helped to unload the milk carts at the end of their rounds. For each one he was paid 2 pence that went towards funding his evening trips to one of the many cinemas around Portsmouth, which charged 6 pence for entry.

At the age of 16, Bill would travel with his manager in their 13cwt truck to deliver extra milk to milkmen on their rounds or retrieve empty containers from them to lighten their loads. Bill would watch how the vehicle was driven and then back at the depot would sit behind the wheel and 'practice' driving. One day the manager hurt his back on the journey and was unable to drive, so Bill hopped behind the wheel and drove the truck back.

Soon after he applied for his driving license. This was the shape of things to come because Poppy helped Bill get a job as a lorry driver when he was 18. He worked a 12-hour shift starting at 6 a.m. and drove to local places and out as far as Petersfield, about 12 miles away.

All this time Percy, Jim and Bill all worked very hard at home to help Nanny and Poppy. As youngsters they had all been assigned household chores and were not allowed to leave the house until they were completed. Now grown up, they pooled most of their take-home wages to help the family.

At the age of 19, in 1942, Bill was called up to join the Army. He joined the Royal Engineers at Aldershot and was assigned to an armoured division where he worked on maintaining army plant and heavy vehicles. He took part in the D-Day battles, joining in on the 6th day of the assault into Europe. At this time Bill earned just 15 shillings a week (that's 75p kids), 10 shillings of which he sent back to Nanny.

After reaching the rank of lance corporal, he left the army in 1947, his finishing wage being the princely sum of 4 pounds 9 shillings a week. Bill returned immediately as a civilian to help look after the Royal Engineers storage depot at Liphook but in 1955 the Co-op was opening a new central 'cold storage depot' to serve around 62 local shops. Bill was offered a job there and he ended up staying for 30 years, finishing as the manager of the butchery cold storage depot. The depot was closed in 1985 and he decided to take retirement.

Bill had married at the relatively late age of 35 to Freda Miller in 1958. He soon made up for lost time and the couple had 6 children. A son Billy, followed by 4 girls and then another son Warren. Apart from my own sons, Bill's boys represent the only other male line carrying the name of Bicheno forward within the branch of the family described in this book.

Bill and Freda lived initially at 70 St Pauls Road in Southsea, later moving to Angerstein Road in North End. They divorced and Bill married Marlene Browne, a lovely lady, in April 1982. Today they live happily together in the Milton area of Portsmouth, in a delightful flat set in surprisingly tranquil surroundings overlooking Bransbury Park.

Getting back to Nanny and Poppy. After 6 consecutive boys, Nanny must have been relieved to give birth to a girl, Mary, in 1924. Mary showed signs of being talented musically and Nanny made sure she had lessons in both piano and accordion. Given their low income it's extraordinary how Nanny found the money for such things, always putting her kids first. She paid Miss Coward in Westfield Road the sum of 6 (old) pence a lesson.

Mary is a lovely lady. She married Fred Castle and together they had 2 daughters (Marianne and Janet) and a son (Alan). Both the girls baby-sat for Madge and I on a few occasions, which was ironic because I actually baby-sat them once when they were little. Alan has a claim to fame as he appeared as a young boy in the 'Jim'll fix it' programme on TV and received the attendant medallion. It's actually one of the more memorable requests in the series. Alan asked Jimmy Saville to provide him with a Rolls Royce in which he could do his paper round, rather than on his push bike and Jim duly obliged.

Another daughter, Mabel, followed in 1926. As a young girl Mabel had a very close brush with death. Unbeknown to anyone, the electrical wiring in the house, which wasn't subject to the same stringent safety checks applying today, came into contact with the metal bath in the bathroom. While she was bathing one day, the family were stunned to hear Mabel's screams. She was being electrocuted and the current was gluing her to the bath. Poppy rushed up the stairs and hauled her out, despite himself receiving a full jolt from the electricity supply. Help was urgently summoned but it seemed as if it was too late as they were unable to bring her round, but Mabel rallied under intensive medical attention and came through.

Mabel married a divorcee from an aristocratic family, Tony Weld, who already had a son Paul and there are now 2 daughters and another son Nigel to whom I am godfather. Paul has a small claim to fame, being the long-standing Club Secretary working at Portsmouth Football Club.

Sister Elsie was born in 1927. By all accounts she was pretty, lively and very popular with all her brothers and sisters. Tragically, at the age of 17 she was knocked down in a road traffic accident when riding her bicycle in the Milton area. My dad was home on leave from the Royal Navy when a policeman came to the door with the news she had been taken to hospital. Nanny asked Percy to go there for her and he arrived at her bedside just 5 minutes before she passed away. He then had to return home with the sad news. The family were devastated.

The next member of the family was Ronald, born in 1930 and sharing a birth date (24th May) with Queen Victoria and my wife Madge. His earliest recollections are of his first day at Reginald Road School when Nanny had to drag him there and bribe him with a promise of a bottle of milk to make him go in.

Like some of his sisters, Ron, at the age of 9, was evacuated during the war, initially to Sandown in the Isle of Wight but then to Christchurch. A rather strange place to relocate children, as any invasion of Britain by Hitler would certainly have meant all locations on the South Coast were quite literally 'in the firing line.'

The children got off the train at the local station and the parents who were to house them simply picked whoever they fancied, usually trying to fit them in with their own children by age and gender. Ron was the very last child left standing on the platform before a woman with 2 girls offered to take him home.

This wasn't an ideal arrangement and he eventually moved next door to be with a family with a single child, a son. Being an only child the boy had been spoiled to some extent with all sorts of toys that Ron became intrigued with. In particular, a large 'No 10 Meccano set' where perhaps Ron's natural practical talents were awakened for the first time and with which he played for hours on end. He joined the boy scouts and collected many badges of achievement and was also a member of the Christchurch Abbey Choir. The father of the family worked as a water bailiff and this gave Ron access to fishing areas in the rivers Avon and Stour, which he enjoyed.

Ron still saw a lot of his sisters who were living only about 100 yards away. All was not entirely smooth with them. Brenda actually received a bad injury when someone threw a brick that struck her in the back of her head and opened a very nasty wound. To this day, the effect caused her to lose some of her childhood memories and in particular her evacuation term. The girls stayed together with a family that ran a 'fruit and veg' business and Elsie, although only 12 years old at the time, actually helped out in the shop.

After about 2 years they returned home, even though the war was ongoing and the area still dangerous. One evening when Ron was visiting the local Eastney Boys Club, a particularly heavy air raid took place. The suddenness prevented the kids going to an air-raid shelter, so they crouched under the snooker tables. When the raid ceased at about 4 a.m. Ron had to make his way home in total darkness, through the stench of cordite and charred materials and pick his way through the ruins of demolished houses that had fallen across the road. Unable to see his way he fell into a large bomb crater and reached home in a dishevelled state where a worried Nanny berated him for being out so late.

After air raids, and oblivious to the danger of building collapse, the boys used to wander around the bombed houses looking for any useful bits and pieces they could take home. They used to throw tennis balls up onto the roofs to dislodge pieces of bomb shrapnel to retrieve as souvenirs.

Like the other boys in the family, Ron had his personal chores. His main one was to take a handcart up to the general tip at Bransbury Park, a fair trek, to collect timber for the fire.

Whereas the other children had left school at 14, Ron carried on until he was 16. This was probably the only cause of sibling disharmony in what was in all other respects a remarkably united family, as the others were effectively subsidising him during this period. But it was all in a good cause and Nanny and Poppy knew what they were doing. At the age of 13, Ron passed the entrance examinations to join the recently opened 'Portsmouth Junior Building School', which proved to be a technical high school of no small degree of excellence.

He was well schooled in such trades as brick laying, carpentry, painting and decorating, plastering and plumbing. With the last subject being selected as his specialist skill for the final year training. Even today, Ron has retained his schoolbooks from the period and treasures them with justifiable pride.

When he reached the age of 16, 'Reynolds', a small local firm operating out of Southsea, offered to take Ron on as a plumbing apprentice. It looked for a time as if he might have a career as a professional footballer and Ron actually had trials with both Portsmouth and Southampton Football Clubs but in those days an apprenticeship was of far more long-term value than the life of a footballer and that decided matters.

During his time as an apprentice Ron also had a spare time job at South Parade Pier working floodlights on the stage. This gave him free entry to the entertainments and the opportunity to see all the top acts and bands of the era in their weekly concerts; such as Ted Heath's band, The Squadronairs, Oscar Rabin etc and enabled him to get autographs from the likes of Dicky Valentine, Lita Rosa and many others.

At midnight when the dancing was over, people would pour out onto the buses lining up in a long queue along the esplanade. Ron recalls one Saturday night when some lads went under the Pier, removed their clothes and went 'skinny dipping' just as the buses were loading up. While they were in the water Ron picked up all their clothes and laid them out in piles along the esplanade.

It didn't take long for the girls on the buses to realise what was going on and they started shouting at the boys to 'come out of the water' and other appropriate comments. The boys eventually emerged under the Pier and after searching for old newspapers to cover their embarrassment they had to locate their clothing Ron had deliberately mixed up within the different piles. There were a lot of red faces that night and I suspect a few dark threats made to Ron!

In 1950 Ron was called up to join the armed services. He was in the

RAF, working in Communications. He was stationed at Tangmere Airport close to Chichester where he worked in the Control Tower. As his shift allowed some evenings off, he continued to study under the sponsorship of the RAF, attending Portsmouth College 3 nights a week. To help him he was granted rail warrants, which he also used as a means of nipping home whenever he could.

One of Ron's chores in the Control tower was to make up sandwiches and meals for the other men and the officer who was in overall charge of Communications. To do this he visited the cookhouse and returned with all sorts of foodstuffs. Food rationing was still in force and the Officer would expect Ron to make up a parcel of surplus food for him to take home. Ron also had a parcel of food, containing things like tea and coffee, which he smuggled out of the camp and back home to Nanny by hitching a ride past the security checks with his officer-in-charge.

After his 2 year secondment, Ron returned to 'Reynolds' but his age and added experience was recognised and he was now given a job in the office doing the estimating for jobs and then managing them, alongside the firms owner. The boss ran the electrical side and Ron did everything else. It was here he met a young girl named Elizabeth 'Betty' Barton who also worked in the office and who Ron then married in 1953. When I was a young lad I remember Betty as being a very glamorous lady.

Ron took an active part in local business affairs and for three years was chairman of the Social Committee of the Portsmouth Chamber of Commerce, among other things organising the very first carnival procession through the city.

In 1968 there was a career and life-changing event when the owner of Reynolds offered Ron the business but he decided Portsmouth had few opportunities and opted to move out. Looking around for jobs he saw an advertisement from the CITB (Construction Industry Training Board). He applied for the post and after an interview at Maidenhead, was appointed as a Training Officer. He and Betty moved to the Oxford area and his initial base was at Reading.

In the early days money was tight and Ron would save on expenses by using his skills to build anything and everything required for the house. The most extreme example was when he demolished an internal wall from the living room into the kitchen in order to install a white marble base unit with serving area above. The problem was white marble cost a fortune.

Then he learned the local cemetery were digging up old and unclaimed graves and dumping the marble headstones. He loaded up a set of carefully selected headstones onto a lorry. Then he cleaned and cut them to size. He positioned the stones carefully to make a beautiful construction but if anyone had opened the housed cupboards and looked in at the reverse side of the stones they would have seen some interesting and somewhat macabre inscriptions.

Ron's role was to look after 15 to 20 companies from the Berks, Bucks and Oxon area, by ascertaining their training requirements and then producing reports, with a 5 to 10 year training plan to enable them to meet their company objectives. As many of these companies were in direct competition it took some time to win their trust and they would reveal their business plans to him, so he could then help them.

Betty acted as Ron's secretary in organising meetings abroad so he could run briefing sessions for Chairmen and Directors in a relatively isolated environment, away from the day-to-day hurly burly.

After working with the Employers for seven years, they presented him with a gold watch, the opinion being he had consolidated 25 years of effort into 7 and thus deserved the accolade 18 years early!

Then Ron was also offered a position as 'Head of Mechanical Services' for the whole of the United Kingdom. The job had not been advertised and he was given just a weekend to make a decision, with the job to start on the following Monday, if accepted. After a lot of heart searching with Betty on the prospect of either moving to London, commuting daily, or living in a London flat (and of course not forgetting their two daughters who were then half way through their examinations at school) a 'no' decision was reached.

Over time the CITB was off loaded and its work was continued as the Thames Valley Training Group, using government grants.

Ron's efforts became recognised as a National model for such an approach to training and when he finally decided to retire in 1996 he was given a grand and glitzy send-off in the buildings and grounds of Blenheim Palace, no less.

Ron and Betty were married in 1953 and had 2 daughters. Betty had ambitions of her own and convinced Ron to move from their luxury home and buy a shop in Woodstock, living above it in a flat. It was a greengrocers and general store, that Betty expanded and built up. Ron's job didn't protect him from additional duties and he would get up at 6 a.m. to prepare the newspapers before he started his 'real' job and again visit wholesales in the evening after he finished.

Ron had also purchased a plot of land alongside the shop and in 1963 took the bold and courageous step of deciding to design and self-build his own house. Even for someone with his knowledge and experience it was a huge task and it occupied all his spare time at evenings and weekends for the next 2 years. When completed, Ron named the house 'coinbeh', an anagram of 'bicheno'.

Later on Betty became even more ambitious and opened a gift shop / art gallery in Abingdon which has been extremely successful. This has now passed to their daughter Janice, who with her degree in Art is further developing the Gallery. Today, after the sad loss of his wife, Ron lives a very active retirement. Still living in his magnificent self-built home and continuing to improve it.

For Nanny and Poppy, another daughter, Brenda, followed in 1932. Like Mary, she also had musical talent, which Nanny nurtured in a similar manner. The two girls often played the accordion together and with a band, including some public performances. It was at such a concert Brenda first met her husband-to-be, Bob Tomkinson. He was a singer who was performing at the same concert. By all accounts it was love at first sight across a crowded room. They were inseparable from that day and recently celebrated their 50th wedding anniversary.

The penultimate child was a boy named Dennis but he regrettably died in infancy.

The final child was Arthur, born in 1935. Being the last baby he was doted on by the rest of the family. He was too young to be evacuated during the war but when old enough was conscripted and joined the Army (Royal Hampshire Regiment), serving in the Malayan wars against the Communist rebels in the 1950's. He was based in Kuala Lumpur and during the fighting in the jungle was badly wounded in the leg. The leg actually turned black and he very nearly lost it. However he recovered and after 2 years returned home.

When Arthur arrived home, Poppy's dog, that hadn't seen him for 2 years, failed to recognise him and wouldn't let him into the house. Someone suggested Arthur return on the morrow with some dog biscuits. The next day he returned and offered the biscuits to the dog. The dog gratefully accepted the biscuits but still wouldn't let him into the house. Dog 1 Human 0.

Arthur married Patricia Thorpe and they set up home in the Fratton area of Portsmouth. Arthur was the first of the brothers to show signs of the heart problems that have plagued the male side of my family and seem to have affected me today. Although receiving treatment he collapsed suddenly and died at the relatively young age of 58.

Having discussed his brothers, now lets take a more detailed look at my father Percy and his younger days.

*   *   *

Percy was born in 1915 and as already described with Jim, it was the norm in those days for youngsters to have jobs to help out with the family income. Percy was no exception and worked regularly from the age of 10.

He helped out Nanny's dad (Amos Foster) on Sundays. Amos ran 3 allotments located near Baffins Pond, close to where the play park now stands. He grew vegetables in one plot and flowers in the other two. My dad was charged with cutting the flowers, bundling them up and then walking around the neighbourhood to sell them for 2 pence a bunch. Amos must have been a bit of a skinflint for he paid my dad nothing at all for his assistance and even moaned if the money was short, which it usually was as my dad regularly 'borrowed' 2 pence to buy himself a sausage roll for lunch on the round.

With other members of the family, Percy also did a door-to-door collection of old newspapers they then supplied to a local fish and chip shop as wrapping material. In return they got a few chips and scraps.

Another little job was getting up at 6a.m. every day and collecting the dirty washing from the Royal Marines barracks and taking it to be done by a local laundry woman; at the same time returning the previous (now clean) batches and collecting the money. Percy also had a job involving scrubbing and cleaning out vacated housing, prior to new occupants moving in.

At home Percy had his own regular chores. Like putting the family's washed clothes through the mangle. I've done this myself and I can tell you it's not as easy as it looks. Turning a big handle to force clothes between 2 big wooden rollers to squeeze all the water out. He also had to chop up wood Poppy brought home from the Destructor or collected from the beach as driftwood. The wood went into the family range that provided cooking facilities and hot water. It frequently coughed sparks and burning pieces of tinder onto the hearth and a small side job was putting out any resultant fires before the house burned down.

With no television or provided entertainment the children had to find ways of amusing themselves. Games were played such as marbles, whips and tops, paper and comb and magic lantern shows. The latter was conducted with a bed sheet, candle and fingers or paper cutouts. Again not without some element of danger with candles being held against sheets. An evening's entertainment was to go and have a fight with the kids in the next street or gather around the man winding the barrel organ on the corner of the road.

On one occasion Jim built a 'go-cart' out of wooden boxes, string and a set of wheels and proved a major hit, zooming up and down the road by kid propulsion. There were few presents, even at Christmas when all that could be expected were apples, oranges, nuts and little else.

Dogs were ever present in the Bicheno household, mainly at Poppy's instigation. As if the kids weren't enough! They were usually mongrels and were generally kept one at a time until they died. You had dog licenses in those days but although Poppy was prepared to pay for the dog's keep he wouldn't spend out on the license. So whenever a license inspector was in the area the incumbent dog got taken on a very, very long walk while any evidence of it's presence in the house mysteriously, albeit temporarily, disappeared.

Dogs weren't the only pets. Always trying to put food on the table, Poppy brought home a group of chickens and several rabbits. The idea being to fatten them up and have them for dinner. Nanny however grew attached to them and insisted on keeping all of them as pets (shades of Madge here). So instead of increasing the family larder they ended up being a drain on it. One of these birds deserves to be singled out for comment. A large white cockerel was a viscous beast that would attack any of the children who approached. Only Nanny could handle it, probably due to her 'no nonsense' attitude, honed by bringing up so many kids. I have a feeling with so many vengeful and hungry tummies around maybe one bird in particular may have eventually made it to the dinner table.

At the age of 14 Percy left school and had a variety of jobs, often more than one at a time. During the week he was an errand boy for two greengrocers and also a chemists. The chemist manufactured many of its preparations on site and my father assisted with this as well. That is, until he spilt an entire vat of 'lung balsam' over the floor while he was stirring it. This was a preparation taken by mouth and was well thought of in the area as a cure for chesty coughs. I'm not sure about this batch though. My dad was told to scrape it off the floor and put it back in the vat.

There were some perks. They also made ladies make-up and my dad collected 'left overs' after the workers had gone home and took them back for the girls in the family where they proved very popular.

Finally Percy got a full time job at the Portsmouth based 'Dorset Dairy' at the age of 17 in 1932. He would leave home at 4a.m. to load up his float with milk bottles. This was the first of 2 daily rounds he was expected to complete in the Copnor, Buckland, Fratton and Mile End areas.

There were no electric vehicles to drive in those days; instead a platform on wheels called a 'pram' had to be manually hauled around. In summer months when it was particularly hot the metal-rimmed wheels would actually sink into the road tarmac, such was the weight they carried. Not only were bottles of milk delivered but some people also brought jugs to be filled from huge 17-gallon milk churns.

Dressed in his breeches and leather boots, Percy cut a manly figure on his rounds and the word was several ladies took a shine to him and tried to entice him into their homes but he rebuffed all such approaches. (The reputation of milkmen is built on such incidents with perhaps a different outcome).

It was at the dairy Percy met Norah Emily Crowley who was destined to become his wife and my mother. For 'dates' they used to go cycling together for miles around Portsmouth and the surrounding countryside, stopping off for picnics.

To earn more money Percy left the dairy and joined the Royal Navy in 1938 at the age of 23. He and Norah married in August 1940. As it was during the war, almost nobody was allowed time off to attend the wedding. Percy himself walked on his own all the way from his home in Eastney to St Joseph's Church in Copnor, where the service took place. (Incidentally, the same church where Madge and I were to be married some 33 years later).

St Joseph's was actually officially opened in 1914, although it had been unofficially 'open for business' from 1908, in an area populated more by cows in fields than by people in houses at that time. It's ironic the church builder, Domenico Marchetti, became the first road accident fatality on the then recently opened Copnor Bridge in 1918 as he left the church.

Several of Percy's younger brothers and sisters could not attend the ceremony as they had been evacuated to Christchurch in Dorset to avoid the bombs. Percy and Bill were in the armed services; Jim heavily engaged in the war effort, Mary at home helping her mum and Arthur just a toddler. Mabel, Elsie, Ronald and Brenda, like other children who were evacuated en masse from London at the same time, spent almost 3 years away staying with volunteer families. It must be incomprehensible to youngsters of today that children were whisked away to stay with complete strangers for years at a time but it happened. All for their own safety of course.

It was just as well the children had been moved as a German incendiary bomb came right through the roof and front bedroom of the house in Landguard Road causing damage and a fire requiring government compensation to rectify.

* * *

Let's just consider Nanny for a moment and what she achieved. She came from a big family and as the eldest helped her mum a lot in bringing up the younger ones. Then, although she herself had an even larger family, Nanny insisted all her children had a proper education and upbringing and worked herself into the ground to achieve it.

Nanny gave birth to 13 children in the space of 24 years. So at any point in time she was either pregnant or caring for young babies or both. Two of her much loved children died as infants, another as a young boy and a most vivacious girl in a tragic accident as a teenager. She brought up her family in an age where there were no domestic appliances or labour saving devices available other than manually driven items. So no fridge, freezer, washing machine, dishwasher, dryers, vacuum cleaners, gas or electric cookers or just about anything taken for granted today. Radio had just come out to the mass marketplace, gramophones were almost inaudible and there was no television.

Nanny had nobody to help her, save when the eldest children were big enough and available. Poppy worked hard with long hours and in keeping with the tradition of the time did comparatively little to raise the children; which was considered to be women's work.

Another tradition was Poppy handed his unopened pay packet to Nanny every week; she would give him back some pocket money and manage the household on the remainder. So Nanny performed the most Herculean feats in bringing up the family. The cleaning, washing and cooking were each full time jobs let alone taking care of the children themselves. She had the heartbreak of losing some of her children while others were sent away from her during the war years. She had the stresses of living through the war, coping with food rationing and had bombs rain about her. Yet all the children received a full education up to the then school leaving age of 14 and they were all well fed and decently clothed.

She would discipline her children but at the same time would stand up to anyone, male or female, in defence of them. Nanny was highly superstitious which accounted for some of her supposedly eccentric behaviour. For example, if she gave a handbag as a gift then it always contained a few coins to indicate future wealth. Whenever Nanny visited somebody, as she frequently did Norah (my mum) when Percy was away at sea, despite the lengthy journey involved, she always took a small gift with her.

Incidentally during the war years this gave Poppy some worries as Nanny would stay and help Norah with the baby (Margaret) and only just make the last bus, arriving home in pitch darkness, due to the 'blackout'. There were of course no telephones then to check on her safety. Incidentally, the blackout also caused Norah grief before she became pregnant with Margaret. When cycling to work in the dark she collided with a bus and broke her leg in two places.

I remember Nanny from my youth. By then she was wizened with age, had deep sunken eyes and heavily lined features but she was always on the go and I rarely saw her sitting down. What Nellie Bicheno (nee Foster) achieved was nothing short of miraculous and I stand in awe of her. Nanny finally died on 23rd February 1967. Exactly 8 years later to the day Poppy collapsed and fell into a coma and was reunited with Nanny the next day, 24th February 1975.

*   *   *

Getting back to Percy and Norah. They set up house in a rented top floor flat at 17 Park Grove in Cosham, just to the north of the Portsmouth boundary. The flat down stairs was occupied by a grouchy individual who happened to be related to the landlady. They lived in uneasy co-existence until the birth of their first child Margaret in 1944. The crying of the baby became a major point of friction between my parents and the grouch. It finished with my dad giving the other bloke a punch on the nose. Given his kinship with the landlady, my parents were obliged to vacate and they relocated to Simpson Road in

Stamshaw to the west of central Portsmouth.

After getting married Percy joined the Navy, much to the chagrin of his uncles who were all Army men. The Fleet Air Arm had only just been formed and was initially staffed by transferring members from other parts of the armed services. Percy was in the very first batch of new, direct recruits taken on as Probationary Air Mechanics (or PAMs). After basic training they did a crash electronics course at HMS Vernon where 3 year's training was crammed into a single year. The same happened with their second years training at Cranwell RAF College. Not, unfortunately, in the posh college itself but in a cluster of Nissan huts nearby.

He passed out as a fully qualified air mechanic; with a wage of seventeen shillings and sixpence a week (that's about 87p kids!) and he still made a weekly allotment home to his mother of five shillings. When he married he was given another seven shillings and sixpence per week out of which (and while still keeping Nanny's 5 bob going) he made another allotment of ten shillings to his wife Norah. This left him ten shillings (50p) a week to live on!

Percy was then posted to his first ship, the brand new Aircraft Carrier HMS Formidable. It was intended for duty as a protector of Atlantic Convoys but was diverted to the Mediterranean Sea in 1941 to cover the absence through bomb damage of another carrier. Percy then took part in his first major action when aircraft from HMS Formidable attacked the Italian battleship Vittorio Vento and 8 escorting cruisers off Crete, stopping her from pursuing four British light cruisers.

Damage was inflicted on the escorting Italian cruiser Pola, which slowed up and caused further ships of the escorting Italian fleet to remain with her. This reduction in speed allowed the main British battleship group to first catch up with and then destroy, the Italian ships. This action became known as the Battle of Matapan.

HMS Formidable went on to cover the evacuation of Crete following the German invasion and there she was badly damaged by Stuka dive-bombers. With a hole big enough to drive 3 double-decker buses through, the carrier put into Alexandria for temporary repair before going on to the USA for a full repair at the giant Norfolk Naval Dockyard.

In the meantime Percy left the carrier at Alexandria and spent the following months in North Africa, maintaining the planes providing air cover for general Mongomery's Eighth Army. He participated in the decisive desert battle of El Alamein in October 1942 before being transferred back home to Lee-on-Solent, adjacent to Gosport. There he serviced the Seafire fighters (the sea going brothers of the more famous Spitfires) that took part in the D-Day landings of June 6th 1944 when the allies finally started the process of wresting Europe back from the Nazis.

He actually came through the war physically unscathed although he was the proud possessor of a 'Certificate of Wounds and Hurts' in 1945. Slightly tongue in cheek however because the 'wound' was in fact a broken collarbone sustained during a game of services football.

After the war Percy spent time on the aircraft carriers HMS Illustrious, HMS Eagle and HMS Bulwark. Then in 1944 his first daughter, Margaret, was born. This gave him cause to consider applying for a shore-based job so he could spend more time at home.

Then came a tragedy. Falling pregnant again soon after her first child, Norah contracted 'pre-eclampsia,' a full-blown and very dangerous form of toxaemia. She went almost full term with the baby, a girl weighing just 3 and a half pounds, but the baby survived just a few hours after birth on 14th January 1945. Her name was Mary Theresa and I was later to name my second daughter 'Marie' in memory of her.

Percy was promoted to Petty Officer and became a land-based instructor at HMS Ariel (later to become HMS Daedalus) in Gosport. He was now earning enough to take out a mortgage on a house. At the time the couple were still renting accommodation in Simpson Road in Stamshaw but it so happened in the Buckland area of central Portsmouth some bombsites were being cleared for replacement housing. In Daulston Road a bomb had flattened the first 3 houses of the terraced row and 2 new ones were being erected on the site (by the way this 2 for 3 replacement explains why there is no house number 5 in that road). Unfortunately both new houses had been spoken for but the word was the people called Mr and Mrs Critchett who were the potential owners of No1 might not move in after all.

Percy wrote to the Mr Critchett politely asking his intentions and explaining his own situation. Later Mr Critchett revealed 3 couples had written to him but Percy had been the only one to enclose a stamped and addressed envelope, so he was the only one to receive a reply. (It's amazing how such tiny details can have such major impacts on our lives isn't it?)

The house on the corner of Daulston Road and Hampshire Street was secured and the family moved in shortly after their next baby was born. This baby was Christopher. (Yours truly). Followed four years later by

Frances, Norah and Percy's last child.

Having just 2 bedrooms and 2 living rooms the house was not exactly spacious but even so the 'front room' was seldom occupied in the early years and kept in pristine condition. Basically the family lived in just the one room and then retired to the bedrooms in the evening. There were no carpets in the bedrooms and the children had to cope with walking barefoot on the cold linoleum floors. Entertainment was through the radio, board games and cards with a black-and-white television appearing much later.

Eventually I reached an age where my parents had to split me away from the girls and the front room downstairs became my bedroom. Well sort of. Everything else remained in there and my bed was a settee that unfolded down into the bed and so the room could be reverted to its original intention within minutes. This forced me to be very orderly and tidy which is a total contrast to my own sons' bedrooms in more recent years.

Percy finally left the Royal Navy in May 1961 after 22 years, with the rank of Chief Petty Officer and in the role of Aircraft Instructor but he continued for the next 20 years as a civilian Instructor Officer. He was highly respected within the services and his work was often held up and documented as the standard to be followed by others. He was awarded the British Empire Medal for his work and presented with it by Lord Strathcona, the Minister of State for Defence, at a ceremony in Whitehall on 18th May 1979.

He was further honoured in 1998 when he was a recipient of the famous 'Maundy Money' from Her Majesty Queen Elizabeth II at a ceremony held in Portsmouth Cathedral. This was in recognition of the many years of hard work (together with Norah) he put in for the church and the local Convent.

Unfortunately the story does not have an altogether happy ending. After being widowed, Percy had his home in Daulston Road broken into by thieves who stole among other items his coveted BEM and war medals. Further vandalism a few weeks later was the final straw and Percy moved out of the long-standing family house and bought a secure high rise flat in Southsea to spend his remaining years.

*   *   *

Now, for completeness, here is something of Norah's background and part of her family history. Her father was Matthew Crowley. Born and raised in Glengarriff, in the west Cork area of southern Ireland; his own parents had been the schoolmaster and schoolmistress of Adrigole village school.

He moved to England while in his 20's as an apprentice in the Royal Navy. He met a young 16-year-old girl named Ada Mitchell whose parents owned a barber's shop in Highbury Street, Old Portsmouth. They also acted as mobile barbers to the military barracks located at Pembroke Park, today an up market residential area. They made a good deal of money from these activities and bought more property in the area. Ada's father, as landlord, would do the rounds of his tenants in a pony and trap to collect the rent but unfortunately he started drinking the proceeds rather than investing them. This led to Ada's father dying through drink at a young age but her mother lived until 1948.

Matthew and Ada were married and set up home in Balliol Road, in the central Buckland area of Portsmouth. They had four children, Vera, Norah, Dorothy and Matthew. The four children were born in as many years and it proved too hard for Ada to cope with them all, so her own mother Emily took Vera and raised her as a surrogate mum back in Highbury Street, although still keeping in close contact with the rest of the family.

Ada and Matthew moved to 66 Shadwell Road and when Matthew retired they purchased a property in Maylands Road, Bedhampton, which is just north of the Portsmouth boundary and coincidently very close to where my family and myself live today. With no telephone and poor public transport, Ada felt isolated and too distant from her friends and family and they moved back after just a few months to central Portsmouth, to 31 Kensington Road.

It's this address I recall well as I often visited Ada and Matthew (known to me as Grandma and Grandad). I have abiding memories of grandma as a short, rotund figure forever chuckling away at something. They always kept a tin of 'mintoes' on their mantelpiece and offered them to all their visitors.

For those readers unfamiliar with such sweeties, they are formidable objects, being very hard and very sticky and although tasting quite pleasant they need a good deal of chewing to get the better of them and being as they are, can easily extract tooth fillings before they give up. I hate to think of the number of visits to the dentist their generosity must have triggered.

I was fascinated by the WWII air raid shelter they still had in their back garden. To a young boy it was like a mini fortress and I frequently played war games in, on and around it, although the high incidence of large spiders and my phobia of them kept me out of the smallest and darkest nooks and crannies.

All of Ada and Matthew's children married and moved out. Vera and Dorothy were married to local men, Alf Seager and Bill Dilley respectively, both setting up home in Cosham just 100 yards apart. Matthew married Peggy and after a short stay in Hampshire Street close to Norah and Percy, Matthew and his family moved away to Newcastle. Their children were to become the usual Geordie manic football fans. In fact, when their son Michael (my cousin) got married one Saturday, the bride, groom, the entire wedding party and guests went in full regalia to watch Newcastle United play at St James's Park that very afternoon straight after the ceremony. Now that's what I call dedicated fans!

Norah got a job in the 'Dorset Milk Dairy' where she met her future husband Percy. She was active in many social areas and was no shrinking violet. As a teenager she even made a stab at fame and glory. Nowadays talent competitions are two-a-penny on the television, many of them exploiting 'reality TV'. The first such remembered talent show on the television was Hughie Green's 'Opportunity Knocks' but you have to go back further to pre-TV days to find the programme that started it all off.

The 'Carroll Levis Discoveries Show' ran on the radio for 3 decades from the 1930s to the 1950s and actually migrated to TV at the end of that period. It featured mainly singers (solo, duo and group), instrumentalists (string and wind instruments) and the occasional comedian. A certain pop group called 'The Quarry Men' appeared on the show in 1957 and got nowhere but they tried again in 1959, reaching the semi-finals this time. In case the reader hasn't realised, this pop group metamorphosed into 'The Beatles'.

My mum's claim to fame was an appearance on the show in 1934 when she was just 19 years of age and the show was a much lesser affair. She was a very passable soprano and entered in her own name as Norah Crowley although there was an attempt to dub her 'the singing milkmaid.' In the contest heat she sang a song called 'My Own' and was in competition with 5 other acts.

She won the heat and went on to the grand final where she won second place behind a young, disabled girl who sang from a wheelchair. (Norah always spoke about this with just a tiny hint of bitterness as she felt she had been pipped by the sympathy vote and I have this vision of a slightly disgruntled Norah assisting the girl onto the stage at the end of the show to receive their accolades and the winner disappearing, chair and all, into the orchestra pit).

As a memento of the event the contestants were each given a record with the entire show recorded on one side. As a boy I often examined this record as the reverse side was completely blank and showed what an uncut '78' looked like, although it was somewhat larger than the standard issue. Margaret has kept this record safe to this date but there's nothing around these days capable of playing it, outside of an Antiques Shop. Years ago I took off it a tape recording of my mum's section of the show I still have in my possession. She retained her superb singing voice until a ripe old age and could be heard every Sunday in church, putting most of the hymn singing to shame.

Norah was a convert to the Roman Catholic faith (as was my father) and she was very devout in her beliefs. She actually seriously considered becoming a nun when in her teens. Had she done so then neither this book nor I would exist. She may have been put off becoming a nun by her father. Matthew was very anti-Catholic for reasons buried deep in his past. He would even threaten violence should the local parish priest show any sign of visiting his house. It was only towards the end of his life Matthew was reconciled with the Catholic faith and he and Ada went back to church and re-took their marriage vows.

There had been a big family bust up over the 'nun' thing and Norah ran away from home. She stayed with a friend who talked her into returning home a few weeks later. It was shortly after she met Percy and their growing relationship finally put paid to a future in the convent. However Norah stayed in close contact with the nuns in the Portsmouth Mile End Convent over the years and once her children were sufficiently grown to fend for themselves she attended every Tuesday as cook for their 'luncheon club.'

Norah's father Matthew died of lung cancer in 1966 at the age of 77. He had been a smoker all his life and my sister Margaret recalls him offering her cigarettes when she was only 10 years old!

After Matthews's death Ada sold the Kensington Road house to her granddaughter Margaret but remained there as a lodger. Ada was unable to adjust to this new style of living and after some friction finally moved out and joined her daughter Norah and her family in Daulston Road. Ada suffered from heart disease and also had several nervous breakdowns over the years, culminating in dementia.

She died in her bed in Daulston Road in 1970. Many years later Norah was also to develop Alzheimer's disease and despite devoted support from Percy over a 2-year period, died in 1993. It was an awful thing to see my mum deteriorate over that time and it's unimaginable how Percy must have felt. The wife he'd been with for over 50 years no longer recognised him and even tried to attack him, thinking he was a stranger who had entered her house.

When Norah took to wandering up the road in the middle of the night she had to be admitted to a secure specialist ward for her own safety. Even then Percy visited her twice a day, every day, for a prolonged period; looking after her and feeding her.

Madge and I also visited from time to time but after a while she only occasionally recognised us, drifting in and out of lucidity. She would go back in time and address me as 'Math,' her brother. Finally, even erroneous communication went and she slowly shut down. The only saving grace was she wasn't self-aware in the final weeks and months and she had her family around her when she was, at last, released from her ordeal.

Some years after Norah's passing Percy met Betty Bennett at a dancing class and they struck up a friendship which gave mutual companionship in his old age. To this day they spend regular holidays together and enjoy 'old ships' meetings at various venues. Percy reciprocates by joining in Betty's 'flower arranging' functions. He is now accepted as part of Betty's circle of family and friends and visits her home on an almost daily basis where he is well looked after.

Matthew, like Ada his mother, suffered mental breakdowns and he and his sisters Vera and Dorothy all seemed to fall victim to 'Alzheimer's' in varying degrees of severity and speed in their twilight years. They say such things may run in families but with a strong presence on my mother's side and a total absence of such things on my father's side then perhaps there is an even chance of such a curse being passed on. I can only pray such a terrible end does not await myself, my sisters or our children.

*   *   *

I would now like to discuss Norah's and Percy's children or putting it another way, my sisters. Margaret was born in the Naval Nursing home in Wickham, a few miles northwest of Portsmouth. She was educated at

Corpus Christi School in North End, Portsmouth.

I have already mentioned the event when she was bitten on the lip by a mongrel, which caused her great distress and affected my own attitude to such animals so deeply. Margaret and I fought cat and dog as children, with me being four years younger usually getting the worst of it. One situation nearly ended up as fratricide. Our parents had gone to St Joseph's church one evening, leaving us to our own devices.

One thing led to another and for reasons I don't recall (funny how the memory blots certain things out) I locked her in the lounge. I don't know why but several of our internal doors had keys on their outside. In fact the only door without a lock of any kind was the bathroom. Which is why everyone in the family learned to sing at an early age. Anyway, when she realised she was locked in, Margaret went apoplectic.

If I had kept her there until our parents returned I hate to think what state she would have been in but if I had released her I feel sure I would not be here today to write this account. I did the only thing I could under the circumstances. I quietly unlocked the door and then ran out of the front door and away as fast as possible. I actually ran all the way to the church and returned home cowering behind my parents for protection.

Happily, all was forgiven which was just as well. When my dad was posted to Lossiemouth and the family moved to Scotland, Margaret and I found ourselves the only English kids at St Sylvester's Convent School. We needed to stick together then, if only for survival. Margaret actually put their noses out of joint by walking off with their Burns Federation Certificate for poetry recital. Margaret being at a reasonably social age then, actually forged some life long friendships with both the nuns who were our teachers and indeed some of the pupils.

Returning to Portsmouth, Margaret was an active member of the church youth club, being one of the few outlets for young people at the time. After she left school she secured a job with the (now defunct) Hampshire Building Society, then based in Guildhall Walk, as the office junior.

Then there was a major turn of events when she had a 'holiday romance'. Margaret met Michael Goldsmith at Butlins Holiday Camp at Clacton. There was instant attraction but with her coming from Portsmouth and he from Herstmonceux in Sussex they had to continue a long distance courtship.

It may have been difficult but it led to marriage in the early 1960s.

They had two daughters in quick succession, Michelle first and then Louise. Initially they lived in Herstmonceaux in Sussex with occasional trips to Portsmouth to visit Margaret's mum. They eventually moved back to Portsmouth full time, to a house in Carnarvon Road, which was fairly close to her mum and dad.

Then when grandad Matthew died, and with some assistance from her parents, Margaret with Michael and the young girls purchased our grandparents house at 31 Kensington Road. However after overcoming so many obstacles, things started to fall apart. Margaret's marriage to Michael ran into trouble; he moved out and divorce followed.

Later she met a rather hypnotic character called David Humphreys. He appeared to be stylish, moneyed and sophisticated but she found out to her cost after she married him he was all front and no substance, and also proved to be a violent bully. They lived at Inhurst Road in North End, Portsmouth. She eventually left him, taking with her Michelle, Louise and a child from the relationship; another daughter named Bernadette. It was her three daughters who were destined to be bridesmaids at the wedding of Madge and myself, several years later.

The solicitor who handled her divorce from David was a very likeable chap named Ian Shaw. He was a bachelor when he encountered Margaret but he became Margaret's third husband. They lived just North of Portsmouth in a large house in Charminster Drive, Waterlooville but when Ian set up his own business in Portsmouth they moved into a town house in the exclusive Pembroke Park area of Southsea. Ironically it was a housing development built on the ruins of much more humble shops and dwellings frequented by the family ancestors many years before.

Margaret and Ian had a son, Jonathan, but despite their shared affection for him their own marriage got into difficulty. Although they divorced they have remained firm friends.

Margaret then met a teacher from St John's College school where Jonathan was a pupil and incidentally where I received my secondary education. His name was Phil Saunders. They initially set up home in Green Lane in Copnor and eventually moved to Craneswater Park in Southsea in 2002, where they remain to the present day. She continues to work, as she has for several years, looking after children's well being in school and looks forward to a well-deserved retirement in 2004(ish).

*   *   *

Norah and Percy's other daughter was Frances. She was born at home in Daulston Road in 1953 and being 5 years younger than myself and 9 years younger than Margaret, she was very much the baby of the family. Her earliest memories are of our time in Scotland and of the hair pulling skirmishes she had with the similarly aged little German girl next door. And of the occasion we met a couple with a St Bernard dog when walking in the woods and Frances, steeped in the story of Goldilocks, thought it was 'daddy bear'.

On our return to Portsmouth, Frances attended Corpus Christi School and after her 11+ went to a small school in Kingston Crescent called St Theresa's Grammar. It was a couple of houses knocked together and Frances loved the close attention that came with the small class sizes. It was a bit of a cultural shock when after 2 years the school was forced to close and Frances transferred to The Convent of the Cross, a Catholic school run by nuns at Waterlooville.

This school eventually became Oaklands RC School, which all of my and Madge's children attended for their secondary education and Madge worked at for many years. Incidentally, for the benefit of my kids who feel put upon to travel more than a few yards under their own steam without calling for a taxi (usually dad's) Frances travelled from home in central Portsmouth out to the Waterlooville school and back, every day by bus.

To be honest she didn't really take to the new school and consequently her academic studies suffered and she left school at the age of 15. But she more than put that right in subsequent years.

She started work at the Hampshire Building Society (later swallowed up by a larger financial group) located at the Guildhall Walk. This was the same company her sister Margaret had worked for a few years previously. She stayed for 3 and a half years before moving on. It was during this time she met and was married at the age of just 18 to Andy Mills who was an electrician and forklift truck maintenance engineer.

They lived together initially in Stowe Road, then in Epworth Road just around the corner from Margaret and finally moved out to the Crookhorn area. Andy was a classic 60's/70s 'hippy' in appearance and manner and therefore came across as very laid back and friendly, if slightly off the wall, and at first Frances very much paralleled Andy's attitudes. But when she resumed her education she seemed to change and become a far more a 'feet on the ground' person. This may well have been down to the company she was keeping at University. She seemed to outgrow Andy and eventually they parted.

As just referred to, in 1977 to 1980, Frances returned to University on a full time basis and in 1979 was awarded a First Class B.A. Degree in Cultural Studies. Then, after a year at Highbury College she achieved a Diploma in Business Studies. Finally she returned again to University and was awarded her M.A. in 1993.

It was while at University Frances met and in 1982, at the age of 29, married Ron Weighell who is a pretty amazing chap. Ron was a skilled carpenter by trade who actually worked at the University but when you met him you took him to be a Professor. He is tall with distinguished greying hair and smokes a 'Sherlock Holmes' pipe. Above all he comes across as a highly educated, thoughtful and thoroughly nice chap. Ron actually writes stories, specialising in the 'P.D.James' style of mystery/horror works. Over the years he has had quite a number of his stories published as individual and in compendium books.

Frances then resumed the world of work, taking on administration type roles, first at PD Fuels in Broad Street, Old Portsmouth, then in 1985 back at Portsmouth University where she had studied for her degree. Over the years she has stayed there, gradually working up the ranks until at the time of writing (in 2003) she has reached the giddy heights of Faculty Manager with a staff of some 90 people.

Ron and Frances initially set up home in Manners Road Southsea and in 1990 at Tangier Road in the first house next to Baffins Pond. Then in 1993 they moved to Winkfield Row, where Ron has created a miniature Italian Renaissance building and garden in the midst of Horndean.

Frances has fond memories of living with the family in Daulston Road. The frequent board and card game sessions. The squashing up of her and Margaret in one bedroom of a 2-bedroom house while yours truly reigned supreme in my own room (that was the converted bedroom downstairs).

Frances recalls the family holidays in caravans and chalets where being the youngest she always got the smallest bed, that in such accommodation seems not actually designed for human occupancy, and she frequently fell out. She also remembers the passing fads of yo-yos and hula-hoops (of which the former has returned recently but for some reason (fast food and child obesity?) not the latter and the manic rabbit called Fred that lived with us and whose personality and quirky behaviour is described in a later Chapter.

Having discussed my sisters, I now need to relate my own story.

2.3 Chris and his upbringing

I was born on 5th June 1947 in the Royal Naval Nursing home in Portsmouth. It no longer exists but was located near the Dockyard main gates end of Queen Street, ironically very close to where my wife's ancestors lived. As implied by my place of birth, my father Percy was employed by the Navy as an electrical instructor in the Fleet Air Arm. I had two sisters, Margaret who was about 3 years older and Frances who was younger than me by almost 6 years. This meant, as a child, I got the worst of both worlds. My elder sister was too big for me to beat up and if I took it out on the younger one then my mum would sort me out.

Life then seemed full of cowpats to be avoided on a regular basis and hasn't really changed since. Apart from my very early weeks as a baby, which were spent in a flat in Simpson Road, I moved with the family to a two-bedroom 'semi' in the centre of the city on the corner of Daulston Road and Hampshire Street.

While I was young my dad frequently travelled abroad with the Royal Navy so I was largely brought up in a household consisting of first 2 and then (after the birth of Frances) 3 females. An interesting contrast to my future wife who was raised without a sibling sister but had 3 brothers, 2 of which were older than her. I have often wondered whether a stronger male presence in my household or stronger female one in my wife's would have changed our upbringings to any significant extent.

I used to look forward to my dad returning from his foreign trips. He usually brought chocolate and sweets with him and I used to raid his luggage to find them as soon as he appeared through the door, often in competition with Margaret who was intent on doing the same thing.

Here are just a couple memories of my childhood. I can remember just before my 6th birthday, Queen Elizabeth II's Coronation took place on June 2nd 1953, there was a street party in my road and a fancy dress competition was included. My mum dressed me up as Sir Edmund Hillary, who (with Sherpa Tenzing Norgay) had conquered Mount Everest for the very first time just days previously, on 29th of May. In the competition I came second to a young lad dressed up as a pageboy in a shop-bought outfit. I thought my thrown together affair with my dad's car towrope over my shoulder was far more deserving of first place. I'd like to say they found the pageboy later, tied up with a piece of car towrope and a custard pie in his face but life wasn't so humbling then, unless of course you were bent on jumping in cowpats.

Also at the age of 6, I can recall listening to 'Children's Hour' on the radio on a regular basis and sending my mother hurtling up the stairs to fetch my teddy 'Edward' whenever the song 'Me and my Teddy Bear' was played.

I grew up rapidly and although I did not develop a large circle of friends, I played a lot with a couple of kids who lived nearby, often in the streets. We raced our tricycles or threw tennis balls onto nearby terraced house roofs and competed as to who could catch them as they rolled back off and plummeted downwards. Indoors, rubber soldiers were the order of the day with a wooden fort my dad built for me and still exists to this day, squirreled away in our loft.

We used to play conkers during October when the 'ammunition' was readily found. My dad had located a 'special' tree out in the countryside in the corner of a farmer's field. It was festooned with enormous conkers we gathered in dozens off of the ground. At the time of writing I don't remember exactly where it was but we returned there like an annual pilgrimage for several years.

*   *   *

When I was eight years old my dad ceased his foreign postings and became 'shore based.' His first posting of this type was to the then Fleet Air Arm station at Lossiemouth, in Scotland (now taken over by the RAF). It was for 2 years and so the whole family went with him and set up home in the nearby city of Elgin, in the locality known as Bishopmill. It was a bit of a physical and cultural shock for me.

Firstly there was the weather. Being a 'Southern softie' I was used to a rather gentler climate. In the Grampians I learned the main weather difference between summer and winter was the depth of the snow and the rain was horizontal during the winter months. We also had the experience of the coldest winter and warmest summer while we were there that the locals could remember.

It was also rather unsettling to experience everyone around me talking with an unfamiliar accent. Some so strong I couldn't understand what they were saying. It took a few weeks for my ears to become fully tuned in. It was then I realised not everything I heard was friendly.

My elder sister Margaret and myself went to a convent school called St Sylvester's and again it was a first experience to be taught by nuns.

My memories of them are they were kind and caring and under their tuition I learned to write. I recall copying out the letters of the alphabet in a small book with the beautiful, flowing example letters written by my teacher down the left hand side of the page and my stuttering efforts replicated several times alongside.

I enjoyed the classes but I can't say the same about the playtimes. It was here I was exposed to the curious attitude some Scots have with regard to the English. Here it was I first became familiar with the name 'Armitage Shanks' as it stared back at me whenever I got my head shoved down the toilet.

When some of the boys decided to play war games, it was invariably the Scots against the English. I was on one side and everybody else on the other. Culloden it seemed had to be avenged at every available opportunity. I was even held as a 'hostage' on one occasion to make my sister emerge from the toilets where she had sought sanctuary. I am eternally grateful to her for giving herself up, as the alternative for me might have been to share a similar fate to 'Braveheart' William Wallace, with all my 'bits' scattered over a wide area of the Highlands.

Overall it was a great 'toughening up' experience and with my dad abroad so much in the earlier years, compensated for the upbringing in a largely female dominated household.

The above events may give the reader a false impression of how I perceived our Northern hosts, but once away from 'mob' situations described above, in a 'one on one' relationship, I fared far better and found both then and throughout my life our Scottish cousins to be both friendly and delightful company.

I made other breakthroughs during our stay North of the border. I learned to ride a bicycle, got 'closer to nature' and developed an appreciation of the environment. There was so much rugged scenery nearby and we had frequent weekend excursions. Acres of heather, ice cold and incredibly clear mountain streams were commonplace in Scotland. Not that we had to go far. Opposite our house was a large field of corn and we used to sit on the dry-stone wall munching at the golden ears. Many years later in 1998 I took Madge and the two youngest children on a tour of Scotland, stopping at Elgin and wandering around my old haunts and was dismayed to find the field of corn had been replaced by a housing estate. Such is the effect of 'progress'.

Just around the corner from where we lived in Bishopmill was 'an area ripe for development' as some estate agents would describe it. It was about half an acre of scrubland down South would have been called a 'bomb site' but local kids christened 'the wilderness.' It was here we made cabins from corrugated metal roofing, waged guerrilla warfare in the long grass and rode bicycles around obstacle courses.

I also had my first experience of a domestic animal that actually belonged to us, although 'belonged' is probably not the right word. Cats rarely 'belong' to anyone. They are very independent and I think would be insulted if they thought we claimed to 'own' them. This one in particular, because it was a stray cat and therefore was even more independent of an owner or family. My dad found it foraging around the camp huts trying to set up home in the Master-at-Arms desk drawer. She was quickly adopted by us children and dubbed 'Tibbles.'

Although we were fond of Tibbles, she didn't really return the compliment and remained very independent of the whole family. Just putting up with us to supply her with food, drink and shelter when she fancied it. I wasn't totally surprised when we eventually left Scotland to return south the cat did not accompany us. My dad found her another home with the camp cook so she could stay in the same locality. Being with the cook and all that food must have been either the equivalent of cat heaven for Tibbles or a quick road to it, depending on the cook's mood and menu.

Although not very successful, the experience didn't put me off cats. I was a couple of years older when my friend at school asked if I would like to see his cat and her new litter of 6-week-old kittens. I went to his house one day after school and sat on the floor, playing with six little fluffy tabbies. My friend then asked me if I would like to take one home. Without any thought whatsoever I jumped at the opportunity. Although she was looking for good homes for the kittens, his mum was less precipitous.

'Are you sure your parents won't mind?' she asked.

'Of course not' I replied. 'How could they turn down such a sweet little thing?'

They could of course very easily turn it down. Once my mum found out what I was trying to smuggle into my bedroom in a cardboard box she went absolutely bananas.

I ended up with the distinct impression my mum had no affection for cats whatsoever and even Tibbles had lived with us under sufferance and mum had got rid of her at the first available opportunity. She seemed to feel the same way about dogs as well. My dad had been brought up with dogs and Nanny and Poppy always had a mutt as far back as I could remember, which admittedly at that age wasn't very far. I was always uncertain of their dog, as indeed I was with all dogs.

The one I knew best was called 'Trixie' who at the time I knew her was a rather moth eaten old mongrel who bayed loudly when anyone knocked on the door. She was at best indifferent to me and at the time simply reinforced my growing anti-dog opinions. My dad would happily have acquired a canine beast if he'd had the choice. It was my mum who wasn't so keen and as dad was away so much she was most affected by the decision and thus had the final word.

What changed matters regarding a house pet was a visit to one of my dad's friends. His name was Albert Munday and he was what one would today call an 'entrepreneur'. He had fingers in so many pies he could have been Simple Simon's Pieman mate. He actually ran a smallholding with animals of all descriptions populating it. On one visit I admired a small indoor snooker table and he immediately offered to sell it to my parents for me, oblivious to it being his own son's pride and joy. He just couldn't stop doing deals; he was that sort of bloke.

However Albert was not just a bit of a wide boy, he also had a heart of gold and treated his guests like royalty. When someone remarked about 'bonfire night' coming shortly he took a cue from this and vanished. A few minutes later he appeared with his collection of fireworks he then proceeded to set off. Giving an amazing, if rather premature, display.

When we eventually made to leave he offered my mum and dad a rabbit from his smallholding stock. At the time and for some years after the war, rabbit was a very acceptable meal although it is much rarer in this day and age. It was no surprise my parents accepted and I saw them exchange pleased glances and he got up and went outside. My parents were rather taken aback when he returned a few minutes later with a beautiful fluffy baby rabbit.

They were clearly not going to reject a gift they had already accepted and it would have been churlish to ask 'can we have a slightly older one with a bit more meat on it please.' Albert clearly had a different idea to mum and dad and had intended it all along as a family pet rather than next Sunday's lunch.

Ignoring the temptation to name it such things as 'dinner' or 'gravy's mate', bunny was christened 'Fred' and went home with us. Exactly what happened to Fred is detailed in the Chapter later on covering 'Pets'.

* * *

It was about the age of 10 I discovered music in a big way. I was bitten by the music bug and went to see the 'Rock Around the Clock' movie with Bill Hayley launching Rock & Roll.

I can honestly say I have grown up liking a very wide spectrum of music, from rock to pop to light opera to classics. I once astounded my teenage daughter by delighting in the rapper 'Eminem's' latest recording. Anyway the foundations were laid in the late 1950s and a pivotal moment was when I was on holiday in 1958 with my family at Rockley Sands Caravan Park. A rather dilapidated hall had been given over to the teenagers evening entertainment and consisted of a jukebox and just about nothing else. However, the place was packed every evening with teenagers listening and dancing to the sounds of the moment.

Elvis had been under way since late 1956 although being challenged by ballad singer Pat Boone; the Everley Brothers were baying their unique harmonies and my special hero Buddy Holly was dazzling everyone with his brilliant but all too brief career. The revolution was on the way and the kids loved it. Me included. With Margaret and many others we formed in a packed but structured phalanx in the hall and with all of us moving as one, we did the 'line bop' for hours on end. I would spend the evenings thus and then strut back to the caravan with the strains of 'Cathy's Clown' serenading me on my way. Fantastic.

Shortly afterwards I bought my first record. It was 'Rave on' by Buddy Holly, still today one of my all-time favourites. I purchased the record in a shop called 'Musical Homes', almost opposite the top end of Hampshire Street. It was a curious place. You could ask them to play a record to you and then decide if you wanted to buy it or not. I was made an offer to either take the record straight away on a traditional '78' disc or wait a week or so and get it on the new, smaller '45' discs made of revolutionary vinyl. I decided to wait and hence became one of the very first owners of a vinyl '45' record.

A few weeks later in February 1959 the world was mourning the loss of Buddy Holly in a plane crash. It truly was as the song goes 'the day the music died'. After that, as I said above, my musical tastes broadened out but the roots were in 'pop' music and still are today.

* * *

I had previously attended George Street Infant School near home, along with St Swithun's School in Southsea and on our return from Scotland picked up my education at Corpus Christi School at North End in Portsmouth. I did well there and was always around the top of the class. We had a good set of teachers and under their influence I also started to really exercise my imagination and initiative and among other things 'published' an unofficial class newsletter. One of the teachers who took me for sports was called 'Mr Plaice' and I recall my mum coming up the school to see him on one occasion and asking to see a 'Mr Fish'. That got a laugh all round.

Like my father and his brothers before me I also was assigned regular household duties, although I'm pleased to say they were not as demanding as they had experienced and I have described in an earlier Chapter. Mine were things like cutting the privet hedge at the front of the house, collecting coal from the bunker at the side of the house then making up the fire using paper and wood to ignite the coal.

It was quite a revolution for me when we bought a gas poker that could just be placed inside the open fire and left to get things burning properly. Note kids, no central heating. In fact we used to huddle around an oil burner that we moved between the bedrooms in the winter months. We thought nothing of it because we knew no better then.

At the age of 11 and following my '11+' examination, I moved from my primary school (Corpus Christi) to St John's College in Southsea. This was a fairly exclusive 'boys only' boarding school with a fair number of 'day' pupils, which took students from all over the world on a fee-paying basis. It was run by the 'de la Salle' brothers, a teaching branch of the Catholic religion, with a sprinkling of lay teachers. Today the school is still going strong but now takes girls into the 6th form and 'brothers' are all too rarely seen.

My form tutors included Brothers Dennis-Mary, Adrian, Cuthman-Francis, Maurice and Richard. My favourite was Brother Charles who was a thickset man about 60 years old with grey-to-white hair. He took 6th form mathematics and was also the chess master. St John's had a considerable reputation for chess in those days and competed at national level. Bro Charles had a lot to do with this success, being a strong player in his own right and also incidentally one of the UK's strongest Crossword Puzzle solvers, working under a pseudonym.

I worked my way through the many St John's chess teams and ended up as a high board in the second team, amassing a lot of wins along the way and regularly getting my name in the results section of the Portsmouth Evening News.

I twice entered and won my age group in the 'Sir William Dupree' chess tournament held at the Portsmouth Guildhall and my parents attended the prize ceremony when the Lord Mayor handed out the cash prizes. It was only a few pounds but represented the most money I'd ever had. As a schoolboy I also went on to play chess for Hampshire but when I eventually started work this activity was firstly curtailed and then dropped altogether.

Back at school, I was a regular in the top half dozen in my class academically, although not strong enough to challenge for the very top place. This led to my participation in a rather extraordinary experiment run by the school. For reasons not clear to me at the time, a handful of 4th year students, including myself, were given the chance of taking their GCE 'O' levels a year early. The object being to miss the 5th year out completely and get into the 6th form a year in advance, although to this day I don't know what benefit that would actually bring.

The problem was we had not completed anything like the full syllabus to take the normal number of 10 or 11 subjects and so we were restricted to just 6. I wish I had turned down the offer but I was 14 years of age and a very young 14 at that. All the other 5 boys offered the opportunity were going for it and my parents were in favour so I just went along with what everyone wanted me to do.

I eventually secured my 6 subjects and went straight from the 4th year into the 6th form to study maths and physics. However there was a knock-on effect. I had missed a whole years study including a lot of knowledge required for the 6th form work. This situation was exacerbated by an injury that caused me to take about 9 weeks off school.

There was no way I could make up so much ground and at the end of the second year I only received an 'E' in Pure Mathematics and an 'O' level pass for my Applied Mathematics 'A' levels, although by some miracle I obtained a grade 'A' in Physics. In the meantime the classmates I had left behind to take the normal course through the 5th form romped away with 10 and 11 'O' levels even though academically, when we had been together, I had been a street ahead of them. They also carried on through to the 6th form and got far better 'A' level results than me, many of them going on to University.

My results were not good enough for a University place so I was faced with the choice of repeating a year at school or seeking employment. What actually happened is detailed in a later Chapter. If I sound a little bitter about all this then perhaps I am. In the end it didn't make a lot of difference to my career but I feel I under achieved significantly at the time.

I think maybe this disappointment and later having to leave my accountancy studies incomplete (due to horrendous work commitments – see later) drove me to want to prove my intellectual capability. Unfortunately I didn't have the time to do this by (re-)sitting exam papers. Instead, I applied to join Mensa, which for those who might not know is a society for those people with an I.Q. of 148 and over. I sent away for a trial pack and then sat the 'mock' test and marked it myself at home. It gave me an I.Q. score of 154. (The same, incidentally, as TV maths genius and thinking man's crumpet, Carol Vorderman).

This encouraged me to go for the real thing. I travelled to London, to the London School of Economics where the test was being conducted. There were about 40 people in a large auditorium. The test took about an hour and a half and was conducted in a very strict manner. A few days later I received an invitation to join Mensa, along with my official score; it was 154 exactly the same as my trial run.

I was delighted and went along to a few local monthly meetings and read the monthly magazine with great enthusiasm. I was very disappointed. At the national level there was nothing but internal bickering and mud slinging via the magazine. The local meetings were populated by cerebral types with little common sense and not really in touch with the real world. However, I stuck with it and things have very much improved over the years. The magazine is fine now and the national people have sorted things out but I have not attended any local meetings since the early days. I have kept it going because it represents a small achievement in my life and one, in my dotage, I would probably be unable to repeat should I leave and then be asked to re-sit the test.

*　　*　　*

My life outside of school was pretty sad. I had no older brother or close friend to go around with, mainly due to my school commitments. My schooling in the later years included a minimum of two and a half hours homework per night, often extending to 4 hours, and in those days we also went to school on Saturday mornings. (This was to compensate academically for a half day of 'games and sports' every Wednesday afternoon). The result of all this was I had little time for socialising and what little I had centred on Chess matches. So I was what you might call a 'late developer', which is a nice way of saying I hadn't developed at all. I was diffident and lacking in confidence.

The exceptions to my seclusion were my occasional Saturday trips up to London. From my early teens I had taken to getting a train to the Capital and spending all day looking around museums and famous landmarks. I hugely enjoyed that and built up a considerable knowledge of where everything was situated and how to get about in London that has served me well through the years when work or leisure have taken me back there.

The only problem I had in making these trips was migraines. I had suffered with migraine from an early age, as did my sister Margaret (although Frances seems to have escaped this particular curse). For me, the main 'triggers' over the years have consistently been stress, bright sunlight, alcohol (even in small quantities) and heavy perfumes.

In those days I had no remedy but to lie down in a dark room and sleep it off. Later I was recommended 'Migraleve' by Margaret and this transformed my life. Up until then I dreaded getting a migraine when I way away from home as I knew I would have to endure it, with the pain and vomiting it induced, until I could get home. My trips to London sometimes induced a migraine and I would have to head home as soon as possible, enduring the pain as best I could. With Migraleve, as long as I took it at an early stage then the migraine didn't develop and I could carry on normally.

My other activities outside school were also a bit cerebral and isolationist. I used to have a fairly extensive chemistry set I supplemented with visits to a chemical and apparatus supplier. I would then treat the house to a wide variety of concocted smells. The extreme of these experiments was when I bought fireworks (a lot more vicious in those days as well I must say), opened them up and mixed the contents together. Sometimes sprinkling the new mixture onto the open coal fire in the living room to see what would happen. Looking back, I'm surprised I didn't burn the house down or at least blow my eyebrows off.

I grew up with the radio being switched on constantly while my mother did her housework. 'Mrs Dale's Diary' and 'The Archers' were her favourites and the forerunners of today's TV Soaps. My mum somewhat surprisingly also listened to the BBC Third Programme cricket commentary. I think this was probably because of John Arlott's interesting and vivid descriptions and his rich, brown Somerset drawl.

For years my Sunday lunchtimes would revolve around a roast dinner and listening to '2-Way Family Favourites' (the British Forces programme) on the radio. So, driven by all this and the absence of a television set, I formed my own favourite list of radio programmes. The comedy shows 'The Goons', 'Life with the Lyons', 'Round the Horne', 'Hancock's Half Hour', 'The Navy Lark' and ' I'm Sorry I'll Read That Again' being my all time favourites and 'Journey into Space' which was the forerunner of science fiction space adventures and scared the crap out of me at the time.

When TV came it was in black and white and very boring, being just the one (BBC) channel comprising things like 'The Brain's Trust'. The most exciting thing they had was 'What's my Line' and that says it all. Even watching paint dry was more interesting than the endless 'interlude' screens constantly put up between programmes.

I was thunderstruck when I was about 10 years of age and we visited someone that had the new ITV channel. Although still in black and white it had things like 'Robin Hood' on it. Now that's what I called children's entertainment. Eventually the Beeb got with it, at least to launch 'Top of the Pops' that became my favourite programme for years. Colour TV finally arrived and with it 'Monty Python's Flying Circus' 'Rowan and Martin's Laugh-in' and 'The Muppet Show'.

You'll notice the vast majority of my favourite programmes were comedies and that just about sums me up. I really enjoy a good laugh and tend to see the funny side of most situations, although if it involves cowpats then the funny side might not register with me until some considerable time later.

One TV event to stick in my mind was the 1966 World Cup Final between England and West Germany. I well recall the agonies and ecstasies accompanying the swaying fortunes, as the game was dramatically played out to its now famous conclusion.

My life during my schooldays was dominated by studies and, in a way, little changed when I left and got a job with the Southern Electricity Board. The studies were still there but the topic had changed to an Accountancy qualification. Even when this finally ceased it was because of excessive workload and masses of overtime working. All in all I didn't really have the time to get a life at all.

At the same time I was trying to become independent of my parents and it was a source of conflict between them and myself on the occasions I left the house that I would refuse to tell them where I was going. Not because I had something to hide but because I was showing typical adolescent behaviour to break free of parental control. (See kids I really **do** know how you feel).

This was why I didn't tell my folks when I booked myself driving lessons and why I went on my jaunts to look around London. All in all I discussed very little with them but if there were ever a whiff of a girlfriend my mum would spring into advice mode.

'If you're serious about a girl then take her swimming. Then you can see what she looks like without most of her clothes on'. You can tell she was nearly a nun.

It's just as well my dear old mum didn't survive to see how the current generation of kids carry on. Jumping into bed seems to be the modern day of equivalent of what shaking hands was in my day. It's just a different part of the anatomy that gets shaken about.

I was following all the natural instincts to make my own way in the world and find myself a partner in life. My parents, likewise, were getting twitchy about my ongoing presence. How I finally broke away, to the delight of all, is the topic of the next Chapter.

Chapter 3

Meeting up

The story of how my wife, Madge and I met, 'courted' (to use the old fashioned parlance) and set up home, has been said to be the stuff of romantic novels and the truthful facts sound like the sort of fiction produced by elderly ladies dressed in pink chiffon.

I was knocking on a bit for an unattached young man, being 24 and still living at home with my parents. Although they were good enough not to say anything outright or drop subtle hints like packing my bags and leaving them on the front doorstep, it was clear they were getting twitchy about my ongoing presence.

My two sisters had already married and left home. In that order too, which in these days seems to becoming unusual, as couples have increasingly long trial periods of living together. I can't help speculating with so much practice going on, how come the divorce rate is still increasing? I believe couples should marry as soon as possible but sign a contract saying the first one to leave the marriage has to take all the kids with them. That'll reduce the divorce rate overnight.

Clearly it was time I moved out of my parents' house and found my own place to live. To me this meant buying my first house, as I had been brought up to believe renting was a waste of money. It would be fortuitous, although not essential, if this could coincide with my also finding a girl willing to put up with me and share this palace of my dreams. I'd had a few girl friends (if not exactly droves of them), but cupid's arrow was yet to strike, although there had been one near miss. Finding a partner who I could fall head over heels in love with and would reciprocate the feelings (difficult as that would be) was going to be tricky to say the least. But I needed to move ahead on both fronts at the same time.

If I succeeded in finding a partner but not a house then I would be presenting my parents with the total despair of me getting married and bringing my bride home to live with them as well as myself (I think under those circumstances **they** would have left home). If I found a house, but no bride, then I assumed life would become a lot tougher with the cosiness of living at home with built-in meal and laundry services being lost. (Actually I was to learn through the experience of my own sons leaving home the above assumption was a complete fallacy. They moved out and yet came home frequently to raid the fridge and food cupboards and leave their dirty laundry as a 'thank you.' Perhaps we were too considerate of our parents or just plain stupid in those days).

Getting back to the search for the girl of my dreams, I needed to make a determined effort to meet up with 'Miss Right' or possibly even 'Miss Wrong' if she had access to a lot of money. One of the most popular places to do this was the local dance hall in the centre of Portsmouth called 'The Mecca'. It was a 2-storey building with a large dance floor downstairs with seating and standing areas all around, a revolving stage, bars and cloakrooms at each end and the entrance in the centre, opposite the stage. Upstairs was a long, elliptical balcony overlooking the dance floor, a restaurant and more bars at each end.

'The Mecca' had special events on for each evening of the week. Mondays was 'over 25's' and was usually populated by spotty teenagers with fake ids (some things don't change eh kids). Wednesdays was 'teeny bopper' night, usually populated by over-40-year-old males with their coat collars turned up.

The big occasions were on Friday and Saturday evenings when mostly normal people turned up to either find a partner, catch a partner out with someone they shouldn't be with or just have a jolly good time. Sometimes all three together.

Past experience of going to 'The Mecca' on my own had been abortive expeditions. The girls never went singly and would not leave their companion(s) in order to go off with some stranger, especially when like me, his looks had more in common with Quasimodo than Steve McQueen. (I never have made pretensions in terms of either looks or height).

I solved the difficulty by persuading a male friend from work to accompany me. John Bloxham was also 'available' if not actually desperate and being tall and as far as I could tell, reasonably good looking for a bloke, I hoped he would bring much needed attractiveness to the partnership.

We selected a particular Saturday evening in March 1972 for our 'wenching' exploits that happened to be the night the clocks went forward, reflecting the change to 'summer time'. We travelled separately and met up outside the building at a decently late hour and then swept in with some panache (or so we liked to think). We spent some time at the bar preparing ourselves with a small intake of alcohol (within the driving limits of course) and surveyed the scene. As usual all the blokes were around the edge of the dance floor or looking over the balcony rails above. All the girls were on the dance floor, facing inwards, away from the blokes and dancing around their handbags in the time honoured ritual.

As luck (or fate) would have it, John spotted a girl that worked with us and we knew well. Her name was Sharon and she was friendly and well, to put it bluntly, a bit of a 'nutter'. I don't mean the latter unkindly. She was very well liked by all (especially her boyfriend) and was great fun but always likely to overstep the bounds of good taste, exceed the legal noise levels or generally cause embarrassment to all in close proximity with her when she was in pursuit of a good time.

She was with several other girls, most of whom we also knew to a degree and a couple we hadn't met before. We decided we ought to say 'hello' to show good manners and, after all, if Sharon was there then things would happen and it certainly wouldn't be a boring time.

Sharon was gushing in her welcome and introduced us to the new faces of Christine Hillman and Madge Lenton. Both were of medium height (i.e. a bit shorter than me thankfully) and 18 years of age. Christine had shoulder length blond hair, she was slightly pale and of a slim build. She wore a dress but I no longer recollect the detail of her clothes that evening. Madge was a brunette with her hair up, wearing an orange dress buttoned all the way up the front (or down, depending on which end you started looking) with knee high white boots. What registered with me was she wore spectacles and had great legs. I was a sucker for white boots, especially when accompanied by great legs. (Perhaps if had I remembered her name was Madge Lenton, an anagram of which was 'Noted Leg Man', I might have seen the writing on the wall. And upon further examination another anagram was 'Tangled Omen' that might have indicated the difficulties yet to come).

We all spent time chatting within the group and eventually Christine and Madge accepted John's and my invitation onto the dance floor. At first we all danced together but when the slow music started and we paired off, I got Madge and John had Christine. I'm not sure to this day how that particular division was decided or even who took the initiative but as I said before, Madge had great legs.

Madge and I spent the rest of the evening together both on our own and as a part of the larger group and I thought we had hit it off pretty well. As people began to drift away I offered Madge a lift home and John did likewise to Christine. Both the girls accepted and went off together to the ladies to do whatever the girls always do on such occasions. (Repair make up, compare notes, vomit etc). John and I waited just outside, where we had arranged to meet up.

The girls didn't show. We waited and still no show. We went back inside and looked around. We even got Sharon to check the ladies loo for us but still no sign. They had disappeared. I experienced a mixture of puzzlement, annoyance and concern for their safety. It was the middle of the night and the area around 'The Mecca' had some pretty unsavoury characters at that time (like us for example). I just could not work out what had happened. The evening had gone so well and I saw no reason to be stood up.

John and I took to the cars. Madge had told me the road where she lived and also said it was in a block of flats but she hadn't told me which block or what the flat number was. So I drove every possible route from the Mecca to her road, back and forth. There was no sign of her so I finally gave up and went home.

It felt a bit like the story of Cinderella. But instead of a glass slipper, I had Sharon. With no phone number as a contact I had to wait until Monday morning at work before I could see Sharon and find out if the girls were OK. Yes, she had seen them on the Sunday. What had happened? Apparently the girls had bumped into Madge's elder brother Richard on their way out to meet us and he had insisted on taking them both home. Exactly as you would expect a caring elder brother to behave.

The explanation seemed plausible, especially as Sharon had brought back with her an invitation from the girls for John and I to accompany them on a 'baby sitting' evening the next weekend. They had given us an address and asked us to get there about 20:30. (That's half past 8 in the evening for those like my wife who have difficulty with the 24 hour clock. ('How on earth can it be 20 something when the clock only goes up to 12 and anyway when are they going to decimalise it?')

The appointed time saw me driving to the address, with John again travelling in his own car. I knew it was somewhere in a new estate under development in the Milton area of Portsmouth. Large areas of the estate were already occupied but building work was still going on. I found the road without trouble and kerb-crawled along trying to make out the house numbers in the gathering gloom. I was looking for No 26.

Peering through the dark I could just make out 20….. 22….. 24. Then a series of partly built homes. What was due to be number 26 had walls currently 4 feet high with a recently fitted door frame but no door as yet and certainly no upstairs, let alone a roof.

My immediate thought was I'd gone into the wrong road or misread the house numbers. I double-checked. There was no mistake. Perhaps I had got the address wrong. A car appeared in the distance driving slowly down the road towards me. It was John coming from the other direction and looking just as confused as me.

We did a few more circuits and met up again from opposite directions, winding down our windows to have a mid road conversation. We decided the most sensible course of action was to repair to the local pub and consider the situation carefully. Surely the girls couldn't have set us up? The more we thought about it the more this seemed to be a possibility. After all we were dealing with friends of Sharon.

If only we had known the girls had given us a fictitious house number immediately opposite the house where they were baby-sitting. At that very moment they were rolling around the floor with mirth at the jolly jape.

If I had known then what I know now; that no respectable baby sitter would allow two scarcely known morons to join them in such a responsible task and no parents would ever allow it in the first place, then I would have guessed it was a set-up from the outset. But in those days I was young, naïve and blessed with a set of raging hormones that tended to block out any vestige of common sense when a pretty face came into view. I just felt I had taken another leap into a fresh cowpat. (Perhaps I should have gone back to the anagrams of her name 'Madge Lenton', where I would have found 'To Dangle Men' was another one of them).

Anyway, John and I decided to write the whole thing off to experience and there the situation would have stayed and my life taken a totally different course and this book also, if it were not for a phone call to me at work the next day. The call was from Madge. She apologised and said the whole thing had been Christine's idea, as she wasn't interested in John and saw the whole thing as being an opportunity to pull a practical joke. Madge had gone along with it to humour her. On reflection, she now felt she was out of order and would like to see me again.

I decided either she was genuine or going for an entry in the Guinness

Book of Records for the number of times a girl could wind a bloke up and he would walk right into it. Even in the short space of time I had known her I had formed the opinion Madge was basically a very honest person, although a bit woolly headed and if she did try to tell a porky then it should be obvious. (This assumption turned out to be true at the time but with the constant practice she has put in since I have become a prime candidate for the Guinness Book of Records over the years, anyway, as she continues to sucker me on every possible occasion).

I agreed to go out with her again but felt a bit guilty about John. He had supported me all the way and now was out in the cold. I thought I owed him something, so as Christine was out of the picture as far as he was concerned I suggested Madge bring another friend along on a double date. She agreed and later so did John.

The event took place starting off in a local pub. Madge had brought a work colleague along called Liz. She was petite, pretty with long dark hair. Madge and I both did our best to break the ice for the other two but it didn't really work out and the evening petered out. On the way home I invited Madge out again on the following Saturday but she said she was going 'ice skating' with her friend Christine in Southampton and would give me a call later. That seemed to be it; the classic brush off after all that persistence.

Come the Saturday I was feeling pretty depressed. I had liked Madge a lot. She was lively and fun to be with but also very caring and despite the initial 'happenings' we seemed to hit it off. I decided to go back to the Mecca for the evening on my own, just to help me snap out of it, not holding out any particular hopes of finding someone else. Things were in full swing when I arrived and cast a look around.

There was Madge! Dancing with another bloke!

I checked them out from a distance for several minutes. Judging by the body language they had clearly not just met but neither were they lovey-dovey. I considered walking out and leaving them to it but I was angry. I felt I had been unfairly treated. When they left the dance floor I marched up behind them and tapped her on the shoulder. She turned and her jaw dropped when she saw me.

'Hello,' I said, 'it's surprising who you meet in here isn't it?' I turned to the bloke.

'I'm just reclaiming my girlfriend,' I said. He made no move to object or interfere as I grabbed Madge's hand and led her off to a relatively quiet nook.

'I don't know what you're playing at,' I said, 'but if you want to stay with me then it gets settled here and now. You can either rejoin your friend or come with me but I'm not going to me messed about any more.' She looked me in the eye, paused and then she took my offered hand.

From then we grew ever more closer together and saw each other virtually every day. So there was little chance of Madge absconding again. Mind you, these days she goes on the offensive over that pivotal Mecca moment and wants to know why **I** was being unfaithful to **her** by being there in the first place. I tell her my conscience is completely clear but she just says my 'clear conscience' is merely the sign of dementia setting in and I obviously can't actually remember my misdeeds.

*   *   *

Getting back to the housing situation, things were looking very bad. This was the time in 1972 when the property market went berserk. I went around every Estate Agent in the immediate and surrounding areas and was given virtually no houses to look at. You simply couldn't find one for love nor money and when one did appear it was snapped up before it could be advertised, sometimes without even being viewed let alone surveyed.

There was a glimmer of hope when my sister Margaret told me of an elderly man who lived around the corner from her. The local gossip machine had reliably informed her he was intending to sell up and go and live his remaining years with his son and his wife. There was a warning the property might not be in a particularly good state of repair. However, the house was not yet on the market and I might be able to get in first. I went and took a look at the place from a vantage point across the road. It was a terraced 3-bedroom house built about the start of the 1900s and did look as if it needed a little work doing on it but it least it had a relatively new tiled roof.

To be honest, having been to several mortgage lenders, I couldn't afford to borrow a large sum on my current salary, even though I had very good future prospects, so the fact it needed work should make the initial cost lower. I needed to contact the owner, confirm he was indeed leaving and establish whether or not the asking price made it a viable proposition for my budget.

As there was no time like the present I crossed the road and knocked on the door. It was opened by an old man who appeared to be well into his 80s. He was of heavy build but stooped. I explained I had heard he was going to sell up and expressed an interest in buying his house. He kindly invited me in and showed me around. His advancing years had prevented him from taking proper care of the place and it was in a bit of a state. This confirmed my hope the condition would bring the asking price down into my price range. We chatted at some length.

Two things he said troubled me somewhat. The first was there was as yet no firm date for his departure which might still be many months away and secondly he seemed quite taken with the idea of letting his property go to a young couple. I did not dissuade him from his assumption that I was half of a young couple, as I feared his view of me would change. He might even see me as a young wheeler-dealer trying to acquire his property cheaply only to sell soon after and turn a quick profit out of his house. Anyway, I thought I was rapidly becoming part of a steady couple with Madge, albeit in a yo-yo sort of way.

I decided to tell Madge what was going on and see if she would be willing to help me. Our difficult early days were now behind us and we had being going out together for a little over 2 months. Even so I knew I had a cheek in enlisting her help and asking if she would come with me on a future visit to the old gentlemen and portray a devoted couple. Madge was enthusiastic and even dug out an old ring of her mothers to put on her engagement finger for the visit. Had I thought about it more, I might have seen more than one agenda running.

The visit to the house took place and Madge's natural innocent charm was a major hit with the old gentleman. Although there was still no date for his departure he insisted we visit him twice a week to keep in touch. We had both grown to like him and so didn't mind this at all. The property market continued to be awful and so the liaison still seemed the best bet of getting something. Just then, fate decided to take a hand. Our visits to the house were disrupted when Madge caught glandular fever.

Just to make matters worse she was given penicillin, to which she proved allergic and came out in a rash. A very extensive and itchy rash. I went to visit her. Madge lived with her parents and 3 brothers in a block of flats. Her dad was a great chap and very friendly but tended to worry over things. Her mum was the dominating force in the household and was a redoubtable woman, being everything Les Dawson would have recognised in his own supposed mother-in-law.

Although we had been dating only a few weeks I had already been to the flat on numerous occasions, either to pick Madge up or to spend the evening in her room. Spending the evening in **my** bedroom with a girlfriend was not something my own parents would be happy about but Madge's mum and dad had no problem with it. Not that any 'funny business' went on; there was no lock on the door.

On this occasion when I called, I found Madge in her bedroom. I looked at her and she stared glumly back at me through tears of discomfort. It seemed anything that wasn't swollen was covered in the rash. I sat on the bed beside her and took her hand and then did the only thing I could think of under the circumstances; I asked her to marry me.

There was a brief pause while she took it in and got over the shock. 'I'll think about it,' was her initial response.

'That's no good,' I replied. 'if you have to think about it then you're not sure and if you're not sure then you should say no.'

She thought for a moment, 'Alright, then …. yes.'

We embraced for as long as the rash allowed before it triggered off the itching. Next time we saw the old gentleman Madge had a different ring on her engagement finger.

Things finally started to move apace. The old man's son met with us and gave us a date for the move to take place. It was only a few weeks away. I put wheels in motion to formally purchase the property. The old gentleman said he was taking little with him and so we agreed an additional sum of money to cover the bulk of the house contents. Not that they were worth much financially but I'm sure some items were of sentimental value and I had no wish to upset him by challenging the added cost. Just before Christmas 1972 and 6 months after getting engaged, we at last exchanged contracts and on completion I finally got the keys to our first house. Little did I suspect the nightmare to come.

Chapter 4

Starting Out Together

The house we had gone through so much to acquire was, as I mentioned before, a 3-bedroom, double bay with forecourt, terraced property in the centre of Portsmouth. It was number 291 in Chichester Road, which is a very busy road running east-west and joins two of Portsmouth's major roads (London Road and Copnor Road). The house was towards the Copnor end and only a short distance from the Portsmouth Dairies plant but sufficiently far away to avoid the clatter and bustle of milkmen organising their round at 04:00 every morning. (The Dairy no longer exists and has been replaced by some town houses now).

As you went in the front gate there was a small forecourt just big enough to park a bicycle and pram by the bay window of the lounge. On entering the house a long hallway stretched ahead, leading ultimately to a back dining room of good size. A few steps in from the front door, the hallway kinked off to the left to give way to the straight flight of 13 stairs leading to the bedrooms. A few more steps and there on the left was the door to the front lounge, followed a few paces further by an open entrance to a small breakfast room.

If you then walked into the breakfast room the kitchen was immediately on the right. I say 'kitchen,' it was so minute it housed only a butler sink with boiler above and a small worktop. A narrow alleyway ran from the back garden up the side of the house, past the kitchen and ended at the window of the breakfast room.

The garden wall on one side of the alley was quite high and the previous owner had effectively 'roofed' it by fixing wooden brackets across from the top of the wall to the side of the house and then putting panes of glass across the top. A door had been fitted against the wall of the house, where the alley led into the garden. The previous owner had then tried to increase the amount of space in the kitchen by removing the door between the kitchen and breakfast room and then extraordinarily, removing the side door from the kitchen into the side alley. The overall effect was to make the kitchen very dark and drafty and almost external to the house. Not an inviting or hygienic place to prepare food.

Retracing steps into the hallway, the door to the dining room was at the far end. Going through the dining room, a small conservatory led into the garden. The garden was the width of the house (about 14 feet) and about 40 feet long. There was a full width brick shed at the far end and an outside toilet attached to the house. A narrow path led from the conservatory to the shed and there were patches of grass, weeds and earth filling all the gaps on both sides. There were no shrubs or flowers, bar a few roses.

Upstairs there was a small landing with 4 doors. The first opened into the main bedroom. It was quite large and had a bay window overlooking the road outside. The second door was to the small third bedroom. It was positioned above the breakfast room and was just about large enough for a cot and small cupboard. The third was the bathroom door. It was the only one of the four to open outwards, as the bathroom was so small that once inside it would was been impossible to open a door into the room space, hence it swung outwards onto the landing. The final door was to the second largest bedroom that overlooked our garden and also those gardens of many other houses on either side of ours and that we backed onto. All the rooms had a fireplace. All the rooms needed redecoration. All the rooms smelled musty.

Although it was still some months to the wedding it gave us plenty of time to settle into the house and apply a bit of decoration, at least as far as our funds would allow.

I knew there were some structural items needing to be sorted as the main priorities for our money, such as the kitchen, but I didn't dream of what was to come. We were about to take a leap into a giant cowpat.

*   *   *

Madge and I were very excited as we took the keys from our solicitor around to the house and let ourselves in for the first time. It was late afternoon and already getting dark. As we went in I turned on the light switch but nothing happened.

'It's alright' I said, he's just turned the lights off at the mains under the stairs. I grovelled about the under stairs area and pulled the mains lever to the 'on' position. There was a loud 'bang' and flames shot up from the wiring. Madge shrieked and I shouted at her to get out. I turned the power off and beat out the flames. When I was sure they weren't going to start again I went outside and locked up. I would come back the next day in the daylight ... with an electrician.

Very handily, my sister Frances was married to an electrician called Andy (that was 'andy!). He very kindly took time out to come with me and inspect the situation. My worst fears were confirmed. The wiring was very old and very dangerous; the entire property needed to be re-wired from top to bottom. Andy would obtain all the materials, which I would pay for and then he would do all the work with me acting as his 'gofer' and 'tea boy'. We worked on the house whenever Andy was available and it was light enough to see what we were doing. I learned a good deal watching him and I learned even more about the house. Most of it pretty bad. Gruesome details are outlined later in the Chapter.

All of the upper floor wiring for the lights ran across the roof space and we needed to spend quite a lot of time up there running new cables about. However, as the loft wasn't boarded, one of the main lessons was 'only walk on the wooden joists'. Part way through the exercise I found out why.

I was kneeling on a four-inch wide joist with my feet braced against another, pulling cables across the loft. As I moved to change my position my knees came off the joist onto the plasterboard ceiling. I got a sinking feeling as both knees went into the plaster. I grabbed a roof beam and levered myself off. There was a substantial dip where I had been. I was roughly central in the roof area and wasn't totally sure where the damage was in relation to the upper floor room layouts, so I crawled across to the ladder and descended.

I went into the main bedroom and anxiously looked upwards. All was well. I then looked quickly into bedrooms 2 and 3. Again all OK. I was beginning to think by some fluke I might have got away with it when I peered into the bathroom. Large lumps of ceiling hung down and plaster had cascaded onto the floor, exposing the laths. I was devastated.

Installing a new ceiling was miles beyond my fledgling 'diy' skills but Madge and I could not afford to pay to have it done professionally and I knew nobody else with such skills that might fix it 'on the cheap.' I resorted to the most heinous of 'diy' crimes. 'If you can't fix it then hide it', a maxim I was to use several times in the coming months. I pushed the sagging ceiling back into the loft and cleared out all the loose material.

At the time, polyester ceiling tiles were all the rage, although over the years they were to prove dangerous in the event of a domestic fire and fell from favour and fashion. In this case they were my salvation. It was only a tiny bathroom; probably constructed in the first place by nicking an area from Bedroom 3. It only needed a few tiles to cover the entire ceiling and by judicious placement across the damaged area I managed to hide my lack of joist balancing skills from view, until we could afford a proper repair and decoration. This last bit sounds good but here I must eat humble pie. When we left this house 6 years later the ceiling tiles were still in place. Sincere apologies to whatever successor in title decided to redecorate the bathroom and found the job considerably greater than they bargained for.

In parallel with the re-wiring we needed to tackle a few more things. The boiler had looked pretty ropy in the first place but after Madge had a go at lighting it, it became a write-off. It was a very old type with two levers that moved horizontally. You moved the first across from left to right to start the gas release for the pilot light. Then you lit the pilot with a match and moved the second lever across in similar fashion to get the full flame. Madge found the levers had seized up and would not move across. At least that was her story. When she finally asked for help I found her with one lever bent and the other one broken off in her hand.

It was an early confirmation, not only was Madge quite strong for a girl but her strength could easily be misdirected. For example, Madge thinks the opposite to 'push' is 'push very hard' which has made the negotiation of doors over the years quite an adventure and has led to several of them requiring extensive repair.

The upshot of the above occurrence was we needed a new boiler. I couldn't bodge around this one. But each time a new expense arose, either the wedding or honeymoon plans had to be scaled back to provide the money. The lavish trip abroad was an early casualty. The kitchen needed fundamental sorting out, so I decided to relocate the boiler from what currently passed as a kitchen into the bathroom that had just endured a new tiled ceiling. I wasn't prepared to take on any work involving gas; indeed it's illegal to do so unless you are properly certified, so I brought in an expert.

He arrived on the appointed day and started work. He explained he would need to make a hole in the wall to fit the flu and this would take a little time. I left him to it, only to be called back 2 minutes later. I went into the bathroom and gazed at a row of roofs and a blue sky.

'Did you know the mortar holding your bricks together has completely gone?' he said cheerily, removing another brick from the outside wall with his fingertips. I was beginning to think maybe I had bitten off more than I could chew with this house but worse was still to come. Much worse.

Andy was in the hallway wiring up the ground floor power circuit when he called me over. ' Can you hear a noise?' he enquired. I listened intently and lowered my ear to the bare floorboards. A strange kind of hissing sound seemed to be loudest beneath one particular floorboard. One advantage of a rapidly decaying structure is it's very easy to lever up a floorboard. As I removed the board a jet of water shot passed me. The noise had been the water striking the underside of the floorboards.

Having a fountain in your hallway may well be novel and an estate agent might even attempt to pass it off as a downstairs shower. However, I was rapidly becoming an expert in knowing a problem when I saw it. In this case it wasn't so much the hole in the ancient lead pipe work I could see, which was about half a meter below the floorboards, it was more the lake that lay beneath it. 'I hope we've got a sound damp proof course,' I mused. What, in a 70-year-old house in this state of repair? No chance.

That night I had a dream I had purchased and was trying to live in, a very large cowpat. It seemed I hadn't fully escaped from being stuck in the smelly mire from that field in Ireland.

Having turned off the water and enlisted help to weld up the holed pipe, I decided to check on the damp proof course. Boy was I a glutton for punishment. High skirting boards and thick layers of wallpaper hid much of the inner walls so I couldn't see much, although I was a bit suspicious about some bulges I could see, now the previous occupant's furniture had been removed.

I called in a 'damp proofing' specialist company for a free estimate. The man went around with a probe in one hand linked to a moisture meter he held in the other. He kept putting the probe against the wall. I didn't like the way it kept sinking in, leaving woodworm-like holes in the plaster. Following him around I wondered if it was a good or a bad sign the needle on the meter kept swinging off the scale. I should have guessed by his 'tut tutting' shouldn't I?

He finished jabbing and tutting and gave me the bad news. The damp proof course had gone completely and all the walls were damp to several feet above ground level. There were 2 major tasks to be addressed. Putting in a new damp course to prevent continuing damage and repairing the damage already done. In that order. The first job was essential and the sooner the better. The second could be tackled room by room as we redecorated and my newly adopted 'diy' maxim invoked as appropriate (i.e. 'if you can't fix it then hide it').

We were given a number of different options to install a new damp course. Ranging from giving the house over to a team of builders while they cut in a new membrane about a foot above ground level, (this approach was undoubtedly the most effective but also the most expensive) to a rather weird method of stapling a copper strip around all the bricks a few inches off the ground. Nobody seemed to understand why this prevented moisture from climbing up your wall but I was assured it did. Not only was this approach the cheapest by far but we could reduce the cost further by removing and replacing the skirting boards ourselves. Guess which option we chose?

A few days before the workmen were due to arrive I started levering off the skirting boards. I was learning as I went along, so decided to start in our dining room at the back of the house; it was empty and dilapidated even in comparison with the remainder of the house. Therefore any mistake I made, as I perfected my technique, would have least impact there. I carefully levered away until I had loosened a complete 8-foot length of skirting board and then lifted it away. I expected to see a coating of plaster or at worse a bare length of wall bricks. What I got was the feet of the people living next door!

I stared in astonishment. There were only occasional bricks behind the skirting board on my side of the partition wall and on the neighbours side there were wide cracks through which I could see their feet. Not only could I see them but I could also hear their voices quite plainly. I gingerly removed another section. This time a proper brick wall came into view. Phew!

I eventually finished the skirting removal and exposed varying amounts of dampness in the walls but nothing quite as drastic as that first section. The contractors subsequently arrived and completed the work without mishap. I replaced the boards without inserting any new bricks in the dodgy section.

The sounds from next door became muffled again but we were always a bit cautious about what we said or did in that area in the house in case the neighbours overheard us.

Mind you, in terraced houses you can always hear a certain amount of what is going on next door, especially when there is a loud argument, so when we heard raised voices we used to race into the back room and put our ears to the skirting board. I even used to keep that famous piece of skirting board loose so we could lever it off quickly should a really juicy row be thundering on. It was better than the television on some occasions and, thinking of more recent programmes, could even have given the Gerry Springer show a run for its money.

I mentioned earlier the back dining room was vacant. Actually when we moved in, there was a large dining table with 6 chairs dominating the room and a Welsh dresser in one corner, next to the fireplace. We decided to keep the dresser but the dining suite went onto the list of things we would try and sell to raise a bit more cash. We looked in the yellow pages and came up with a local firm that did everything from buying individual items to clearing entire houses. I gave them a ring and a man came around.

He looked over our assembled collection with a grimace on his face, often shaking his head. He seemed most interested in what seemed to be a silver coloured knick-knack box with a broken hinged lid. He sighed and tutted as he turned it over in his hands. 'I'll give you £5 for the lot,' he said. We were both naive and no match for a professional. All attempts at negotiating on price or contents list was met with a repeat of the original offer. Although I was pretty sure we were being done, £5 to us in 1973 was a lot of money. I consoled myself with the knowledge he hadn't checked the furniture underneath where he would have seen it was heavily infested with woodworm.

Turning to the Welsh dresser, Madge decided it needed to be moved into the breakfast room. It didn't look too heavy and so the two of us attempted to lift it. After several seconds struggling to get it off the floor there was a crack and the dresser lifted. At least some of it did. Three of the feet remained rooted to the spot and everything else moved. We propped it against the wall and examined the feet. Not only had the dining suite been affected by woodworm but also the dresser. So badly, the feet were rotted through and had simply dropped off.

For the first time I peered very carefully at the dresser. It looked as if a thousand woodworm had attacked it, each holding a miniature machine gun. Riddled with holes, it had to go. Madge was upset at losing the dresser she had liked so much but suddenly I went cold at a thought.

I walked into the corner where the dresser had obviously stood for many years. Suddenly I got a sinking feeling, in more ways than one. The floorboards where they joined the wall were bending under my weight. I fetched a screwdriver, pulled the carpet right back and poked the floorboards all around that area. There was little resistance. In some places the blade went straight through the boards as if they were paper.

I took the carpet up completely and went on poking. A combination of damp and woodworm had taken their toll. Two corners of the room were in a bad way. I knew it wasn't just the floorboards themselves. The fact they acted like springboards from a swimming pool meant the supporting floor joists had gone underneath as well. I gingerly levered up a couple of floorboards and shone a torch underneath.

My worst fears were realised. Two joists had crumbled to powder and four others had badly deteriorated. This was going to be expensive and our meagre savings were already stretched to breaking point. Bearing in mind the cost of all the other house repairs and providing a spare kitty for any other emergencies, there was but one thing for it. The wedding evening bash and disco were cancelled and the Honeymoon got downgraded from a four star hotel to a much more modest place.

With all the other costly activities going on in the house and a small matter of a wedding to pay for, Madge and I held a council of war. We decided the priorities for our money were the key elements of the wedding itself and those parts of the house we needed to live in. Other rooms would be disregarded until we could afford to deal with them. The only exception to this would be if we felt a structural condition was dangerous, in which case I would carry out some form of 'holding action' at minimal cost.

Downstairs, the back dining room, conservatory, breakfast room and hallway would be ignored while we sorted out the front lounge and kitchen. Upstairs bedrooms 2 and 3 would be used as storerooms while bedroom 1 and the bathroom would get our attention.

My dad volunteered to paint the hall, stairs and landing which was very good of him. He believed in meticulous preparation, so I knew it would be done well. In fact, far better than I could manage. The only problem was his insistence he remove all the old paint first with a blowlamp. I was terrified as, knowing my luck, the house would probably go up in flames. A little earlier and perhaps I wouldn't have minded as it was well insured but we had already invested a good deal of time and money which would be wasted and I suspected the neighbours wouldn't be too pleased.

One advantage of taking over a house falling to bits, previously owned by a carpenter-handyman was there was a wide range of wood pieces in the shed unaffected by damp or woodworm and there were lots of house bricks lying about. I tried not to think of where the bricks may have come from (like the internal walls of the house) and started putting them to use. Although it was on the 'ignore' list, the back dining room floor was dangerous. One step in the wrong place and there was danger of disappearing through the floor.

I took up all the ravaged boards and a few good ones to give me access to the joists below. I tracked along the joists until I located sound wood and then cut out the bad sections. After I measured and cut the new joists pieces, I either butted them together, linked them with brackets and supported them with stacks of bricks or I overlapped them and bolted them together, again providing supporting bricks. I then nailed new floorboards onto the top after cutting them to size. No doubt the professional builders will hold up their hands in horror at my bodged up efforts but it was meant purely as a temporary stopgap and we were very careful not to put substantial a weight on the 'repaired' areas.

After so much pain and trauma over 'structural' issues, I eventually turned to a bit of light painting and decorating with a sigh of relief. 'It should be downhill from here on,' I thought to myself. By now, I should have known better! It wasn't just my lack of practical experience in such matters. I had done a spot of painting before and I had found it relatively simple but I had only partially observed at a distance my dad doing the wall papering at home, without any direct involvement myself. In fact, in my teens, I had tried to have as little direct involvement in just about anything, except girls, and that had been less than successful most of the time.

I started upstairs in bedroom 1, where I blocked in the fireplace with some hardboard, covered it with matching wallpaper and drilled some holes in the board to give a bit of air circulation in the chimney to prevent dampness. Considering how damp the rest of the house was it seemed a bit of 'too little, too late' but there you go. I painted the ceiling with emulsion and then, before I started to paint the woodwork a nice bright white colour, I started to remove all the existing wallpaper. Although in my parent's house I hadn't actually hung any wallpaper, I couldn't avoid getting roped in to remove the old paper. Hot water and scrapers seemed to do the job and this is what I employed here.

The first thing I discovered was my predecessor had not been over fond of wallpaper removal and had simply put new wallpaper layers on top of the old. The result was a huge thickness of paper to scrape off. The next thing discovered was to haunt me in room after room as I struggled to decorate. The adhesion of the paper to the plaster was greater than that of the plaster to the brickwork. Or in other words, as the wallpaper came off it brought huge lumps of plaster with it.

I looked aghast at the large hole in the wall the first bit of paper removal had caused. For a moment I considered simply adding another of paper to the surface layer but this was already rippling over the multitude of layers beneath. Besides the whole room couldn't be this bad surely? Again, I should have known better by now. It turned out this room wasn't as badly affected as some of the others but I wasn't to know that at the time.

I went around the room, tapping at the walls. I should say, at this point, I became a great 'tapper' through my work on this house. They say people working in some of the old breweries can tap the wooden casks and tell not only how full they are but also whether or not the contents is ready for drinking yet. I am equally proficient! I can now tap walls and floors and give you a pretty good idea of whether they are sound or not and just how extensive any problem is.

I had been on my hands and knees tapping floorboards and now, in the bedroom, I had my ear to the wall tapping away to sound it out. If the plaster was sound and adhered to the bricks then the tapping gave a relatively high-pitched sound, if the plaster was loose then the note dropped much lower. I was almost like a doctor using a stethoscope on a patient's chest and it was by means of trial and error I learned the black art of 'tapping' over the following weeks and months.

(It's something I have put to good use over the years. Like helping me find the position of joists in the ceiling, deciding which wrapped Christmas present had the most interesting contents and proving Madge's head was indeed empty).

Back to the decorating. Although I was happy to bodge around and cover up faulty areas in the 'low priority' rooms, I wanted the 'high priority' rooms to be sound in all respects. So I decided I would 'make good' as I progressed.

I bought some bags of plaster and carried on tapping the walls. The plan was any bulging parts or 'hollow sounding' areas got belted with a hammer until I was satisfied the remaining plaster was sound. I would then trowel in a mix of new plaster and level the surface. In bedroom 1 I set about 'tapping' and 'belting' as I went up, down and around the room.

I was about half way round when Madge came into the room to see how I was getting on. At least I heard the door open and then a lot of coughing and spluttering. I couldn't actually see her because of the amount of plaster dust in the air. It was a bit like getting trapped in a desert sandstorm. Head down and blazing away, I hadn't realised the amount of devastation I was causing. Fortunately I was wearing a facemask and goggles; otherwise I might not have got out of the room without being asphyxiated.

You may be wondering where all the tools and equipment were coming from, we being low on funds and therefore not being able to afford to buy any. The answer was - from the shed. The old man had been a carpenter and I believe a shipwright as well and the shed was crammed full of useful items. Admittedly many were in a poor state of repair and rusted up but they were still useable and I employed them with gusto.

It was while I was searching in the shed for further useful items I spotted mouse droppings. I had not encountered such things before but I was pretty sure that's what they were. If mice had taken up residence in or near the shed it was too close for comfort. I did not want the house invaded as we had enough on our hands sharing the house with the woodworm.

I bought a couple of traps and set them, using the traditional cheese as bait. The next day I checked the traps and found I had caught two victims. I threw away the traps and their grizzly contents and set several more. I gave my sister Margaret a ring. She had lived in several houses and I recollected she'd experienced a similar problem at one time. She listened while I described what I had found and what I had caught. When I'd finished she said quietly,

'Chris, they aren't mice. They're rats!'

Madge freaked out and I was pretty shaken. I thought they had been pretty large mice. Come to think of it, a mouse caught in a trap would probably be well into the trap area and have its back or neck broken by the sprung bar. What I'd caught had been hit by the bar across the nose and the body was several inches long before you got to the start of the tail. I kept going with the traps and caught 3 more; then nothing further. I fervently hoped they'd either run away or been exterminated. Madge however would not be satisfied. As far as she was concerned they could easily come back and no way was she going to live and raise children near a nest of rats. There was only one solution. The shed would have to go.

Before this, the shed had not been a priority to tackle. We were busy enough inside the house. Now things had changed. In some ways I was quite pleased. I managed to borrow a sledgehammer and a pickaxe. Every bloke has a bit of a destructive side and any destruction I had performed to date on the house, although perhaps considerable, was purely incidental. Now however was my chance to vent my true feelings on this property.

The shed actually utilised the back and side walls of the garden. Hence the demolition would mainly involve only the roof and front. The rubble would not be that great a volume but much of the inside shed contents would also have to go and that was considerable. We invested in a large skip.

There were plenty of other things from inside the house we needed to throw away, in case the shed didn't fill it completely. The only problem was there was no access from the back garden to the skip outside in the street, apart from through the house. Not that the house décor was any great shakes, in fact it was in a pretty poor state but the shed and it's contents were still a couple of notches down in terms of desirable contents of one's rooms and hallway.

The roof was made up of corrugated sheets and I resolved to take them down as whole pieces as far as I could. It was easier to transport to the skip, as I had no wheelbarrow. It turned out this was a wiser move than I knew. I was totally innocent of asbestos at that time and did not realise this was the material I was dealing with. If I had attacked the roof with my sledgehammer and sent up clouds of asbestos dust then I probably would not be around now to write this book. The only other parts of the shed to avoid my swinging sledgehammer were the windows. There were several pains of glass I removed whole in their frames.

At this point I should mention I have a phobia of spiders. I can stroke snakes, tolerate rats and even get friendly with a lizard but show me a spider and I'm off to the hills. The shed of course had more than its fair share of these monstrosities but they generally ran away from me when I approached and I was equipped with my trusty wellies.

Anyway, I picked up the window frames to take them through the house to the skip. I held them horizontally in my arms, supporting them with my chest, so they were just under my chin. Off I went through the garden and into the house. At which point I became aware the largest spider I had ever seen in my life was sitting on the top pane of glass about six inches from my nose.

I couldn't back up as I couldn't see where I was going and my eyes were frozen on the apparition in front of me. I daren't drop the frames, which is what all my senses were screaming at me to do, as to have glass all over the place plus the spider itself roaming around the house presented it's own problems. Instead, with eyes glued to the spider and following my homing instincts to the front door, I staggered out to the skip.

Forget that coach trip to Disneyland Paris, which stopped 17 times on the way to Dover to pick up people in every remote nook in the South of England. The walk through the house with 'gargantua' staring at me was the longest journey I have made in my entire life.

You might well inquire how I got into this mess with the house and whether or not I'd had the house surveyed. Well, the truth is I hadn't engaged my own surveyor. The reason being the cost and I erroneously assumed if there were problems the Building Society surveyor would report them and we would have some kind of conditions to have work done, placed upon the loan.

I learned valuable lessons here I went on to apply to my working life and resulted in spectacular benefits. Firstly, assumption is the mother of all cockups. Secondly, cutting corners to save costs may well result in even greater costs occurring.

*   *   *

Concurrent with all the shenanigans with the house, there was a small matter of the wedding to plan and organise. I could not expect too much from the bride's family. Madge's dad was a great bloke who I liked very much but he hadn't two ha'pennies to rub together and with all due respect would have found organising such an event beyond him. He gave us £20 towards expenses, which to him at the time was a lot of money and we very much appreciated. My own parents chipped in with the flowers and wine for the meal and toasts. After that we were on our own.

Madge's stipulation was she wanted a 'proper' white wedding. Mine was it should be in St Joseph's church, which had been my 'local' parish church for many years and you may recall from an earlier Chapter in the book, the place where my own parents had been married.

So all the usual things were needed in terms of church, brides dress, bridesmaids outfits, flowers all round, organist, posh car and of course the reception. After the 'mandatory' items the only thing we could trim to keep within our budget was the size and extent of the reception and of course the honeymoon.

We were able to hire the hall next to the church which assisted with our and everyone else's logistics and the priest discounted the cost to us. Then we made a list of family and friends who we wanted to invite but even with a critical eye the list ended up in the eighties. As I said before we had already decided on certain 'cuts' and there was no way we could afford to pay for an evening 'do' so we settled for a wedding reception 'sit down' meal and that was it. The honeymoon was confirmed as a week away in the 'West Country.' We booked a small hotel in a rural setting, just outside sunny Weston-super-mare, near a village called Brean.

Madge and I had met on 18th March 1972 and we were engaged by mid-June of that year. The wedding ceremony was booked for 28th July 1973 at St Joseph's church, Copnor in Portsmouth. I had my stag night a few days before the big day and Madge did likewise for her hen night.

The actual night before the wedding we both stayed at our respective homes with our parents. I was spending a quiet evening when there was a ring at the door. It was Madge's brother Mike. Typical Madge, always looking for the down side of everything, had despatched him to check up on me. Just to make sure I hadn't got cold feet and I was still intending to turn up at the church the next day. I assured him all was well and we had a good laugh but I reckon Mike had a shotgun back in his car, just in case.

The next day was beautiful with sunshine and blue sky. The wedding was at 13:00 so there was plenty of time. I contacted my sister Margaret, whose husband was the best man and checked the arrangements. Everything went like clockwork from my perspective.

Unusually the bride and her bridesmaids got prepared at separate locations. There were five bridesmaids, 3 of whom were my sister Margaret's daughters and she had to get them prepared at her own house. Madge's sister-in-law Lyn was the fourth bridesmaid and she joined them there, along with my sister Frances who was the fifth bridesmaid. With his wife busy, brother Mike went to Madge's parents flat where the bride was getting dressed. Mike was to generally help out and later take the bride's mum Rose to the church.

Madge had looked after herself from an early age and her wedding day was going to be no exception. She went to the hairdressers in the morning and then dressed. Of course, donning the wedding dress too early is usually a mistake as nervous visits to the loo result in massive logistical problems. However, Madge was never someone to leave things to the last minute, so she was ready well before the large, black Rolls Royce turned up to whisk her to the church with her dad.

When Mike, looking out of the window, heralded the approaching wedding vehicle, Madge was haring down the stairs from the fourth floor flat before the car had even come to a standstill. Ted, running along behind, arrived at the car door and had to be persuaded to get in the back with Madge, as he'd always wanted to travel up front in a 'Roller' and saw this as his big chance. Despite Ted's assertions, it was no contest; you don't want to trifle with a bride on her wedding day, especially not Madge.

You hear about brides being late for the ceremony, Madge was so early the chauffeur had to do a tour of Southsea to kill time, otherwise she would have been at the church before anybody else turned up. Actually, she would have been early enough to make it as a second bride at the wedding preceding ours. That would have been interesting. As it was she passed several of the wedding guests who all thought they were late and sprinted off to the church.

Anyway, all was well and the familiar tune of 'Here comes the Bride' rang out as I waited by the altar. Madge looked beautiful in her dress. She'd told me it was cream in colour, just to totally mislead me as she extended the superstition of the bridegroom not seeing the bride in her wedding dress until the big day, to the bridegroom not having a clue about what the dress actually looked like. It was, of course, pure white. I gave her a smile as she joined me and I could see she was petrified. The priest noticed as well because he asked for some chairs to be brought out for us before Madge collapsed on the spot. The ceremony went off well. I don't think either of us fluffed our lines. We signed the official documents and were husband and wife.

Everyone trooped outside for the official photographs and then into the adjacent hall for the reception. The only regret I had was the Rolls Royce had long gone by then and the photographer didn't get any pictures of Madge's dad helping her out of the car when they arrived at the church. Ted would have liked that and it would have given Madge a memento she would have treasured.

The reception went off very well with no inter family punch-ups and all the regulation speeches. I suppose Madge and I share a second regret; that we didn't have an evening 'do', which you may recall we had to cancel due to lack of funds. After the food and drink ran out and people started to think about going, we took our leave and I'm told things petered out once we had gone.

After the reception we went back to our house in Chichester Road. As we walked in, Madge tossed some stuff onto a table where lay a couple of glass doors I needed to fit to our new kitchen cabinet and there was a loud crash. Oops. Perhaps a sign of more cowpats to come.

We changed and set out on our journey to Brent Knoll. It was about a 3-hour drive and we arrived in the early evening. The hotel was not easy to find, being set back from the road up a long track and surrounded by fields. It looked very nice and secluded and the people who ran it gave us a warm welcome.

Our room was small, basic but spotlessly clean. There was no en-suite bathroom but shared facilities close by, including a shower cubicle. Neither of us had ever seen a domestic shower cubicle before and over the next few days it proved to be a great novelty. Madge even managed to flood the shower room.

I didn't make myself too popular with my new bride by nipping downstairs for something and accidentally leaving the hotel room door ajar. She was reclining on the bed wearing not a lot when another guest walked past. Madge said she couldn't look him in the eye at breakfast after that. I bet he enjoyed it though.

Although it was nice being located literally in the middle of the countryside, we 'townies' didn't fully appreciate everything else that comes with such seclusion. Like the frantic and continuous mooing from the cows at all hours. Whether they needed desperately to be milked or they just fancied the bull in the next field, we never found out. Another novelty was the smell of fresh cowpats as we took a morning stroll, hand in hand, up the grassy knolls. Despite an almost magnetic pull towards them, I made a point of not jumping in any.

In the mornings we also had the great luxury of a full, cooked English breakfast. They always gave us a choice. It was either egg bacon and sausage, sausage egg and bacon or bacon, sausage and egg. Although over the years, both before and after I was married, I have always breakfasted on cereals and toast, this experience of a cooked breakfast affected my life forever and every time I went away on business and stayed the night at a hotel, I always luxuriated in a 'full English breakfast'. Which just goes to show what I pig I am and confirms the way to a man's heart is most definitely through his stomach.

As well as spending time in the hotel (don't ask!) and enjoying the countryside, we also had day trips around and about, including to Weston-super-Mare, Brean and Cheddar. We bought a large whole round of really creamy homemade cheddar cheese to take back home with us. Then we went back to the hotel and sat on the bed stuffing our faces with the stuff until it was all gone. Luverly!

Time passed quickly but the weather took a turn for the worst midway through the second week. Madge and I decided we would cut the honeymoon short and get back home. Although we'd bought the house months before we hadn't actually been living in it and there was lots of sorting out and settling in to do.

So that's how Madge and I got off the ground. However, before I develop our story further I thought it might be an idea to pause and go back in time. To track Madge's family back and take a look at her ancestors, who they were and where they came from, just as we have already done with mine.

Chapter 5

Madge's Family Background

5.1 Ancestors

Firstly, just a brief word about how we went about our research into Madge's ancestors, whose surname was Lenton. The start point was anyone living today and what they could remember but this gained virtually nothing on the Lenton side. The only information was Madge's paternal grandmother's maiden name was 'Martha Beatrice Colbourne' and she died in a fall at a relatively young age when Madge's dad was barely old enough to bring up his younger brothers.

The initial research was to look at the 1901 census survey recently available on the Web. This showed there were a handful of Lentons' living in Portsmouth at that time. The thing that caught my eye was one was named 'Richard', a name shared with both Madge's dad and her brother. If it was a family name then we had a connection. A search on 'Colbourne' showed a few candidates, one of who was named 'Beatrice' (note not Martha) but who was about the right age in 1901 to have been Madge's grandma.

The Census also told us who was living in the same house at the time and what the address was. The Portsmouth Library has microfiche records covering the whole country for Births, Deaths and Marriages from 1827 to (then) 1996. It is organised by Year and within each year by Quarter. Within each quarter the names are arranged alphabetically. Some of the old records are hand written and very difficult to read at times whereas the microfiche from the late 1980s onwards are typed but in some instances still rather difficult to read.

So to do a 'birth' search for a name like Martha Beatrice you need to know the relevant year. Then look through each of the 4 quarterly microfiche foils to find the name against the registration town of 'Portsea'. Once you have this reference then the Registrar of Births, Deaths and Marriages can make a copy of the certificate. In Madge's grandmother's specific case we determined her Christian names had been transposed (apparently not uncommon in those times) and she was in fact 'Beatrice Martha.'

You can guess approximate wedding dates from the age of the eldest child (people in those days generally getting married before the kids were born, unlike the trend today) and then search records either side of the suspected date. To identify people and link them together we needed birth certificates, that would give us not only the baby's name but also the parents names and address; together with marriage certificates that gave us the couples names, addresses and ages as well as parents names. Subtracting the ages of the people getting married from the year of the wedding gave approximate birth dates, and so you went on, going backwards in time.

Another useful source was Kelly's Directory, an annual record for each major town. An alphabetic list of streets in Portsmouth with a record of the head of the household at each house number, within separate lists of odd and even numbers. Armed with address details from the above certificates we were able to establish approximately when a family moved into that address and when they moved out. We could also tell what close by addresses were used for if they were not domestic dwellings.

*   *   *

We spent about 20 hours across several sessions in Portsmouth Library tracing back Madge's ancestry, just to get a bit of a family background. It seems her family name of Lenton originally came from the parish of Lenton close to Nottingham but we have no means of linking back to that part of the country.

More recently, the family hailed from Salisbury in Wiltshire in the early 19th century before moving to Portsmouth and Portsea in particular. A William Lenton from Salisbury filed a 'Last Will and Testament' in 1773 so the family name was established in the area at that time but we have no proof of a direct line to Madge's ancestors.

Although I have briefly mentioned places in Portsmouth during the story of my own ancestors, the Lentons' and in particular the Colbournes' lived in the area prior to the Bichenos' and were more centred on the area of 'Portsea' within the overall 'Portsea Island.'

Before I go any further I need to give a thumbnail sketch of Portsea as it was in those days so you can understand the background to the way they lived and the terrible struggles they must have had just to survive.

Portsmouth was founded back in 1495 when King Henry VIII decided to create the world's first large dry dock there for the building and maintenance of his fleet. It grew slowly over the years to around 1698 and then expanded rapidly to fill about 300 acres of the southwest corner of Portsea Island.

The area adjacent to the Dockyard was known as Portsea and apart from a few isolated farms elsewhere, made up the entire population of the island. About half the male population worked directly for the Royal Navy and most of the rest did indirectly, in support of the population.

As the Dockyard grew in importance and the amount of work it did, the area of Portsea became very, very overcrowded. It also supported the main pastimes of the sailors, which were booze and women. (No change there then lads, apart from football and cars being added later!) During the middle of the 1800s, those people less closely connected with the Dockyard moved slowly outwards into other parts of the island. So places like, Landport, Kingston and Buckland gradually became built-up.

Note the area of 'North End' was indeed at the northern end of such development even though it is slap in the middle of Portsmouth today as the remainder of the island has been fully filled up. However, much of the overcrowding and bad habits of Portsea, although present in the wider Portsmouth area, did not exist in anything like the extremes as in the immediate area around the Dockyard.

Mains drainage was generally installed around Portsmouth starting in 1865 although the people in Portsea might not have been aware of it. Drinking water was available from pipes from 1875 for all those able to afford it. However, in general the Portsea inhabitants continued to rely on communal stand pumps and the barrow boys selling water from containers ferried around on hand carts, as they had done from the middle ages.

The road thrusting out northwards from the main Dockyard gate, through Portsea was Queen Street. This was what you could describe as a throbbing ribbon of life with every shop imaginable along its length. It was, however, reasonably presentable with colourful displays and decoration; the problem areas were the numerous, dank, narrow streets and alleys branching off Queen street on both sides. It was there by

1922 up to 20,000 people lived in poverty and squalor. The only exception was a small island of decent accommodation in the area of St George's Square and Lion terrace. (It was close to here, in Britain Street, Isambard Kingdom Brunel was born in 1806).

In the late 1800s, some of the most notorious places were the likes of White's Row (where both the Lenton and the Colbourne family would live – see later), Blossom Alley and Southampton Row. After a nasty fight in White's Row had led to a death the Hampshire Telegraph newspaper of the day, under a headline of 'Fatal Affray', wrote:

'White's Row, that is the scene of abominations which neither the mind can conceive nor the pen describe, now has another crime of murder added to it growing list.'

Southampton Row was 627 feet long but in that distance there were no less than 14 brothels. The passage between the buildings was only 7 feet wide and people would throw rubbish and human waste out of upstairs windows onto the road and possibly onto unfortunate individuals passing below; conditions in which epidemics of Cholera were not unknown.

None other than the Chancellor of the Exchequer, no less, actually mentioned another notorious road, The Hard, in Parliament in 1895. The Hard still exists today and follows on from the bottom of Queen Street just by the Dockyard main gate and runs alongside the waterfront. It appears permission had been given to build 27 dwellings there but a subsequent check had shown only 10 were actually domestic dwellings. There was also 1 Post Office, 1 Hotel, 1 Wine and Spirits store, 1 Beer House and 13 pubs! There is no indication how many of the remaining 10 dwellings were actually brothels but it was probably several. I think these statistics sum up the Portsea of the day quite well.

Housing was old and dilapidated throughout the middle and late 1800s right up to the middle of the 1920's. Gas was available but there were no toilets in the houses, let alone modern conveniences such as central heating and get this kids – no electricity!!

As far as community services were concerned, in Portsea there were no Fire Stations (outside of the Dockyard), no hospital for infectious diseases, no parks, no public baths and few schools. A charitable organisation set up schooling for the area, called 'Free Ragged Schools' which started in 1849 (and believed to have evolved from the John Pound schools) and went right through to the period between the World Wars.

The food people ate mainly consisted of potatoes, suet pudding and bread with small amounts of fish, meat and cheese. Things like tea, butter, jam and fresh vegetables were non-existent. (It makes one almost grateful for the likes of McDonalds and Pizza Hut). Fresh milk was unaffordable and people made do with tinned milk.

The mortality rate in Portsea was almost 3 times the rate of the wider Borough average, 1 in 3 dying of tuberculosis. Many children died in their early years due to gastric and intestinal illness. It was no surprise when in 1872, Smallpox spread across Portsea and over 500 people lost their lives.

The average wage in the early 1900's was 20 shillings a week (that's £1 exactly for the post decimalisation innocents and 70 Euro cents for those readers coming from the future). Lodgings would take about 5 shillings of that and to feed each child would cost about 4 shillings. So it's not hard to see how poverty was sustained. Even skilled craftsmen in 1914 such as shipwrights, plumbers, carpenters and bricklayers were only paid about 40 shillings a week.

The working week was about 58 hours in the early 1900s although this reduced to about 50 hours in 1920 and 44 hours by 1944. Women were paid just over half the wages of men doing the same job and wherever possible they would take work home so the kids could help with it. Children were expected to work from the age of 8 or 9.

The slums and ghettoes of Portsea were finally demolished, starting selectively in 1912, with the main clearance within Portsea beginning in the late 1920's and going through to the late 1930's. Many displaced people were offered accommodation in other parts of the city and new developments in Cosham were amongst these.

Even after rebuilding, Portsea remained a dangerous place to live and visit. You still wouldn't venture off of the main streets unless you lived there or had very pressing business. This situation was made even worse during WWII when the German bombing took a heavy toll both inside the Dockyard and across the adjacent area.

The worst experience was on 10th January 1941 when 171 people were killed and over 3000 made homeless in a single night. (I could make a joke about Portsea's continued overcrowding problem by saying over 100 people were injured when 5 houses were damaged but that would be a bit tasteless).

Poverty continued to be a problem right up to my day. In the 1950s and 60's when I used to take the ferry going to Gosport from the bottom of Queen Street near the Dockyard main gate, I recall seeing the 'Mudlarks'. These were boys (and very occasionally girls) from the local area who waded about in the stinking mud underneath the landing jetty that ran out to the boats. People walking over the jetty would lean over the railings and throw coins down into the mud and the youngsters would delve into the mire for them. Madge's brother Mike was actually a 'Mudlark' and can vouch for the foul smelling stuff as being far from hygienic.

So given this bleak background how did Madge's ancestors fare?

*   *   *

Hendy Lenton was a farmer in the Salisbury area and was married to a lady named Rosa. This is all we know of them; other than they had a son named Richard and attended his wedding in 1878. We have searched fruitlessly for further information about Hendy and found none, so we will move forward to his son.

Richard Hendy Lenton was born in 1855 or 1856 in Salisbury and as a young man seeking his fortune moved to Portsmouth, probably around 1877. Although raised on a farm Richard became a licensed victualler (a supplier of provisions) and then a shoemaker (also described as a bootmaker - journeyman) by trade, working mainly from home.

He was married in 1878 to Louisa Palmer Snow (who appears to have been of good class, although born in Portsea) and they lived at 18 Kilmiston Street in Portsmouth. This street no longer exists but was almost opposite the top of Hampshire Street, which is the road I was brought up in.

In the 1870s and 80s the Dockyard was expanded and the tall outer walls, some of which still evident today, were erected by conscripted convict labour. With the increase in activity and associated personnel, Richard Lenton, being a skilled craftsman, must have found plenty of work in the area, both from Navy and Dockyard personnel and civilian families. In those days shoes were often repaired rather than replaced and it was commonplace to share shoes within a family.

It was probably uncomfortable in Kilmiston Street as they lived almost opposite a small slaughterhouse and the smell must have been horrific at times. This may have (at least in part) caused then to move to 42 Hanover Street in Portsea in 1880. It was here that they would have encountered the Colbourne family for the first time as they were living almost opposite at No 35. Both couples had their first babies around then and this would have formed a common bond between them.

In 1887, possibly prompted by the growing family needing larger accommodation, Frederick and Louisa Lenton moved to 3, Albion Street which today has no dwellings but is the approach road to the Portsmouth Continental Ferry Port. This stay did not last long however and a further move in 1888 to No 50 in the notorious White's Row brought them back into contact with the Colbourne's, who by now were living a few doors away at No 30.

Tragically in 1889 Louisa died from tuberculosis but within 3 months Richard had re-married. His new wife was Jane Rex, 6 years older than him and a widow whose maiden name had been Vincent. She also lived in White's Row, at No 8 above a fishmongers shop, and Richard joined her at that address to help her run her deceased husband's business. Jane was to bear him no children and died in 1895. The cause of her death was 'cirrhosis of the liver', which one normally associates with heavy drinking. Enough said.

Richard moved his family in 1899 to 70 Frederick Street (today opposite the infamous 'Tricorn' concrete development and now a supermarket car park) where they remained, until 1906. We know they lived there with others, as 2 of them were included at the 1901 census survey as 'boarders', a young man named James Voller, who was a bricklayer and an elderly lady, Francis Woodman.

Richard himself died in 1903 at the age of 47. The cause of death was 'tuberculosis' and 'exhaustion', which is scarcely surprising given his difficult circumstances. His children by then were almost all grown up and able to fend for themselves.

Richard had seven children, all by his first wife Louisa: the eldest named Richard after himself, born in 1879, followed by Ellen Louisa (born 1880) who was destined one day to report her father's death, Rose Letitia (born 1881) who was to die in childhood, then Francis (born 1883), Clara (born 1885), Frederick Arthur born on 17th July 1887 and finally George (born 1886) who was destined to die as a child. It is Frederick, the last but one named, we are most interested in for he was to become Madge's paternal grandfather.

Frederick Arthur Lenton would in due course marry Beatrice Martha Colbourne but before telling their story we will first trace the Colbourne family roots as far back as we are able.

George Kervell Colbourne, born in 1830, was a licensed beer retailer living at 35 Hanover Street in Portsea in the second half of the 19th century. The road still exists today but with flats and a car park on one side and nondescript commercial buildings on the other, it's but a pale shadow of its colourful past. In the late 19th century it was a main shopping street with no domestic dwellings but the narrow road was crammed on both sides with shops of all descriptions. George, his second wife Harriet (who was 20 years his junior) and their family actually lived in a flat above what we would now call an 'off license' that he managed.

George attended the wedding of his son Frederick George Victor Colbourne (hereinafter referred to as 'Fred Colbourne') to Martha Swayne on 9th November 1879. Fred Colbourne and Martha were Madge's great grandparents.

All we know about Martha's family is her father's name was John Crabb Swayne, his wife was named Caroline and John worked as a baker in the Royal Navy. They lived at 19 Hawke Street in Portsea, which is the next road along from where Fred was living with his parents.

The Hampshire Telegraph of the times said a survey of number 33 Hawke Street (only a few doors up) had shown the only brickwork within the building was the fireplace and chimney, the rest of the house being constructed of lath and plaster with some wooden panel dividers, although these had been damaged by rats. This gives some idea of the desperately poor quality of housing in the area.

Fred Colbourne was 23 years old at the time of the marriage and Martha just 19. Fred is described as a cab proprietor on the wedding certificate but it is doubtful he actually owned any such thing, especially at such a young age and more likely he was a coachman/driver, which he was some time later at the time of his daughter Beatrice's marriage (in 1919).

Fred and Martha had a large family of 8 children, comprising 5 girls and 3 boys. The first, Elizabeth was born in 1881. Then followed Charles, Charlotte, William R, Beatrice (the key link), Ruby, Lillian and a second William E. One of the 'Williams' was destined one day to be the one who registered his sister Beatrice's death.

So Beatrice Martha, born in 1895 (and Madge's grandmother), was the fifth of eight children born to Fred ('John/Jack') and Martha Colbourne. It was she who linked the Colbourne and Lenton families when in 1919 she married Frederick Arthur Lenton. Coincidently,

Beatrice's father Fred Colbourne and the Richard Lenton from Salisbury shared the same year of birth, 1856, which is also the year the Crimean war ended and the first railway was opened in Africa between Alexandria and Cairo.

Both Lenton and Colbourne families lived in Portsea, which you will recall from earlier descriptions is the area of Portsmouth adjacent to the Royal Naval Dockyard and the thriving hub of Portsmouth at the time. As I have described before, the main thoroughfare north from the Dockyard, Harbour Railway Station and Ferry landing terminals to the City Center was Queen Street. About half a mile long, it teemed with shops and thronged with people in the early 1900's. Portsea was the area to the east and west of Queen Street. The scenes there today are but a pale shadow of their frantic past.

At the time, the Royal Navy was re-inventing itself from an age of sail to an age dominated by the huge ironclad dreadnoughts and so there were plenty of jobs available for both skilled and unskilled workers in the construction, repair and maintenance of those titans of the sea. In fact about 23,000 people were employed in the Dockyard during WWI and slightly more in WWII, but numbers fell between the wars to around 8,000.

In those days Portsmouth had more pubs per square mile than anywhere else in the country. Apparently, over 300 alehouses and almost 400 beer-houses (don't ask me what the difference was between them) slotted in among the fairly miserable domestic dwellings.

In the late 1880's the Colbourne family lived in rented accommodation at number 50 in the notorious Whites Row. This address no longer exists but the street was a narrow but long alley, leading eastwards off of Queen Street and ironically close to where the Freemantle Flats were later built and lived in by Ted Lenton and his family (my potential in-laws).

Beatrice's father Fred worked for a Hansom Cab company as a carriage driver. In those days motoring had barely begun and horses still produced the basic means of transport.

With the Portsmouth Harbour railway station and both the Isle of Wight and the Gosport ferry landing stages just 2 minutes walk away from the Dockyard main gates, there were plenty of paying customers travelling into the business centre of Portsmouth. The well-heeled customers headed a mile eastwards to the up-market holiday resort of

Southsea, with its shingle beaches and entertainment piers jutting out into the water.

Portsea was the closest point to the Dockyard for workers and sailors and here the alcoholic watering holes were at their densest. Brothels, pawnshops and other mini industries were attracted to the immediate locality and the whole area was what you would call pretty rough. The sort of place where the patter of tiny feet didn't mean toddlers were walking around but rather you were about to be mugged by a gang of 10-year-old footpads. Not an ideal area to settle into when looking to raise a family but it was at 38 Cross Street, a short stone's throw from the walls of the Dockyard, Frederick and Beatrice set up home after their marriage.

The house was probably chosen as it was close to Frederick's place of work in the Dockyard and also because both sets of parents' family homes were nearby. The Lenton's were living near Cross Street and the Colbourne's about 100 yards away at 67 North Street, both off of Queen Street, the main Portsea thoroughfare. The Hampshire Telegraph had an article that said there had been an infestation of bugs and fleas at 73 North Street, which was only 3 doors up and probably a source of concern for them at the time.

As well as domestic dwellings, Cross Street also contained a wide variety of shops including grocers and a launderette. Eventually most of the domestic dwellings, shop and pubs in Cross Street were demolished and a brewery built in their place. Nowadays even the brewery is gone.

Having had a look at the ancestors and Madge's family origins, at least as far as we have been able to do to date, let's move forward in time to her grandparents and parents.

5.2 Recent Family

Getting back to Beatrice and Frederick, the first skeleton rattles in the closet. For, prior to their marriage Beatrice became pregnant out of wedlock and on 16th January 1919 produced a baby boy named George ('Frazie') Victor Colbourne. The exact circumstances of the pregnancy are today unknown but we know Beatrice was still living at home with her parents when she married Frederick and the baby has no declared father on the birth certificate.

Although the law at the time differs from today and made it more difficult to accurately register births out of wedlock, Frazie was referred to as a 'half-brother' within the Lenton family and so it is assumed Frederick was not his father.

Illegitimacy in those times carried huge social stigma; it says a lot for Frederick he was prepared to take on a young mum and tiny baby as his own, in very difficult circumstances. Frederick and Beatrice were married in the Parish Church, Portsea in December 1919.

Some years later, in 1930, the family moved to rented accommodation in Colwell Road in Cosham, which lies within the northern outskirts of Portsmouth, just off the 'island' itself. The move may have been precipitated by the size of the growing family or the general slum clearance, taking place in Portsea around that time. It was a good, middle class area indicating they were climbing the social ladder and the house (No 13) exists to this day and, at the time of writing, is actually undergoing renovation.

Evidence suggests Frederick still worked in the Dockyard in a skilled workers role and cycled the 4-mile distance to work every day. Brought up in a rough environment and strengthened by adversity, Frederick would have thought nothing of the 8-mile daily round trip on his pushbike.

Incidentally, 'Bicycles' and 'Dockyard' were 2 words very closely linked for many years. Until the Dockyard was drastically run down between the wars and the numbers of workers reduced, all the local residents would avoid being anywhere near the Dockyard two main Portsea exit gates at 4pm when the hooter sounded to announce the end of the day shift. As the loud wail rang out, from the Lion and Unicorn gates at the two ends of Queen Street, literally thousands of bicycles would appear through the gates about 20 abreast. All surrounding roads were filled with a   seething mass of bikes for several minutes.

Pedestrians were like islands with the river of bicycles flowing all around them.

By the time they settled in Cosham, three more boys had been born. Edward ('Ted') in March 1921, William ('Blidge') in early 1924 and Ernest ('Ernie' or 'Nobby') much later at the end of 1929. The last two were due to lead relatively uneventful, brief and rather lonely lives as bachelors, in rented accommodation and with few possessions but Edwards's life took a more positive turn, partly by intent and partly by good fortune. It was he who was destined to become Madge's father.

Edward (from herein after known as 'Ted') Lenton had been born back in Portsea in 1921. Ted moved with his parents and older brother to Cosham, into larger accommodation after Ernie was born towards the end of 1929. However it was here in 1935 the first major blow struck the family.

Ted's father Frederick became seriously ill and was taken to St Mary's hospital in Portsmouth. Shortly afterwards he died of what was commonly known then as 'consumption.' However, it was also noted on the death certificate he was in the latter stages of syphilis. Another skeleton rattles in the closet but given the social state of affairs in the Portsea locality where he was brought up, such ailments would have almost been an occupational hazard. Indeed if family rumours are true then Beatrice may have been the source of Fredericks ailment as she was said to 'entertain' the night shift down near the Dockyard main gate to supplement the family income. With her husband gone, from the mid 1930's, Beatrice brought up the children on her own.

To give some idea of the environment at this time, it was only in 1933 the first set of traffic lights was erected in Portsmouth and it was the next year trolley buses were first seen on the roads. For those unfamiliar with such vehicles, they were not like the trams that ran on ground rails. Trolley buses were powered by overhead electric cables running the length of their route and the buses were connected to the cables by a pair of connecting rods from the vehicle roof.

I travelled on them myself as a boy and experienced a number of breakdowns when a connecting rod came away from the overhead cables. The conductor had to get off the bus and pull down an enormous long pole from the roof he then used to lift the arm back onto the overhead line.

Interestingly, when the trolley buses appeared they largely replaced the trams and most of the tram rails were taken up. The straight sections of rails were recycled as metal support girders for the new shops and buildings being erected throughout the city.

Getting back to Beatrice, for some reason, possibly to be closer to her own family for their support, she moved back to Portsea, into Abercrombie Street. This street no longer exists but was positioned very close to the Dockyard wall at the Northern end of Queen Street. Unfortunately, she also fell foul of long term illness but battled on alone with the boys until 1940.

She finally succumbed to what appears to have been a combination of multiple sclerosis and/or cancer. According to the death certificate she died in the house in No 32 Abercrombie Street. Family rumours she fell down the stairs and broke her neck are not substantiated by the death certificate, although it is entirely possible her weakened state caused her to take a fall prior to her death. Her demise left her sons Frazie, Ted Blidge and Ernie to battle on by themselves.

Ted had left school when barely a teenager and got a job with the local railway, working both in Portsmouth and on the 'Billy Line' (the section that ran from the mainland down through Hayling Island). A railway video on the 'Billy Line' actually includes footage of Ted shovelling coal.

With his mum gone and also her income, to make ends meet for the family he took on a second job, working at a fishmongers in Surrey street, in an area now occupied by the main Post Office. He got up at 4am every day to do the fishmonger job then walked through to the Fratton goods yard to do his railway job.

Ted's job gave him free rail travel over a wide area and he went on frequent excursions, even to France, and he took such trips throughout his life. He would leave his wife Rose (who wasn't keen on 'walking' holidays) at home, then lead the children round Guernsey, Jersey, London or Paris, always walking everywhere and having little food on the way round.

Madge remembers them sitting on steps in Montmartre, each with a meat pasty in one hand and a bottle of milk in the other. It may sound harsh but the kids loved it and doted on him, especially Madge. But I'm getting a bit ahead of myself in relating this tale.

The boys were now on their own, living in rented accommodation at

61 St Paul's Road, with the half-brother Frazie the eldest at 22 and Ted, at 19 years of age, trying to bring up the two younger ones, who at the time were aged 16 and 11. Remember in 1940 the war had started and the Portsmouth Naval Dockyard was a prime target for enemy bombers. There were no accurately guided weapons in those days and indiscriminate bombing caused havoc in the civilian areas close by. So living in Portsea was extremely hazardous to say the least. Scavenging from damaged and demolished domestic and commercial premises was an ever-present occurrence and a way of supplementing meager incomes by either using or selling whatever was retrieved.

Further blows were then delivered. Firstly, Frazie was 'called up' to join the army. This was in 1940 after the British Expeditionary Force was formed and two years later it was Ted's turn. He considered his place was at home; helping to bring up his brothers but HM Forces didn't see it that way. After he ignored several letters to report for duty a couple of burley military guards paid him a visit and he was unceremoniously carted off. Ted ended up in the Pioneer Corps and served as a prison guard, looking after German detainees and POWs at a camp near Ashbourne in Derbyshire.

We know he wasn't a particularly strict guard because, feeling sorry for the prisoners, he slipped them chocolates and cigarettes. This was typical of Ted, always soft hearted. However, the story was to take a happier turn. While based near Ashbourne he met a girl called Rose Jones. She had worked in the local corset factory along with her cousins and aunts but at the outbreak of hostilities had moved to an ammunition factory that started up. (I'm not sure which of the factories had the more lethal product).

By today's standards such jobs appear to be a rather curious occupation but during WWII they were quite commonplace. Rose was about 5 years Ted's senior (being born on 27th February 1916) and she lived with her 3 sisters and 3 brothers in Ashbourne. She was the second youngest in a family of 7 born to Charles Jones and Annie (nee Fearn). The first 3 to be born were all boys, Charles the eldest (in 1903) then Neville and Jack; then followed 4 girls, Lilly, Frances, Rose and finally Madge (after whom my own wife was named).

Going back in time a little, we have traced the Jones family as far back as Mary Jones who was born in 1826 in a small village near Ashbourne called Kniveton. We do not know what her maiden name was or the Christian name of the Mr Jones she married in the early 1850s. We do know their children included William Jones who married Mary Bridgwood and they were parents to Charles, or to put it another way, William and Mary were my Madge's maternal great, great grandparents.

We also know at the turn of the century Mary Jones was living with her daughter and 4 grandchildren (including Charles) in Can Alley Station Street in Ashbourne. Charles married Annie Fearn on 30th April 1904 and they had the 7 children listed above, including Madge's mum Rose. At some stage they moved to 39 Cokayne Avenue and the address has remained the family home to this day. (I have visited it a few times with my wife Madge, on one occasion taking some of our children).

After a relatively brief courtship and with the war finally heading towards a conclusion, Ted and Rose were married on 17th April 1945 in Ashbourne Registry Office. Rose was by then employed as a packer in the Nestles condensed milk factory but left her job after Ted was discharged from the forces and they both returned to Portsmouth, to 61 St Paul's Road where Ted's younger brothers were still living.

Unfortunately Rose did not get on with Ted's brothers (what was to become an increasingly familiar trend) and eventually Blidge and Ernie moved out. Frazie also returned after his wartime service but one day left supposedly to get a pint of milk and they never saw him again.

The union of Ted and Rose was subsequently blessed with three boys and a girl - Richard, Michael, Madge and Stephen, known within the family as 'Bigsie,' Mike, 'Dayde' and Steve. 'Dayde' was a corruption of 'Daisy,' which baby Steve was unable to pronounce properly. Why 'Daisy' in the first place, I just don't know.

Ted was a simple type but the nicest bloke you could wish to meet. He didn't have much but was always prepared to give what he had to another needy person and especially to his own family. He was so easy going people could sometimes take advantage of him and Rose, in particular, tended to do this.

As his family grew in number, Ted decided he needed a car to transport the family about and started taking driving lessons. He bought a car in anticipation of passing but unfortunately was unable to pass the test initially and gave up lessons for a while. Needs must, however, and during this lull he could still be seen driving around in his car alone or with the family. He actually taught his sons Richard and Mike to drive to a standard where they passed their tests while he still didn't have a license. None of this can be condoned of course but in his defence the roads were nowhere near as busy in those days.

Having gained more driving experience, Ted finally passed his test. As he couldn't afford a lot, his cars were consequently not up to very much and tended not to last very long. He once bought a car (a Ford Prefect) for twelve pounds, then took it back for a discount when he found it a bit imperfect. Eventually it clapped out and his daughter Madge volunteered to buy another car for him on condition he taught her how to drive. She paid £70 for an old Ford Popular and he gave her a few lessons.

Unfortunately one day she removed a parked lorry's tail lights when trying to steer round it. Ted carefully wrote a note and left it under the windscreen wiper. It said 'Sorry Mate.' It was mainly for the benefit of onlookers; he certainly wasn't going to give his name and address. This incident shook Madge's confidence and shortly after she packed in the lessons. A legacy I was to pick up and take to fruition about 10 years later.

Raising a family of 4 children in difficult circumstances will tax anyone. It was therefore no surprise to learn Ted suffered from his nerves and occasionally got depressed. Perhaps made worse by allowing it to bottle up inside him. A couple of times he admitted himself into St James's mental hospital for treatment but he pulled round after a while. One of these bouts was brought on just before Madge and I were married and was possibly brought on by his work colleagues suggesting the attendant wedding bills would be coming his way. If that is so, if only we had but realised this or he had said something to us, then we could have put his mind at rest.

Rose was a loving mother to her kids, defended them rigorously against all 'outsiders' and brought them up with good values. However, she had major weaknesses, supposedly brought on by her upbringing and the perception of her achieved lifestyle against her aspirations. Rose always seemed to be driven by the twin evils of money for herself and jealousy of others.

She collected sizable sums of money for their 'keep' from her children and then squirreled the money away while Ted still paid some of the bills. She insisted her family spoil her with presents but bought them little in return. I can say with certainty my children, her own grandchildren, never received either a Christmas or a birthday present from her. Not even a card; although I can imagine Madge's mum sending out a single Christmas card with a list of names and a note attached saying 'please read and send to next person on the list.' Contrast that with Ted who was always slipping the children bars of chocolate and whispering, 'Don't tell Rose.'

Rose was always at war with her neighbours bordering all directions around her flat, above, below and to the sides. Given this was always so at the various locations they lived, I am tempted to reach the conclusion the common factor as to the root cause of all these hostilities was Rose herself.

There was some excuse for her. She had left all of her family behind in Ashbourne and felt rather isolated in Portsmouth and had no telephone in the early days to contact them easily. When her own mum died, Rose's sisters sent her a pair of curtains as her sole legacy. Perhaps it wasn't surprising she became embittered.

When the neighbours weren't in range, poor old Ted caught the brunt of her bitterness. He often used to walk the streets, rather than stay in and be ear bashed. Often he would walk to the railway where he was happy and relaxed.

He spent most of his working life on the railway and it was on his very last working day before his well-earned retirement he keeled over in the street with an instant and fatal heart attack, just days short of his 64th birthday. This was on the 8th of February 1986 and 3 days later our second daughter Marie was born in St Mary's Hospital. Madge actually left the hospital 2 days after the birth to attend her dad's funeral just over the road in Milton cemetery, then returned to look after the baby.

The night before the service Madge said she had awoken to see her dad framed in the doorway to the ward. He was dressed in his working gear and just looked across at her and the baby. When she was standing at the graveside she experienced a warm glow inside and knew her dad was sending a message to her he was OK. Madge loved her dad deeply and was very moved by this experience. Later she would later undergo a conversion to the Catholic faith and her experiences around the time of her dad's death were one of the main drivers for this.

The whole family were devastated by Ted's death and he was deeply mourned. However, true to type, Rose didn't want to stump up the money for a headstone for his grave but faced with a family mutiny she gave way. Rose didn't change her attitudes and behaviour but just swapped in her son Steve for Ted as companion and sparring partner.

She went on to the age of 87 before capitulating to dementia and finally passing away.

I admit to feeling angry when the extent of her 'savings' came to light. Both in official bank accounts and hidden in the roof of her house were tens of thousands of pounds. When I think of Ted, wearing second-hand clothes in the cold winter and struggling to start his old car to go to work, I just wonder at her mentality. She could have hugely improved their standard of living and allowed Ted to drive a half decent car by putting the money up and barely denting her 'savings.' But she preferred, like a classic miser, to have bundles of banknotes instead. So sad.

* * *

What of Ted's brothers? There are some points of note we have discovered about Frazie. He was called up to the services during the second World War as part of the general recruitment of 'over 20 year olds,' following the dispatch of the British Expeditionary Force to France in October 1939 to shore up the French defences against Hitler's advancing blitzkrieg. He joined the 53rd Regiment of the Royal Artillery after basic training and was evacuated from the beaches of Dunkirk along with 338,225 others as part of 'Operation Dynamo' in June 1940 while Nazi bombers screamed overhead.

It is difficult to imagine the trauma undergone by these troops while they were waiting to be rescued, under constant bombardment by bombs and artillery and it obviously affected Frazie deeply, as through his life he was to undergo frequent mental breakdowns and spent much of his time in St James's mental institution. Frazie completed the war as a guard at a POW camp set up on Kempton Park horse racing course. After discharge he returned home but could not get along with Ted's new wife Rose and left.

Ted kept in touch with him, as he did his other brothers but after Ted's death the last heard of him was an attempted contact from an old peoples rest home in Southsea. Unfortunately Rose gave the caller short shrift and at the time told nobody else in the family; it only becoming known much later, after Frazie had died.

Through our research, Madge and I discovered Frazie had died of peritonitis in 1999 at the age of 80 in Red Lodge Residential home at 61 Clarence Parade and was buried ironically quite close to Ted and Rose in Milton cemetery, in an unmarked grave. Madge did some ferreting around of her own and contacted the person named on his death certificate at the Council Offices.

It transpired a few of Frazie's personal effects were held in the stores there and we collected them. They consisted of 2 photographs of himself (the first time Madge had actually seen what he looked like), 2 postcards featuring Field Marshall Montgomery and a simple watch.

Even less is known of Blidge and Ernie. Blidge reached his 20's during the war and was called up to serve with the Royal Air Force, alongside the 8th Army (the famed Desert Rats) in North Africa. He contracted cancer and died at the age of 29. This was also the fate of Ernie, the youngest of the brothers who died of the same cause when he was also 29. With her grandmother and two uncles contracting cancer it is not surprising Madge to this day lives in constant terror of the potential threat.

But what of Ted's children? There were 3 boys. Richard was born on 26th March 1946. As the eldest, much was expected of him as he grew up and he turned out to be a pragmatic and practical chap. After 6 months working in a timber yard, he joined the railway as along term career like his father before him and remains there to this day. He was still living at home until well into his 30's and eventually went to live with his long term partner Annette Orriss and her 2 children (Shana and Midul) from a previous relationship, in a flat that was part of band of housing between Portsmouth and Cosham.

This was a curious parallel with Frederick taking on Beatrice and her child and I take my hat off to him for taking this courageous step. One day Richard knocked on our door and in casual conversation announced he and Annette were to be married the next day. It was typical of Richard, not wanting to make a fuss.

Over the years he developed hobbies in both 'diy' and car mechanics and is one of those people it is generally recognised as being very 'handy,' often doing little jobs for friends and family alike.

His younger brother Mike was born in January 1952. He was more gregarious at an early age and was the first to leave home after he met and married Linda Earley in 1972. They started out in a small flat above a fruit shop in Osbourne Road, Southsea before moving to Millbrook Drive in the West Leigh council estate just north of the Portsmouth boundaries. Back to a flat in Portsmouth in King Albert Court and then they bought their first home in Tokyo Road, Copnor, quite close To where Madge and I were living in Chichester Road.

Mike then moved to St Swithun's Road and finally to Cosham to a large property in St Michael's Road.

As a youngster, Mike had earned money by being a 'Mudlark' (as described earlier), by directing cars to spaces in congested car parks and by carrying passengers' luggage as they alighted from the ferries by the Dockyard main gate.

After leaving school at 15, Mike started working at Fyffe's banana factory by the Fratton railway station, and then was a meat delivery driver with Frederick Wains. He delivered to schools, factories and other places. During this time he had an accident and was thrown through the windscreen of his van, receiving cuts and scars that he still has to this day. Mike made additional money on the side by acting as an agent, selling clothes and fancy goods to the people on his delivery round.

In 1973 he left and became a milkman, giving up his part-time 'selling' activities. However, in 1974 when he heard that his old employers had gone bust and the business taken over by Christofoli Hunt, he approached them and offered to organise the delivery rounds, based on his knowledge of the customer base. He resumed there as a driver and also picked up his sideline of selling goods, but this time buying direct from wholesalers himself, rather than act as an agent for someone else.

In 1982 Mike took the plunge and made his part time entrepreneurial role his main job and started working for himself with Lyn as his secretary/accountant. As a self-made man he did well and soon bought a detached property in Cosham. It was high up on the slopes of Portsdown Hill, which overlooks Portsmouth that Mike and Lyn brought up their family of 3 girls; Sammy, Susie and Louise.

He received a setback when the recession kicked in during the latter part of the 80s and early 90s. Many individuals and firms in similar situations folded but Mike struggled by. He had the support of most members of the family, especially Lyn's brother Trevor, who as a car mechanic kept Mike on the road during the whole period of difficulty.

Mike's dad Ted had already passed on, otherwise he would have undoubtedly bailed Mike out. But his mum Rose refused Mike all but the meanest of financial help, even though she was sitting on her piles of money. Despite this, Mike survived and once more started to prosper as the recession finally lifted. At the time of writing he is still in the same line of work and doing very nicely.

The youngest brother Steve remained at home. After Ted's death

Rose bought her Council flat on very favourable terms and in 1988 sold it and moved with Steve into a small 2-bedroomed house in Southsea. Steve's job was as a deck hand on the Isle of Wight ferries, which he enjoyed. However his social life was gradually squeezed and virtually eliminated as Rose became more demanding of his time and attention and sent away his friends that came to call.

A major turn of events came when she had just turned 80. Steve phoned Madge to say their mum was feeling unwell. Madge hurried to see her, took one look and decided she needed to go to hospital. Steve wanted time to lock the house up and so Madge put Rose into the back of her car and started off for the A&E at the Queen Alexandra Hospital, 5 miles away. They had barely got going when Rose complained of chest pains and collapsed. Madge dived into the nearest building with a phone, that happened to be the railway station, and dialed 999. Paramedics quickly appeared and Rose was rushed by ambulance to the A&E.

The doctors examined her and said it appeared her main artery had ruptured and an operation would most likely be pointless. They said it was best to pump her with morphine, make her comfortable and just let her go. Steve finally arrived and was like a rabbit caught in car headlights, stunned by what was happening. He was prepared to go along with the recommendation and let nature take its course but Madge wasn't willing to give up so easily. She refused to accept the situation, had a row with everyone in sight and insisted the doctors try to save her mum.

They operated and found the initial diagnosis was incorrect. Her spleen had ruptured, still potentially fatal but operable. It was removed, and after a period in intensive care she was moved to a regular ward. If she had been left alone, as was suggested then she would almost certainly have died.

As it was she still wasn't out of the woods. The family were taking it in shifts to be by her bedside and Madge and Mike noticed when asleep she periodically stopped breathing, only to start again a few seconds later.

The doctor took the family members aside and told them their mum was unlikely to survive the next 48 hours. However, Madge had noticed the breathing symptoms had only started when a new form of medication had been introduced and she queried with the doctor whether there could be an association. The doctor said nothing but the new medication was withdrawn and Rose sailed through the critical 48 hours, improved by the day and was finally allowed home 3 weeks later. She was certainly a tough old boot.

Rose's ongoing care was a problem as she was now unable to properly fend for herself. Richard, Mike and Madge all had families as well as jobs and none had either the time or accommodation to help her. Rose was adamant she would not go into an old peoples residence and wished to remain at home.

The solution was Steve, who had no commitments and was living at home anyway. He would give up his job and support Rose, aided by state benefits and the family when they were able. He was at first reluctant but then saw the scenario contained some attractions and readily agreed.

After this traumatic event, how did Rose then reward her family for saving her life and being so attentive? She cut Madge, Mike and Richard out of her will and left her entire estate to Steve. Hmmmm.

After Rose's death, Steve lost all his financial allowances and Madge and I assisted him in applying for a job at the Portsmouth Commercial Docks, which he secured. He was also concerned it was taking a long time to finalise the execution of his mum's will and again turned to us for help in accelerating matters on his behalf, which we did.

He showed his gratitude to Madge by telling her she wasn't really a 'Lenton' any more. Perhaps that's why he hasn't to date offered her a piece of her mum's jewellery as a keepsake. All that didn't go down well. Madge is enormously and justifiably proud of her bloodline and family name. He didn't treat his brothers Richard and Mike much better either.

As soon as he got his hands on the inheritance money, Steve packed up work and to the date of writing has been living a life of leisure ever since. I imagine we won't see much of him until the money finally runs out. Perhaps one day he will find out in this world you end up reaping what you sow.

Having taken a look at her immediate family, including her 3 brothers, let's now talk about Madge and her upbringing.

5.3   Madge and her upbringing

I have already mentioned Madge in the context of her family and now I must describe her more fully. Madge was born on 24th May 1953, a few days before Queen Elizabeth II was crowned and Mount Everest was conquered for the first time, in the year battery powered wristwatches first made an appearance.

She was born in a rented flat above a shop at 35 Railway View in central Portsmouth where the family was living. She was the third child after her elder brothers Richard and Michael. Her mother, Rose, later told her she had attempted to terminate the pregnancy by taking various medication concoctions. Nice to feel wanted.

Whether it was caused by Rose's efforts or not, Madge was born with a damaged eye, which she could barely see with and had it's eyelid partially closed. An operation on the eyelid as a child had only limited success and for years the 'droopy eyelid' caused her to self-deprecate her appearance and undermined her self-confidence. The problem was to be finally and successfully resolved many years later as you will see if you read on. Madge also had hearing difficulties and at the age of 9 attended a series of tests to help identify the problem. Fortunately, it seemed to resolve itself over time and did not recur.

However one childhood ailment has stayed with her and dogged the whole of her life. Madge suffers from dyslexia. Made worse because in her day at school it was not recognised and her education suffered accordingly. Teachers labelled her 'slow' or 'thick' and gave up on her, rather than getting to the root of the problem and giving support.

Her parents didn't pick up on this although they were supportive of her in other matters. For example, when she had her coat stolen at school, Rose let loose her full wrath upon the teachers and other parents alike. The coat was discovered in a second hand clothes store half a mile from the school.

The environment in which Madge and her brothers was brought up was also difficult. A series of anonymous blocks of gray flats with clanking metal lifts that were forever breaking down. Experiences of being trapped in lifts have left Madge with a deep horror and distrust of such contraptions. To this day she will always use a staircase rather than a lift, which has given rise to some interesting situations (see later).

Like when her friend Jennifer Lawson broke her toe and

Madge took her to the hospital. With Jen in a wheelchair and needing to go up 2 floors, Madge realised it meant taking the lift. To give her full due, she tried to be brave about it. She wheeled Jen into the lift and pressed the floor button but just before the doors closed she bottled it and leapt out. As the doors finally shut behind her she just caught sight of Jennifer's astonished expression as she set off on a lone ride into the unknown. Madge hurtled up the adjacent staircase and just got there in time to take the wheelchair back out through the open lift doors before someone on another floor called it and sent Jen off on another voyage of discovery.

There was a follow up to this. Madge was so flustered she didn't release the wheelchair brakes properly and after struggling to push it, finally gave in and parked Jennifer in a nearby corridor and went off to get some fresh air to recover. In the meantime Jen was causing a major traffic bottleneck, as they couldn't wheel beds past her. When Madge returned, a porter had moved Jen round the corner, out of the way, and Madge couldn't find her. It sounds more like a comedy sketch than real life but I often feel like that when Madge is around.

Anyway, as I was indicating, to put Madge in a lift is to invite a blind panic attack. However there were other, more serious horrors for a young girl. She once discovered the body of the resident of the flat above them when he hanged himself on the communal stairwell and on another occasion a man followed her home into the flats and attempted to sexually assault her. Madge just gave him an earful of abuse and he ran off. Such things were not uncommon in the seedier reaches of Portsea and Madge had to fend off at least two other attempts to attack her. She told her elder brother about them but he counselled her to hush the episodes up, otherwise even more trouble might be stirred up.

Not all anecdotes of the time have quite such serious connotations. There was the time Madge, then about 10 years old, asked her big brother Richard to fetch her ball that had ended up on the roof of a shed adjacent to the flats. Richard kindly left his dinner on the table and went downstairs. He climbed up onto the shed roof, watched by Madge through the upstairs kitchen window. As he threw the ball down the roof gave way and Richard disappeared in a cloud of dust. Seconds later and in the best traditions of comedy the shed door opened and he walked out, totally unhurt and brushing the dust off his clothes. He just walked back upstairs and continued eating his dinner. Three weeks later a letter arrived from the Council with a repair bill for the shed roof.

Rose just tore it up.

On another occasion, Madge wanted a bicycle but couldn't afford it so her brother Mike and his pals got hold of a dilapidated boys bike that had been dumped and did it up for her. Madge was delighted, except it had a crossbar. She complained to Mike who obliged by sawing it off and Madge went for a triumphant ride, only to have the weakened frame come apart and leave her mourning over a bicycle in two pieces.

Madge's fear of lifts through claustrophobia was exacerbated one day when she tried to change the film in her camera. Seeking as dark a place as possible, she went into her mum's walk-in wardrobe and pulled the door to. Unfortunately she pulled a little too hard and the door actually shut, locking her in. Her shouts for assistance went unanswered as only her mum was in the house and she out of earshot of the muffled cries. It was a test of Madge's desperation against a very solid lock and door. No contest. The door was splintered and off its hinges in no time flat.

Mike also had his moments. He yearned for a pet of some kind but Rose was not at all in favour. This led to animals of various descriptions being smuggled into his room and kept secretly under his bed. This included pond creatures, lizards, a sparrow and a small duck he pinched from Baffins Pond.

At the age of 11 Madge attended Kingston Modern School in Portsmouth and was put in the 'dregs' class. Populated with miscreants, troublemakers and dyslexics like Madge the girls were a real life St Trinian's group. When not playing truant and going shoplifting they got up to all sorts of tricks and generally wrought havoc. Like writing graffiti on classroom roller blinds so when they got pulled down a rude message was revealed.

One poor trainee teacher was locked in a walk-in cupboard for an hour (we all know how Madge would have handled this, don't we) and on a separate occasion the classroom door handle was removed so the teacher was unable to open the door. She eventually left the school in a flood of tears. That's not to say I condone such actions but I narrate them to show the environment within which Madge was supposed to be educated.

Madge has protested she was a follower rather than a leader and was not really to blame for the class behaviour. However she did pick up some very bad practices and it took an episode when she was caught shoplifting to bring her to her senses. Madge's friend had demonstrated how easy it was to steal from shops and Madge had already 'had a go' and taken some items home. Then one day Madge and another girl were both caught as they left a shop and taken to the manager's office.

The reprimand from the manager and his security guard is emblazoned upon her memory to this day and nipped in the bud any blossoming life of crime. She told her dad about the episode but he told her 'leave it with me and don't tell your mum.' Madge threw away all her ill-gotten gains and never stepped out of line again. Rose found out about 5 years later when she bumped into the other girl's mother who chatted about the episode and left Rose open mouthed. (Joke: Madge went to the doctor and said she was suffering from kleptomania; he told her to take something for it).

Like most girls of her age, Madge was keen on pop music, however she had no money to buy either a record player or records. Then one day she heard one of her friends had acquired a new record player and was about to throw out the old one. Madge secured it and took it home to her bedroom. The problem was she only had enough money to buy just the 1 record. After much thought she carefully selected 'It's the same old Song' by the Four Tops. She then proceeded to play it ad nauseum at home and drove everybody mad. Finally Richard gave in and bought her a second record, just to save their sanity.

At school, Madge never had pretensions to be the 'Brain of Britain'. It was rumoured her head didn't cast a shadow but there was no need to do what one teacher did. Just before she left school, Madge's form teacher took her to one side and told her she was a completely lost cause and would never amount to anything.

The teacher may have had a point academically, although Madge was not really to blame for that. But she totally overlooked Madge's personality and nature. If she had really known her pupil as she should have, then not only would she have picked up on Madge's learning difficulties and supported her, but would have also recognised that beneath the slightly mischievous and tom-boy façade there was a very loving and caring girl who just needed a bit of guidance.

Interestingly, some deep friendships must have been forged between the girls as in 2003 Madge was contacted through Friends Reunited to have a re-union with about 20 of her ex-classmates, 34 years on. I hope the bar/restaurant has adequate accidental damage insurance.

In an earlier Chapter, I made reference to my admiration for Nanny (Nellie Foster) who brought up a large family, through a combination of love for her children, putting the family before her own interests and sheer hard work. It reflects well on Madge she has been compared to Nanny on more than one occasion as possessing similar qualities.

Over the years Madge and I have been motivated always by doing what we think is best for the children although sometimes they have not appreciated this and put it down to 'interference' on our part or the actions being too controlling. Madge in particular has always been hurt by such comments, as it has never been her intention to do anything other than guide her kids and protect them, in some cases from themselves.

Madge has always been very self-deprecating, frequently putting herself down and believing her sole purpose in life is to serve as a warning to others. She does have a few other idiosyncrasies however.

Her dyslexia leads to some interesting situations, like her predilection for opening cereal packets at the 'wrong' end, then putting the packet on it's side in the kitchen cupboard. On many a morning I've struggled bleary eyed to prepare breakfast; retrieving the cereal box and holding it up the 'right' way. Only to find myself paddling in Rice Krispies.

After many years of working in a canteen kitchen, Madge has a strong dislike of flies. Which is a bit strange because they seem to like her a lot. I'm not saying she attracts them in some way but nevertheless they seem to realise she does not appreciate their proximity and just for the hell of it insist on buzzing past her nose as frequently as possible. Madge reacts at home by demanding the offending insect is banished forthwith. This is usually easier said than done and results in bruised shins and skinned knuckles as whoever received the order careers around the room with a rolled up newspaper, eyes on the fly and tripping over the furniture and dogs.

On one occasion after being dived bombed a few times by her unwanted friends, Madge insisted I open a window. I did as she bade and immediately 3 more flies flew in and joined in the aerial display of contorted manoeuvres. It was of course all my fault. I've come to the conclusion the only way to stop flies going into the living room is to put a bucket of manure in the kitchen. I should also have looked into the anagrams of Madge's maiden name (Madge Lenton) a bit further where I would have found 'Nag de Men Lot'.

Madge herself tried to solve her problem with flies by purchasing several 'Venus fly traps' and leaving them around the house. It didn't work however and the plants all died. Probably from starvation.

When it comes to doing you partner's bidding, you can be the most gallant man in the world but you are putty in the hands of any woman when it comes to their picking holes in what you do. A woman can make or break a man using just 3 little words. Either 'I love you' or 'Is that it?'

Of course men don't help themselves either by putting their feet in it. Usually, slowly and up to the groin. Witness the following monologue following the well known chivalrous gesture of opening a door for a lady (in this particular case - my better half) to pass through.

'Honestly dear, when I opened the door for you to walk through I did not open it a bit wider than I usually do in order to infer you're putting on weight. Your figure is positively sylph like and if anyone says different then I'll personally fetch them a knuckle sandwich. Really. You're not even approaching plump, let alone the 'f' word. No I'm not saying you're plump, just the opposite. No you're not skinny either you're just right. Now don't get upset about it. Come on now cheer up. Chin up .... both of them ....doh!'

Notice the 'doh' then. This has entered the English language courtesy of Homer Simpson, of whom I am a great fan and, as my kids assure me, someone who closely resembles myself both in personality and physically although he is minus the hairy bits.

Although I also have similarities with Homer's girth, I have tried to persuade Madge although when we got married she could get her arms all the way around me and now she has difficulty in doing so, is because age makes your arms grow shorter.

That I even got a flicker of acceptance of the above contention is down because Madge can be very gullible at times. ('Yes I may be gullible but at least I have this magic potato the man sold me.') Madge is so open and honest herself she assumes the same in other people and hence gets misled on occasion. The kids know this and wickedly tend to take advantage and wind her up (especially Mike).

*   *   *

Madge moved with her family from Railway View to a series of council flats in the Lake Road / Arundel street area. Including Titchfield House (1954), Fareham House (1958), where Steve was born and Hambledon House (1966), until ending up in Freemantle House in

Portsea (1970) where they were living when I entered the picture.

There are stories of Ted organizing the house moves using only a 2-wheel handcart borrowed from a trader in the street market in Charlotte Street and with the assistance of his two eldest sons. Hauling everything including cookers, beds and sofas down and up several flights of stairs at each end.

Madge had a close circle of friends, including Christine, who she met at school, mutual friends Sharon and Glenda and Pearl from her place of work. Together they formed a local 'mafia'. Madge was actually a bridesmaid to Pearl when her friend got married and I was with her and attended an infamous reception where a huge fight took place between the two families.

Madge's concerns over her physical appearance were not helped by her mum's comments. Whenever Madge as a teenager would be getting ready to go out for the evening, her mum would say: 'I don't know why you're spending so much time trying to look nice, nobody's going to be looking at you'. What a charming woman she was.

Boys occasionally entered the picture. Madge had actually been going out with a sailor for a short time when he had to go away for a while and it was in his absence Madge and her mates made that now famous trip to the Mecca dancehall and the meeting with yours truly, described at length in an earlier Chapter. I occasionally mention to Madge she was two-timing the young sailor when she met myself and warn her not to make a habit of it now she's with me. That's after 30 years of marriage of course.

Her mum wasn't keen on me, at least at first. Mind you Rose was never keen on any 'outsiders' at the best of times and even immediate members of her own family felt threatened on occasion. Ted dubbed me 'Esci' because at the time I drove a Ford Escort car. Her brothers made me welcome once I appeared to be more than just a flash in the pan and I saw Madge just about every day.

So eventually Madge and I became engaged and were married in July 1973, again as described earlier. What happened after is the subject of another Chapter both in our lives and in this book.

Before we move on to that, I've put together a few of the anecdotes involving Madge over the years, in the form of a spoof quiz. The intention is not to laugh **at** my dear wife but to laugh **with** her and enjoy some of the predicaments in which she has found herself.

5.4 Madge Quiz

Madge is well known for somewhat eccentric behaviour on occasion and her friends refer to her fondly as 'mad' Madge. As an illustration of the point, this quiz is based upon actual events and gives examples of Madge jumping into a few metaphorical cowpats.

I would here like to apologise to anyone who feels they have in any way been harmed or embarrassed by these anecdotes, just in case they recognise themselves within the descriptions and happen to know a good solicitor. Also please note I am not poking fun at my wife but relate these events as examples of her general dottiness, that is one of her very many attributes, that make me love her even more.

1. A glazier is giving you an estimate for replacing a large window in the conservatory, which became cracked in mysterious circumstances ('not us dad'.) Unbeknown to you, the puppy has left a deposit on the conservatory floor the glazier unwittingly steps in.

    Do you? -
- (a) Point out what has happened, apologise through a mist of embarrassment and clean the man's shoe for him.
- (b) Point it out and accuse him of bringing it in from outside. Your justifiable rage can only be assuaged by a heavy discount applied to the window repair estimate.
- (b) Ignore it and let him tread it back through your house, and then have major carpet cleaning exercise. (Oh well, they needed doing anyway).

Answer assessment:
- (a) You are a very kind and possibly gullible person. Please send me your name and address on the back of a £20 note.
- (b) You are a despicable and probably very rich person.
- (c) Your name is 'Madge.'

2. You are out walking your dogs. A man pulls up in a car and asks you for directions.
Do you? –

(a) Give concise, logical and accurate directions to his destination.
(b) Give him a complex web of instructions orientated to local landmarks such as the ladies hairdressers, auntie Mabel's and the place where the woman up the road tripped on the kerb and spilled her shopping the other day and you know how much bananas cost these days although Tesco's does have a special promotion on at the moment.
(c) Innocently send him completely in the wrong direction and about 10 miles out of his way.

Answer assessment:
(a) You are a perfectly normal man.
(b) You are a perfectly normal woman.
(c) Your name is 'Madge.'

3. You are walking the dogs and they have stopped dead by a bus 'request' stop. Their eyes are glued to a little old lady stranded on the other side of the road and desperately trying to get across to the request stop before the bus arrives. The heavy traffic is preventing her crossing and the bus appears in the distance. It's 2 hours to wait for next one and the reverse trip back home to wait if it's missed.

Do you? -
(a) Watch with interest and fall about laughing when the bus goes past.
(b) Stop the traffic and help the old lady cross. Then wave down the bus and assist her on board with a word of encouragement and a departing wave.
(c) Stop the traffic and help the old lady cross. Then thrust a conversation upon her, extolling the attentiveness and curiosities of a bunch of Westies, while brushing aside her flailing attempts to break free and get the attention of the bus driver. Finally notice the bus as it disappears into the distance and politely enquire if she needed that one.

Answer assessment:
(a) You are a despicable person and probably either a double-glazing salesman or an estate agent.
(b) You are a kind soul who probably gets taken advantage of by double-glazing salesmen and estate agents.
(c) Your name is 'Madge.'

4. You are out walking your dogs. A man who you don't know stops you and admires them. While you are chatting one of the dogs does a 'Number 2' on the grass verge. Before you can move in to remove it, she scrapes the ground, flicking her back feet, as dogs are wont to do. One of her paws catches the smelly deposit, throws it into the air and it plops down onto the man's shoe. Absorbed in conversation, he does not notice.

Do you? -
(a) Apologise profusely; produce suitable materials; remove the offending article; buff and polish the man's shoe until it shines.
(b) Keep quiet and hope he doesn't realise what has happened until he is well out of range, in the knowledge you are unlikely to meet him again.
(c) Sidle up closer to him and try and knock the deposit from his shoe with your toe without him noticing. Then overbalance so that you tread heavily on his foot, squelching the object and working it well into his laces and the underside of your own shoe. Realise you have just given birth to a new reality television game show – 'Talk your way out of that one, mate.'

Answer assessment:
(a) You are a perfectly normal woman.
(b) You are a perfectly normal man.
(c) Your name is 'Madge.'

5. Your son's pride and joy is his car; a black Ford Escort. He has recently had a body kit fitted; the car has just been delivered and is sitting resplendent on the front driveway. While manoeuvring a double pushchair, complete with grandchildren, past the vehicle you scrape the car right along the newly fitted bodywork.

Do you? -
(a) Immediately own up. Beg your son's forgiveness and offer to pay to have the damage repaired.
(b) Ignore the episode and hope he doesn't notice until at least one trip has been made to a car park or to his friends, which will provide an alternative culprit to blame.
(b) Grab a tin of black boot polish and smear it on to cover up the scratched area.

Answer assessment:
(a) You are a person of the highest moral integrity. You also have a death wish.
(b) You are a perfectly normal coward.
(c) Your name is 'Madge.'

6. You have heavily pruned your conifers and are loading the branches into your estate car. They run from the windscreen to the tailgate. The end of the thickest and longest branch is sticking out of the back and preventing the tailgate closing.

Do you? -
(a) Unload the protruding branch and put it back having sawn it into two more manageable lengths.
(b) Rearrange the branches so the longest is aligned diagonally and now fits.
(c) Slam the tailgate down to ram the branch into the car, driving the sharp front end straight through the windscreen.

Answer assessment:
(a) You are a very sensible and practical man.
(b) You are a thinking person who doesn't own a saw.
(c) Your name is 'Madge.'

7. It is a cold winter evening and snow is on the ground. You have enjoyed an evening out with 3 of your closest friends. Now it is your job to drive them home.

Do you? -
(a) Walk to the car and then stand chatting for 20 minutes before getting in.
(b) Walk to the car and then usher everyone inside quickly, ensuring they are comfortable before driving off.
(b) Walk to the car. Yell at everyone to get in quickly while leaping behind the steering wheel and driving off. Suddenly notice the back door is wide open and one of your passengers, still half outside the vehicle and hanging onto the door handle for grim death, is running alongside the car shrieking.

Answer assessment:
(a) You are a typical woman.
(b) You are a very considerate woman who has forgotten her coat.
(c) Your name is 'Madge.'

...ographs borrowed from the Bicheno book by Jean Nelson and Eileen Webster.

...left: Hemington Bicheno. My great, great grandfather. This is the earliest picture that I can find of an ancestor ... direct line. *Bottom left:* Hemington's son Warren and wife Clara. My great, grandparents.

...right: James Ebenezer Bicheno (who gave his surname to the town in Tasmania)

...re and bottom right: James Ebenezer's memorial and crest in the grounds of parliament house. It is not clear ...her the crest is related to our family surname or the position in government that he held.

Top left: My great grandparents Warren and Clara with daughters Mary and baby Mabel (note the similarity to my own daughter Emm and granddaughter Chloe) and sons James (standing) seated left Charles and right Percy (my grandad Poppy). (c. 1898).

Centre right (below): Wedding of Poppy's elder sister Mary.
Front: Mabel (Poppy's younger sister), Mary Unknown, Clara (Poppy's mum).
Back: Percy Fryer (Mabel's husband), Charl (Poppy's brother), unknown, Bill Youngs (groom) who as a musician played for the ki and queen on the Royal Yacht, unknown, Warren (Poppy's dad). (c. 1914).

Centre left (above): Nanny with her first 3 children. Percy (my dad – notice the resemblance with me!) Rita and baby Charlie. (c. 1917).

Bottom right: A composite picture that someone in the family put together. It depicts a very young Nanny and Poppy (my Bicheno grandparents).

118

Above: The Zeppelin (L15) medal.
This is the medal specially struck for shooting down the first Zeppelin of WWI and presented to my great uncle Charlie Bicheno and 2 other A.A. artillary gunners.

The inscriptions read:
Reverse: Presented by the Lord Mayor of London, Colonel Sir Charles Wakefield.
Obverse: L15 Well Hit. March 31st April 1st 1916. C Bicheno.

Left: Believed to be a picture of 'Aboyeur' who won the 1913 Derby. Also thought to depict my grandad's brother Jim Bicheno (in hat) who was the stable's Head Lad and the horse's trainer Tom Lewis.

Views of the town of 'Bicheno' in Tasmania as catured by Canadian relative Albert Bicheno and his wife in 196

Top left: Albert trying to find his way to the township. 'Let's see. If Swansea is 55 miles that way and Derby 6 miles the other way, then I must be in Hereford and the town of 'Bicheno' is close to Stratford-upon-Avon.'

Top right: The town's 'Wecome' sign. The 'Please Slow Down' is thought not to be indicative of the arrival of the motor vehicle there but more likely refers to the very fa Aborigine runners.

Centre left: Albert has found the Bicheno service store and appears to be utilising the Bicheno outdoor urinal facilities.

Below left: The Bicheno church. Looking pristine.

Below right: The diminuitive 'Bicheno Finch'.

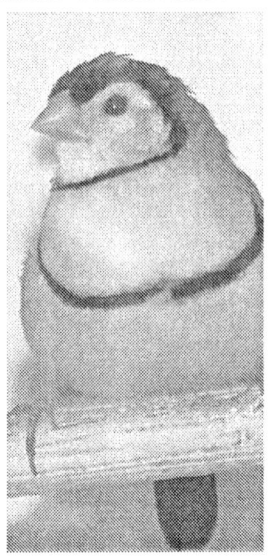

...vs of Nanny's and Poppy's generation.

...left: My dad's sisters Rita and Mabel with their mum.

...right: Dad's vivacious sister Elsie, taken just before her tragic accident.

...re left: Nanny and Poppy with my mum Norah.

...re right: Poppy's brother Alf, pictured as a Captain and prior ...s further promotions.

...om right: Possibly the only photograph of Poppy's brother ...y who was shell-shocked during WWI and had his left hand ...led.

121

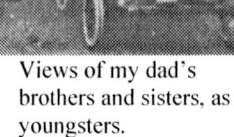

Views of my dad's brothers and sisters, as youngsters.

Top left: Jim with Ron (c. 1934).

Top centre: Elsie and Mabel pushing Arthur. (c. 1938).

Top right: From the left. Arthur, Brenda and Ron. (c.1942).

Centre left: Brenda, Elsie and Ron, outside the famous home in Landguard Road. Note the styles of the time.

Bottom right:
Ron with Poppy and dog Peggy, with Brenda in background.

Bottom left: Brenda. Note the exquisite doll and pram. (c. 1935).

Bottom centre: Ron with another dog, Bonny.

122

Top: The 'Mafia' picture. My dad and his brothers, photographed with Poppy at a family wedding. Left to right. Bill, Percy (my dad), Jim, Ron and Arthur. (c. 1968).

tre: Picture taken at a heno reunion shows ny's and Poppy's legacy talwart Bicheno's.

 left to right:
, Bill, Ron, and Percy (my
.

ies left to right:
ıda, Mary, Rita and
el.

Bottom: A wedding group.
From left to right:
Percy (dad), Jim (uncle), Poppy (grandad), Bob (aunt Brenda's husband), Ron (uncle), Arthur (uncle), Fred (aunt Mary's husband), Bill (uncle). (c. 1955).

123

Top left: My mum (Norah) as she was when she entered the 'Carroll Levis Discoveries Show' and sang her way through to the grand final.

Top centre: My dad (Percy) receiving his BEM from Lord Strathcona the then Minister for Defence (1978) and *Top right:* (1998) displaying his medal and receiving the Maundy Money from Queen Elizabeth II.

Below: Norah and Percy, over the I.o.W. before they were married.

Above centre: Norah and Percy with a little yours truly at a reception. (c. 1953).

Centre right: An elderly Norah with my wife Madge.

Bottom right: Percy in the North African desert during WWII. Cuddling up to a 500lb bomb in lieu of Norah. (c. 1942).

124

vs of my close relatives.
kwise from top left.

mum and dad with my kids
e and Richard. (1984);

re picture, my sisters Frances
and Margaret, dad Percy,
Norah and myself (complete
basin hairstyle). (c 1979);

p holiday at Butlins Minehead. My lot with my mum and dad and his sister Rita, plus my sister Margaret
usband Ian with their son Jonathan;

num's side of the family. She is centre back with her brother Math and sister Vera either side while her other
Dorothy is front right;

ister Frances and her husband Ron while on holiday in Egypt.

Views of Madge's relatives.

Left: Uncle and Aunts.
Frances, Lilly, Don (Madge's husband) with our daughter Marie, Madge and Rose (Madge's mum). (1986).

Above right: Madge's brothers. Steve shows a nasty growth of balloons on his knuckles and Mike thinks it hilarious.

Left: Madge's brother Richard's wedding. Left to right. Madge, the bride Annette, groom Richard and his brother Steve. No, the picture's not lop sided. The Lenton's always stand like that, normally up against a bar. (2002).

Bottom: Our wedding picture. From the left. My sister Frances, my dad and mum, me (notice the hair!) and Madge, Madge's parents Rose and Ted, Lyn (Madge's brother Mike's wife) and the little bridesmaids are my sister Margaret's daughters Louise, Bernadette and Michelle. (1973)

Various views of Ted and Rose, Madge's parents.

Above left: Ted cuts a dashing picture in his younger day.
Above centre: Ted with Madge's younger brother Steve as a youngster. (c. 1965).
Above right: Rose relaxing.

Left: Ted and Rose with Stephen, our first baby.

Bottom left: Madge and Ted when Madge and I were married. (1973)

Bottom right: A rare picture of Ted's brother 'Frazie'. Taken during the war when he was a gunner in the British Army. The photograph only came to light when Madge went searching for him in 2002 only to find that he had died in 1999 in an old people's home in Southsea and left this among his meagre belongings.

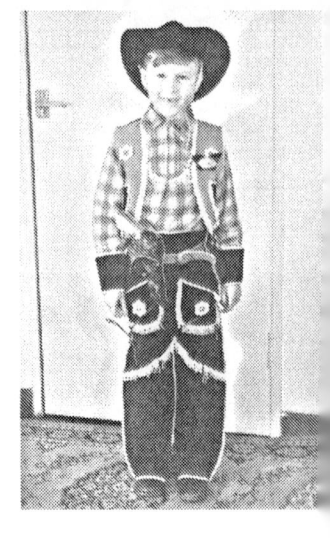

Views of yours truly.

Top left: Droopy drawers and obviously not yet potty trained. (1949).

Top centre: Earliest picture of me, with my dad. (1948).

Top right: Cowboy Chris. Taken in Elgin, Scotland. (1954).

Left: In the Daulston Road garden with school Chess trophy. (1963).

Centre: In my St John's College uniform (Note: Strictly speaking trousers at half mast weren't actually part of the uniform spec) (1960).

Below Right: Watching bubbles. (1950).

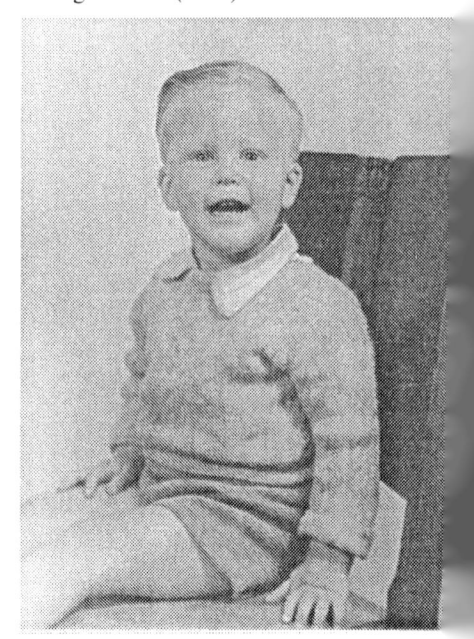

...re pictures of me.

...o row, left to right.: Picture taken in the kitchen of our ...se in The Keep. 1980. Notice the absence of facial lines ... eye bags as the full impact of the kids was yet to catch up ...h me at that time; A sketch of me made by a London street ...st (1987); ...oung dad getting stuck in. The baby is Marie (1986).

...ht: Being presented with another pot. One of two ...asions that I won the 'Player of the Year' for highest ...age score in the SESA skittles leagues (c. 1983). After ..., the beard slowed me down.

...ow: Left, just before I retired (2001). Right, as I am now, writing this book. Note the inane expression (2003).

129

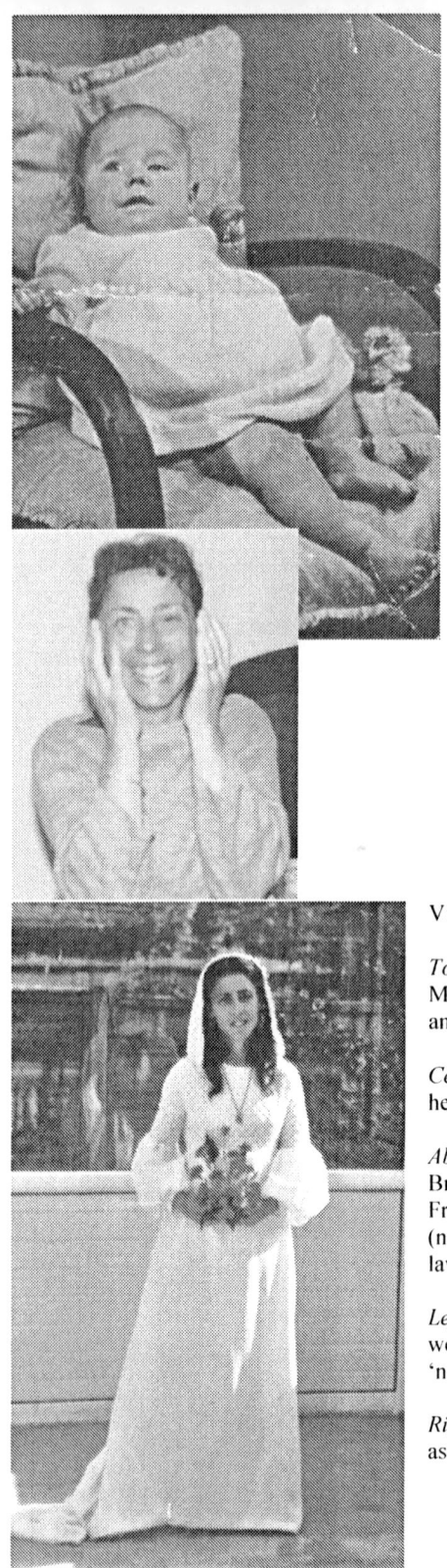

Views of my wife, Madge.

Top row: The only picture of Madge as a baby; as a young lady and a ladette.

Centre left: Madge, just before her eyelid operation (1987).

Above: Wedding photo. Bridesmaids Louise (my niece), Frances (my sister), little Bernie (niece), Lyn (Madge's sister-in-law) and Michelle (niece).

Left: Proving she still fits her wedding dress. Taken in our 'new' conservatory (1984).

Right: Madge displaying her assets in Majorca (1997).

More views of Madge.

Top left: Shy and demure at our honeymoon hotel (1973).

Top right: Standing in the Cupola of St Peter's in Rome (1998).

Left: 'Well judge, I saw it parked there and I thought ….' (1998).

Right: A rare picture of Madge on a school trip to London. (1966).

ow: Fearsome lineup of Dinner Ladies. From the left.
la, Josephine, Barbara, Gwen, Madge, Theresa, Jean, Barbara, Hettie,
, Jennifer. Josephine and Jennifer are featured in the book (2001).

Top and right: Togetherness. Pictures of Madge and myself taken in 1973, 2003 and 1983.

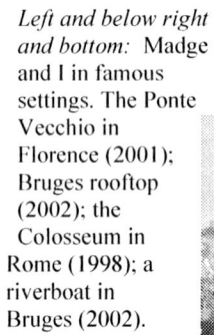

Left and below right and bottom: Madge and I in famous settings. The Ponte Vecchio in Florence (2001); Bruges rooftop (2002); the Colosseum in Rome (1998); a riverboat in Bruges (2002).

Chapter 6

Our Life Together

They say facing adversity together can bind couples closer. In which case the many disasters in our first house in Chichester Road certainly did Madge and I a favour, although it didn't seem so at the time. Having got the house in a reasonable state or putting it another way, a state within which a baby might be able to survive and thrive, we decided we should make moves towards having a family.

We had already discussed, at length, the size of family we wanted. We had started off by deciding we wanted at least one boy and one girl. However, having experienced being the only boy among girls, I was keen there should be more than one boy and Madge for a similar reason, being brought up the only girl among boys, wanted more than one girl.

There were also a couple of other agendas running. I wanted boys to keep the unusual family name going. It had survived hundreds of years and I didn't want to be the one who had to explain to my ancestors when I joined them in due course I had poured weed killer over the family tree. Madge, with her very powerful maternal instincts, simply wanted lots and lots and lots of babies. For the purposes of planning however, remembering whatever size family we produced we would have to support on just my wage, as Madge was going to be a full time mother, we settled on a target of 2 boys and 2 girls.

Madge was keen to start the family as a matter of urgency and as soon as I said the house and finances were in a sufficiently good state, that was it. Madge has never been renown for her patience, as many damaged doors opening the 'wrong way' will testify, and she wanted to get pregnant the very first month we tried.

I won't go into private details at this point but sufficient to say for me it was a pretty amazing month and for Madge too when she took a pregnancy test and found it to be 'positive.' I wanted to rush out and buy lots of outrageous toys that would only make sense to children over 10 years of age but Madge put her foot down. She did not want to tempt fate by buying baby things, in case things went wrong. She did not even want to tell anyone she was pregnant until the first 3 months had elapsed; when the greatest risk of miscarriage had passed.

After just a few weeks it wasn't too hard to guess anyway, as Madge was positively glowing by then. Both our mums noticed and word gradually trickled out. I finished decorating the smallest bedroom, although the intention was to keep the cot (and baby!) in with us for the early months. Madge left her job with just a few weeks to go to the big day and then she allowed us to start buying things.

Many items that would be required from day 1 were rapidly accumulated and Madge also packed her suitcase, as all prospective mums do, so she would be ready at a moment's notice. The baby's clothes were a problem, as we had no idea what gender it would be, so Madge bought the sweetest little garments in white and lemon colours.

The official date came and went and still there was no sign. Madge had had enough by now. While visiting her mum, she noticed the children's play park over the road and waddled off to play on a few things to see if it shook the baby into making a move. Still no luck.

A week later, in the middle of the night, things started to happen. (Why do babies always insist on making their move to be born at such unsocial hours?). I was alternating between enforced calm for her sake and the wild excitement of the unknown. Madge rang ahead to the G.P. Unit of St Mary's Hospital, where she was booked in and I took her suitcase to the car.

Contractions were regular if not frequent and we had been warned several times first-born babies took longer than average, so there was no frantic rushing about. In fact it took until 10 pm, 19 hours later before Stephen made his first appearance before two very proud parents. He was named after one of Madge's brothers.

When it comes to looking at a baby and identifying which parent it most resembles, I'm pretty hopeless. Although I do recall Nanny declaring after seeing a certain baby for the first time 'That baby definitely looks like a Bicheno.' I think she was using the baby's nose to judge by, but as all babies' noses look alike to me I need a clearly marked label to tell me what's what.

I know I'm biased but I thought Stephen was a very beautiful baby, especially for a boy. And as he had a nose, he was most definitely 'a Bicheno'. Madge was exhausted and delighted but got little rest, as it wasn't long before the new arrival wanted feeding. Madge had decided well in advance she would feed the baby herself but I don't think she realised the discomfort attached to the decision. Anyway she stuck to it for the baby's sake and kept it going for several months. Something she would repeat for each and every subsequent baby.

After a few days they were both allowed home and we could start getting used to a routine that went with our new roles. Madge proved to be every bit a natural mother I suspected she would be. The only problem we had was Stephen turned out to be a rather difficult baby. I think I spent more nights walking around the bedroom trying to get him to sleep than I did with all the others put together. It was 2 years before Stephen would sleep through the night.

If I had a rough time you can imagine what Madge had, as she was very much bearing the brunt of tending to the baby. (Note for the modern kids: Disposable nappies were relatively scarce then and very expensive so we used the old terry nappies all of the time. These needed constant washing and of course we had no washing machine in those days. I had the easy role; I went back to work).

We didn't realise how difficult a time we were having. Stephen was our first baby and we had nothing to compare him with; we just accepted it as the norm and only later when Emma and then the others came along did we fully realise how hard it had been.

Parents always spoil their first child; they tend to get the best that can be afforded for all their needs. The second and subsequent children tend to get the discarded items from the first time around and hand-me-downs from the first child, as well as from the children of other parents who are befriended along the way. Stephen was no exception.

We bought a beautiful coach-built pram. It was great. It was also very heavy. In fact it proved to be too heavy for the chassis and one day it collapsed when we were out. Mind you when it happened we had a baby inside it, a seat with a toddler on the top of it and a load of shopping on the tray underneath. So I suppose I can't moan too much. It just made getting home from there a bit tricky. Another small cowpat you might say.

Stephen grew up with our rabbit called 'Sid'. They got on well together apart from the time Stephen decided to eat Sid's currant droppings. Madge rushed him to St Mary's Hospital where they checked on Stephen's injections and then, satisfied he was in no danger, fell about laughing.

Our neighbours were a young couple with 2 little girls. They didn't have much money and decided to let part of their home to a lodger. Their house was the same layout as ours but a mirror image. The breakfast room downstairs we extended into our kitchen, they turned into a livingroom/ bedroom and the lodger had this and a share of the kitchen and bathroom.

The first occupant was a girl in her early 20's. We used to see her visitors come out into the garden to access the outside toilet. And boy, did she have a lot of visitors, several times a day and they were all men. Then some very interesting and unusual items started to appear on next-door's washing line. Especially as there were no Ann Summers shops then. It was such a topic of local gossip it was almost a disappointment when the neighbours cottoned on and asked her to leave. Mind you, for all I know it may have been totally innocent and she might have been a fortune-teller. ('You're going to get a very strange disease …').

When Stephen was 13 months old, we proceeded with our plan to extend the family. Once again Madge was impatient to 'get lucky' and once again I managed to do my bit on cue. Nine months later a beautiful baby with dark hair and long curly eyelashes was with us and we named her Emma after my mum's middle name of 'Emily'.

As a baby, Emma was every bit as docile and well behaved as Stephen had been hyperactive and a handful. All of which meant I was lulled into a sense of false security. One day while shopping down Portsmouth's Commercial Road for a new carpet, Madge was looking around and I was minding the two children when Emma started to play up in her buggy.

She was about 16 months old, usually well behaved but like any child prone to the odd 'benny.' I tried to quieten her by giving her what I had in my pocket to play with. Starting with my car keys, which she hurled across the shop. I thought it prudent not to risk them disappearing and searched for something else.

To my endless shame and without thinking what I was doing I pulled out some coins and gave them to her. It appeared to do the trick as she stopped screaming straight away. A few minutes later Madge returned to find Emma coughing violently and spilling a handful of coins onto the floor.

Both the air and Emma then turned blue as Madge realised the toddler had a coin stuck in her throat. I grabbed Emma and turned her upside down, smacking her on the back. With a clatter, a coin dropped out of her mouth. I sat her back in the buggy. 'Gone' she said. She seemed

OK but Madge thought it prudent to have her checked out.

The Royal Hospital (now demolished and turned into a supermarket) was nearby and so we took the kids to the A&E department. They decided to give Emma an X-ray. A few minutes later a doctor returned with an X-Ray photograph in a large, brown envelope.

'You'd better see this' he said, pulling out the picture. We looked at the shadowy negative. At the base of her throat was something small and round and the size of a penny piece.

'She'll need an operation to remove it,' said the doctor. 'Can you take her to Queen Alexandra Hospital yourselves? It'll be quicker than waiting for an ambulance and I'll ring ahead and warn them you're coming.'

The next 20 minutes were a blur. Madge was screaming at me to put my foot down and overtake everything else on the road but I knew we had to get there in one piece and to jolt Emma around might dislodge the coin and block her windpipe.

We reached the Q.A. Hospital safely and Madge rushed out of the car and into the building while I parked. By the time I got back Emma was already in the ward and Madge was helping to get her ready for the operation. Madge took Emma's clothes off and put her into the operating gown. It was several sizes too big and she looked so tiny as they took her away on a trolley.

Apparently they tried to pull the coin out of her throat without success and ended up pushing it down into her tummy. They gave her another X-Ray to make sure things were OK. A rather pale doctor approached us with the resultant picture. The coin had moved out of her throat but there lying in her stomach next to the coin was a large safety pin, like you use on a baby's terry nappy.

Madge brightened. 'I used a safety pin to fasten her operating gown because it was flapping about too much' she explained. There were huge sighs of relief the pin was on the outside and not the inside.

We took Emma home with strict instructions to monitor her 'number 2s' for the coming days. Sure enough 2 days later the coin appeared in an Emmapat to everyone's relief. We kept the coin and cleaned it up. Eventually we had the infamous penny mounted in a pendant and many years later presented it back to Emma on the occasion of her wedding to Wayne Hine.

*   *   *

Although I would never call myself a 'fit' person, I used to keep in reasonable shape by playing table tennis, a deceptively energetic sport. I was quite good at it too. I represented the SESA (Southern Electricity Sports Association) in the Portsmouth and District league. There were 15 Divisions and I usually played around Division 5 although I had won games as high as in Division 2.

I actually went through one season winning 50 out of 51 games (the one I lost was avenged in the return) and won the 'player of the year' trophy from the SESA. Madge would come and watch me play but she wasn't an enthusiast for the game and usually got bored. However there were to be dreadful occurrences that led to Madge insisting I gave up the sport.

The first was when we were playing away against the Civil Service in their sports complex. I was matched against a very heavily built bloke who tried to knock the cover off the ball with every shot coming over the net. I adopted my usual defensive posture, standing well back from the table and simply sending back everything that came my way. It was a tactic that wore down the opponent and induced errors into their game.

I had won the first set and we were well into the second when my opponent just collapsed in a heap. He was unconscious and breathing heavily; then as we watched stunned, he started to turn blue. Someone called for an ambulance and he was taken away in a wheelchair but I understand he died from a heart attack on the way to hospital. We were all deeply shocked by the event but even worse was to come.

One of my team-mates was a Scot, called (inevitably) 'Jock'. He had been really good in his day and was still a very useful player although he was now well into middle age and overweight. Jock and I had been drawn against each other in an internal competition. We knew each other's game well as we often practiced together. The match was intense and exciting and I just about managed to come out on top. We both sat down and Jock produced an orange and started to peel it. Suddenly he pitched forward off the chair and collapsed onto the floor, unconscious. He was rushed to hospital but died the next day, again from a heart attack.

Madge decided as everything came in 3's, I was to give up the sport before it claimed me as the third victim. Somewhat reluctantly I did, as I could see how worried she was.

I turned to a less energetic sport. The SESA were trying to put a Skittles league together. I became a founder member of a Team called

'Bottoms Up' that won the inaugural league and cup competitions, after which it disbanded. I set up my own Team drawn from the Computer Programming Department and our partners. It performed poorly but gave us a great social night out every week. Madge was actually quite a good bowler.

All this time the club section was expanding so it ran 4 separate leagues and a knockout competition. When my Team folded I joined what turned out to be the most potent Team that existed during all my years of playing the game. Initially called 'Pond's People' after its captain Bob Pond, it changed its name to 'Pond's Cream' and swept all before it. Not losing a single game for a couple of years. I won loads of trophies.

Eventually the Team broke up and I joined with some mates under the captaincy of Ged Pratt (a great bloke with a sharp wit) to form 'We Used to be Good'. The team started by including our spouses for a muck about and then got a bit more serious and eventually became one of the dominant Teams of the era and left me with even more trophies. Even when it became more serious the wives and the children all came along to watch the matches and the kids got spoilt with drinks and crisps all evening.

* * *

When Madge became pregnant for the third time it was obvious we were going to run out of space in our house. Not immediately but the third bedroom was very small and could only accommodate one child. We could double up in the second bedroom for a while but to be honest I'd had enough of the house and by that time (mid 1978) we could just about afford something a bit better. We started looking around and soon realised all Portsmouth had to offer was fairly elderly properties.

There was no way I was prepared to take on another old house and start fixing things all over again. I had been spending almost all of my free time, evenings and weekends, clad in overalls and doing something on the house, while Madge needed me to help her out and I wanted to spend time with both her and the children. So we started looking a bit further afield, the distance being constrained by the location of my place of work. I was well established at the Southern Electricity Board, in the Computer Department (see later) with good career prospects and had no wish to leave.

We looked at the major areas of Fareham and Waterlooville and many other places around and about. We finally settled on a place in a relatively new housing estate in Portchester between Portsmouth and Fareham.

The estate was called 'The Keep' and was very close to the Portchester shopping precinct and located at one end of Castle Street; the other end being the site of the Roman/Norman built Portchester Castle.

The house was No 61 and had 3 reasonably sized bedrooms, a large 'L' shaped lounge and kitchen. The garden was about 30 foot square, with a small shed. There was an adjacent pathway down one side and external to the property that led to some more houses behind us and on the other side of the house was a garage. The garage was not ours unfortunately, although the word was it went with our house when first built but was traded by the initial owners for one in a separate block round the back as they were non-drivers.

It was a rather strange looking property with almost slit windows at the front from the living room and a large window looking out from half way up the staircase. Huge windows overlooked the back garden. It was nowhere near as large as the old house but was much more modern and with central heating and a garage (albeit in a separate block) we felt a lot better off. We had bought the Chichester Road house for £6,500 including furnishings and spent thousands on it, making it somewhere near habitable for a family of young children. We had sold it for £11,700 and bought the house in The Keep for £18,500, which was the limit of what we could afford on my salary at the time.

When we left 291 Chichester Road, it was with a feeling of great relief and with a wish our successors in title to the property did not experience anything like the troubles we'd had. I also hoped I hadn't left them too many problems to sort out.

The new house was on an estate of about 100 homes and almost opposite the pedestrian precinct with a reasonable range of shops. We quickly settled in, although we were somewhat taken aback to learn the couple living next to us, adjacent to the garage, were both 'naturists' and had a predilection for sunbathing 'au naturale' when the weather suited. And before you blokes start the 'Whey Hey Heys' I have to tell you, although she was a pleasant lady, the wife was somewhat overweight and not youthful by any means.

In any event they were sheltered from view in the garden by a screen and you could only see them by climbing onto the top of the wardrobe in the third bedroom. (Oh what a giveaway!). Madge said the husband was a bit on the scrawny side, although I kept noticing her wandering around upstairs with a ladder whenever it was a sunny day.

When the neighbours went on holiday they left their keys with us and asked us to check out their house and feed their cat while they were away. We couldn't resist a sneak look into their master bedroom. There were extensive wall murals featuring naked people together with mirror tiles on the ceiling. Boy was I intrigued. Madge was just embarrassed.

The time this happened was when Stephen was 4 years of age, Emma was 2 and Richard was due to be born very soon. Madge was performing miracles as usual, bringing up the little ones while coping with a pregnancy. She seemed to revel in it and was very much a natural mum.

There was a school along Castle Street just 5 minutes walk away and as soon as he was old enough, Stephen started there. It became apparent quite early on he was having serious learning difficulties and after seeking expert advice we decided to pay for him to have tuition at a small private school. Fortunately it was quite close to us and in walking (or rather pram pushing) distance, just the other side of the shopping precinct. Unfortunately it wasn't the breakthrough we hoped for.

It wasn't easy for Madge at this or, in fact, any other time. She always had infants on her hands and my early starts off to work meant she also had to get the children ready, then take them to school, virtually on her own. I know many mums do this and we dads don't really give them enough credit for what they achieve. The men only do the tasks occasionally when mum is ill and we expect accolades whereas the mums do it day in and day out, largely without praise.

We always tried to get out and about, especially at weekends and took the children to all manner of places over the years and only once did we 'mislay' one of them. We were looking around a large garden centre when Stephen (then aged 4) wandered off without either of us seeing him go. When we realised he was missing, panic set in and with the other kids in our arms we flew around calling his name and looking for him. He turned up very quickly and all was well, apart for Emma then standing in the middle of a very large and muddy puddle, getting herself stuck fast and screaming blue murder. It made a change from a cowpat.

On cue, two years after Emma we had Richard, again named after one of Madge's brothers. He was a very good baby and quiet little lad. He had a shock of blond hair and was a daddy's boy.

Although the children were a fundamental part of our lives and took almost all of my non-working time, I occasionally tried to create a little breathing space for myself by burying my head in the newspaper. On one such occasion, I was busy reading when Richard toddled up to me. He was barely 2 years old at the time. 'Build me a plane please Daddy', he asked. Rather than put the paper down, I unfairly tried to fob him off.'

'I can't Richie, I haven't anything to build it with'.

His little face went down and off he went. Ten minutes later he was back. He had gone around and collected together an armful of bits and pieces. None of which were any use for plane building.

'Here you are Daddy' he said, handing over the ensemble. His eyes shone bright and the look he gave was of total confidence his dad could somehow conjure up a plane for him out of what he offered.

I felt ashamed I'd let him down in the first place. I dropped the newspaper and with the aid of a few extra pieces to go with his collection, Richie got the best damn plane dad could make.

Emma was off to school by now and quickly established herself as a bright pupil, much to our relief, then Richard followed in this vein.

In the meantime, Mike arrived as our fourth baby. The largest of all our babies, he was again named after one of Madge's brothers and like Richard he had very blond, almost white, hair. We had a bit of a scare with Mike at a few months old when he was taken seriously ill and this story is told in a later Chapter.

However Mike quickly recovered and proved to be just as robust as the other boys. He was not as quiet though, often proving to be the 'black sheep' of the family and getting into all sorts of scrapes. (He has retained this trait right up to the day of writing).

*   *   *

One of the features of our stay in The Keep were the children's parties. Twenty or so children was normal for such a gathering of initially Stephen's friends and latterly Emma's and Richard's. We would spread rugs out over the floor and have an indoor picnic as we had no table to accommodate so many. After the usual food fight I would put on a film show, using my movie film projector and/or we would play games, depending on how old the children were and how violent the conduct was getting at the time.

Another tradition starting up at that time was the annual pilgrimage to Butlins at Minehead. We would bung everything bar the kitchen sink onto the roof of the car, chuck the kids in the back and then put up with their bickering during a 4-hour drive. The children loved it there and Madge and I even found time to have a bit of fun. It was there my close association with 'teddy machines' started. These are the increasingly popular challenges found in amusement arcades where you guide a 'grab' to pick up soft toys.

I won over 50 on our first visit and many hundreds over the years, in arcades around the country. I just enjoy the challenge but our kids, grandchildren, church fetes and local charity shops have all done well out of my addiction, as well as the arcade owners.

Madge and I were always keen radio listeners, especially in the mornings while we were preparing and eating breakfast. Our favourite being Radio Victory, the local Portsmouth station. When our 10th Wedding Anniversary was due I wrote to the programme and requested they dedicate a record to us. Not only did they do this on the day but also they actually read my letter out on air.

I actually got the whole thing on tape and it's lying around somewhere today. The record the disc jockey selected for us was 'December 63 (Oh What a Night)' by Frankie Valli and the Four Seasons. Ten years out, but what the heck. The tune became 'our song' from that moment. Radio Victory packed up broadcasting a few years later and was much mourned, although several of its staff became national radio and TV personalities.

The attentive reader will have noticed we got it wrong with Mike. According to the grand plan our fourth child needed to be a girl to even things up. However when Mike came along we had to revise the plan, especially as Emma desperately wanted a little sister to play with. So we didn't 'shut up shop' but decided to extend the family even further.

Time went past and again Madge was heavily pregnant, this time with Alan, although at the time we didn't know the baby was a boy let alone what his name was going to be. We tended not to decide on names until our babies were actually born. This was largely because Madge thought it would be temping fate to do so. She's like that, always expecting things to go wrong. I reckon in a previous life, as well as this one, she managed to jump or fall into quite a few cowpats.

Anyway, not having names ready sometimes gave us problems and we sometimes ended up with 'baby Bicheno' on the baby's nametag. Thank goodness for an unusual surname, at least we didn't get the babies mixed up with people of similar hang-ups with the same surname. Mind you Madge would tell you it wouldn't surprise her to find out one or two of ours got swapped in hospital, as at times they behave more like aliens than either of their genetic parents.

We usually resorted to family names as a way out of our predicament. Stephen, Richard and Michael were named after Madge's 3 brothers and Emma after my mum's second name and Marie after my sister who died. Alan was pot luck although he had the family name of 'James' added for good measure. If I had guessed that his brothers would address him by the anagram 'Anal' we would have picked a different name.

Perhaps we should have done what the Native American Indians used to do. When the dad came out of the teepee after his child was born he would name the baby after the first thing he saw. Hence you had romantic names like 'Running Deer' and 'Laughing Water.' It wasn't such a good idea though when you ended up with names such as 'Pile of Buffalo Crap' or 'Dog Licking Bollocks.'

By now Madge was very close to her delivery date for Alan and we were both on tenterhooks. What happened on the evening of 11th January 1983 varies according to whom you listen. Either Madge's version or the true facts I will now relate to you. I was due to play in a works skittles match that evening and to be fair to Madge's version, yes I was a very keen player with a number of trophies on my mantelpiece to show for it.

However, I would not have gone had I thought Madge was close to going into labour even though I was only about 15 minutes away by car and she had the phone number of the clubhouse. She assured me everything was fine and there were no signs. What she didn't tell me at the time was she was already getting contractions. If she had informed me of this fact then no way would I have disappeared.

After I had gone the contractions started getting stronger, with shorter intervals between them. Madge realised the baby was on the way and got Stephen to run to the house behind ours and fetch her friend. Stephen was only 7 years old and I have to say he was magnificent in a very difficult situation.

Unfortunately her friend wasn't in and her husband came instead, nearly passing out when he realised the situation he'd walked into.

Fortunately there was a midwife on the housing estate. Stephen ran to get her while the neighbour phoned for an ambulance. Everyone was too busy to get around to letting me know.

Over the next few minutes 3 things arrived; the midwife, the baby and the ambulance, in that order and with about 4 minutes between each. Alan was born on the floor under a cheese plant, rather than a gooseberry bush. I eventually got a phone message to say Madge had already had the baby and all was well. I rushed home at breakneck speed and just caught the ambulance paramedic tidying things up before leaving.

I won't say what he did with the placenta but we were a soup plate short after his visit. (Yes I appreciate how full of goodness such things are but you really have to draw the line somewhere). Anyway, both Madge and the baby were well enough to stay on at home and all was well that ended well.

Alan was our fifth child and the fourth boy. Before he was born both Madge and I recognised with such a sized family we needed a fourth bedroom, as well as a lot more space in general. With typical foreboding and fear of cowpats Madge had decided it would be inviting fate to take a hand if we were to look for a property before the baby was with us.

Now Alan had arrived safely (just!) we started looking for another house. I'd received promotions at work and could now afford a much more substantial mortgage. Again I was insistent we bought something no more than 10 years old. The scars of the house in Chichester Road had still not healed and my worst nightmare was we would end up back in a similar place. We actually looked at a few brand new properties (most of which we couldn't afford) before we found something ideal.

Situated at Bedhampton in Hulbert Road, only one and a half miles from my place of work. It was a 6-year-old detached four-bedroom house with a partially integral double garage. Built with 2 other properties on a plot previously occupied by a cottage in extensive grounds, it was numbered 91B.

It didn't have anything as fancy as an en-suite bathroom to the main bedroom but it was exceptionally spacious. All four bedrooms were 'doubles' and it had a very large bathroom and a downstairs cloakroom. The lounge and dining rooms were good size and adjacent with connecting doors, so if you opened them up you had a huge area 30 feet long by 12 feet wide.

The property was 40 feet wide with a front drive 45 feet long and a back garden 90 feet long. The only small drawback was the back garden was totally overrun with weeds, with not a flower in sight, save for a few wild bluebells. There was also a large mound of earth and builder's rubble, accumulated from some time back when the house was built, taking up the back half of the garden area.

We went to our bank, which was the TSB (before the link-up with Lloyds) and applied for a mortgage. They carried out a survey and got back to us. There was no problem with the financial side but the mortgage had a condition that I redecorated internally. This we were happy to do as Madge wanted to change some of the colour scheme anyway.

The house was being sold to us by a couple but we only dealt with the wife. It wasn't entirely clear but the impression we got from her was they were separating and one of them had found another partner. After our offer for the house was accepted (negotiated down to £52,000 after an initial price of £58,000 and an interim reduction to £54,000), I started to drive past the house on the way to and from work.

Then I noticed something rather peculiar. The lady owned a pair of statuettes that when we visited her were displayed upon a cabinet shelf. They were a matching pair of dogs. Sometimes I saw as I drove past, these dogs had been moved onto the window ledge and were clearly visible from the road. A car I knew did not belong to the husband was sometimes in the drive when the statuettes were present but when they weren't on the windowsill the car was never in the drive. Then the penny dropped. She was using the statuettes as a signal to her fancy man. When the dogs were displayed in the window it meant the coast was clear for him to stop by. Ingenious, in the then absence of mobile phones.

After we moved in I spent the first 6 months carrying out the redecoration that had been a condition of our mortgage offer. Then I took on the garden and cleared the huge mound of earth and rubble overgrown with weeds. I levelled the ground next to the house and laid turf to form a lawn for the children to play on. We had brought with us the small shed from our house in The Keep and I erected this close to the side door of the garden.

We had to buy carpets and curtains for most of the rooms, as we had not purchased the delicate white fluffy decor owned by our predecessor. They just weren't practical enough to sustain the impact of our family.

Although we had brought just about all of our furniture, moving into a house with double the floor area meant we were somewhat rattling around in it. But now we had a house with plenty of space, Madge decided to fill up a bit more of it. She has always fancied she has an eye for a bargain (and to be fair generally has) and regards herself as a collector of 'antiques'. She loves nothing better than pottering around a Car Boot Sale (for the uninitiated it's an informal sale of unwanted goods that people just bring along to a common location and sell out of the back of their cars or from paste tables) or rummaging through the contents of Charity Shops. I think Madge's idea of heaven is a high street that's composed entirely of Charity Shops with a Car Boot sale at each end.

Unfortunately some of the 'antique bargains' she finds are not small and light which can either take pride of place on a shelf or be discretely tucked away on a window sill, depending on the degree of nudity (I haven't yet worked out why Madge buys so many naked statues). Madge's 'bargains' are sometimes 6 foot long, made of wood, weigh a ton and invariably act as hosts to several families of woodworm, wood beetles, several interesting species known only to 'RentoKil', as well as various forms of rot.

Anyway, back to the point. Madge as I say loves a bargain. One of her favourite places is a shop selling garden statues in Petersfield. Not the expensive versions but rather 'rejects' having various degrees of imperfection. Some are just chipped while others may have limbs or bits of features missing. It's usually the noticeable bits too. Like noses and ears that are gone. I suppose it's because extremities are more vulnerable to being lopped off. It makes a bloke shudder just thinking of it!

Our garden is subsequently full of all manner of stone figures. Like 'The 3 Graces,' a figure of a small boy looking sweet and a rabbit with an ear missing because Madge felt sorry for it. Actually some of them look quite good as the garden has gradually encroached upon them and they now peep out from within leafy bowers or to put it more accurately, they are overgrown with weeds. We also have our fair share of dog statues and on one occasion when browsing at the shop we spotted a couple of Westie figures which looked in almost perfect condition, going for a tenner each. I had a slight issue with the dog's designed pose; physically impossible for a Westie, but beggars couldn't be choosers.

Incidentally this place is also very good for getting a hernia if your partner takes a fancy to anything much bigger than a stone Jack

Russell. On this occasion we had to buy these as Madge decided they would look great at the entrance to the drive. We took the two stone Westies home. The next day I cemented a paving slab onto the top of each of the stone pillars at the drive entrance and then cemented a Westie statue on top of each paving slab.

I wish I could say it looked good but it was an amateurish job, with cement clinging where it shouldn't. I think the local yobs didn't appreciate the statues either because a few days later we awoke to find one of the statues was gone. I found it in a hedge 50 yards up the road with one of the ears missing. Overcome with rage at what the vandals had done to my work of art, I replaced the statue using a fresh batch of cement and stuck the ear back on.

A few days later the other statue had its head knocked clean off, possibly by the same morons. I racked my brains to think of some way of effecting a repair. It's amazing what superglue can do. I glued it, replaced the head onto the Westie body and bound tape around the neck like a collar to help hold it while the glue set. I mounted a security light above the garage to detect movement inside the drive to deter encroachers.

Madge had the bright idea of putting electrical wire around the Westie statues. This not only helped to hinder them being removed but with the security lights gave the impression there was some form of alarm attached to the stone dogs. We haven't had any problems since then but every time I look out of the bedroom window I check the statues are still there and in one piece.

Although the vandals were kept at bay from the stone dogs, we nearly lost them on three further occasions. Once after Stephen had just passed his motorcycle-riding test. In his euphoria, the 10-foot wide drive opening wasn't wide enough for his motorbike and he rammed a pillar with the stone dog sitting on the top.

Mike also struck the same pillar a glancing blow in his car when he attempted too acute an entry, but Alan came closest to a demolition job when his car bounced off it. On each occasion the dog survived, which is more than can be said of the insurance 'no-claim bonuses'. However our neighbour unwittingly put paid to the pillar when he engaged some builders and they accidentally rammed it, causing it to crack above the base and moving the tower of bricks askew.

As well as furniture and statues, Madge has also been a very keen collector of pictures and ornaments in general. She likes 'mezzotint' pictures and ones featuring studies of people and children rather those just showing scenery. I seem to have filled most walls in the living rooms and hallways with her selections. She also has a thing about Sherlock Holmes and loves murder and detective stories. For her 50th birthday I bought her a framed and authenticated copy of the famous 'Jack the Ripper' letter to the police which, although macabre, she was very pleased with.

*   *   *

We settled into our new house in early 1983 and our lives, although with the occasional glitch, proceeded without jumping into further large cowpats. My mum visited us occasionally before she went downhill with Alzheimer's. She loved being 'out in the country' as she saw it, because our road is rich in trees and hedges. That tens of thousands of people lived just the other side of the greenery didn't seem to change her perception of the locality.

The children converted over to a new infant and junior school. St Thomas More's, which was the local Catholic primary school, with a very good reputation. They all liked it there and formed new circles of friends.

A few months later and for the first and only time in our lives, one of the children strayed out of the house. Madge was taking Mike (then aged 3) up to the play school. She got him and baby Alan ready and went out into the front drive. Just as she was about to leave she popped back indoors for something and when she came out Mike wasn't there. She ran screaming out of the drive and when there was no sign of him, quickly searched fruitlessly around the house.

Desperate, she brought Alan back inside and popped him into the pram to keep him safe and then charged out and up the road. Just before the road started to bend, taking it out of her line of sight, she saw an old man. She rushed up and asked if he had seen a 3 year-old dressed in a blue and red checked coat, all on his own. He said 'Yes' and pointed up around the bend.

Madge says she has never run so fast either before or since. Rounding the bend in the road she saw Mike in the distance. He was just approaching the place where Madge always crossed the busy main road to go to the playgroup. Screaming his name she closed on him rapidly and he just heard her in time. It appears Mike thought she had left without him and had set out to catch her up. A close shave.

Then in 1984 we had what was the saddest occurrence of our time together. Up until then we'd had a baby every other year and remember we were still trying to give Emma a sister. So when Madge fell pregnant again we were both delighted.

At the '3 month' milestone Madge went for her routine scan and check. She was really happy at the time and was not prepared for what was to come. When they examined her there was no heartbeat and they told her the baby had died in the womb. Madge left the hospital totally devastated and went missing for several hours trying to come to terms with the news.

I was also frantic, as I didn't know what had happened and had no idea where she was. Eventually she came home and to this day I don't know how she managed to drive a car without hurting herself or somebody else, she was in such mental turmoil. She told me the news and we mourned together for our lost little one.

Years later when we sold the pram, with the money we bought a tiny statuette in memory of the baby and this is still one of our treasured possessions. But at the time, the foetus was still inside Madge and she had to endure walking around with it while they decided what to do and when to do it, in order to remove it.

Fortunately, Mother Nature took a hand. A couple of nights later Madge became doubled up with pain. I called the doctor who examined her and immediately summoned an ambulance. There wasn't time to bring anyone in to look after the kids and so I had to reluctantly let Madge go into hospital on her own.

The next morning I went to see her and she was in a pretty bad way. She'd had a rough time overnight and had been in the operating room 3 times. Just to make things worse the hospital had tactlessly put all the mums who had suffered miscarriages in the same ward as those having voluntary abortions. I'm surprised World War 3 didn't break out.

Madge returned home in a very shaky state both physically but more particularly mentally. That our children needed her helped Madge to come to terms with our loss and we swore as soon as she was strong enough we would try again.

*   *   *

Although I would not for one moment claim we are a musical family, the children had the usual participation in the school music activities and concerts. Emma was probably the most advanced, getting into playing the clarinet and doing quite well at it. At school the music classes were divided into 2 groups, the wind instruments and the stringed instruments or the 'blowers' and 'scrapers' as they were known.

Mike and Alan opted for the violin, in my view a much more difficult musical contrivance. We bought the actual instruments for them to practice on, the violins only being one-third of the normal adult size. Their practice at home was usually a pretty torrid affair and they made little progress before giving up.

One consideration for a large family was the space available and the number of bedrooms. Another was the older children were growing up and showing signs of wanting to spread their wings, the problem being they didn't have the finances to move out.

Of the 4 bedrooms, one was mine and Madge's, one for Emma (being the only girl); the other two being split between the four boys. An additional child would give logistical difficulties if it were a boy as to cram 3 into a bedroom, however large, would bring territorial friction.

All these factors, combined with my own escalating position and salary at work, combined to put the idea into my head we could move again as long as we remained in the area because of the strong ties. Madge agreed and we started to look around. I worked out how much I could afford to extend our mortgage commitment by and with this in mind we searched around the local district.

It quickly emerged the additional money would only get us at best, one more bedroom, an en-suite facility and possibly a larger garden. This was a poor return for such a large outlay. Then I had a brainwave. The amount of money we had to play with, although well short of Havant house prices in general, was sufficient to purchase another house in a relatively depressed area not too far away from where we lived.

We could get a lot more space, including 3 more bedrooms and provide subsidised accommodation for the eldest kids, at a stroke. So that's what we did. Unfortunately, it turned out we were buying at the market peak, which then collapsed; leaving us with 'negative equity' for many years. However, that aside, we managed to get a 3-bed semi with a garage for about the same we would have extended the mortgage by.

As each of the children became ready to leave home they moved round to the 'other house' to give them a measure of independence while being supported financially. Rarely were any of the children living there on their own. Usually partners or other of the kids cohabited with them.

The only ongoing issue was as part of the deal, those in residence were supposed to maintain the property but in practice little was done and the place deteriorated. This caused friction between we parents and the kids in residence, as we had to be mindful of the siblings, yet to have the same opportunity, taking over a hovel.

*　　*　　*

Alongside all the above happenings, we finally got the news we had been waiting for. Madge was pregnant again! We were over the moon. I had researched and acted on all the means of influencing the baby to be a girl, short of leading-edge gene technology and so we had our fingers crossed Emma would finally get the sister we had promised her. Even so, Madge didn't want to be told the baby's gender, even when this became known, in case it wasn't what we wanted to hear.

So, in 1986, our last child (Marie) was born. Named after the sister my mum had lost at birth. Like the other babies, she was very beautiful although as a little girl she was rather reluctant to smile, especially when she was having her photograph taken. But being the baby of the family everyone still spoiled her rotten. Marie joined the well-trodden paths to the usual schools and performed reasonably academically. She turned out to be very self confident and rather loud in public, especially after a smidgeon of alcohol. She always looked much older than she was and had no trouble getting into places she shouldn't have been in.

*　　*　　*

Although our house was basically what we wanted, there was still some room for improvement and after the initial decoration work to satisfy the mortgage lender, over time we did a few more things. We had originally brought the small shed with us from the house in 'The Keep' and I later added a much larger one. By the early/mid 90's we had added a large conservatory to the rear of the premises, a front porch and a small side porch to house the washing machine and tumble dryer.

Although I hadn't done any really heavy duty 'diy' since vacating our home in Chichester Road, I had the opportunity to have a bit of a go when the gas company moved the meter box to accommodate the front porch. A large hole was left where the box and equipment had been and I decided to brick it up myself. Armed with bricks and mortar I did what I thought was a reasonable job, except I left smudges of cement on the exposed surface. Being tidy, I decided to wash the bricks off using water from the hose. Unfortunately I underestimated the water pressure. As well as cleaning the bricks, it blasted out the cement between them and they all fell out. So much for my resurrected 'diy' skills.

I continued, but this time on safer ground, with the garden. I planted some fruit trees but I was never one for flowers. Madge was the one with green fingers but she tended to plant shrubs with various shades of green foliage with a splash of colour here and there. I don't know how Madge does it. She breaks twigs off of various bushes while we are out walking (no, she doesn't invade peoples gardens and butcher their flora) and just pushes them into the soil. I don't know if she uses some kind of mystical incantation, like Harry Potter, but it certainly works.

I dug out a wavy border to make the lawn and borders look a bit more interesting but I'm no landscape gardener and I'm sure lots could be done to improve upon my poor efforts. The front garden was already very presentable with a sweeping piece of concrete separating two areas of grass with attractive shrubs and roses.

We added privacy by putting some quick growing conifers along the front wall and a weeping willow in the centre of the front lawn. Unfortunately the willow eventually tried to take over the garden and the roots threatened the house and so it had to go. I well remember cutting the main trunk down with a hand axe. It was going OK until I took a rather wild swipe and missed the tree completely and struck myself on the shinbone. It took weeks for the swelling to go down.

As time moved on, being practical, we had to say goodbye to the grass and flowers in the front drive. Hulbert Road is very narrow but is a major road in the area, so there is no sensible parking along the road outside the house and all the cars need to be accommodated somewhere in the drive. Plus, as the reader will see later, there were times when we also had to fit in 2 caravans as well.

We needed motorbike and car parking space as the children grew into teenagers and adolescents. Before long there were 4 or 5 cars in the drive and a couple of bikes. (It sounds impressive but they comprised a company car for myself and an array of old bangers for Madge and the kids). So the whole front drive area was covered in tarmac.

* * *

Our respective 40th birthdays were celebrated rather differently. Mine had coincided with a 'skittles' social evening down the clubhouse. The only specific reference to my big '40' being when someone tipped off the DJ and he called me out in front of everybody and ceremoniously presented me with a Des O'Connor album. At least that's my excuse if anyone stumbles over the recording in my record collection.

For Madge's 40th we had the works. She hired the hall adjacent to St Joseph's Church in Havant, hired a 'Disco' and provided lots of food. About 90 people attended. Madge suspected I would get her a 'kissogram', which of course I did. In the middle of the festivities she was accosted by a 'Tarzan' figure who proceeded to put her through his routine.

To my surprise Madge not only entered into the spirit of the thing but also joined in with some gusto, bringing the house down. When it was all finished and she was relaxing, safe in the knowledge the dreaded bit was over, a policeman turned up to speak to her and when he had her attention, promptly took his clothes off. Yes, I had booked a second 'kissogram' to make sure she was really surprised. I was laughing so much I nearly dropped my camcorder.

Something else happened when I turned 40 also worth recording here. I took the momentous decision to grow a beard! Partly driven by the inconvenience and time it took to shave before going off to work and partly by looking to the future. I reckoned by shaving it off again when I reached 50 I would instantly look younger at a future time in my life when I would be worrying about getting old. Looking back, how vain can you get?

I had heard it said there are only 2 types of men who did not grow beards; those who can't and those who daren't. I had some concerns I might fall into the former camp but as it turned out I managed it, albeit rather slowly.

So, did I shave it off at 50? No. Perhaps I wasn't so vain after all. But I might shave it off at 60 if and when I get there in 2007.

*   *   *

You may recall me mentioning in an earlier Chapter Madge had a damaged eye since birth. Her sight was very poor through it and the eyelid drooped down, despite partially successful operations during her childhood to raise it. It always made her self-conscious and every now and again she would say she would like to have something done about it. She didn't though because she was afraid it would not rectify the problem and might even make it worse.

Some people, Madge included, would prefer to live in hope something might be done in the future to resolve a problem, rather than pursue a solution and risk being permanently disappointed and left with no hope at all.

Finally, after a bit of encouragement in 1986 she went to her GP and after a delay was referred to 'Moorfields Eye Hospital' in London. These were the top people in their field and if anyone could help Madge it was they.

For the next few weeks she was constantly on edge, waiting for the appointment day. When the date finally arrived I went with her to London. Her brother Richard was kind enough to look after the children and Madge and I went on the train to Waterloo. After a slight flurry as Madge tends to class the London Underground along with lifts as a claustrophobic experience to be avoided at all costs, we arrived at the hospital.

After careful examination she was told the previous operations on her eyelid meant no more could be done on her 'bad' eye. However they suggested to her the overall appearance could be improved by slightly lowering the 'good' eyelid so it matched the faulty one more closely.

You can imagine how that went down with Madge. After years of worrying about her 'wonky' eye it was now being suggested that her only good eye be put at risk. We made our way home with Madge being terribly upset and disappointed. It looked as if all her hopes and dreams of looking 'normal' (to her that is, I had never really noticed her droopy eyelid unless I specially looked for it) had been swept away.

For a full 12 months Madge brooded on the situation and then she decided to go ahead with the operation on her good eyelid. On the appointed day, I stayed at home with the children this time and her brother Richard took Madge up to Moorfields, which by now had relocated from central Holborn to more northeast London. He left her there, quietly panicking. After a while a nurse came and put a big cross on her forehead above the eyelid to be operated on. Madge looked around and saw everyone else in the ward had crosses on their faces in one place or another. It looked as if some nutter had been let loose with a crayon.

Once the nurse had disappeared from view, the girl in the next bed said to Madge 'Cover for me will you, I'm off to the pub down the road'. And with that she was gone, crayoned cross and all. She returned a couple of hours later, giggly and with a smudged cross above her eye.

To make Madge's stay even more trying, the lady in the bed opposite couldn't speak a work of English (so does that mean her chatter to the nurse might have been 'you've just put the cross against the wrong eye, stupid?') Also the lady in the bed next to her (on the other side from the absconded alcoholic) appeared to be a bit confused and every time Madge went to the toilet, on her return she found the woman trying to climb into Madge's bed.

Eventually Madge was collected to go to the theatre and there received her next shock. She had been told they would put her under but now they decided to do the operation under just a local anesthetic. You can imagine what Madge went through. Her head in a 'vice' and some bloke with her eyelid rolled up hacking it with a scalpel. To make matters worse the surgeon was actually a trainee. The main man was just keeping an eye on him from another table. ('Hack a bit more off the middle there, Jeremy').

Some 3 days later I went to London to collect Madge, taking baby Marie with me; the other children being looked after at home. Madge had her eye covered with a patch but there was heavy bruising and puffiness all around it, clearly visible. As we made our way back on the train I had a few looks from people that clearly had me down as a wife beater.

As the puffiness started to subside Madge began to panic. It looked as if the surgeon had overcooked the job and her 'good' eyelid was now significantly lower than the old 'bad' eyelid. Madge of course was very upset but I encouraged her to wait until the swelling was completely gone as the surgeon had warned her a good deal of 'adjustment' would take place as the eye area became normal.

Eventually, after a few weeks, we could make a final judgement. Madge tried very hard to find a fault with it but the eyelid was perfect! The surgeon at Moorfield had calculated things with great accuracy and had fulfilled all my expectations of them as being the UK centre of excellence for such treatment. Madge's expectation was they'd cock it all up and she'd have leapt into another cowpat. So having been proven wrong, she was absolutely delighted with the results.

*   *   *

Madge had been riding a pushbike for years. Before I had the luxury of a company car I always used to take our one and only car to work, so she had little choice but to use a bicycle.

When there was just Stephen she would plonk him in a child seat on the back of her racing bike. Later, with two kids, she bought an adult tricycle and rode around the Portsmouth and Havant area with the two of them sitting in the rear seats, facing backwards and waving at bus drivers, lorry drivers and anyone else Madge was holding up from overtaking at the time. In fact, Madge became quite famous in the local area riding her trike around with the kids on board.

On one occasion she was hooted at by a bus following her. When she turned and looked, the driver in the cab was waving a teddy bear at her that baby Richard had dropped further back down the road.

Once the number of kids reached 3 and more, the two youngest got the tricycle seats and the older ones had to ride their own bicycles either in a row behind her or alongside her on the pavement, depending on whether or not there were any old ladies to skittle over. People used to say she looked like a mother duck and her ducklings in a line, weaving about in her wake.

It's probably worth recounting how we got the tricycle, as it may be enlightening for anyone also contemplating buying this invidious device. When I got home one day Madge was bubbling over with enthusiasm. She had just seen a tricycle with 2 children seated at the back. Wow, she just had to have one, it was obviously so useful. I made enquiries and found out the cost of a new one was around £600 and as they were very rare anyway, the chances of picking one up second hand were pretty remote.

So I filed that one away under 'to be quietly forgotten about' and went onto other more pressing matters. Just my luck, Madge found an advertisement offering one for sale for £180 in Emsworth, only about 3 miles away. We made arrangements to view the trike and went over there the next evening.

The lady owner was very nice and the machine seemed to be in very good order. Madge seemed a bit reticent to try it out but the lady, rather mysteriously, insisted we did as she said it was difficult to ride! Difficult to ride, whatever could she mean? I hopped on and peddled forward. Only the bike didn't go straight, it veered off the side. I then tried to turn left but the damn thing just carried straight on and I had to brake frantically to avoid going into a hedge.

I thought we had been presented with a trick cycle from a visiting circus but the woman explained that unlike with a conventional bicycle where you leaned your body into the corners, with a tricycle you had to sit up straight and steer with your arms. I tried the advice and it worked but it was still difficult curbing all my natural cycling instincts.

Madge refused to ride the trike home, as even with the new approach she still couldn't quite manage it. So I gingerly rode off and eventually arrived home safely. With a bit more practice Madge got the hang of it and spent the next few years riding all over the place, frequently with one or two children seated on the back.

*   *   *

Our 25th wedding anniversary was approaching and I wanted to make a big thing of it. Madge had made it quite clear she didn't want a 'do' of any kind but she would like to go away for a few days to somewhere special. I was aware Paris was the ultimate in romantic locations but France is a country populated by French people and French people seem to have it in for the English almost as much as the Scots (e.g. French Air Traffic Controllers, Farmers, Lorry Drivers, Waiters and anybody you ask directions from – need I say more?). So I had little inclination to expose the success of our celebrations to the whim of a frog.

I gave it a bit more thought and booked a trip to Rome. I wasn't entirely sure she would like it as Madge had shown little interest in historical events and artifacts but it was, after all, the 'eternal' city and supposedly very romantic. To be on the safe side I kept the trip down to 4 days. Long enough to get a taste but not too long to put up with should she hate it. As it happened, Madge absolutely loved Rome, as did I and in fact we returned there a few months later to see more of this amazing city.

Madge, like me, had a fear of flying but the flight time to Rome was only about two and a half hours. By the time we had settled in, read the magazines and had a meal we were most of the way there, which minimised the fear factor for us both. Madge also befriended the girl who was the third passenger in our particular section and chatted with her for a good deal of the trip.

On arrival, after some difficulty, we found our reserved taxi that took us the hour-long journey to our hotel, passing a few interesting sights along the way. We had booked into the Metropole, a 4-star affair and close to the Main 'Termini' Railway Station. The accommodation was small but very nice and the champagne and flowers I had ordered were in the room waiting for us.

We had a couple of coach tours booked to give us a quick look around the main attractions but the problem was so much was crammed in we had only a few minutes at each location. For example, at St

Peter's we barely had time to get inside the massive cathedral before we had to return to the coach, so it topped our list when we made the return visit a few months later. The second time we went we had a good look around and Madge and I even whispered our wedding vows to each other again in front of the main altar.

Towering above us inside St Peter's was the immense dome; the largest in the world and around the bottom rim ran a narrow walkway. We could just about see people walking around it, way above our heads. Madge decided she wanted to walk around the base of the dome as well. With my poor head for heights I didn't want to go but it looked like a considerable trip and so I didn't want to leave her to do it on her own.

We asked someone how we got up there and he indicated a sign that read 'Cupola'. I wasn't exactly sure what 'Cupola' meant but off we went and queued for a ticket. There were 2 types of ticket; one meant you got the lift to go up and one that you walked, which of course was cheaper. Madge hates lifts, so we decided to take the challenge of the walk up and got a pink ticket each.

I was a bit concerned as I would regularly get breathless climbing even a few stairs but we could go at our own pace and stop as frequently as we liked, but if I have known what lay before us I might not have even started out. I looked around at the next queue that presented itself and noticed everybody was clutching a yellow ticket. It dawned on me. We were the only suckers going to walk; everyone else was waiting for the lift.

Of we went and I admit sheer adrenalin and challenge sent me up the spiraling staircase of very shallow steps at a considerable rate. Madge got into a panic in case I had a coronary on the spot. We eventually emerged onto the flat roof of St Peters and could see the dome above us. The lift terminated on the roof and the exit was nearby and to my astonishment, there was something else. A souvenir shop. Right there on the roof of the Cathedral was a shop!

We had a look around the shop and bought a couple of things and then went outside for a rest and to admire the view, which unfortunately was heavily obstructed by statues and other architectural bits and pieces. Finally we pushed on and ascended some external steps and went inside the building.

Through a door and we were onto the narrow walkway circling the inside base of the dome. There was a high guardrail but I still couldn't look down and just walked slowly round, hugging the inside wall.

Madge was in her element and gave me a running commentary on how great it was to look at the sheer drop under our feet and the microscopic figures scurrying about below us.

I wanted to head back the way we came in but a uniformed man gestured we take an exit further along. When we reached the way out I saw the stairs leading on down but just to the right was a narrow flight of steps disappearing upwards in a curve, with a sign that said 'Cupola'.

I looked Madge. 'How about it?' I enquired.

'We've come this far,' she replied 'so let's go for it.'

'Are you sure you can manage?' I enquired caringly.

'Of course,' she retorted with hurt pride, 'I'm not a bloke you know!'

We were both feeling pretty good after the rest and stroll around the souvenir shop and the adrenalin rush was still with me. Up we went. We were clearly inside the outer skin of the actual dome and I dare not think but for a few inches of stone I was leaning into thin air with hundreds of feet of nothingness under me.

The walkway leaned more and more over to the right and became so narrow my shoulders brushed both sides at the same time. I wondered what would happen if someone came the other way. We'd just have to crawl over the top of one another, like the lizards used to do (see later Chapter). I didn't realise at the time the architect had thought of this and arranged a separate corridor to descend around the dome.

Every so often there was a small window with an internal ledge widening the passageway out. A useful passing point if you caught up with the people in front and also a good place to stop, get some fresh air and peek out at the incredible view. We stopped more than once at the windows in the dome and gawped at the amazing view while sucking in the fresh air.

Up and up until we emerged above the dome but still inside the building, onto some wide wooden staging with more wooden flights of steps going up. Finally there were spiraling stone steps so narrow there was no room for a handrail but a central rope hung from above to cling on to. I emerged into the glaring sunlight and turned around to help Madge. We took in the breathtaking view. We were on a tiny stone platform with a low guardrail. I backed into the stonework and took a few pictures with one hand while hanging on for dear life with the other.

So that's what the Cupola was, a tiny, domed 'lookout' platform perching above the actual dome of St Peters. About 6 other people had made it to the top and all stood panting with exhaustion.

We exchanged glances of mutual respect for having made it and I flashed my pink tickets with a grin. We had really done it the hard way! Just to put the icing on the cake we also scorned the lift on the way down, to do the entire trip on foot. Something I fear I could never manage again if, and when, we again return to Rome and St Peters.

We also got to see the Vatican museum (where incidentally I got short changed at the pay kiosk!) and the famous Sistine Chapel. It proved to be a very arduous hike through a huge number of rooms and hallways ending up with a football-stadium-like crush in the Chapel itself. It was really quite dangerous and I thought the authorities needed to sort something out before someone fell over a pew and got trampled.

Later we visited the Colosseum with its mesmerising history, brought alive by such films as 'Gladiator' (one of Madge's favourites; she's had a thing about Russell Crowe ever since) and the Spanish Steps.

It was at the latter location we saw a couple emerge from the church at the top of the steps having just got married and pose for their wedding pictures on the stairs and terraces beneath. The crowds of locals and tourists broke out into spontaneous cheering and applause. It was a stirring experience to be there. Eventually and all too soon we had to come home but Rome remains one of our most favourite places to return to again and again.

I hadn't finished with the 25th wedding anniversary just yet. To celebrate such a major milestone in our marriage I had decided to do far more and spoil Madge rotten as she had definitely earned it. On one of my business trips to London I found the time to go to Hatton Garden and in the long line of jewellery shops I found a beautiful gold and diamond bracelet. I bought it and hid it way for the big day.

I'd also saved up a lot of points on my credit card giving money off a new Vauxhall car. Bearing in mind how much we'd liked the Opel car in our trip to Majorca, I had in mind to buy a Corsa for Madge, which was the UK equivalent. I could hardly keep this a secret as it involved active participation from her and we went to the car showroom together. We bought a very basic model which the 'deals of the moment' and with my points discount reduced the cost from £8000 to just under £5000.

I still hadn't finished; I wanted to buy something very different we could both share in and would give Madge a real boost.

A short time before, I had noticed an advertisement in the Sunday newspaper for 'Effective VIP Titles'. Some investigation into what was being offered revealed in the UK you can not only change your own name by 'deed poll' (a well known fact) but you could also change your 'title' by a similar legal mechanism.

So, for example a deed poll change could be used for John Smith to become Fred Smith but under both circumstances the title would still be the 'Mr' as in Mr Smith. However Mr John Smith could become Sir John Smith or Lord John Smith by applying a 'Title Deed poll' change. It's legal as long as you don't pretend you are the real owner of a hereditary title or some form of honour. Also it's not transferable and cannot be passed on to one's descendents; although there's nothing to prevent other members of the family doing likewise on their own account.

I discussed it at length with my mate Jim Tickner at work and we had a great time going through all the options. At one point Jim himself was flirting with the idea of becoming 'Sir James' and we cast the rest of the office in similar lofty positions that would have made the morning greetings rather spectacular ('good morning Sir James..... good day your ladyship, hello Lord Jones, greetings Duchess' etc).

I decided to go ahead with a change of title for both Madge and myself, just for a giggle. Obviously I needed to tell her and gain her agreement, as this was a legal matter. But which title? I didn't want to take on the equivalent of a true English title or honour as it seemed pretentious and sailing a bit close to the wind from a legal standpoint.

However the titles 'Count' and 'Countess' had a certain appeal. They were more European than English and seemed to go with the Italian sounding surname. All the Counts I could think of had surnames like mine, ending with a vowel, like Cristo, Basie, Dracula and the like.

So we went ahead and changed our titles, so today Madge and I are truly Count and Countess Bicheno and we have the framed certificates over our bed to prove it. So far I haven't had the bottle to change any official documentation to that effect; if anything it might wind a policeman up to see it on my driving license, but putting it on our passports is a tempting idea.

*   *   *

Emma has always been a particular source of anxiety for us with a constant stream of misfortune dogging her. Some of the situations she has got into have been at least partially self-inflicted and some have been not at all of her making. One instance of the latter now struck home. A routine check indicated she might have cancerous cells present and a more detailed examination confirmed this. On a scale of 1 to 10 indicating the increasing level of severity, Emma was an '8'. There was no time to mess about.

We paid for her to be examined and treated as a 'private' patient. She underwent laser surgery under an expert consultant named Mr Woolas. He proved to be a very pleasant, sympathetic and able professional, whose path we were to cross again a few years later. Happily, Emma was cured by his treatment and subject to ongoing and periodic tests, has not had a recurrence.

Other than relatively minor and transient treatment, the other kids have remained healthy over the years. Long may the situation continue. Unfortunately I am not able to make the same positive report for our grandchildren (see later).

I would never really describe myself as a 'fit' person although I believed I had been reasonably healthy. It came as a bit of a shock to find out I wasn't. I knew I was a bit overweight and was aware I couldn't run any distance more than a few yards without getting breathless but put this down to a lack of exercise going back many years to when my in-growing toe nail had curtailed my sporting activities.

When I was 50 I thought the age represented a bit of a milestone in life and I decided to give my body a full MOT as it were. So in the summer of 1997 I booked myself a full head to toe health check with BUPA. It cost in the region of £250 at the time and involved some 'sampling' that doesn't bear thinking about but it was all in a good cause.

All the checks seemed to go well until we got to the ECG (electrocardiogram) that checks out the heart. I had electrodes stuck to my skin in various places around my chest (which when removed left a circular red mark on the skin and made me look as though I had contracted a rare disease).

The machine hummed away for a minute and then started to produce a paper trace of whatever it is they measure. When the test was completed the doctor seemed to take an inordinate amount of time to study the graphics and then turned to me.

'Mr Bicheno, I've noticed a bit of a glitch on your readout here. I think it advisable to refer the results to an expert cardiologist at St Mary's Hospital.' When I heard the words my heart sank, or at least it would have done if it hadn't been enlarged to a degree there wasn't enough room for it to head downwards.

Off I went to St Mary's and some more detailed tests, including being wired up again, this time while on a treadmill. This was to test the heart when under the stress of walking and running. I got a bit bothered when the treadmill operator said to the doctor 'What setting do you want doctor' and got the cheery response –

'Put it on the low setting for just walking. I don't think he can handle much more than that.'

Finally, when all was completed the doctor sat me down and gave me the news.

'Your blood pressure is extraordinarily high and I suspect it has been like that for some time. The extra work your heart has had to do against the increased pressure has caused it to grow, just like any other muscle in the body will grow when it is heavily exercised.'

'So, what does that mean? It sounds not too bad.'

'The problem is the heart is a hollow muscle with four internal chambers which hold the blood before and after it has been pumped around the body. The less blood these chambers hold, the less oxygen is carried around with each heartbeat, and the more quickly you become tired or breathless when exercising or just moving about. The sort of exercise your heart has been getting due to the blood pressure is bad because the heart muscle is not just growing outwards but inwards as well, constricting the space inside the chambers,

'So what can I do?'

'I'll refer you back to your GP. He will prescribe tablets that will bring down the blood pressure. This in turn will exercise the heart less and like any muscle in the body it should reduce in size when exercised less forcefully.'

That all sounded fine, so I went to my GP who put me on a 5mg daily dose of Enalapril with a six monthly review. At the subsequent review he took my blood pressure and after a bit of humming about, decided it was on the high side but I was probably a bit stressed out at the surgery so he would see me in another 6 months. Next time around the 6 months grew to 12 months and the level of medication remained the same.

Looking back, I was being mega stupid. This was my very existence I was dealing with and should have been far more assertive and probing as to what was being done to me and why and how was I getting along?

The basic problem was from a very young age I had been brought up to have total faith in doctors. To accept what they said unquestioningly, because they always knew best. Even into my middle age that attitude was deeply instilled. The doctor at St Mary's Hospital had diagnosed my problem and the GP had addressed the matter, so all was well. If I was dealing with any other profession or trade (except dentistry with which I was equally trusting) I would have been challenging the other person to fully satisfy myself the matter was being dealt with correctly and effectively.

If I had thought about it I would have realised; armed only with a stethoscope and blood pressure measurement device, the GP did not have the range of monitors that would tell him in much more detail what was going on inside me. I also didn't question the level of dosage of medication being given me. For all I knew it was a maximum dose whereas I now know it was only the minimum. I stayed on that level for over 3 years and I don't like to think what additional harm may have been done. I now know at some juncture, possibly even at the outset, the dosage should have been increased.

So I carried on, still getting breathless but by then I had accepted it as 'normal' in my life and didn't really think any more about it. That is, until things started getting really bad. I couldn't even climb the stairs without almost ending up on my knees at the top through exhaustion and I was getting more and more pains in the chest. I attributed it to the increased stress I was having at work. Things were going badly for me under a new regime, as I describe in a later Chapter.

It was early in 2001 I decided to go back to the GP practice outside of my reviews and this time see a different doctor. I saw a GP who was relatively recently qualified, very thorough and enthusiastic. He examined me in more detail than I had experienced since the initial test back in 1997 and at the conclusion he suggested I see a cardiologist again.

This time a sense of urgency had instilled itself and so I decided I would 'go private' for the examination in order to speed things up. I was a member of BUPA at the time as a company perk. Within a few days I was having a range of tests again. The consultant was very concerned at the results. He told me although only 53 years old I had the heart of a 70-year-old. He would carry out more active and invasive tests, but only when my blood pressure had reduced to a much safer level, as otherwise the strain would be too great.

Anyone with my condition had to tackle 5 things, 4 of which were clearly assessable and measurable.

1. Give up smoking. No problem for me as I had never smoked.
2. Lose weight and get fit. I wasn't quite medically obese but I should lose a couple of stone.
3. Change to a healthier diet. My cholesterol level was bordering on unacceptable.
4. Check on heart conditions within the family, as they can be hereditary. My mum had a heart problem, as did 3 of my dad's brothers, one of whom had died from heart problems at the age of 58.
5. Reduce stress.

I had a few problems with number 2 as I have always loved my food and in large quantities. Up until then, as far as '3' was concerned, my idea of a balanced diet was a packet of crisps in each hand. The good thing was I actually enjoyed eating things like fruit, vegetables, fish and white meat. The bad thing was I liked all forms of junk food and dairy products as well. I ate 3 square meals a day, along with elevenzies, threezies and supperzies. So I needed to suppress my additional snacks and cut down (if not actually out) the naughty things. I also started to use lashings of a special margarine that promised to massively reduce your levels of cholesterol.

Number 5, the last one was the really difficult item. No clear advice can be given medically as different people react differently to stress. Doctors agree stress can be very harmful indeed, but it's not like things such as smoking and diet where the rules are universally the same for everyone. Some people thrive in stressful conditions while others might collapse and to some degree 'stress' is inevitable and even necessary in today's workplace and living environment.

In my case the Consultant suspected stress was playing a significant part in my condition. He would spell out in a letter to my GP what treatment and dosage was to be given and when I had achieved a target blood pressure of 145/90 he would progress the tests.

My new doctor juggled a little with the medication within the parameters the consultant laid down, according to the results being achieved. I bought my own blood pressure monitor and I used it daily and recorded the readings. I reported back to the GP every 2 weeks for him to confirm or tweak the medication.

Finally, after about 3 months, I got to the target levels and stayed there for enough time to prove it was no fluke. Remembering my only medication had been Enalapril at 5mg per day, I now found myself on the following daily cocktail of medication:

Enalapril	- 40 Mg	(8 times more than before!)
Atenalol	- 25 Mg	(A Beta blocker to slow the heart)
Bendrofluazide	- 2.5 Mg	(To shed water from the body)
Aspirin	- 75 Mg	(To thin the blood)

After a year of this I had my blood pressure and cholesterol re-measured. The BP was well down but the cholesterol hadn't changed much. I imagine the 'good' margarine had roughly balanced the 'bad' food I had consumed. I just had to bite the bullet and take a firmer grip on my diet. Out (or at least somewhat reduced levels) went crisps, some dairy products, cakes and pies. I increased fruit and vegetables and also reduced the size of the portions on the plate.

One problem with having a heart condition is you sometimes jump to erroneous conclusions. One evening I was sitting on the sofa with my arms folded when I looked down and saw my hands had turned blue. In a rising panic I rolled up my shirtsleeve, revealing my arm was also blue. 'Madge' I yelped 'I've got a problem!' Madge was sitting beside me and looked across.

'My God,' she said, startled 'your neck is blue as well.'

I was starting to feel as if my last hour had come then Madge leaned across, licked her finger and rubbed my forearm. The blue came off!

'It's that shirt' she said.

I had bought a cheap shirt the previous day and was now wearing it for the first time. I ripped off the offending article of clothing and Madge curled up in laughter. My torso was blue as well. I looked like one of the ancient Britons who used to paint themselves with blue woad. Boy was I relieved as I headed off towards the shower.

*   *   *

It was during my battle to drive down my blood pressure I was given early retirement from work. Immediately afterwards and at a stroke most of the stress went out of my life. I was able to shed about half a stone in weight; still not enough but a start and I cut a lot of the 'wrong' foods from my diet. It's to all these things I attribute my blood pressure reducing to more acceptable levels.

I returned to the Consultant for more tests. The ultimate was to be an angiogram. This is where the surgeon shoves a wide tube or 'sleeve' into the main artery at the top of your thigh and then feeds a wire through it, up through your arteries into the chambers of the heart. A dye is then pumped through the wire and the way the blood containing the dye is then dispersed around the heart is captured on a monitor screen and readout. By squirting the dye several times with the camera at different angles any blockage in the arteries, the heart itself and its valves, can be detected.

I lay there and watched the screen, fascinated. When the dye was injected it rushed through the arteries and momentarily lit up the heart connections. It looked rather like a flash of forked lightening, lighting the sky during a thunderstorm.

I was also told to expect a hot sensation passing through my body as another test was done. I understand it's about as close as a man can get to experience the 'hot flushes' women often have during the menopause. If so, you can keep it. I felt like I was being cooked from the inside but thankfully the feeling passed after a few seconds.

After the angiogram the sleeve was removed from my leg and a nurse pressed on the hole in my artery until it sealed up. Or at least she was supposed to. My leg remained numb, even after the injection had worn off and turned purple from hip to knee.

Although I was discharged I went to the Q.A. Hospital and to my own GP. They both told me I had had severe internal bleeding and the leg nerves had been damaged. I went at my own expense to intensive 'sports' physiotherapy to massage large lumps of congealed blood away from my thigh and although this was largely successful I remain to this day with a degree of numbness and tightness in my leg. It actually came in quite useful a few months back when our dog Tasha got over excited and bit me in the leg. I didn't feel a thing.

Apart from sorting out the physical side of my life, the early retirement from work had quite a few financial implications. I had been on a very good salary, amounting to over twice the average national wage. Although by no means 'rich', we had got used to not having to count the pennies too closely.

Now my pension gave me a monthly take-home pay of less than half of what it had been. Even with the mortgage paid off from my lump sum, the difference between what I was getting compared with what I used to have was significant and it meant an adjustment to the way we lived, to get by within our means.

I further dented my lump sum by splashing out on the very first new car I actually paid for myself (see later Chapter). The remainder of the money went on a few things for the house I had promised to Madge, and subsidising our way of life while we continued to try and adjust our lifestyle. It proved to be harder than I had imagined and was a source of some friction within the family.

* * *

As I mentioned before, two of Madge's uncles had died from cancer and she was always petrified of contracting the illness. You can imagine her response when a routine test showed she had some abnormal cells that could turn cancerous. Although I had recently retired from work, part of the exit package was to let my BUPA membership continue until the end of the year and we took advantage of this and arranged for her to see a specialist consultant.

His name was Mr Woolas, a very proficient and understanding man and the same consultant who had successfully treated Emma for her cancer some months before. His examination found Madge had extensive fibroids and taking everything into account he explained all the options. Madge pressed him to say what course of action he would recommend if it were his own wife in this position and he chose a hysterectomy.

We went away and thought it over and then having agreed it was the best thing, the operation was arranged to take place almost immediately. At least this didn't give Madge the time to worry about it so much. The operation went well and after she had been returned to her room, I spent the first night sitting next to her bed while she flitted in and out of uneasy sleep and pressing the morphine pump every time she showed the pain was getting to her.

The next morning a relief contract nurse came in and tried to bully Madge, totally ignoring the fact she'd had a major operation only a few hours previously. I was in the refreshment lounge when I received a message to return to her room. I found Madge in very distressed state trying to cope with a woman who was a disgrace to her profession. Fortunately we didn't see her again and the other nursing staff were magnificent.

The next day Madge managed to hobble into the shower. Suddenly I heard a bang and rushed to the bathroom door. A bolt from the showerhead had been blasted off by the water pressure and buried itself in the wall opposite. It had missed Madge's head by inches. We complained about it and all I got was an 'oh my' and a promise the maintenance man would fix it. So much for 'going private'.

As the operation had also removed her ovaries, Madge went onto HRT, preferring to take it in the form of patches, as she didn't like taking tablets. We heard one hilarious story from a nurse who had been on a similar prescription. Her husband had started to behave in a peculiar way. After a few days he discovered his wife's hormone patch had fallen off in the shower and in stepping into it after her he had managed to get the patch stuck to the underside of his foot. For several days he'd been getting a liberal dose of female hormones. He's lucky he eventually noticed it or he might have ended up on 'page 3'.

Madge literally stuck the patches for a while but then had to give them up as her skin reacted to the glue and she came out in a rash. After that she lost interest, partially because she was concerned about possible side effects. She preferred to put up with the 'hot flushes' that came instead, although these sometimes led her to open all the windows in winter and leave the rest of the family with chattering teeth. She is still putting up with them to this day.

Madge is still undergoing annual checkups with Mr Woolas to ensure she is fully clear of any cell abnormality but everything appears to be fine. Although the BUPA membership ran out some time ago, we want to stay with the consultant who knows Madge well and in whom we have a lot of confidence, so we put our hands in our pockets to fund the visits and tests ourselves.

I found myself forking out more money a few months later when I was struck down by another unexpected ailment. I'd had a sore throat but thought nothing of it until it persisted and got worse. After 6 weeks I consulted my GP who prescribed medication that had no effect. I returned to him and asked him to refer me to a specialist, which he agreed to do, suggesting my appointment would take place very quickly.

When the date came through it was 7 months away. I just couldn't stick it out for that long. So I returned to the GP and asked for a referral to a 'private' Consultant. The initial contact proved to be of no use at all and just made a hole in my pocket but the woman Consultant at least referred me onto someone who could help.

To cut a long story short I was diagnosed with a 'hiatus hernia'. Every time I ate something my stomach convulsed and sent a jet of stomach acid back up my throat, thus burning it. After a camera was shoved down my throat to confirm there were no further complications, I was put on stomach acid reduction medication for the remainder of my days. This was preferable to an operation, which might cure the problem, but had side effects I didn't fancy.

The whole process took just under a year, during which I was constantly ratty with my wife and family because of my continuing discomfort. God knows how long it would have taken under the NHS. I might have topped myself through despair if I had gone that route, long before the condition was diagnosed. It has largely done the trick to date and not otherwise affected my day-to-day living, which an operation would have done.

Madge had taken many months to recover from her own operation, which of course was a major one, during which time she was supposed to desist from lifting things but occasionally disobeyed to cuddle the grandchildren.

*   *   *

Madge and I had always looked forward to having children and as I will explain later, the dogs to some extent were there to bridge the gap from looking after our own kids to the grandchildren coming along. When they finally did, we expected to see the grandchildren a couple of times a week each and take them out now and again. That's not the way things have worked out however.

In fact, Madge and I have seen a great deal of our first grandchild (Chloe) since she was born. With both Emma and Wayne working, we initially looked after her as much as 4 days a week and then their next child Lewis got added later for half days, when we had to collect him from his child minder a few miles away.

Then catastrophe struck with Lewis becoming seriously ill. With Lewis in hospital (see later Chapter) and at the doctors so much; again we helped out by taking Chloe, including many overnight stays. Emma correctly decided to leave work for a while to look after Lewis and also take maternity leave when she was pregnant with her third child, Jessica, but we continued to take a bit of the pressure off her by being there when she needed us, which was pretty frequently.

Richard's partner, Sharon, used her own mum in a similar way to help them out with their daughter Lauren. However when she took on other commitments we started to collect Lauren from Playschool once or sometimes twice a week and look after her until Richard got home from work, as well as having her all day on some Fridays.

Over time we amassed a huge collection of toys and videos to keep the grandchildren amused, as well as the usual paraphernalia such as cot, beds and the like. The new carpets and furniture we bought just before I retired quickly showed the ravages you associate with children and the poor dogs got increasingly neglected.

Since I retired the grandchildren have to a large extent taken over our lives and Madge and I have had very little time for ourselves, even restricting and cancelling holidays when arrangements didn't fit in. We have tried to preserve Sundays just for us but even then sometimes when we get home from a nice day out the front drive is crammed with cars and the grandchildren are all indoors, wrecking the place. We love them to bits but sometimes feel that you can have too much of a good thing.

So why don't we assert ourselves and get a little of our lives back? Well, Madge's feelings of guilt usually interfere. She feels she has to be there whenever our kids, or the grandchildren, need us. If she is not around and something happens then she tears herself apart with remorse. So I guess that we'll just soldier on and take each day as it comes; relishing the good days and forgetting the bad. And trying to squeeze the odd break in here and there.

*   *   *

I think I've given a reasonable précis of what our lives were like over the years but I've concentrated solely on the aspects of life 'at home'. Both Madge and I had careers. Mine going on for 37 years, with Madge not quite so long and interrupted by doing her bit as a mum. So let me now go on to recount our lives away from home.

Chapter 7

Careers

Rather than mentioning our jobs here and there throughout the book, I decided to devote an entire section to the topic. Strictly speaking while I had a career, Madge had a number of separate jobs running before, after and during her true career, which was of a wife, mother and grandmother.

7.1 Chris's Career

I should start this section by giving an apology. Living in the world of computers for so many years it's difficult to describe my career without at times slipping into the old familiar jargon. So I am faced with a quandary. To omit certain 'jargonised' sections would be to miss out significant parts of what I consider to be some of my key lifetime achievements but to simplify them would not do justice to my ex-colleagues who will know exactly what I am talking about. So I'll just try and keep the technical content to a minimum.

I suppose my career kicked off at school. Remember I had sat my 'O' levels a year in advance of normal timescales which meant effectively omitting a whole years schooling when I went forward to the sixth form to study for 'A' levels. That alone would have been hard enough to catch up but my subsequent accident then effectively laid me up for about 9 weeks, caused further significant inroads into my study time and affected my eventual 'A' level grades.

This is turn meant my results were not good enough for University unless I re-sat the exams. I consulted with my 'Careers Tutor' and we worked out a career in accountancy, possibly with a company allowing day release for further study, might be a good idea, rather than go through a re-sit. I was then summarily despatched to the local careers information office to see if such a thing existed in the local area.

The Youth Employment Officer (a Mr Chiles) at the Careers Office was very helpful and told me Southern Electricity Board (SEB) offered such placements. He picked up the phone and made an appointment for me to have an interview later that same day.

Unbeknown to me, my uncle Bill Dilley (married to my mum's sister Dorothy) actually worked in the local SEB offices in a middle management capacity and the request to interview this young lad actually got routed to him. He immediately realised who I was and disqualified himself from the interview panel but obviously he put in a good word for me.

I was actually interviewed by Bill's boss the District Accounting Officer, Mr Wood and offered a job there and then as a clerk in the accounts department, with day release to study for a professional qualification in accountancy. I like to think I obtained the position by having an excellent interview but have a sneaking suspicion there was a touch of nepotism about the appointment.

So that's how I got started on 12th May 1964, taking up the offered appointment on 24th August 1964 at the age of just 17, with the Company with whom I was to spend the next thirty-six and two thirds years.

I was initially placed in the 'cashiers' office, receiving account payments through the post from customers, as well as taking money from our own prepayment meter cash collectors. (In those days there were no key-meters but lots of cash was collected instead from the pre-payment boxes).

The office was also responsible for making up and distributing the wage packets to the weekly paid company employees. With just 5 of us it was a very small team but I got on well with the others. There were the two top cashiers, (Mr Tovary and Mr Passalls) quite elderly gentlemen who had been there since the nationalisation 'vesting day' in 1947, a much younger man named Eddie Hurford who was the real engine of the Team and another chap a little older than myself.

I thoroughly enjoyed the work, including trips to the bank to pay money in, as well as tours around both town and countryside to pay the shop staff and external workers. I got a kick out of handling quite large sums of money actually many times in excess of my own meagre wage. I started out at just £19 a month, which was substantially less than my hourly rate when I eventually retired.

The only part of the job I didn't enjoy at the outset was the direct contact with some of the customers. We still didn't have a telephone at home in those days so it was a strange instrument to me. To have what were sometimes very angry and frequently confused customers on the other end of it gave me the eebyjeebies at times. Eventually I got the hang of it and learned to be very helpful and tactful, as was appropriate to the call.

A few of the customers were highly questionable and I got know some of them quite well through their regular payments (or excuses) and correspondence. Like the bloke that always deducted the cost of his postage stamps from the electricity bill charge before he sent it to us as he didn't see why he should pay extra just to give us our money; the numerous people who sent us their gas bills and thought the gas, electricity, telephone and water companies were all the same and interchangeable (wow, those people were just years ahead of their time as it turned out); and the people who just sent a cheque with no account, letter or any other means of identification (actually these were the most interesting as they led to some great detective challenges on occasions).

After a few months I moved on the 'Costing' section that dealt with the paperwork associated with the entire minor to major electricity distribution projects in the area, from the laying of cables to the building of new electricity substations. I used to file all the documentation for the jobs and through this got to know all the activities going on. I also got to see all the little wheezes the engineers used to divert costs from their jobs to go elsewhere and thus not appear to be overspent. (Some of the techniques were to come in very useful many years later when I ran my own budget within the Computer Department).

Of course this doesn't happen nowadays when everything is computerised and foolproof. (Excuse me while I remove my tongue from my cheek. The only problem with things being foolproof is fools keep stumbling on new ways of defeating the system). During my stay with the 'Costing' section I was loaned out to other groups to broaden my experience. Why did they do this? Well I was part of a select group of youngsters who were on a 'development programme' designed to help those who were taking day release to study for an accountancy qualification.

There were four of us who used to attend college both during the day and in the evening, twice a week. In those days I couldn't drive. The good news was one of the others did. The bad news was he drove a tiny minivan and muggins, being the only other bloke, drew the short straw to travel in total discomfort in the non-seated rear part of the vehicle.

I had passed the first set of Accountancy exams and was busy on the second set when an opportunity arose to join the hated Internal Audit section. I say 'hated' because the work of the auditor was to check on everybody else. The checking was primarily to detect any fraudulent activities but also to note poor practices. In other words to check on people and of course people don't like being checked up on.

In 1967 I managed to get selected for the Audit team along with another young chap called Alan Purchase. Our boss, named Alex Aitchison was a great character and I'm sure the detective 'Columbo' (the great Peter Falk made famous) could have been modelled on him.

He appeared somewhat dishevelled in dress and a little confused but in reality he had a mind as sharp as a razor. Alan and I spent some months travelling around with Alex and this was an experience it itself. Alex's driving was casual to say the least and he seemed to spend scant attention to the road while he turned his head to talk to his passengers. Alan and I quickly learned not to engage him in conversation while in transit.

We actually made a bit of a name for ourselves when Alex had an extended bout of sickness and was off work for two weeks. Alan and I were only trainees and could have just marked time but we pushed on in his absence and conducted a full audit. Boy was Alex pleased and impressed when he got back. He was able to report to his boss the audit programme had not slipped at all in his absence and was still on track. We looked good and so did he for training us so well.

This taught me a lesson in my working life, to be proactive and take initiatives in trying to anticipate what one's superiors required. If you please your boss and you help your boss look good to his superiors then you are clocking up 'brownie points' towards promotion. An approach that was to come in very useful over the years ahead.

Then in 1964 my career underwent a major change, setting the direction right through until the day I retired. The SEB had created a Computer Department about 6 months previously. The Computer Centre was being built at Havant and the current staff numbering about 10 was deployed in temporary accommodation above the SEB electricity showroom in Havant. I knew one of the people (Rodney Farmer) who had already been taken on and had a chat with him. It certainly seemed this new fangled 'computer' thing was the bees knees and both Alan and myself decided to apply to join.

My preliminary interview took place with two managers named

Gordon Rogers and Ron Bellinger, of whom more later. I did well and even successfully answered 'what's the number 17 expressed to a base of 7.' (That's 23 for the readers who are not 'anoraks').

I was invited to attend a final interview with the Chief Accountant from the Company's Head Office at Maidenhead. There was just one small problem. Years before I had started suffering with an in-growing toenail on my big toe. Various treatments had failed and the problem was getting worse, to the point where I could no longer run and I was even having trouble walking.

My operation had been fixed to remove the whole nail bed in my big toe and I was due to attend for this just a few days before the date given to me for my interview. There was no way I could cancel the operation having waited for so long and being so inconvenienced, so I just hoped I would be OK. As it turned out, the operation resulted in an infection creeping in and it felt like I had an elephant standing on my foot. I had to go back to the hospital every day to have it cleaned and re-dressed. I ended up attending the interview on crutches and must be among a select few who have a conversation with their big boss with only one shoe on.

However all went well and both Alan and I were appointed, along with 2 others, Dave Merwood and Dave Daley. Although the latter left a few months afterwards (and Alan after a few years) Dave Merwood stayed the course and only left a couple of years after I retired, umpteen years later.

After a month in London on a training course for programmers, we started work with the others above the electricity showroom in North Street, Havant. As it was only temporary accommodation it had been fitted out with all the furniture cast offs from other offices in the area. The rock hard wooden chairs were chronic and I would go home at the end of each day with the flower carved into my chair seat imprinted onto my bottom.

As there were no support staff, we had to look after everything ourselves and the most junior (which at this point was my intake) had to take turns in making the tea and running the telephone switchboard. Before I got the hang of it I managed to cut off a few important people and poison a few others.

Our task in the new programming department was to prepare a system to hold our customers records, read electricity meters and prepare the bills, post payments and chase debts. It was pretty daunting as the entire system had to be designed from scratch by a group of people with little prior experience and be delivered in just 2 years.

The key people at the top were the man in overall charge Fred Webster (a very nice and able man but a chain smoker who regularly poisoned his own office and all the meetings he ran); Ron Bellinger, who was head of the operational side that actually ran the computers; and Gordon Rogers who was in charge of the programming department and my ultimate boss. Ron is a man for whom I have the greatest respect and who eventually took over from Fred many years later, then got into politics in a big way and left to become a Liberal Democrat Councillor and eventually the Lord Mayor of Havant.

Gordon ruled with a rod of iron and although he was unpopular he welded us all together as a Team and was a prime mover in our ultimate success in meeting our target on time. Gordon was also a keen footballer, although perhaps past his prime in this respect and in the early days we would all join him for a kick-about in Havant Park after work, a couple of times each week. Depending on who he had upset that day there were some pretty vicious tackles flying in but to give him his due he never complained about sore shins; he just served out extra mundane duties the next day to the perpetrators.

So we all beavered away in very difficult practical circumstances. We had no computer on site and so had to send all our work to the computer manufacturer's offices in London. The programs were held on punched cards that had to be packed into trays and sent off with accompanying instructions and the whole process took 2 weeks to turn any single piece of work around. So we all worked on several jobs simultaneously to keep us busy.

Such a delay was particularly galling when you waited a fortnight and got work back which had been rejected because of a tiny syntax error or the operating instructions were incorrect. However it taught me the importance of work quality and attention to detail together with the benefits of getting a piece of work correct at the first time of asking; something that has stayed with me all my life since then.

The technology in those days was very primitive and the programs written virtually at machine code level (that means program instructions mapped onto the basic computer 1s and 0s almost 1:1, rather than giving instructions close to English or selecting things off of a screen). We had no PCs of course in those days, all communication with the computer being via punched card or paper tape, apart from the actual master operators console.

As a further illustration, the bloke working next to me was a programmer who was given the task of working with a new invention for computer storage that had just come out. They were called **disks!!**

Eventually we moved into our plush new building. By then the group had grown to about 40 strong but we still rattled around in an 'L' shaped building built for 300. Eventually, many years later an additional wing was built to turn the 'L' into a 'U' and over 700 people crammed into it.

Our first computer was delivered. It was an ICL 1904 machine. With all the processing power, memory and storage that would be out performed by the average washing machine of today.

Unfortunately, as we progressed towards our target deadline we had to work later and later. I was in a group that had to work to 21:00 every day but some groups went right through to midnight. One of the casualties of the increased hours was my college work. At first I dropped the day release, postponed my examinations and switched to a correspondence course but even that proved impossible after a while.

With some misgivings I gave up my accountancy studies but I was becoming increasingly committed to my change of career to computing and an accountancy qualification was becoming less useful. Incidentally, in those days it was called 'Electronic Data Processing' (EDP), the term 'Information Technology' (I.T.) came much later.

Following the success of the initial system, further implementations were initiated and the organisation began a rapid expansion to handle the necessary work. I was promoted several times as I grew in experience with the department. I simply loved the work and on one occasion when I was due for a holiday, took the work home with me and wrote a whole computer program while 'on leave'. I can therefore claim to be an original computer nerd.

Despite this rather sad indictment of my social life it did my career prospects the world of good. My Team Leader boss, Roy Harding, was delighted to be about 2 weeks ahead of schedule and sang my praises to the big boss who awarded me some additional leave and lots of 'brownie points'.

The next milestone was when I moved up to the Team Leader role. This was still a technical post in the computer programming department but meant I had much wider responsibilities and a small (about 6) staff to carry out the work. This was probably my favourite post up to that time as it retained a high measure of technical work but also gave a fair bit of power in terms of getting things done and, of course, experience in a fledgling management role.

When I had first joined the department, the British Computer Society (BCS) was being set up and now, a few years later, they were going on a drive to increase membership that was normally achieved via examinations spread over several years. To speed things up, they had waived the exam requirement and were going for established people in the fledgling industry that had the right level of knowledge and experience.

I applied to join and presented a paper, accompanied by samples of my work. My position in the company organisation and my responsibilities had to be underwritten by an existing BCS member and Ron Bellinger very kindly agreed to sponsor my application. In a few weeks I became an official member and to this day can use the letters 'MBCS' after my name.

As a Team leader I also got to go to external meetings and events. As such, occasionally something crops up which sticks in your mind or to put it another way has you cringing with embarrassment for years to come. What I describe now is one such happening.

I was to accompany my immediate boss (a Project Manager named Eric Yates) to a conference being held in Canterbury. It was quite a long distance to travel and rather against the natural direction of the main roads from the Portsmouth area. It was due to last 2 days so we took overnight cases. We travelled in Eric's motor caravan which was somewhat slow and that, plus the winding 'B' roads, made the journey particularly lengthy.

There came a point when both of us received a call of nature but there were was nothing but flat, treeless countryside around us and no sign of a town for many miles. However the need became pressing and we looked around as we motored along for a temporary 'loo'. Suddenly Eric spotted what appeared to be a deep but dry ditch just set back from the road. Beggars can't be choosers, so we came to a halt and hopped out.

We both climbed down into the ditch with Eric turning to the right and myself to the left and we both walked on a short distance to preserve some measure of privacy. The first thing to happen was there was a yell from Eric, followed by a thump. I turned and called out to see if he was alright. 'I'm OK ' he shouted back 'I've fallen over a dead animal.' I'm afraid I was laughing so much I was not quite as attentive as I should have been.

The next moment my foot broke through the surface of the supposedly 'dry' ditch and I felt myself sinking up to my knees in mud and ditch water. I made a grab for the grassy bank to prevent myself falling forward and sinking lower. I managed to get a good grip on the grass and hauled myself out. The problem was it wasn't grass I was clinging to for dear life but a clump of stinging nettles.

My hands were throbbing with pain as I sat gasping on the verge with wet and muddy trousers to the knees. Eric appeared soon after and didn't look to be in much better shape. He was white as a sheet and covered in mud. As we sat there a car went past and the kids in the back seat waved to us enthusiastically. In our dazed condition we automatically waved back to them as they drove into the distance.

We pulled ourselves together and took stock. Fortunately as we were prepared for an overnight stay we both carried changes of clothes and being a bit of a cautious person, I generally carried a small range of medication in my case. This included some antihistamine cream and with this thoroughly applied and some fresh clothes, we were on our way again with nothing but spoilt clothes and damaged pride to remind us of our adventure. I thought ditch water made a change from cowpats.

Despite this event my career continued to blossom. One day the department head, Gordon Rogers called me into his office. A major new departure in our type of computer operating system was planned, would I like to lead the technical side of the work, with Eric Yates leading the project as a whole? It would mean I would have to attend 3 months specialised training in the new system, along with Eric Yates. On our return, Eric would be in charge of the implementation project and I would lead it in the technical nitty gritty. This was undoubtedly a pivotal moment in my career. A 'yes' would put me in a unique position but make me more specialised, while a 'no' would put me back with the pack and mark me with a refusal of an offer from the boss. I didn't hesitate. 'Yes' I said enthusiastically.

The training was to take place in Reading and being a significant distance away Eric and I would be staying overnight for the 3 months. I was somewhat concerned at this because Madge was pregnant at the time with our first child (Stephen) but fortunately she was nowhere near her due date and was keen for me to take this career developing opportunity. At least, or so I thought, I would be in a fairly comfortable 2-star hotel. Some hope.

I reckoned without Eric and his motor caravan. He much preferred to live (cheaply) in the van and claim a much higher sum for 'living expenses' instead. Of course I profited likewise but I wasn't as used to the Spartan existence as he clearly was. What surprised me was being expected to leave my own car at Eric's house (fair enough) but then his wife got to drive it all week when we were away as she had no vehicle of her own with the motor caravan gone.

She was good enough to pay me for the petrol used but the car usually had mud up the sides when I collected it again each Friday. God knows where she was taking it to get in that condition. Anyway, I said nothing, as Eric was my boss after all.

The training itself went very well, despite the man in overall charge being a maniac. His name was 'Micky X', just to preserve his anonymity in case he reads this and works out my address. He would sit in his office strumming on a guitar and leafing through porno mags, while every now and then leaping out of his chair, grabbing an air rifle that he kept by his desk and blazing away from the open window at passing pigeons. I surprised that he wasn't sectioned under the mental health act, let alone arrested for injuring some innocent passer-by.

While I'm talking about maniacs, my department boss Gordon Rogers always fancied himself as a provider of innovative solutions to problems. I recall one day he wanted to summon one of the team leaders (Rodney Farmer) to his office but became frustrated when Rodney's telephone was constantly engaged. He decided to invent a communications device that was more immediate.

The programming department was on the third floor of the building. This was in the days before 'open plan' offices had taken hold and Gordon's office was about 5 along from Rodney's. Gordon had Dave Merwood's brother Tim, who was the incumbent 'gofer' at the time, dangle string from both their offices to the ground. Tim then went down and tied the two string ends together. He made the joint string taut, securing one end to Gordon's chair and the other to Rodney's waste paper bin that was then balanced on the edge of his desk.

When Gordon wanted to summon Rodney he just pulled the string and the bin came crashing off the desk. Rodney put up with this for a few days and then the string was mysteriously severed.

Gordon had got the bit between his teeth by this time. Me and my Team were located in the office next to Gordon. He invented a 'knocking code' on the thin partition wall between us. If he banged once on the wall he wanted to see me, if twice he wanted Tim to go in and do something for him. It worked OK until one day there was a big, single bang on the wall. Assuming he was in a bad mood, I leapt from my desk and rushed into his office. Only to find that he has just fallen off his chair and banged his head on the partition. It may not have been as professional but life was far more entertaining in those days.

Anyway I have digressed. The training completed, Eric and I returned to the Computer Centre only to learn the department manager Gordon Rogers had resigned. A short time later Eric was appointed to take over from him.

In terms of the new Project, Eric had now been promoted above the level of managing it and was not replaced, so as the sole trained person left I became responsible for the entire technical implementation, from the programming department standpoint.

Much to my relief everything worked out fine and the project was considered a great success. Time passed and our computer manufacturers (ICL) came out with yet another radically different approach to the computers they built. It implied a major change for us and a lot of work by more than one specialist implementation team. Having done something similar before with some success I was chosen as the right person to lead on it again. I was promoted to be a Project Manager and given 2 teams to run. I even had my own office. Was I chuffed.

However there was a down side. I had to ease myself out of the technical role I had enjoyed to that date. I was now exclusively a manager and I had to achieve things, not through direct means but through other people. It took some getting used to and I missed getting my hands dirty but adjusted to it and gradually took to the new role. It meant I was involved with staff recruitment for the first time and I have great pleasure in remembering some of the names that graced the Computer Department in those days.

One name I didn't bring on board, as she was recruited only a short time after me from within the Company, was Jenny Dean. Jenny became one of my Team Leaders and she was feared throughout the department for her abrasive personality and acid tongue. This tended to mask the fact that she was very capable, nearly always right in her opinions and drove things through with a single-minded (and indeed bloody minded) persistence.

This turned out to be very fortunate, given the company had a high dependency on its computer department and the new machine we had been provided with (a 2900 series) was relatively unstable. It needed a great deal of looking after, by both programming and operations staff. A small handful of people became key to the computer department continuing to function effectively through a very difficult period. Jenny was one of the key people and only those closely involved with what occurred at the time can fully understand what the Company truly owed her.

Shortly after this last project and having presided over his final major change, Fred Webster retired as overall Computer DP manager and Ron Bellinger, the Operations Manager, took over from him. Ron was a very good manager who got all sections of the computer department pulling together effectively. However after a few years of increasing stability and churning out more and more systems, a major revolution was in prospect, and with the departure of Ron to further his political aspirations, the new broom came in and boy did it sweep clean.

*   *   *

The head of the Computer Department assumed the more senior position of 'Director of Information Technology' and a chap named Peter Woodhart was appointed. He was medium height and of slight stature, wearing a heavy moustache that would have looked good under a sombrero. Peter was a visionary and his personal charisma also made him a natural salesman. He had huge personal and departmental ambitions and only the best would do. The best that is, both by us and for us.

Peter dragged us out of being a very insular set up with virtually all promotions being internal into a whole new world of competitive commerce. Why was this necessary? It was because the Conservative Government had decided the whole Electricity sector was going to be privatised and we had to be taken out of our relatively cosy nationalised world into one where very cold financial wind blew.

The new I.T. department was to be quadrupled in size and Peter started to introduce all the things needed to control an empire of that size. Like project management methodologies, change control procedures, problem management techniques and the like.

We also had a second computer room built at our Portsmouth offices to act as a contingency site in the event of the main I.T. centre being destroyed or made inaccessible. We did have an arrangement prior to this but it was in Leeds, some 250 miles away and highly impractical to use if called upon, although we had done a couple of practice runs. I try not to think of this because these practices were my first ever flights on an aircraft and convinced me if God had wanted me to fly then he would have attached a British Airways pass to my birth certificate).

Peter opened our eyes to a bright new world and we came along, slightly reluctantly at first but then running fast to catch up. The initial problem was expanding the numbers but retaining high staff quality. Peter brought in several people from his previous job and slotted them in very senior positions in the new organisation.

Eric was upset about this arrangement, as he was effectively demoted and left soon afterwards. The rest of us could see the new people had much to teach us about business in a whole new set of circumstances and readily accepted them. Although there were new people above and alongside me, I was adopted into the newly created management team of about a dozen members.

Peter also sanctioned the use of contract staff for the first time. These people were generally very expert at what they did but cost the company a fortune; earning several times my salary for example. However they were meant to be a short-term investment just to get us up and running.

That still left us with large numbers to recruit in the medium to low level technical posts. We did this by advertising, running 'open evenings' and taking part in recruitment fairs in London. The latter proved to be great fun with competitions between us to see who could attract and then recruit the most people that visited our stand and met our criteria.

The following months were a frenzy of gelling the new, enlarged department and coping with a host of additional systems deemed necessary for us to be successfully released from government control. I was given 4 teams of technical staff to run and I got a larger office as well. At this point I would like to single a few people out for special mention. Steve Spurgin, Dave Dunton and Mark Taylor were all fantastic technicians and demonstrated a flair and dedication to their work that made them an example to all. My Team Leaders - Jenny Dean, Neil Farmer, Alan Jamieson and Brian Tee all did an excellent job and took care of technical matters and the day-to-day organising of their Teams but I was still run off my feet. In order to keep my head above water I was working deep into the evenings during the week and a good deal of every Sunday as well.

As I indicated above, although I had 4 teams of people and up to 38 staff in all, they were all highly technical and required to spend all their time on specific functions whereas most of the management and administrative functions (e.g. budgets, financial reports, recruitment, software acquisitions and contracts) fell on my shoulders personally to a very detailed level. This was one of the reasons I was working excessive hours, coping with relatively mundane work. My technicians too were overworked, partly because of the high level of interruptions made in an unstructured and informal manner, by people from other departments requesting them to do things.

I plagued my boss, David Mengham (one of Peter's imports), with requests for more staff but at first received flat refusals and then what at first I regarded as a silly suggestion. The computer punch card department was being run down and several 'punch girls' were to be released and he offered for me to pick one of these. I considered it nonsense to take a punch girl (who had been recruited on the basis of dexterity for operating a keyboard to punch cards, rather than academic qualifications) into what was one of the most technical and demanding sections in I.T. and use her on work requiring years of training and experience.

In desperation, as it was all that was on offer, I decided I might be able to use one person to handle the filing and other donkeywork generated by the section. I interviewed a group of the girls and was surprised by the high standard and especially when one of them convinced me that far from being a bimbo, she was more than capable of handling anything we could train her to take on. Her name was Elayne Cox.

I appointed Elayne to my section and initially put her on helping to unbury me from some of my mountain of dross, which she did very effectively. Then I set up a 'front desk' for her to run that would control all external contact with the technicians in my teams. Elayne's engaging personality and ability to handle difficult people had as much to do with its success as the process itself. Suddenly life was transformed. The interruptions to the technicians stopped and they became more productive and I was able to reduce my evening working and got my Sunday's back for Madge and the children.

I have dwelt on this story because it taught me an important lesson. People often turn out to be far more able than you might expect. All they need is to be given the opportunity to try and the authority and trust to enable them to succeed. Elayne went on to train as a full technician and became a valued member of the I.T. department.

In 1990, out of the blue, I received an unexpected bonus. Somewhat typically of his style, Peter had arranged to go to a conference in the USA but at the last minute the CEO had demanded his presence. It was too late to withdraw from the visit without having to pay much of the costs and so the invitation went down to his two deputies. Again both of them had unbreakable commitments and were unable to attend.

Down to the next level which included yours truly. The key thing was the content of the conference had much more to do with my area of responsibility, rather than any of my peers. So guess what. I was offered the place. I consulted with Madge who gave me her blessing to fly off over the pond for a few days. Then I got my next nice surprise. The flight would be 'club class' and the destination was Anaheim in California. This location didn't mean much to me until I saw I was booked into the Disneyland Hotel.

It turned out to be a very strange experience. The first long flight (which incidentally scared me to death); the first time abroad on my own; the first time I had driven on the 'wrong side of the road'. I expected a fairly large cowpat to come my way but it all went surprisingly smoothly, except for my body clock. I was only there a few days and didn't fully adjust to the jet lag. I would get up at about 04:00, make notes about the previous day, have breakfast, go to the conference at 09:00, return at 18:00, have dinner and go to bed at 20:00.

It was very frustrating living in the hotel and being surrounded by people, 99.9% of whom were there to go to Disneyland, while all my waking hours (i.e. when the park was open) were fully committed. In an effort to make the best of serendipity, I delayed my return flight by 24 hours and booked a coach tour of Los Angeles and the Universal Studios back lot.

Also, as the Conference finished early on its last day, I hurried back to my hotel, hired a camcorder (that turned out to be a huge device you had to carry on your shoulder) and set off around Disneyland for a few hours. The next day I took the camcorder with me to Universal Studios where I infuriated all around me on the tour bus by waving the huge contraption about and blocking their view whenever something interesting happened.

There was a follow up to this. The camcorder had recorded in the 'USA' version of the VHS format that wasn't the same as the European version. Hence when I brought the tape home it wouldn't play on our recorder. I found a company that would carry out a conversion for £25 per tape and all was well in the end.

When I eventually got back to work, there was a mountain of tasks waiting for me but you couldn't get the grin off my face for weeks. Just to placate the other managers (or was it to wind them up) I bought each of them a small souvenir and handed them out on my return.

I had become an established manager and as such applied to join the British Institute of Management (BIM). Although I hadn't taken the examination route, I was able to qualify due to my company position and years of experience in the job. So with some pride I was able to add a few more letters after my name. Since then, the organisation has been awarded 'Charter' status and been renamed the 'Chartered Management Institute' (CMI).

Eventually the electricity privatisation happened and we took our place in the FTSE100. Staff were given the opportunity to buy shares in the new company through a 'sharesave' scheme and I made the maximum level of savings allowed. This turned out to be the best financial investment I ever made, apart from buying the house in Hulbert Road, and I paid a great chunk of our mortgage off when the scheme came to maturity.

Shortly afterwards, Peter Woodhart left. It was very sudden and as far as I could see under somewhat mysterious circumstances. I can only assume his ambitions somehow fell foul of the Chief Executive and you certainly didn't take on that particular gentleman and survive.

We all wanted his successor to be David Mengham. He was one of Peter's 'imports' from his previous job and was my immediate boss. He was hugely respected; a big man in every sense, with a deep authoritative voice seeming to rumble up from his boots. I found it easy to work for him because we shared similar principles and work ethics, although he possessed an enormous drive and ruthless streak I didn't have.

Unfortunately this was not to be. Instead a man named Stan Kay was appointed from the business side. Clearly this was an attempt to get I.T. to become more 'business driven' but as an experiment it turned out to be questionable to say the least. Stan had no previous computer experience except his own 'PC' at home he used extensively. The big problem was he seemed to imagine the huge commercial 'mainframe' machines we ran were just very big PCs and so erroneously assumed everything he knew about his little PC also applied to the behemoths.

Stan started off by changing the organisational structure and getting everyone to apply for the new posts, including those not actually changed by the new hierarchy. This was fine and is a common practice in organisational reshuffles.

The means of assessment was by psychometric tests. He called a group of us together and heavily emphasised he was looking for people who would be 'team players' above all. Fair enough. When it came to the tests I carefully ticked all the boxes indicating being a member of a team was my main driving force and no way would I be off ploughing lone furrows.

Then the consultants running the tests told me my results showed I was a team player whereas to be a manager, needed to indicate I preferred to be an individual and not a member of a team. Stan, it appeared after all, wanted people who could plough a lone furrow in his top management team, not 'team players'.

I was rather hurt when I heard this, as I believed the briefing he had given misdirected the way I (and others) had approached the tests and answered the questions. So, although I was still a senior technician I was effectively demoted and had only one team of people to run and was no longer a part of the upper echelons.

My place was taken by Isobel Thomson, who had originally come to us as a contractor and who I'd had a small hand in converting to a permanent staff member and also in progressing her career. I had a great deal of respect for 'Izzy', who seemed destined for much higher things, and this took the edge off of my disappointment. It was a bit ironic when she eventually left to take on a Europe-wide role in a global company she would become David Mengham's boss.

Stan continued to run the department in what appeared to be a somewhat eccentric manner. For example, he reportedly used coffee cups to decide how big our new computer should be. I might well say to have what amounted to an 'enthusiastic amateur' at the helm drove the professional I.T. staff potty but you will have guessed my opinion of him was a little biased and perhaps just a touch unfair.

One of the main reasons for Stan to be in charge was his experience in relation to the major deregulation change within the industry; to be able to supply not only electricity but also gas and potentially water and telecommunications services as well. With his business background Stan would be able to guide us through this major transformation. To give him his due, Stan recognised (as we all knew anyway) the shantytown of I.T. systems that had been built and added to since the late 1960s were not in a good position to handle the new and ongoing situation.

The Board agreed a completely new and fully integrated system was required and put their money on the table. The question was which computer supplier(s) would be used to deliver it. Stan set up a working party I was not a member of, but was involved with on the fringes, inputting information. They concluded IBM was the most suitable partner. This was a bombshell to I.T. as this was a complete change of direction and effectively meant going back and re-developing our technical skills again from square one.

Having said that, it was undoubtedly the correct decision. We were shooting for the moon and in my view only IBM had the know-how and expertise in depth to enable such a thing to be delivered successfully. Then, just at the point where we needed to start to make it happen, Stan disappeared. The word was something had gone wrong; he had been accused of misleading the Executive in some way and involved in an acrimonious discussion with the CEO. If so, nobody survived such a clash.

We progressed leaderless for a short while and did what we could. IBM had identified the Company's I.T. Department needed to have a more strategic view of things and a complete technical architecture on which to base the new system. Such a task was beyond the members of Stan's working party who were largely theoretical in computer knowledge and so David Mengham, as acting top man, turned to me to tackle it. It meant leaving my current responsibilities and leading a small team, from both our company and also IBM.

Just as we were about to start work a new Director of I.T. was appointed. His name was Matt Devereux and he proved himself to be, by some way, the finest leader we had in all the 33 years I was with the Company's I.T. department. He endorsed what David had put in place and gave me the teeth needed to get the co-operation from everybody else for the work to succeed.

The next 3 months included some of the most rewarding experiences of my career. Myself, Mark Hindry from what was now called Southern Electric, together with Mark Croft and Simon Treen from IBM, pooled our own knowledge and interviewed every other I.T. expert and a range of Business managers. We came up with a complete blueprint of what we had, what we needed and the guiding strategic and design principles required to get us to the Promised Land.

Matt, in the meantime, had set up a full strategy group within I.T. led by a chap named Gurmel Bansal. Matt enthusiastically adopted the work my team had produced and made me the technical design authority within the I.T. department, through whom all technical proposals would be passed. I was to report to Gurmel and I had Mark Hindry to assist me.

Although I no longer had the large numbers of staff it meant I could influence the entire I.T. infrastructure and also actually get directly involved in things myself, rather than just be a people manager. The nature of the work made me extremely happy, because in the previous weeks I had undergone a 'Road to Damascus experience'.

If I can explain. Every 'techie' (i.e. technician) believes the best organisational structure comprises his/her technical group and just one manager to go to for decisions, all other levels and departments being superfluous. I went for years holding this very view and I knew of some strategic "thinkers" whom I regarded as totally dispensable to getting the work done.

What I realised in a flash of insight one day was the technical work needed a higher level of coordination and direction going beyond simple written 'standards'. For example, a man might be able to dig a hole in the ground very effectively but others were needed to tell him where exactly to dig it, to what dimensions and what the most suitable tools were; and to ensure everyone else digging similar holes followed the same best practice. After all, builders are not given free rein to put up just any old building; they have to follow national building regulations and local byelaws.

I had finally discovered my true niche in I.T. I was to be the function guiding the practitioners and establishing the 'rules'. In the past I had been the hole digger and I had been the builder. I had the know-how to ensure the rules for building I.T. systems were effective, efficient and sensible in practice.

I was in a team of like-minded people under Gurmel. Mark Hindry helped me, Neville Clough looked after security matters and I worked especially closely with him. Roger Freeston was responsible for the 'corporate models' of how I.T. mapped onto the business processes and we had a small 'futures' group headed by a most remarkable chap named Dr Philip Gartshore, along with Phil Jones and Jill Bowen.

Philip suffered from motor neurone disease and was confined to a motor-driven wheelchair, having very little use of his limbs. However despite amazing disability he insisted on being treated as a normal member of staff and did just about everything other people did, including going to meetings on his own, many miles away.

Phil was an extremely able technical analyst and PC expert. A very fit chap who had a cupboard full of tennis trophies. His sidekick Jill was an ex-teacher, which might explain the enormous patience and diplomacy she displayed while sorting out problems and the people that went with them.

The group as a whole was a catalyst within the I.T department for 'excellence' and with strong direction and support from Matt Devereux a new, much more effective but cost saving regime became pervasive.

Against this background the 'IBM Customer System Project' was the main focal point of the department's work. The system being delivered to us was new but had it's roots in an application already being used in the USA by an energy company called NIPSCO based in Gary, Northern Indiana. It was decided to send a small working party to the States to study this system and report back. Armed with our Technical Architecture I was in an ideal position to draw technical comparisons and identify potential impacts and unforeseen costs and so was included in the visiting group.

Off we went, however, this was not to be like the previous visit I made to California. We were driven from Chicago O'Hare airport to a hotel in a small town called Merrillville and then bright and early the next day we drove a few miles to the city of Gary where NIPSCO had their offices.

We were told the city was the murder capital of the USA; there being more killings per capita than anywhere else. It certainly explains why we hadn't stayed in Gary the previous night. We were warned it was vital we stayed within the company premises at all times.

Any thoughts our hosts were exaggerating were dispelled when we crossed the city boundary. The streets seemed largely deserted as we drove along, with views of shop windows boarded up and lampposts leaning over at crazy angles. The odd drunk or cokehead lay in the gutters here and there and small gangs of black youths hung around street corners. The car pulled into the company car park and we were told to remain there until an armed guard appeared and escorted us the 50 yards or so to the building entrance. Boy, was I glad I didn't work there! All the glamour of a trip to the States seemed a million miles away.

The visit itself went very well and we came away with our confidence in the potential of the new system boosted high. The only problem was the version of the system we were to get didn't actually exist as yet and two other British Electricity companies had already signed up for it about 6 months ahead of us. Both South West Electricity (SWEB) and South Wales Electricity (SWALEC) were already working in close tandem and having regular meetings with IBM to refine their specifications and monitor progress. Southern Electric was to join in these discussions and I was selected to represent the I.T. department and my colleague Richard Collings represented the SE business interests.

It says a great deal for how far our company had come in terms of efficiency and conciseness, we discovered the representation from the other 2 Electricity companies was in double figures for both, compared with just the two of us and we more than held our end up in the discussions.

In the final event both the other 2 companies pulled out of the deal leaving just us. In my view this was the best thing that could have happened. IBM's effectiveness was being diluted by having to work with 3 separate companies, each of whom was trying to maximise their own interests. The withdrawal meant all their efforts were concentrated on Southern Electric and what we wanted.

As the 4-year project moved forward I was asked to take on firstly a Project Assurance role where I validated all the technical aspects of the product against our expectations and the formal contract. Then I moved into a design/planning role where I worked with IBM to determine the computer infrastructure Southern Electric would require to run the system. Obviously I could not know everything about everything myself and needed to obtain assistance.

Around this time there were several significant developments. Firstly both Gurmel Bansal and Roger Freeston left the company. It was no great surprise regarding Gurmel as he had been commuting to Havant every day from the Maidenhead area and we knew all the travelling was getting to him. Roger was really an I.T. consultant and he wanted to re-join one of the big consulting companies.

Then Neville Clough retired earlier than expected and was not replaced, his security responsibilities falling on myself. Finally and totally unexpected was the tragic death of Phil Gartshore. He had been taken ill following an external trip that had been a particularly difficult journey. He was rushed to hospital but went downhill rapidly. We were all distraught, especially Phil Jones and Jill Bowen who had both worked closely with him for years and always kept an eye on him at work when he needed a little assistance.

I was asked by Matt Devereux to take over the group and to build it up again both to support the IBM Project and all the numerous other projects going on. Phil and Jill looked after themselves to a large extent and I brought in a contract worker, Jim Tickner, to assist me with IBM on the Database side.

Jim moved into the IBM Hursley complex where the early system development was taking place and he was my eyes and ears there while I was based back at Havant. A business manager named Mark Knight led the SE group at Hursley. He looked a bit like a mad professor but he was very able indeed and an amiable character who lent me much support in my work. His presentations were famous for being not only informative but also hilarious and not to be missed.

Jim was a really nice bloke and proved himself to be sufficiently versatile that I ended up getting him to work on all sorts of things beyond his original remit, which he did enthusiastically and effectively, becoming in time a fully fledged 'I.T. Architect'.

The IBM Project then moved to Havant and although matters were going reasonably well from the technical standpoint, the target date was slipped by several months, mainly due to data problems. The CEO was very irate at this and demanded an investigation as to what had happened and why he had not been better informed of the probable slippage.

An independent external team was wheeled in from IBM to conduct the investigation and Matt Devereux volunteered me to join this high-powered group of troubleshooters as a local 'facilitator'. The group leader, a very high powered manager named Jim McClure, asked me to be a fully-fledged member of the team and this I very must appreciated. Jim had overseen (for IBM) the earlier work with the system at Bristol and Hursley and was very familiar with such mega-developments.

The team reported back within a matter of days with a list of problems and proposed solutions. Unfortunately, one or two people were made to carry the can, as the CEO was expecting an element of blame to be laid and the most significant victim was David Mengham. He had been heavily involved but was very unfortunate to be labelled as a fall guy. Shortly afterwards he left the company and we were the worse for his ongoing absence.

As I said above, Jim McClure had managed the initial development of the IBM system when there were multiple Electricity Companies involved. Now he was asked by our CEO to take over the development just for us at Havant.

Jim was an amazing guy and one of probably only a handful of Programme Managers in the world that could have delivered something as big and complex as this. Although nearing retirement age himself, he tackled his responsibilities with a drive and determination that blazed a trail for all to follow. With him in charge of development etc and Matt handling the infrastructure implementation etc we had an excellent chance of success.

The only problem was Matt and Jim didn't get on too well. Each had a very difficult job to do and any attempt to make things easier for the one usually made it harder for the other. Hence some blazing rows. I could see both points of view and sympathised with each of them, so I was mightily relieved when, all together, the joint Project Team finally hauled the System over the finishing line.

As the publicity bandwagon began to roll I was asked by Matt to write an article about the new system, subsequently published in the company magazine. The editor said it was the first article from I.T. he had ever understood! The system finally went into very successful production in a wave of fanfares, although I had regrets at the passing of the old programs that had served us well for so many years and had personally had a hand in developing. However, the new system was ground breaking and would put us in a better competitive position than any of the other companies in the Energy sector.

My personal position was consolidated and I and my group received further plaudits from Matt Devereux for the completion of a full I.T. Corporate Architecture, that also won praise from our external auditors and other external consultancies engaged from time to time, to check up on the I.T. department.

Things never stay still and the next challenge was on the horizon. Competition between energy companies was to be opened up far more and we had joined a consortium to take a set of core programs from a national agency, then add our own bits and pieces for a competitive edge.

I was offered and brought in an IBM consultant named Paul Booth. Paul was one of the most extraordinary characters I have ever met. He had the brain the size of a planet, was hugely productive and basically did the work of several lesser mortals. He represented IBM at global events and despite all the accolades poured out to him was one of the most approachable, unassuming, unflappable and polite people you could ever wish to meet.

One of Paul's early recommendations was to establish a test-bed as a final step for systems to undergo prior to deployment. This made perfect sense, as PCs in those days and especially early versions of the Microsoft Windows operating system, were highly vulnerable to applications clashing with one another. We were expecting to have to run dozens of them concurrently on the Company PCs and hence could expect a lot of problems. Phil and Jill designed, created, and ran this testbed system (dubbed TIAS).

Initially TIAS was opposed within I.T as it was seen as an unnecessary additional step that would delay deployment of new or updated systems but it soon proved its worth. Phil and Jill's quiet thoroughness and professionalism won people over as they soon realised identifying problems behind closed doors was preferable to having them discovered by our users in the field and causing complaints to be directed from the business into the Director of I.T.'s office.

Mark Hindry supported this initiative by developing a 'Style Guide' that ensured all our systems had a 'common look and feel' for our customer-facing users. Mark also introduced me to my own first PC and gave me some basic training. By this stage of my career most technologies had overtaken my initial expertise at the detailed level, although in terms of breadth of technical knowledge I could more than hold my own. In other words, whereas techies tended to know a lot about a little, I knew a little about a lot. Regrettably Mark left soon afterwards to pursue a career opportunity and was sadly missed.

Another expert, this time in Telecommunications, named Adam Bowie joined our group. Adam was a tall, lanky, canny Scot with an extensive practical knowledge of his subject and a cutting dry wit. Adam was as famous for his diligent and accurate designs as he was for his hatred of producing supporting documentation. He proved to be a valued and popular member of the group.

I managed to secure the services of Julian Wakeland, a contractor I had recruited many years before for Jenny Dean's Team and who had an extensive practical knowledge, allied to wide vision and excellent presentation skills.

Paul Booth, in the meantime, was taking the lead in designing all of our systems for the new competition regime and also frequently attending national design meetings on our behalf to plan the detail of the system. There were a handful of National Forums to steer the whole thing through and although I was not a regular attendee I was called upon occasionally to represent the company when our business representative felt the meeting content warranted an S.E./ I.T. presence.

I was always on the lookout to strengthen the group as I had vacancies to fill since Neville and Roger had left. Some people were being released from the famous millennium bug 'Y2K' project and I looked to take advantage of this. I was very fortunate to obtain the services of Richard Green, an ex-telecomms colleague of Adam's and a very able and thorough designer. Richard was a talented architect and Paul took him under his wing to further develop his skills. Then a little later I managed to recruit Jim Warren, a Project Manager and ex-contractor from the same Y2K stable who took on our Applications Architecture work.

In the meantime our test-bed manned by Phil and Jill was going from strength to strength and the amount of work lined up for it necessitated another pair of hands. The sort of person we needed had to possess a high degree of technical thoroughness and dedication, as well as being able to communicate clearly and firmly with our 'customers'. An unusual combination of talents difficult to find internally but we were very fortunate to discover an ideal external candidate; John Vince, technically able and a very nice chap who fitted in well both personality and work wise.

The industry competition system went into production, again very successfully and with Matt's backing my group continued to be extremely effective and the individuals within it well respected. Independent industry watchers put Southern Electric at or close to the top of their efficiency measures. I.T. were playing their part in achieving that accolade and our group was playing its full part within I.T.

Perhaps I should mention here some of the other terrific people I had the privilege of working with, in addition to those already mentioned in the course of my story. Rodney Farmer, a founding member of the original Computer Department and the person I had consulted many years previously when I was considering applying to join. He carried on for many years and left at the completion of the Y2K project. His wife Carol Farmer was one of the early joiners above the showroom at North Street and ran the section handling user liaison, change control, problem management and the like. She left shortly after Rodney.

Sue Murphy who assisted Carol and took over from her and finally left a little while after myself. Neil Farmer, Rodney's brother; a model of thoroughness and dedication who was one of my team leaders for several years. Ged Pratt who was a very able and inventive techie and who had a wicked sense of humour, still there today as is Paul Edney who with Ged and I ran one of the most innovative projects (called Maestro) ever carried out in I.T. under Peter Woodhart. The three of us also played in the same skittles team which Ged captained and we won many trophies together.

I would also like to list a whole host of people who stayed in or passed through the Software Support Teams and the Operations Department but they are too numerous to narrate. They know who they are. (Having said that I'll single out Mike Eaton, Pete Edgar and Steve Cleverly for special mention; all very able colleagues). They were often the unsung heroes and heroines of I.T. over many years keeping machines and systems running when everything else seemed to be dropping to bits around them.

And of course the senior managers secretaries without whom the I.T. department would have collapsed. Pat Bradshaw, a lovely lady who retired some years ago. She used to rush about when things went wrong but had it all under control really. Then more recently and still there when I left; Sue Long, a very vivacious lady, who was unflappably professional, must have been a real stunner in her heyday and still retains her good looks; and Liz Hall who was ever so slightly scatty but with a heart of gold and such a sweet, demure personality you felt you had to give her a cuddle every time you saw her. All these ladies were so helpful to me.

Although very much the boss, who at times could be ruthless in pursuit of his objectives, Matt himself was always approachable and gave you a hearing. He also wasn't above mucking in either on social events. On one occasion he joined myself, Madge and a few others manning a 'water station' supplying refreshments to cyclists taking part in a charity bike ride in the New Forest. The sight of him rushing about was almost as good as seeing the CEO collapsed with exhaustion across his handlebars. I take my hat off to the CEO for participating but the rumours were, having just about made it to the first check-in, his chauffeur driven car was just around the corner to take him around the rest of the route.

Things were never settled for long and we hardly had time to breath before the next challenge emerged. This time, after several abortive attempts to acquire another company in the rapidly consolidating energy sector, it was announced we were to merge with Scottish Hydro-Electric. There were some concerns as we were at opposite ends of the country and were so similar that most functions were duplicated. Where there are 2 groups of people doing the same thing, in a company merger one of them has to go, irrespective of geographic location.

Somewhat surprisingly the two I.T. organisations, although overtly providing the same service to the main business, were completely different. In the south we were highly centralised with a single highly efficient unit serving the entire business. In the north each business area had it's own computer unit, with consequential costly duplication between them and little common policies or shared technical standards.

Matt was put in overall charge of I.T. with a remit to merge the two departments. The north based I.T. staff saw the writing on the wall and while some left straight away, others decided to stay on. Some of these decided to resist any form of change to their way of doing things. While plans were being put in place, the two management teams served in tandem under Matt and just as Matt had placed me to work with IBM to look after his interests, so he turned to me again to work very closely with the north based managers to keep an eye on things and report back.

At this time our management team, spearheaded by Matt and his most senior managers, Dave Merwood and Steve Harding, were spending huge amounts of time in Perth. I was going once a fortnight for meetings and to see the staff that had been allocated to me. Management meetings commenced at 09:30 in Perth on the days we travelled and as I refused to fly in the very small planes from Southampton, I had to get up at 03:00 to drive to Heathrow in order to arrive on time.

I had a collection of some excellent people in the North, notably Jim McGee (who I had known for several years as an industry contact), Anthony Glen, Iain Bremner and John Evans. I also had a few hangers on, including a number of expensive contract staff who were unable to justify their activities and I made plans to discard these as soon as possible.

The good ones I wanted to keep on, as they all had a lot to offer and a group such as mine issuing guidelines and advice to others, would have found a local presence in Perth very useful. However time would show I was to be denied this.

When we formally announced the merger, the CEO declared the savings to come out of the merger would be so many million pounds. In fact the I.T. savings from the plans Matt and his management team had drawn up almost met this figure on their own and hence the company was able to revise the cost savings upwards by a considerable amount.

Then just as we started moving the plans into action, there was a terrible blow. Matt Devereux resigned. It appears he felt his post in a merged company merited a place on the Board as in fact happens in many large organisations but our CEO did not agree. So Matt went.

Matt's nearest I.T. manager equivalent in the north (Alistair Forbes) was put in temporary charge while a replacement was sought. Alistair had some top management qualities and was a useful senior manager but he was also a frustrated techie to some degree with one or two bees in his bonnet seeming to warp his judgement at times.

There was great concern for a while in case the northern stopgap appointment turned the whole I.T. strategy on its head but fortunately there was already a lot of momentum from Matt which the southern part of the management team were actively carrying through and Alistair seemed to have had his cards marked by his Executive Director not to deviate too far from existing policy.

However, Alistair was more vulnerable to the rearguard action taking place in some quarters up north and things became somewhat watered down and took longer than they would have done under Matt. However Matt's old southern management team, lead by Dave and Steve, had the bit between its teeth and eventually I.T. was all but shut down in Scotland and centralised at Havant.

One thing I did manage to achieve around this time was my first and only presentation at a National Conference. The computer company 'BMC Software' were one of our major suppliers and we had spent a good deal of money with them in support of our IBM customer system. We had a close relationship with their Account Team and they had poured free consultancy into some of our biggest problems and saved us a lot of hassle and money in areas I cannot really go into.

At around number 5 or 6 in the software company world rankings, they ran an annual conference in the UK for their existing and potential customers and on more than one occasion asked Matt or myself to talk at this event about our experiences of using their products. Although Matt seemed sympathetic towards doing it, the timing was never right due to our company commitments. As Matt had now moved on I regarded it as my responsibility to fulfil the obligation. So I found myself in Birmingham doing my first (and what turned out to be my only) major conference speech.

I had attended dozens of such events on the floor and had always been a little intrigued when I saw doors marked 'presenters only' from where people with special 'speaker' badges emerged. Now I became one of those rather special people who got to go into the designated room and I got a small kick out of joining the 'club'.

Actually the speakers' room at this particular venue was a complete let down. It was very small and furnished with a table, a couple of chairs and a PC, with papers strewn all over the floor. It looked like a junk cupboard pressed into service at short notice. The only redeeming feature was a coffee percolator I availed myself of. Still, at least I found out what it was like in such esteemed places instead of just wondering about it.

Finally an appointment was made to the vacant Director of I.T. post. It was a chap named John Berney. He was an accountant who in his last job had taken over as I.T. manager for the previous 18 months. It had been a very tiny department in comparison with ours and we had some concerns he might not fully appreciate the impacts and complexities of scaling up. We had grown with it as both the department and the I.T. infrastructure had gradually expanded since Peter Woodhart's day but for John it would be an instant change.

John proved to be totally different to his predecessor in terms of his interpretation of the role of Director of I.T. and also his Management style. Matt was a true leader who gave a clear direction and then challenged people to meet his exacting objectives and standards. John had less leadership qualities; preferring to let others make the running and then criticise with the advantage of hindsight. He adopted a very confrontational stance on all aspects of our work and with his entire management team. Everything was turned into a battle he always had to win and on his terms.

This might be taken as a sign of a strong manager perhaps but it certainly didn't help him make friends either inside or outside of I.T. Relationships with key suppliers and with our business users, carefully cultivated over the years, were thrown into disarray or broken.

Anyway that's how I saw it; doubtless John saw it as jolting us out of complacent relationships and sharpening us up. Although I couldn't really see why an I.T. department such as ours, that had gained a reputation within the industry as being one of the most efficient and was already pretty sharp, needed to be shaken about quite so much.

Although not an inspiring leader, John was certainly a true accountant; trusting far more in numbers than in people. Again in comparison with Matt, who would always question the numbers and the rationale behind them in the context of the business proposition, John seemed to attack the numbers for themselves and endlessly had them re-worked, constantly trying to disprove them. Consequently, all progress ground to a halt except on absolutely critical matters and even they were significantly delayed. Projects incurred continual and critical slippage and I could see early signs of things falling apart.

I believe John's main problem was he found it extremely difficult to trust anyone already in post when he arrived. Peter Woodhart had brought a small legion of trusted cohorts with him, which he was able to do as he came from a very large I.T. organisation; he then adopted some of the 'natives' into his circle.

Matt hadn't brought in anyone at all but he quickly commanded the loyalty and respect of the incumbent management team. John came from a very small organisation with relatively few people and so couldn't bring a lot of trusted staff with him, just 2 technicians in fact.

Even with this ongoing situation I was able to continue to strengthen my own group as I still had vacancies against the organisational structure established in Matt's era and not revoked. With Steve Harding's help (the Operations Manager) I managed to recruit the services of Paula O'Toole who was a very experienced practitioner and who ran the PC/server support team for our outsource suppliers. Paula was very able with both a strategic view and with 'hands on' knowledge. She could also hold her own at meetings and annihilate people on a squash court.

She in turn brought with her Lisa Grover, a PC and Server expert, and together they formed what was the last link in the chain of total infrastructure expertise within my group. The only negative point was the loss of Adam to the now separate Telecommunications group but as I.T. had lost most of its responsibilities in that area since the merger with 'Hydro', his departure was not too serious, although he was personally very much missed.

Things never stood still for long and the next task became the acquisition of the SWALEC supply business. Ironic as it was they who we had worked with in the early days of the IBM system. This was no 'give and take' merger. The plan was we would just roll our I.T. solutions straight in and that was that.

I referred earlier to the 2 techies John brought with him. One was a young guy called Stephen. He was technically talented, a bit headstrong but with a good deal of drive and I could see how in a small set-up he and John had got on well and developed the mutual trust John was having difficulty establishing with the rest of us.

I recognised in Stephen a likeness to myself in my early days of being a Team Leader and I welcomed the opportunity to pass my knowledge on to him. He seemed daunted by the sheer size of the department he had joined and had no experience at all of the issues that go with a large and complex I.T. installation.

However, protected from any comeback by John, Stephen didn't really want to listen to or learn from anyone and constantly got into hot water with the big department heads (Dave Merwood and Steve Harding) for not following procedures and doing things precipitately that impacted other people adversely. In other words, it was typical behaviour from an unconstrained techie who had his head down and ignored everything else outside of his personal remit.

Then a bombshell struck home. John promoted Stephen to a level effectively making him a department head and one of his direct reports and at a point in the organisational structure that meant I would have to report to him. I was dumbstruck. Stephen was a talented techie and was good Team Leader material but a Manager he was not, even though he might have had the potential to grow into such a role over time, if he matured and changed his attitudes.

When I thought of the giants that had occupied Stephen's newfound senior position in the organisation, like David Mengham, John Williams, Terry Finch and Isobel Thomson, to name but a few, he was a pygmy by comparison. It seemed I had been demoted by this move although I retained my previous membership in the management forum.

I was still prepared to support Stephen and help him grow into his new role but the conversations I had with him filled me with dismay. He was still totally blinkered and saw everything in purely technical terms, being unable to raise his vision to more strategic thinking or take wider implications to I.T and the Business into account.

He didn't see my group as a key resource for all of I.T. to share and exploit to the general good of all, he simply saw a collection of very highly skilled individuals, some of whom had knowledge he could use on his own pet subjects and he promptly removed them for that purpose without even enquiring as to what implications and impacts such precipitous actions would have.

A very successful I.T. department was being damaged by someone who didn't know any better and wasn't prepared to listen to either myself or my management team colleagues. I despaired. For the first time in my career I felt the incumbent Director of I.T. and his new right-hand man were taking both I, and the whole of I.T, a big step backwards into the chaos of the past and there was no prospect of retrieving the situation in the foreseeable future.

My stress levels rocketed and I started to get the particularly bad pains in the chest and the breathlessness described earlier. I went back to the doctors and checks by private consultants showed my heart was not in good shape. My weight and diet were far from ideal and there was a strong record of heart disorders on both my mother and fathers' sides of the family.

Work politics and now the stress was literally killing me and I knew I had to get out. I remembered Madge's dad dying on his last day before retirement and some senior managers within our Company that had died in post before they reached retirement age.

My kids shouldn't have to cope with me collapsing at work. Madge and I had striven very hard all our lives and we deserved a long retirement together to enjoy ourselves and catch up on all the things we gave up to raise 6 children and 3 dogs.

I went to see John Berney and explained my medical situation. To my surprise and relief he was very sympathetic and caring. For the first time I saw behind the obdurate accountant was a person that could and did have compassion.

He agreed I could go and said he would try and obtain for me as favourable terms as possible. He also said he would progress the matter urgently and indeed within a week he concluded a deal that was acceptable to me and meant I would be leaving in as little as 3 weeks. This would be at the end of April 2001, after joining on the Company on August 24th 1964 and the I.T. department on April 1st 1968.

I got my little group together and, in what for me was one of the most emotional experiences of my life, I told them I was going and explained my medical condition. They were all magnificent and gave me every support. In the next 3 weeks I pulled out of virtually all active topics so I could concentrate on preparing notes for my successor to help him/her pick up the reins.

I had hoped Phil Jones would succeed me but Phil had problems of his own with his wife's medical condition and the last thing he needed was additional responsibility at that time, so I didn't push the point too hard. In the event it was decided a chap named Chris Wickham who had been appointed to another post but not yet taken it up would take over from me. Handover was made more difficult because he didn't start until after I was gone and couldn't see me at any time beforehand. I wasn't too troubled by this as my handover notes were fairly copious and all my team members would see he was well briefed.

I tried several times to take Stephen through the notes and act as intermediary with my successor but he was always too busy to do so; that is until my very last day when just as I was leaving to go down to the pub to celebrate my career with my friends, he turned up and asked for a handover session when I got back. I told him if I could find him when I got back I would do so. Guess what. I didn't manage it!

I went out on a quiet note. I didn't want a big fuss. Many of the people I cared about came to see me earlier in the day and others joined me in The Curlew at lunchtime. I did a tour of the building to say my goodbyes. I had already said farewell to people at the other offices and with our major supplier contacts over the previous couple of weeks.

My group had already taken me out for a meal and given Madge and me a terrific present. Just before we went to the pub, Madge joined me for the formal presentation the secretaries Sue and Liz had arranged. I had brought in a few mementos of years gone by (like punch cards, paper tape, old electricity bills etc) just to show people what life was like then. The place was crammed with people to hear my old mate Dave Merwood give my farewell speech and I responded with what I hoped were appropriate 'thank you's' and some 'words of wisdom' to those I was leaving behind.

I was showered with gifts and Madge was presented with a large bouquet of flowers. A number of ex-employees sent me very kind messages and e-mails, including Matt Devereux who also offered me some consultancy work! Then it was down to the pub and farewell to the people and the Company I had been with for so long.

* * *

I had a concern that with me gone, a lot of what I stood for in terms of appropriate planning and design up front, quality workmanship and professional conduct, would be cast aside by the 'new regime'. 'Do it quick and fix it later' seemed to be the growing order of the day. It reminded me of how we worked in the 1970s. Processes, rationale, experienced people and lessons learned had been deliberately put in place to avoid errors, delays and increased costs. These good things were all now being cast aside in the headlong rush towards short termism and false economies and therefore the problems they resolved were bound to re-appear.

I kept in touch just to find out what was going on, just for curiosity really. I certainly wasn't bothered about it once I had gone. In fact Madge said she was amazed that after so many years when I was totally dedicated to my work, even putting her and the kids second to it on occasion (that's how sad I was), I had been able to switch it off like a light. I think it shows just how much I had been turned off by the events towards the end.

After I went, there was a bit of an exodus. Jim Warren and Julian Wakeland had already been poached to further other pet projects. Julian left soon anyway, as he believed he was being unfairly treated in his new role. Jim Tickner had his contract terminated almost immediately I left. Jim was highly competent and the only person in the group to have both mainframe and database knowledge. He had been closely involved with and understood the detail of the new Customer System data repository. To get rid of him without any skills transfer just goes to show how little this key area was understood and appreciated by the new management.

Paul Booth was phased out rapidly. Paul was an expensive consultant but understood the design of the new competitive market system better than anyone as he was part of the national group that produced it. His knowledge was unique and his contribution both to the Company and the Industry nationally was enormous.

I was told that both Paula O'Toole and Lisa Grover became disillusioned with the newly exposed attitudes and activities and left of their own volition; Paula with her partner setting up a vehicle business and Lisa preparing to marry and start a family. Phil Jones needed to leave in order to look after his wife who by then was very seriously ill. Sian was a lovely lady who had battled incredibly bravely against impossible odds and now needed Phil to be with her.

Jill Bowen was due to retire in a few years and so stuck with it. John Vince had made a major career move to join and could still benefit by staying on and learning more. Richard Green was in it for the long haul and gritted his teeth against the more nonsensical goings on. His being a voice of common sense in an increasing hubbub of incoherence.

Many outside my group also went within the next 12 months, including Jenny Dean and Steve Harding (who endured constant pressure from above, was taken ill and took retirement through poor health). Ex-colleagues I bumped into told me the I.T. department had badly deteriorated since my day there and I could consider myself well out of it.

Then I heard John Berney had been removed as Director of I.T. which after all that had happened was really no surprise to me. I was told it was down to 'failure to deliver' what was expected of him but anyone who constantly takes a very negative stance, trusts virtually nobody and says 'no' to almost everything will never produce much.

The 'trust' John needed within the department and found so difficult to give or obtain is a sensitive thing. I have likened it to a house of cards. It's difficult to build up but easy to undermine and send crashing down when people feel betrayed or let down. Without mutual trust a lot of things go out the window like loyalty, teamwork, credibility and productivity.

I feel somewhat guilty about criticising John who came through for me and let me leave on favourable terms but, as I did at work, I give my assessment based not on the rights and wrongs as they affected me personally but rather as they impacted my section and the I.T. department as a whole.

My own group had such a strong bond that, at the time of writing, 2 years later and the individual members scattered to the four winds, we have still met up for a reunion meal now and again. A team like that can move mountains and it served the Company well.

*   *   *

Despite the slightly sour end, I still look back on my career as one I hugely enjoyed. I may have spent it with a single company but over a long period of time I saw many manifestations of it. I was involved with Nationalisation, Privatisation, a merger, an acquisition and a total reorganisation of the energy sector. I served under a wide range of managerial personalities and styles and I experienced just about every major computer hardware and software supplier in the world.

Considering everything, I feel I made a worthwhile contribution to a very successful FTSE 100 company. I also met some very wonderful and talented people and as any manager worth his salt will tell you, a Company is only as good as its people, and I was privileged to work with some really good ones.

7.2   Madge's Career

Madge didn't have a career in the same sense I did. Rather she had a succession of jobs leading up to when she left work to have our first baby (Stephen). She was then very much occupied as a wife and mother for many years until she started to get some free time after our last child (Marie) started school.

She then got a job at the infant school Marie was attending, just to keep an eye on her. The involvement with schools expanded until she ended up with 4 concurrent school-based jobs. However, she gave all her jobs up when I retired so we could look after our grandchildren together but she then started getting involved again with the schools as she began to miss the social exchanges.

*   *   *

Madge had her first job at the age of 12 as a newspaper delivery girl working for Wrights Newsagents. The shop doesn't exist today but was located about half way down Arundel Street, close to the 'Hambledon House' block of flats where Madge lived with her parents at the time.

When she left school in 1968 at the age of 15 she was offered a job inside the Newsagent shop, behind the counter. Madge loved children and delighted in serving them their sweeties when they came into the shop and brandished their pocket money. She was also well up on the little dodges some would get up to, to purloin a few freebies and occasionally had to have a sharp word.

The shop was family owned and Madge felt as though she was part of the family, however that didn't stop them exploiting her. For very low wages she was expected to start at 07:00 and work until 18:00, from Monday to Saturday.

She stayed there until the end of 1970. She had become needlessly worried about a small cowpat called 'the change to decimal currency', not realising it actually made calculations easier to do. She also needed a job with better wages so she could save for the things girls of 17 think they need. This forced her hand, much to the disappointment of the shop proprietors.

Although, as said before, her teachers predicted she wouldn't amount to much, Madge had a steely determination to carve out some sort of niche rather than just hang around and wait for something to happen.

One day Madge's friend Christine, who you may recall from a previous Chapter was with Madge when I first met her, decided to go for a maid's job at a posh hotel on Southsea sea front. She asked Madge to go along with her for company and moral support. She was sitting in the waiting area when Christine was called in and interviewed and when she finally came out; Madge was astonished to be asked in for an interview as well.

Madge tried to explain she wasn't there for the job but the manager would have nothing to do with such trifles and interviewed her anyway. The upshot was Christine didn't get the position but it was offered to Madge. Christine was pretty peeved about it and it came down to a choice between the job and Christine's friendship. Madge turned down the job offer.

Shortly afterwards, when returning home one day from the 'Eye and Ear Hospital' in Southsea, Madge walked past the Guards factory on Fratton Bridge. She noticed an advertisement for workers and on the spur of the moment went in and applied.

She was taken on as a trouser presser. She had to operate a huge machine fitted with a large steam iron she had to wield. Steam was pumped to the iron through a hose running down from above and Madge frequently got her arms burned as they came in contact with the red-hot hose. If work ran low then she went onto sewing or button holing machines.

The other girl machinists were not much better off. They were all on 'piecework' and to make money worked at breakneck speed, such that 2 or 3 times a day a piercing scream could be heard. It meant a girl had mistimed the passage of the garment under the needle and had skewered herself.

The needles used to go right through fingers and the male supervisor had to carefully disentangle the girl, who might well be passing out by then, before taking her to the first aid room. Patched up, they usually just went back to work again. There was money needing to be earned and Health and Safety regulations in 1972 were not as they are today.

Unlike at the shop, there was little opportunity to chat amidst the frantic activity and the girls were not particularly friendly. Madge hated it there but couldn't afford to just walk out and of course there was precious little free time to look for another job anyway. She was still working there at the time of my famous meeting with her at the 'Mecca' dancehall.

Fate came to her rescue when the Company went bust. Now she was an experienced machinist Madge found it easy to find another similar job, which she did in the Cockerills plant at Southsea. The hours were the same, being 08:00 to 16:00 but she had further to travel, which she did by bicycle every day.

Madge remembers flashing her ring around her fellow workers there shortly after we became engaged in the summer of 1972. She often had lunch with Christine, who worked close by, the two of them cycling the short distance to Southsea where they sun bathed on the beach and ate their sandwiches.

Madge would have stayed at Cockerills had (in 1972) she not heard some of the middle managers from Guards, and a handful of the girls Madge got on well with, were planning to set up a new enterprise making men's clothes. It was called 'Clokes Menswear' and was located in Twyford Avenue near to where the Mountbatten Centre stands.

The new premises was little more than a large hut but had 2 floors. The machinists were upstairs and Madge worked downstairs on a pair of back-to-back Hoffman pressers. These were different from the ones at Guards and safer too. They were more like very large domestic trouser pressers.

Madge needed to lay out the trousers on one press, bring the top down and while they were 'cooking' lay out the trousers on the other press. Not many people had the speed and accuracy to work two presses together as she did and her skill was highly regarded. The only problem was the constant smoothing down of rough material played havoc with her hands and there was no way Madge would have been able to do the Fairy Liquid advert for 'soft hands'.

It was a small set-up, employing few people but Madge got on very well with all of them. There were only a few girl machinists, plus Bernie the cloth cutter, Ray the supervisor and Arthur who was in overall charge. Quite a few of them attended our wedding when Madge and I were married on 28th July 1973.

Madge remained there until she became pregnant with our first baby and finally left just before Christmas 1974 to prepare for the birth.

*   *   *

Over the following years Madge was fully occupied with raising our 6 children and doing the 1001 things housewives do. She finally started to get a little free time as Marie began playschool. She also had a reciprocal arrangement with 3 other mums to look after each other's children on different days. This effectively meant Madge got the mornings free while the other women looked after Marie and their own children and in the afternoons Madge took her turn to look after the kids. It suited all parties equally well and Madge was able to take a job as a 'supervisory assistant' at Crookhorn Junior School.

The only problem was one of the other women was Madge's sister-in-law Lyn who lived at Cosham and had no transport of her own. Madge had to do all the travelling about with the 2 kids on her adult tricycle. Incidentally, for those who might not know, the 'supervisory assistant' role entailed supervising the children out of class time both in the playground and the general school premises.

After 6 months of this arrangement, Marie finally started school at St Thomas More's School in Bedhampton and Madge left Crookhorn to be a dinner lady there. This meant she could keep an eye on Marie's well being from the kitchens. Madge liked the work but always seemed to get lumbered with the dogsbody duties such as cleaning out the huge ovens directly after lunch while they were still very hot. She often came home with burns and blisters on her wrists, hands and arms.

Financially back in 1991 we were struggling a bit. The children were growing rapidly and constantly had new and expensive needs, and we'd taken on the second mortgage for the 'other house'. Although I was paid well, I was not able to claim overtime pay for all the excess hours I worked, as I was told the more senior people like myself should be setting an example of unpaid working to the other ranks. I wasn't happy about this arrangement, but to refuse to work the hours would have meant I would simply be swamped by the workload so I had to carry on.

Madge bravely volunteered to take on a bit more work to earn extra cash. She didn't mind too much as all the time she was working with children, she was happy and she liked not having to depend on me for her 'spending money'. Like she said 'If it's my money then I don't feel guilty about spending it'.

So alongside the dinner lady job, Madge took on an early morning cleaning job at Oaklands School where our older children attended. A few months later, getting the bit between her teeth, Madge also volunteered for an evening cleaning session at the same school. After holding down this permutation of jobs for around 3 years, Madge went the whole hog and also became a supervisory assistant at Oaklands.

Cleaners are rarely recognised for the work they do and Madge used to work particularly hard, not stopping for a break. Most of the teachers and especially the Headmaster would look down their noses at her but after she eventually left and her high standards were not retained by her successors, she got stopped in the street by those very same teachers who bemoaned her absence.

The dinner ladies were only just above the cleaners in the school 'recognition' pecking order but woe betide the teacher who was rude to one of them. You sometimes hear stories about restaurants when a diner makes a complaint and sends his meal back and what happens to the replacement dish before it reappears before him. Well I can tell you such stories are absolutely true when it comes to dinner ladies and rude teachers and especially very rude head masters.

Let me just have a re-cap here for the benefit of my children who have sometimes said about Madge she was lucky doing all the part-time work because this meant she didn't have a 'real' job. This was Madge's normal daily timetable at the time and for several years, while I was working at Southern Electric.

05:15	Get up
06:00 - 08:00	Cleaner at Oaklands
08:15	Rush home and get kids to school
09:15 - 11:45	Walk dogs and do housework
11:50 - 13:00	Dinner lady at St Thomas More's school
13:00 - 13:10	Cycle the 2 miles to Oaklands school
13:10 - 14:10	Oaklands supervisory assistant
14:15	Home for more housework
16:00 – 18:00	Cleaner at Oaklands
18:15	Rush home to prepare dinner
20:00	Bed

I would be leaving for work just as she got home at 08:15 and getting back home again around 19:15. The load was eased when the Oaklands headmaster started to get the teachers to carry out the supervisory duties out of lesson times. This was not a good idea, however, because firstly the teachers had to be paid more than people like Madge to do the job and secondly the teachers were subject to a very strict code when it came to dealing with pupils. Their hands were very much tied, whereas Madge was able to bend the rules slightly.

For example, the boys in the 4th year upwards were frequently strapping 6 footers but cowed in terror if they did anything wrong and Madge found them out. They got subjected to Madge's 'let's tidy you up routine' which basically meant brushing them down and straightening their ties. I couldn't possibly say any more than this for fear of litigation, but believe me you would not want to be on the end of one of Madge's 'tidy up' sessions. Suffice to say nobody got seriously hurt and the local gangs held Madge in very high esteem.

As grandchildren started to appear, Madge started to get roped in more and more to look after Chloe, in particular, but the others too on occasion. There was no way Madge could hold down all of her jobs and also spare the time to devote to the grandchildren.

The 'supervisory assistant' job had already gone and the dinner lady job was the next to go. Then the big change came when I retired and within a few weeks Madge underwent a hysterectomy operation. She was clearly unable to do the cleaning jobs after such major surgery and I persuaded her to give up her remaining jobs and join me in retirement.

At first she welcomed this. The operation had really knocked the stuffing out of her and she needed many months to fully recover. Plus she liked the additional time she could spend with the grandchildren. Emma was back to work full time and the more we were able to help, the easier things were for Emma.

The problem was neither Madge nor I were as young as we were the first time around and we found looking after the grandchildren very onerous and quite exhausting. Also, after the first year or so of retirement, I had to start tightening the purse strings. We simply hadn't adjusted sufficiently to the new income level of my pension, which was less than half of my salary when working.

I was very reluctant to start up a new job and re-introduce a level of stress into my life, having striven so hard to remove it. Everyone said how much better I looked since giving up work and I wanted things to stay that way. However Madge was missing the social side of working with all her friends and volunteered to earn some pin money by getting a part-time job. It meant with Madge tied up I would have to bear the brunt of the grandchildren for at least part of the day but for me this was still preferable to a 'real job'.

Madge contacted St Thomas More's School and was put on their rota as the 'relief' dinner lady when someone went sick, which happened on average about 1 day a fortnight. This wasn't enough to provide her with a decent and consistent level of pocket money and so after casting about Madge applied for a position as a School Crossing Attendant or 'Lollipop Lady'. They said they'd let her know when a vacancy arose but she heard nothing for months, despite rumours they were desperate for such workers in the area.

Slightly disillusioned, Madge applied for a 'School Escorts' job. This meant travelling to and from schools in a taxi, escorting to school those children who had some sort of physical or behavioural difficulty. Madge attended an induction day at Hampshire County Council offices in Winchester and then waited to hear if she had been accepted.

During this time I had to have a quiet word in her ear when she ran around telling her friends she was going to become an 'escort' for some extra money and then wondered why her words were met with a stunned silence.

Several weeks went by and lo and behold she was offered a job as a School Crossing Attendant. It was about half a mile away in a rather rough area, extremely busy with traffic. Still she was prepared to give it a go. A week after starting her new job she was offered her first assignment as a school escort! The day after she was told one of the dinner ladies had resigned and she was in line for a permanent lunchtime role at St Thomas More's. Suddenly from no job at all, she was being inundated with them.

There was a sting in the tail however with the lunchtime job. A new headmistress decided to have a clear out and redefined all the positions, leading to existing staff having to re-apply for similar jobs to those they were already doing. Several of them were not successful and Madge was having kittens before her appointment to the dinner hall (where she could keep an eye on our grandchildren) was finally confirmed.

Madge is at her happiest when kept busy and if these jobs give her some money to buy whatever she wants then even better. It certainly eases the finances a bit. The grandchildren are another matter but Emma is talking about going part-time, or even giving up work altogether, in order to be with Lewis and so on that basis, and with a bit of luck, we might be able to handle the reduced load asked of us.

The only thing that has suffered since my retirement is what we have always suffered over the years, myself and Madge not having enough time together; relaxing and taking holidays in sun drenched and romantic locations. It used to be because of my work but now, at the time of writing, between the children, grandchildren and dogs, I just don't see any let up in the demands being made of us. We'll just have to settle for being buried in the same plot I suppose, with a joint gravestone inscribed 'Alone Together at Last – and about bloody time'.

Having just referred to the next 2 generations, let's move on and take a closer look at the individuals concerned.

Top left: At the Tower of London. Left, Madge feeding baby Alan, Richard and Emma messing around, Mike asleep in the buggy and Stephen looking bored (1983).

Above: Posing with the guard (he's real, honest). Me with Stephen (lining up for a free kick), Emma, Mike and Richard. I assume baby Alan took the picture, as I wouldn't have a head if Madge took it.

Left: An informal shot of all of us together when Mike did his first Holy Communion at St Joseph's Church, Havant. (1989).

Left: Next to Lord Nelson's flagship, HMS Victory in Portsmouth Naval Dockyard. Madge with our boys, Alan, Stephen, Richard and Mike. Just before they got arrested for damaging an antique cannon. (1990).

Our kids posing in groups.

Top left:
The first 3. Stephen Emma and Richard.

Top Right:
The second 3. Alan, Marie and Mike.

Centre left:
Stephen, Emma, Richard and Mike in 'Bohemian Rhapsody' pose (1981). (This picture got into the SEB staff magazine).

re right: Alan, Richard, Stephen and Mike acting as tough guys (2003).

m: My boys going out on Mike's 21st birthday celebrations with some friends. Stephen as Superman, Alan as naman, Mike as Batman and Richard hiding inside a Darth Vader costume. Friends include Ian as The er and someone who thinks that sticking a can of lager up his nose is costume enough.

217

Our kids having fun. Clockwise from bottom left.

Stephen, Emma and Richard on a motorbike (1985);
Mike with Emma crawling out of the real igloo we
built in the winter of 1986 with its heavy snows;
Emma's 6th birthday party with Richard and Steph
Pontin's holiday, with cousins Sammy and Susie,
Stephen, Emma and Richard (1984);
Dressing as clowns at Butlin's, Minehead. Alan,
Richard, Mike and Emma (1987);
Mike, Marie and Alan in American Football huddle
Emma with baby sister Marie. (1986)

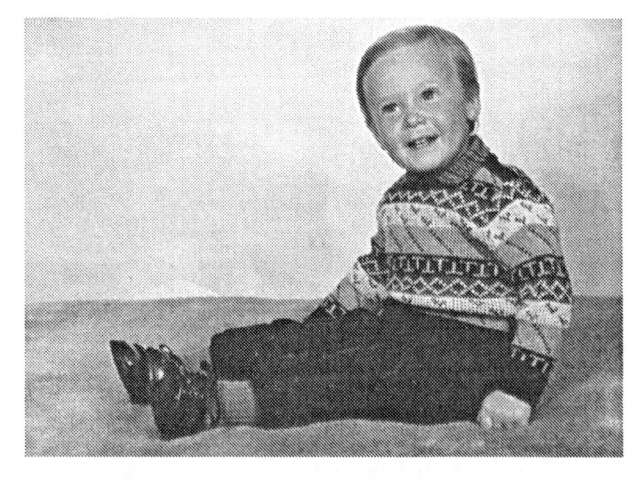

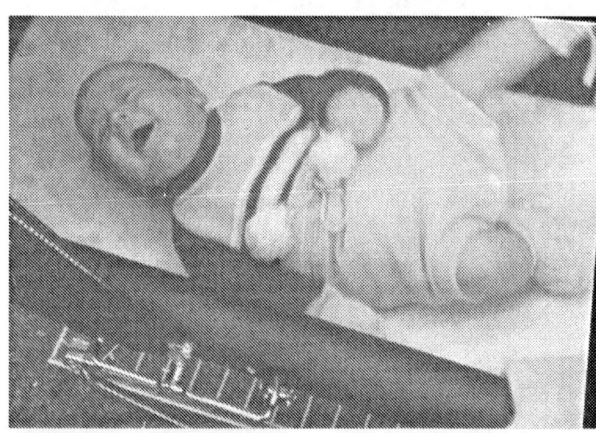

Views of Stephen.
Clockwise from the bottom.

On holiday with mates (1992);
As a 'Mr Man' at Pontin's Holidays (1983);
At Junior school (1971);
Smart little lad (1976);
Had a sense of humour since a baby (1975);
Growing up (1986);
Partying at secondary school (1991).

219

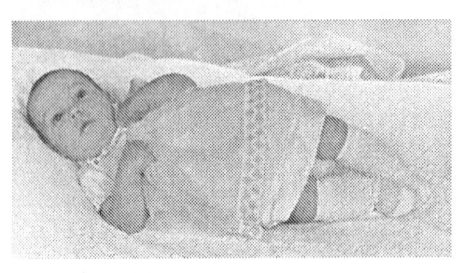

Views of Emma.

Top row: As a baby (1977); A Christmas Fairy (1979); as Noddy at the Pontin's fancy dress competition (1982)

Middle row: A 'chubber', around the time that she swallowed the penny and was rushed to Q.A. (1978); a little madam growing up fast (1980).

Bottom row: From the left. A lady regrets asking Emma what 'Table-D'Hote' means at the Company party (20 Emma having fun (1994); Emma at her marriage to Wayne (2002).

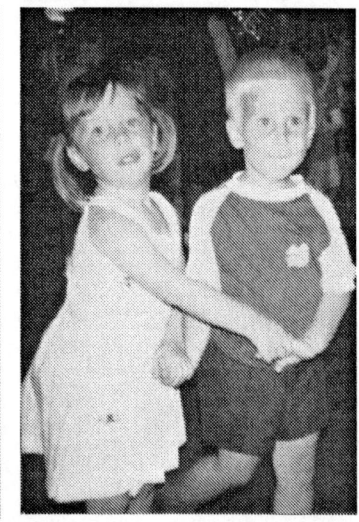

Views of Richard.
Clockwise from top left.

As a baby with Madge (1979).

Cute blond toddler (1980).

Dancing with cousin Susie at Pontins (1985).

At senior school.

After joining IBM.

With daughter Lauren (2003).

After receiving a First Class Honours Degree from the University Chancellor and Portsmouth Lord Mayor.

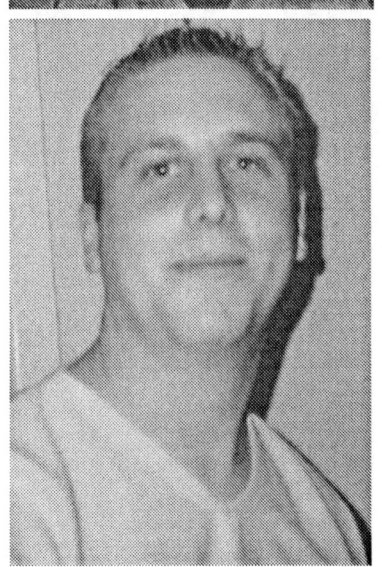

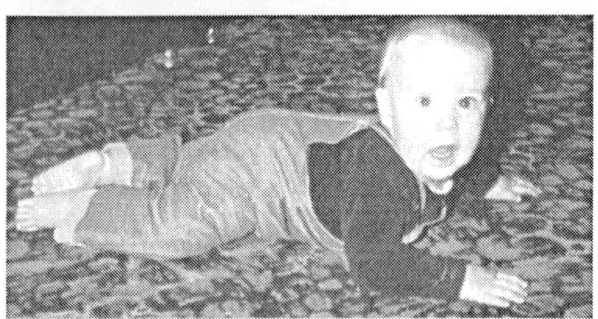

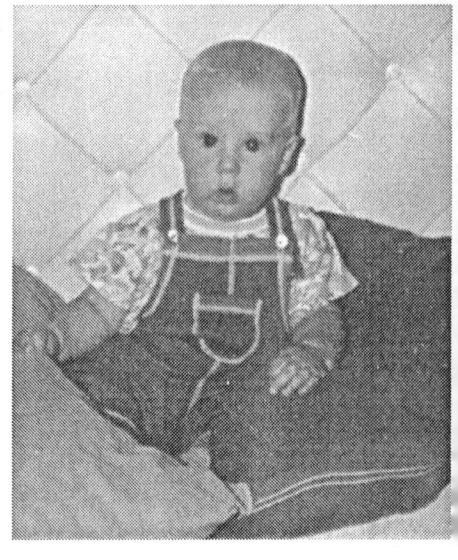

Views of Mike. Anti-clockwise from top right.

Looking a bit stunned to be here (1981);

Cheering up a bit (1981);

Nice snapshot of a caring brother with Marie;

The real Mike practicing his fierce look for American footb

Mike grown up and looking for mischief;

Holiday picture in Greece where he first met Cheryl. Now they are engaged to be married and live together.

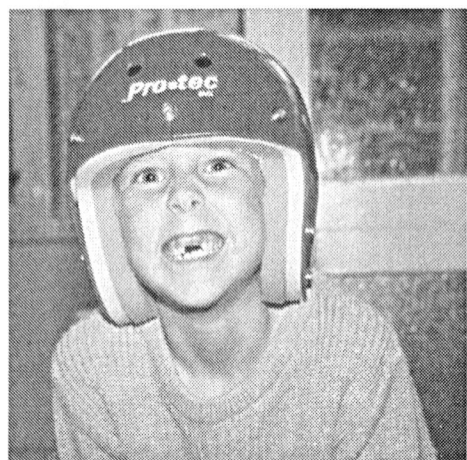

222

Views of Alan.

Top row: As a baby with Madge (1983); Almost ready for junior school (1987); with a clinging friend (1991).

Middle row: Typical happy smiling face. (I wonder what he's just broken or spilt?) (1985).

Bottom Row: At 'Village Holidays' stables. (c. 1996);
A serious lad starting secondary school. (1994);
Impish and sticky (1985);
Getting into computers at a young age (1986).

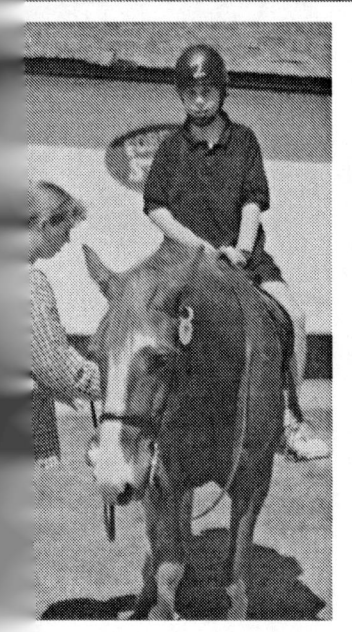

223

Views of Marie.
Clockwise from bottom left.

Emma's bridesmaid (2002);
Pony riding at Oakdene;

Little Miss glamorous (1989);
Rudie nudie (1986);

What's this water stuff? (1988);
Practicing her skateboarding;

Miss Punk (1990);
Hot stuff. Growing up (2003).

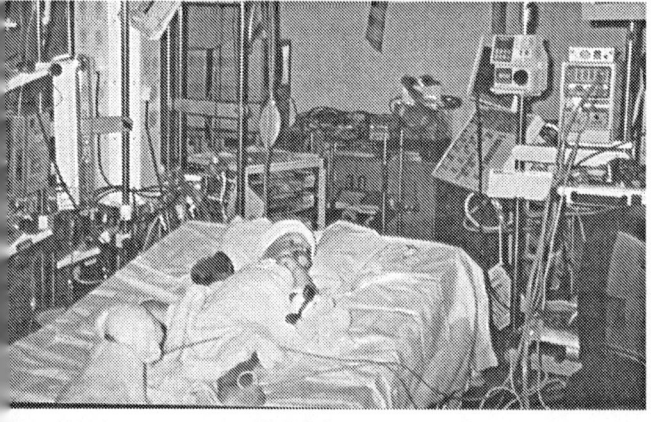

...vs of the Grandchildren.

... Lewis battling in 'Intensive Care' after his brain tumour operation (2002) and later in his Pompey kit.

...tre: More of Lewis, coping amazingly well with adversity and Chloe being photogenic (2001/2).

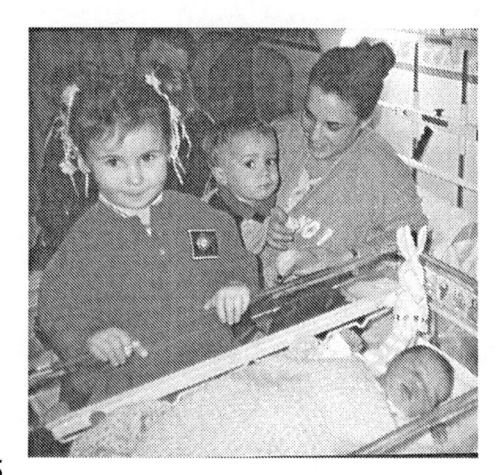

...w: More Emma and her children, Chloe, Lewis and baby Jessica.

225

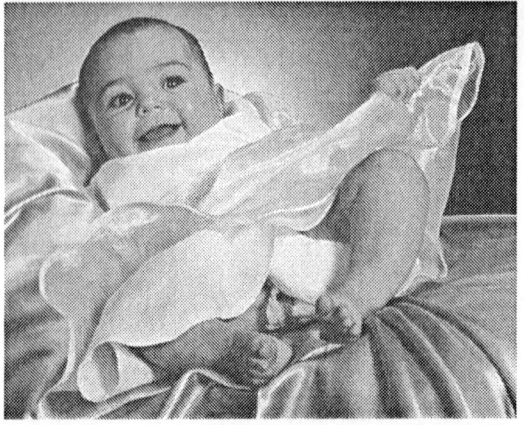

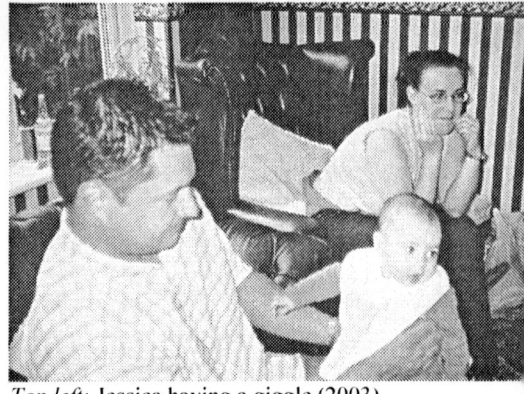

Top left: Jessica having a giggle (2003).

Top right: Jessica with mum and dad (Emma and Wayne).

Left: Chloe and Lauren – butter wouldn't melt (2000).

Right: Lauren as a picture of innocence (2001).

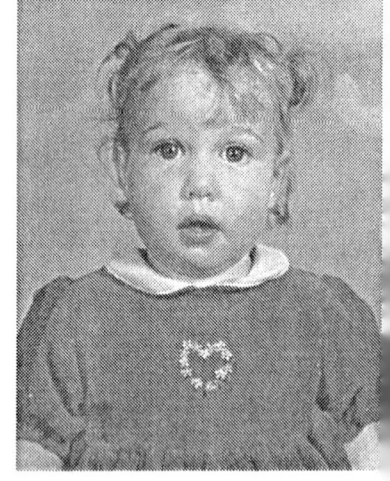

Bottom left and centre: Lauren again. A little girl full of fun (2003).

Bottom right: Lauren with mum and dad (Sharon and Richard - 2003)

Above and left: Views of Fred, the manic rabbit that I was brought up with in my parents house in Daulston Road. Managing to lose a race with Jerry the tortoise; eating my mum's best rose bushes; dancing around with a piece of paper. (c 1961).

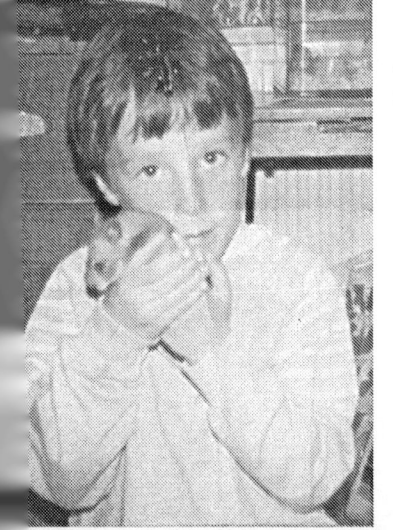

Centre left: Mike with his golden hamster, Bertha. (1985). No he's not about to do a 'Freddy Starr' and eat it.

Bottom left: Popular 'babbits' Dolly and Fudge (2000)

Bottom right: Mike with Tyson the Bosc Monitor lizard standing next to the vivariums that he built.

227

Dogs with the family.

Top left: Mike with Tasha (1994).

Top right: Marie with Daisy (1996).

Centre left: Granddaughter Chloe sweet talking Daisy to no effect (2000).

Centre right: Me with Tasha (1994).

Bottom left: Marie with a boisterous Monty. (c. 1997).

Bottom right: Madge with Monty. He was very much her 'baby' (1994).

Westies galore.

Top 3 pictures: Left to right: As puppies. Tasha (1994), Daisy (1996) and Monty (1993).

Second row: From the left. Tasha, Daisy and Monty on leads in the park. 2003.

d row left: Monty with Tasha as a puppy (1994) bigger but she is definitely in charge. (What do mean, just like me and Madge?)

d row right: Tasha, keeping an eye on things.

m right: Monty celebrating Christmas 1996. opped up onto the chair when it's occupant ed it, hoping that he might get served a turkey . I seem to remember that he did, but just the lass of wine.

Above: My parent's house in Daulston Road in Portsmouth where I was raised. (1947-73). You can just make me out standing by the gate.

Above: The notorious house in Chichester Road, Portsmouth where Madge and I set up our first home (1972-78). Actually, it doesn't look too bad from the outside. Stephen is perched on the wall.

Left: Our home in The Keep, Portchester (1978-8 Parked outside is the green Lada that served us s well.

Below: Our home in Hulbert Road, Havant (198: Present). Pictured shortly after we moved in.

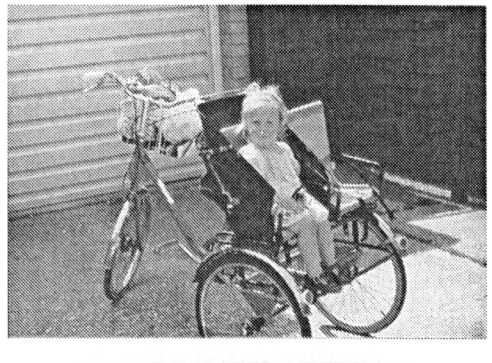

Top left: Madge stands proudly beside her first 'real' motorcycle, a Suzuki RSX100 which she passed her test on. Notice the 2 caravans on the drive in the background. These were the days when we went on holiday in a convoy.

right: The famous adult tricycle, with Marie in a makeshift rain-cover arrangement. (1988).

tre left: Madge on her biggest ever motorcycle, the Suzuki GSX600, which had 6 times the cc of the RSX100 hine above. It went like lightening and offered seating with a commode as an optional extra. (1996).
tre right: Madge on the original Honda Melody that started all the trouble with motorcycles.

om left: Marie gets ready for her school-leaving Prom. Now which car to travel to it in? (2002).
om right: Madge washes the Datsun Bluebird but there's not much room on the washing line to hang it out.

Chapter 8

Offspring

Although I have mentioned our children and our grandchildren in various places in this book, I thought it appropriate to have a section that could be sub-divided and dedicated to each one in turn.

With apologies for omissions to those grandchildren, great grandchildren and beyond, not yet born at the date of writing. To those I say 'Hello, I'm sure you're a credit to our family and I hope you read a few Chapters of this book to find out about your (Great....Great) Nanny and Grandad who both send their love to you across the years.' School age readers might even find a few snippets in this book they can lift for their homework projects. (e.g. 'How **not** to raise a family ....')

Incidentally, I would like to explain why we are 'Nanny and Grandad' and not 'Nanny and Poppy' as my paternal grandparents were or 'Grandma and Grandad' as were my maternal grandparents.

It's quite simple; Madge had strong feelings about wanting to be a 'Nanny'. Something about the word being associated with the bringing up of children, I believe. I concurred with this, as the thought of my sleeping with a 'Nanny' seemed somehow preferable to sleeping with a 'Grandma'.

I had assumed Madge's title automatically landed me with being a 'Poppy' but Madge didn't like the term and thought 'Grandad' had a more cuddly sound and given my growing girth seemed to suit me better anyway.

Going back for a moment to the time we were parents and before we were grandparents, I thought I would include some words of wisdom about what I learned from achieving that particular status. So, with my tongue planted firmly in my cheek, here are a few truths and guidelines.

A father needs to be expert in many other professions other than his main job. e.g.

- Taxi driver (when the kids don't have a car),
- Garage mechanic (when they do have a car),
- Toolshop owner (when they work on the car themselves. But don't expect to ever see the tools again, or if you do they will be all rusted up).
- General fixer (when they damage the car, break something important etc),
- Custodian of the money tree in garden / Moneylender (and don't expect any repayments),
- Form filler inner (and don't they always need it completed urgently after they've been sitting on it for the last 3 weeks),
- Telephone service provider (all calls are free of course).

A father is someone who carries children's pictures where his money used to be.

A father needs to be aware the easiest way to find something the kid's have lost around the house is to buy a replacement. The original item is then found about 5 minutes later.

A father must not be surprised if anything his child succeeds with is entirely down to his or her own hard work; but anything they fail with is always dad's fault.

A father should be aware insanity runs in families; you get it from your kids.

So, having been forewarned, lets take a look at the offspring.

8.1 The Children

Stephen:
I know every parent is biased towards his/her own offspring and the first-born is especially favoured and I have to say Stephen really was a beautiful baby. Unfortunately as an infant he was very unsettled and Madge and I spent many sleepless nights with him. I recall walking up and down the bedroom with him in my arms in the middle of the night, for what seemed like hours on end. Probably because it **was** hours on end.

Stephen was a very bright toddler and a very mature and responsible young lad. Evidence his heroic actions at the age of 7 the night Alan was born (described in an earlier Chapter) and the occasions I witnessed him holding conversations with adults on financial matters, such as mortgages, at the age of 12. He also did Richard a big favour when Richard was a toddler and choking on a sweet with Madge out of the room; it was Stephen who whacked him on the back and dislodged the obstruction.

However I cannot pretend things didn't go wrong for Stephen. Like Madge, Stephen turned out to be dyslexic but we didn't realise this when he was young, up to the point he was formally tested at the age of 8. In the meantime he became frustrated by his inability to learn certain things because of his dyslexia and this manifested itself in what was interpreted as him having 'learning and behavioural difficulties.'

We hoped educating Stephen at a small private school in Portchester when he was 6 years old would give him more of the individual attention he needed. We couldn't really afford the fees but we were desperate to help him develop. However the extra attention didn't seem to improve things for him very much.

When we moved to Havant, Stephen was just 11 years of age and went to Oakland's school. Unfortunately he still seemed to have difficulties and so we accepted an offer from the Social Services to send him to a boarding school called 'Brickwall House School', specialising in teaching boys like Stephen, with dyslexia and personal difficulties.

Madge was very reluctant to send him away (it was almost 100 miles away from us) to a location near Hastings in Sussex but after discussions with the experts we concluded it was in Stephen's best interests. The placing was subsidised but we had to pay a certain amount of fees and provide him with spending money.

Madge insisted we bring him home for a weekend stay every two or three weeks so he didn't feel too isolated from us. I made the almost 200 mile round trip on the Friday evening and again when I returned him back on the Sunday evening, dozens of times in my trusty Datsun Bluebird Estate. The distance involved was also the root cause of our getting into caravanning when Madge decided that occasionally we should visit him rather than the other way around.

Stephen actually did quite well out of this arrangement academically and it arrested his decline down the slippery slope of dyslexia. So now, in adulthood, it scarcely holds him back at all. However, emotionally it did him no favours. He did feel rather abandoned by his family and despite making a few friendships, was not really happy there. He has always shared Madge's over active imagination the worst will always happen, if not actually in the process of happening at the time. Also being a rather shy and timid lad he got picked on to some extent by some of the other boys.

At home during one of his 'exeunts' Stephen started some home brewing, making a gallon jar of ginger beer. When it matured he poured it out into bottles and some of the liquid spilled onto the dining room table. As we looked at it fizzing away, the shiny table surface started to disappear. We decided if it could do that to a table then pity our stomach linings. It was a toss up between pouring the drink away and trying to sell it to a paint stripping company.

At the end of his stay at Brickwall, Stephen left with some good qualifications and also walked off with a trophy at his very last end of term ceremony, presented for excellence in spoken English.

Stephen then attended Southdowns College to gain even more diplomas and qualifications and then through the YTS training scheme secured a job as a trainee 'Microwave Oven Engineer' with a small company. Although he enjoyed the work and learned a good deal, the pay there was frugal and in time he decided to leave and get himself a job with more money.

Back home there was some friction within the family. They say 'opposites attract' which by implication means 'alikes repel'. In Stephen's case he was so similar to Madge in many respects they simply didn't get on. Madge's attempts to help him were seen as 'interference' and trying to deny him control of his own life as he grew up.

After some fill-in, bitty jobs, Stephen then secured a position as an electrician, wiring up large commercial refrigerators in a production factory. At last this gave him a good deal of self-respect and much better pay and for a couple of years he was happy.

The only problem was one particular moronic individual working there who for some reason picked on Stephen and made his life a misery; among other things cutting Stephen with a penknife and announcing he had given him 'AIDS'. Such things not surprisingly played on Stephen's mind and his keeping it all bottled up and not telling anyone magnified the effect.

Matters finally exploded one day at our house when Stephen was visiting Madge, with Emma also present with her children. I was at a lunchtime 'farewell do' for one of my ex-work colleagues and received a hysterical call on my mobile to get home urgently.

I won't go into further details but it took Stephen around 6 months to fully recover from the situation that had built up. During this time he returned home and Madge looked after him with the love and dedication only a true 'mum' can provide.

Unfortunately, just as he became fully fit again and able to resume his job, the Company he worked for went into liquidation and the workers, including Stephen, were made redundant. Stephen made do with a couple of shelf-stacking jobs at local supermarkets while he was waiting for a skilled position to come up.

Fortunately, about that time, Rolls Royce started recruiting for a new assembly plant near Chichester about 14 miles away, with a fast dual carriageway as the connecting route from Havant. Stephen applied and after a rigorous selection process and to his great credit, managed to secure a job there.

Stephen has had only a few girlfriends but has an active social life including playing 10-pin bowling, at which he performs very well.

He also followed Madge into motorcycles, although unlike her he became proficient in their maintenance. He is into tropical fish keeping but came a bit unstuck when he branched out into buying piranhas. ('Where's the other fish gone?'). He is also an avid computer boffin, loving to do his own PC upgrades and playing about with the technology.

Firstborns always bear the brunt of breaking new ground for the other children in the family. They are also the ones the parents make the mistakes with that get corrected with the others. As such Stephen has had a bit of a rough deal and under the circumstances has done very well. I'm pleased to say he has put his difficult past well behind him now and is looking forward to a far more rosy future. He not only has a good job but also at the time of writing is buying himself a flat, being his first step onto the property ladder.

We were somewhat relieved when our next baby was a girl and initially Emma was an ideal baby. However she soon proved she was to be the drama queen of the family and seemed fated to move from one crisis to the next. As such, of course, she has become queen of the cowpats.

* * *

Emma:
I wasn't at Emma's birth as I was looking after Stephen but I was there soon afterwards. She was a very pretty baby. The thing that most struck me about her was the long, curly eyelashes and mass of dark hair.

As she grew up she turned out to be much quieter than Stephen had been at a similar age, much to our relief. However this didn't stop her, as a toddler, occasionally feeling sorry for herself and coming out with the immortal line – 'Nobody loves me' while sobbing dramatically.

Emma always seemed to be accident and incident prone from an early age. We had the famous occasion at the age of 16 months when she swallowed a coin described in an earlier Chapter but that was my fault for giving it to her. When she was 2 years old she fell off the end of a slide in a children's playground and caught the back of her head, needing stitches. At the age of 3 she grabbed a bottle of liquid plant fertiliser and got a swig from it before being stopped. (Fortunately the hospital said it would do her no harm and some wag even suggested it might even give her a growth spurt).

Stephen added to her list of incidents, as elder brothers tend to do with younger sisters. He pulled a bookcase down onto her at the age of 7 and later burned her with an iron when Madge turned her back for a second. She wasn't even safe going on school trips. She came back from a day trip to France with the school needing head stitches, following an incident on the cross channel ferry.

Emma was always very confident, even from an early age. I recall once when we were on holiday in a static caravan, on a site having a large entertainment complex, Emma went missing. She was 11 years old at the time. I eventually found her on the stage in the main hall, clasping a microphone and singing. She'd entered herself in the talent contest and was being auditioned.

Emma was schooled at St Thomas More's primary and Oakland's secondary, which set the pattern for the rest of the family. Her exam results did not do her justice as she discovered boys and started to pursue an extensive social life just at a critical time in relation to her studies.

However, she was very proud when she wrote a letter to the Queen and a few weeks later actually got a reply 'Her Majesty has commanded I write to you on her behalf and ……..'.

Emma did the usual teenage rebellion bit but at the age of 17 there was an older man lurking to take advantage of her naïve and impressionable state. He was a 'bouncer' named Alec. They lived together for a time, during which he was seen with other women. By the time he left her, he had a posh car and lots of other nice things, with the accounts for them in Emma's name, saddling her with thousands of pounds worth of debts she couldn't pay.

Credit companies are only too willing to lend money at the drop of a hat to inexperienced youngsters but they are pretty ruthless when it comes to getting it back again; Emma was out of her depth and dragging her own and the family name down with her. Unfortunately Madge and I were not aware of the situation and even when we got an inkling, Emma would not at the time let us in on the scale of her problem.

Her financial worries were compounded by illness over the next couple of years and stress may well have contributed. A test for epilepsy, following fainting fits was merely a prelude to a far more serious condition when she was diagnosed as having cancer.

Fortunately this was treatable by laser surgery and Emma was declared 'clear' although she still has annual checks up to the time of writing.

She secured a job at my Company, Southern Electric in 1996 at the Portsmouth Call Centre, where she worked on the telephones as a Customer Advisor. She then became a trainer and her undoubted talent was recognised by a promotion to a management position in 1998. She moved to the Havant I.T. centre in 2001, shortly after I retired but then the severe illness of her son Lewis, followed closely by the birth of daughter Jessica has put her career on hold for the time being.

Her life had taken a new turn when in 1998 at the age of 21 she met Wayne Hine. He was a tall, good-looking bloke a few years older than her. He worked at the local Water Company and was also a semi-professional footballer. Nine months after they met, Chloe was born (see later). They bought a 2-bedroom house in Leigh Park, however this proved to be too small by the time Lewis (again see later) was born in 2001.

Wayne and Emma were married in April 2002 and moved into a new house shortly afterwards. The massive leap in house prices, together with Emma's pay rises accompanying her increases in responsibility, meant not only could she and Wayne afford a much larger mortgage, but the proceeds from the sale of the old house enabled her to finally clear her financial debts.

Emma has experienced more dramatic episodes and endured more stress during her first 26 years (at the time of writing) on this planet than most people experience in a lifetime and she deserves all the sympathy and assistance she can get.

After all the dramas that went with Emma, it was a relief to get a smoother ride with our next child, Richard.

*   *   *

Richard:
Madge was pregnant with Richard when we moved from Chichester Road to The Keep. His birth was uneventful and he proved to be an amazingly quiet little boy who was relatively well behaved.

He had a shock of blond hair that very gradually darkened over time and was devoted to his little blue teddy bear and his 'bot bot', which was a bottle of milk almost permanently clenched between his teeth.

His favourite television programmes were 'The A Team' and ChiPs'. I well remember when he was a toddler his favourite occupation was zipping about astride his A-Team van, pushing like mad with his little legs. He was a 'daddy's boy' and liked me to carry him about.

Richard grew up to be particularly hard working and studious at school, obtaining a very good set of qualifications. He even had a poem accepted for publication in a children's book of poems, called 'Squat

Diddley' but we were never able to get hold of a copy of it.

On the run up to his 'A' level examinations, Richard applied for a Graduate Training course with IBM. The Company then took about 20 of the most promising students a year from the length and breadth of the country and subsidised them through University, mixing their studies up with practical experience. At the end of it, then suitably qualified, students obtain a position within IBM with excellent career prospects.

Madge and I took Richard up to the IBM buildings in Southbank, London for his preliminary assessment and interview, while we had a day out in the Capital. This was followed by further stages in the selection process and at the end of it Richard was offered a place, depending on his 'A' level results. We need not have worried. He produced 4 grade-A's in his 4 subjects and joined IBM's scheme.

Richard progressed his studies and at the end of 3 years came away with a 1st Class Honours Degree. Madge and I were ecstatic and we attended his special IBM presentation ceremony, attended by the University Chancellor and Lord Mayor as well as my own dad Percy and sister Frances.

Richard was also one of the more 'sporty' members of the family. He represented his school in Rugby and Tennis and has been a keen footballer up to the present day, taking part in tournaments with his mates. He has also supported Portsmouth Football Club since he was small and was rewarded by seeing them win the Division I Championship in 2002/3.

In his spare time Richard developed an interest in motorcycles, following on from Madge and Stephen. However he was more gregarious than Stephen and collected a wide circle of friends.

His girlfriend, Sharon Burgess, had actually been at school with Richard, in the same year but not in the same class. At the time they scarcely knew each other but were introduced by mutual friends at a nightclub and from there started to go out as an 'item'. Although they were living together, as such things happen, a baby came along somewhat unexpectedly. She was a beautiful little girl, with a shock of golden curls, whom they named Lauren.

Richard selected an initial role within IBM and went to work at their offices in Hursley where he remains up to the time of writing, as a Software Engineer.

Richard was a hard act to follow at least academically and Mike, as it turned out couldn't have been more different in just about every respect.

*   *   *

Michael:
Mike was the biggest of all our babies at birth, being a fraction over 8 pounds in weight and was later dubbed 'The Hulk' because of it. He'd already had one close shave in making it into this world when Madge had started bleeding following an over enthusiastic examination by a midwife during her 3 month check. Then he contracted the serious condition of bronchiolitis at the age of 4 months and for a short while it was touch and go for him. It was just before he was due to be christened and we actually got the hospital visiting priest to baptise him, just in case.

After he recovered, Mike went from strength to strength and was to become the tallest of the kids, although this distinction is currently being challenged by both Richard and Alan. Mike was always the black sheep of the family, being the one who would take on the 'dares' of his schoolmates with frightening frequency and some pretty hair raising outcomes.

He was also the family entrepreneur, daredevil and entertainer, taking it upon himself at a very early age to pester people at bus stops for 'penny for the guy mister' after nicking his mums and brothers' clothes out of their wardrobes to dress his 'guy'. He also persuaded us to let him do a Car Boot sale at the age of 11 where he manned a stall by himself and sold old his old bits and pieces and if the truth be told, probably a few family heirlooms as well.

Mike's schooling was always a bit fraught. After the problems with Stephen, Madge and I were relieved to have Emma and Richard sail through their early years academically but on one school 'open day' we went to inspect Mike's work and after being shocked at what we saw, I ended up having a major row with the headmaster for not advising us on the poor standard of Mike's work.

We were terrified Mike would have similar learning difficulties to Stephen and after we saw early signs of it Madge and I pulled out all the stops. Fortunately it turned out to be just a blip and after that the only reason for Mike's work suffering in secondary school was because he was a lazy monkey always looking for a wheeze to escape doing anything.

Mike's extra curricular activities were something else. When he was 17 and was learning to ride his DT50 motorcycle, Madge would let him ride it to school for practice. Unfortunately the school rules only permitted 6th form students to ride such vehicles and so Madge told him to hide the bike when he got to school and keep a low profile about it. When she went subsequently went to check on him (she was at the school as a supervisory assistant at the time) she found him doing 'wheelies' in the school car park. So much for keeping a low profile.

When the kids had races at break time, pushing shopping trolleys around the grounds, Mike was the one who just had to be in the trolley. He was also the one who had his hair all shaved off for a sponsored prank but neglected to mention to the donors the money would be used to acquire under-age alcohol for himself.

There were also a number of 'incidents' at school when Mike was attending there and caused the teachers to complain there was a large gang of students operating in a disruptive manner.

Things like poking old pieces of egg and fish into a hole in the wall so a rotting smell wafted round the cavities and into the classrooms and giving an ideal excuse to abandon lessons. Like the large number of missing homework books (of which Mike claimed to be one) so work couldn't be marked. Like the missing attendance register that would have indicated Mike's absence from school was bad enough to merit a note to his parents. And finally, like the entire set of school wall clocks that went missing on the last day of school before the summer holiday and led to the annual ritual of the caretaker removing all such clocks when the anniversary came around again.

If anyone from the school is reading this then I am implying no connection whatever with my son and would point out he was never blamed for any misdeed while at school, save for being accused of forging his parent's signature in his homework diary, that turned out to be Madge's genuine handiwork. I am only saying when Mike was about, things tended to happen. I think, like his parents, he has a strong connection with cowpats. I would also say Mike is pretty good at finding things some time later that have gone missing; and you can always tell the time in our house.

Apart from the homework signature, I believe the only other occasion Mike has been wrongfully accused is when he was detained by the police for being in possession of a threatening haircut. He was out with his work colleagues for a drink down the Guildhall Walk when police stopped him because of his somewhat aggressive appearance (he looked like a 'skinhead' even though he wasn't).

A 'sniffer' dog drew attention to him and he was hauled unceremoniously back to the police station where a strip search revealed a suspicious silver chewing gum wrapper, screwed up and obviously containing something. After carefully photographing the 'evidence' they opened the wrapper to reveal.... chewing gum. Mike fell about laughing at the whole thing but still wrote a stinking letter of complaint to the Chief Constable. Good for him!

There are other anecdotes concerning Mike from both his school days and afterwards (I could mention clues like 'bishop', 'milk float', 'orthodontist' and 'garden hopping' and I'm sure there are other happenings that haven't seen the light of day) but these tales are best left untold in this book. Such things are usually down to a combination of high spirits and alcohol in teenagers but no malice or criminal intent was ever present.

Mike is also fairly well travelled for one so young. When just 14, he was invited by his friend, who had a wealthy father, to be his companion for a 2-week holiday in Antigua. He also made shopping trips with his mates to Spain on the boat from Portsmouth when just 16 and a holiday, again with his mates, to Ibiza when 17.

He still won't let Madge and I see his holiday photos but the rumours are they are quite spectacular and one or two actually got pinned up on the notice board at his place of work. Certainly Mike has become a bit of a legend at work in the few years he has been there and is very well liked, especially by droves of young females.

Holidays abroad can be very educational and we always encouraged Mike to learn a few useful local phrases before he went. Like the Greek for 'excuse me officer but are these handcuffs really necessary?' or 'I'm sorry sir, I'll clean it up if you bring me a mop and bucket'.

It was on a holiday to Greece in 2002 he met Cheryl Cade and the pair clicked. On their return they spent every weekend they could in each other's company, made particularly difficult by he living near Portsmouth and she in Manchester, 250 miles away. Eventually Cheryl moved down south to live with Mike and at the time of writing they have just got engaged and Mike has also calmed down ..... well just a bit perhaps.

When Mike left school he got a job at the Southern Electric Call

Centre as a Customer Advisor on the phones, just as Emma had done before him. He progressed from there and has held down a number of roles on the 'complaints' and 'training' side. He recently landed his first 'manager' job, based at the Company's Basingstoke offices. Since joining Mike 'down South', Cheryl has got herself a job (guess where) at the Southern Electric Call Centre at Portsmouth.

So, having blazed a bit of a trail, how did Mike's activities impact and influence his younger brother Alan?

*   *   *

Alan:
Alan of course had that amazing start in life described in an earlier Chapter when he was born at home on the floor. He was always seen as another 'Richard' in his boyhood as he closely resembled him facially. He was also very quiet and shy and although he had the intellectual ability, he didn't (at least at first) have Richard's level of commitment and enthusiasm.

Alan was popular with his schoolmates in the infants and juniors but due to his diffidence, he was always very reluctant to attend the kid's parties that took place. Although my family think Richard is the one most resembling me, I was more of a mixture of both him and Alan at their age.

At school Alan was competent but rather under-achieved his full abilities, getting a reasonably good level of examination successes. He had no clear idea of a career and decided to go to University; his 'A' level passes being good enough.

Typically, Alan didn't want to cut loose on his own but preferred to remain in Portsmouth so he could still have home comforts while he studied. He selected a course in Computer Studies with a bias towards 'Internet' working. However, to be fair to him it was the first year for that particular syllabus and the course did not meet the description very well, being heavily biased towards the hardware engineering side. Somewhat disillusioned, Alan kept it going for a term and a bit before deciding the course was not for him.

He had already secured a part time job in the local ASDA store as a shelf stacker to get a bit of pocket money and he retained this job to keep his bank balance ticking over while he looked for proper employment.

Alan didn't follow the other boys onto motorcycles, much to my relief but he was an addict to cars and avidly devoured any car magazine that came his way. His advice and information was often sought when someone (even me) was looking to buy a new vehicle. It was Alan discovered the personalised number plate on the Web I ended up buying. He didn't have a lot of luck with his own vehicles. He had 3 crashes in as many years, two of which he was totally blameless for, with the other party admitting full liability. He was slightly injured in both events although eventually recovering fully and getting a few quid in compensation.

Going from school days to getting a 'real' job actually proved to be a bit of a crisis for Alan. Like many teenage boys he had trouble adjusting his body clock. In other words you had to plant a bomb in his bed to get him up before mid-day.

However, I am delighted to say he eventually saw the light and got himself a very good job as an engineering apprentice with Southern Electric Contracting (SEC). The job transformed him and he became completely self-motivating. Getting up very early in the morning to travel to Swindon once or twice a week for college studies and working very hard during the day at manual tasks while he was learning the ropes. In a strange reversal, he would come home from work, devour his dinner and then collapse into bed, completely exhausted.

Alan is still somewhat diffident although he has a reliable circle of friends and goes out most weekends to socialise. He has customised his car with some add-ons and takes great pride in it, although not to the extent of washing it very often. After a somewhat late start, he seems to be getting his life in order and has very good future prospects.

He is finally spreading his wings and has taken his first holiday abroad with his pals, to Greece. However, as it was an 18-30 holiday I think it was a bit of a cultural shock for him (not that there's any 'culture' on such holidays). He got into practice for it by getting drunk and chucking a bottle through a pub window down in the Portsmouth Guildhall Walk; leading me to I hope he isn't metamorphosing into Mike.

So after having (at least initially) a shy and retiring little boy, would our last child, a little girl, be equally demure. Like hell! Baton down the hatches, here comes Marie.

*   *   *

Marie:
Emma desperately wanted a sister and after the disappointment of a miscarriage, Madge and I were delighted when Marie appeared. She was born a little prematurely, probably as a reaction to Madge sadly losing her dad 3 days before.

At the time of her birth she was named 'Rosebud' in the ward because we didn't have a name ready. Madge had decided to choose a girls name in advance was tempting fate too much and although we had a boy's name ready, 'Rosebud' it had to be for a few days until we made our minds up. For me the name was obvious, being based on 'Mary', which was the name of my sister who died a few hours after she was born.

As a toddler, Marie loved watching videos. The only thing was it was usually the same video, again and again and again. Then after total saturation had taken place she'd move on to another one and watch that countless times. There are certain animated films I know the dialogue for, almost by heart.

Like the others, Marie was schooled at St Thomas More's and Oaklands. Every time we went to a parents open evening we heard the same thing. 'Marie is bright and capable of good work but boy does she chatter.' She had no problem at all finding like-minded souls within the other girl pupils and was always a member of some cadre.

On one occasion, Madge and I were away on one of our rare escapes at the time Marie was sitting some exams at school. Without us to turf her out of bed she woke up too late to sit her French paper. So she went to the Doctors, faking illness to get a sick note to excuse her non-attendance. (Nought out of ten for punctuality and honesty but ten out of ten for initiative and cunning). However despite the chattering and shenanigans she emerged with reasonable GCSE results, including a grade 'A' in English literature.

We also have Marie to thank for starting us down the road to dog ownership. While a little girl, it was her incessant badgering of Madge set the ball rolling in that particular direction.

Growing up, Marie was a quiet but serious little girl. It's a real job to find a photograph of her smiling, at least before she discovered alcohol. Initially, as a teenager she matured rapidly and was fairly loud and a bit 'pushy'. Now, approaching the end of her teens she is very loud and very pushy.

Madge and I have a running battle with her over smoking. All of the kids experimented with cigarettes but only Marie stuck with it, much to our chagrin. Madge occasionally looks around her room and throws away any packets of fags she finds. An action that always leads to a big row about Marie's privacy and self-determination versus worried parents trying to stop her poisoning her lungs.

It seems there always has to be a bout of serious illness with children just to worry the parents and in Marie's case it was Glandular Fever she contracted when she was 13 years old. She had to take 4 weeks off school and then for the next 2 months only went back on a half-day basis. The rest of the day she spent in bed asleep as she was constantly exhausted by the illness. Even today, four years on, she goes to bed sometimes after she gets home from a particularly hard days work.

Perhaps it was down to sympathy for her but a few weeks after she had been laid up we agreed, against our better judgment, to allow Marie to get her belly button pierced. It seemed our misgiving were being proved justified when she proved to be allergic to the piercing and had it removed, leaving a nasty mark. However she went ahead again a few weeks later after it was healed up and had it done again but successfully this time.

More recently, Marie wanted to get her tongue pierced but Madge absolutely forbade it. But just as happens when I absolutely forbid Madge to do something, she went ahead and did it anyway.

The next worry was when after many bouts of sore throats she had an operation to remove her tonsils. This was a case of going through some short-term discomfort to avoid more and greater problems in the longer term. The surgeon at the time told her to give up smoking but she still doesn't listen.

Marie left school and went to Highbury College to study Hairdressing. This accounts for her hair changing colour from time to time with various (to my view) garish streaks appearing. The course provided for a large amount of practical work where she was seconded to a local hairdresser.

Early on in her training, Richard very bravely volunteered to have Marie cut his hair for him. I pass no comment as to the results except to say nobody else made a similar offer! Actually we could have done with Marie's skills being developed some time earlier when both Mike and Alan displayed long 'girly' hairstyles.

Marie actually isn't too happy with the hairdressing career at the time of writing but is prepared to see the course through to the end and obtain her qualifications. After that it remains to be seen what direction she will go in.

She is always very much up with the fashions of the time, which like many parents has cost Madge and I a fortune over the years but at least she earns some pocket money herself now to offset these expenses. She has a particular obsession with boots, which if you read the earlier Chapter on how Madge and I originally met shows she has at least one thing in common with her dad.

Marie's social life has been extensive and this has been the direct cause of my phone bill going through the roof and our car getting worn tyres as we ferry her about. To our great joy, Marie recently passed her Driving Test, which means Madge and I are no longer required to provide her transportation on a regular basis.

Marie is extremely self confident, as well as being physically robust and rather than sailing through life she has taken it by the throat. Madge and I just hope she doesn't come unstuck.

So that just about takes care of our own children. However, the time lag to the grandchildren appearing proved to be merely the calm before the storm. With the new generation of children came a whole new set of cowpats and it seemed not only Madge and I but the whole family started jumping in them.

8.2 The Grandchildren

Chloe:
After all the scares Emma might not be able to have children, it was almost a relief to find out she had become pregnant, even though (in old fashioned parlance) she was 'out of wedlock.' The result was Chloe. She was a carbon copy of Emma when she was a little girl but perhaps with a little more 'attitude'.

Chloe was born at St Mary's Hospital and within seconds she was looking round the delivery room rather than just bawling. There had been some concerns during the final 6 weeks of the pregnancy the baby was not getting sufficient nourishment and this proved to be the case. Chloe was under-weight at birth but she rapidly put on the ounces and pounds. She turned out to be the spitting image of Emma as a baby and a little girl, and every bit the drama queen as well.

The early signs were confirmed when she turned out to be very bright. So bright she sometimes gets a bit bored and into mischief, as tends to happen with the clever ones.

At the time of writing, Chloe is 4, going on 10. She not only has a vast vocabulary and chats freely on a variety of topics but she has also mastered the art of people manipulation and a way of expressing the words to get her own way. Witness the following statements and conversations:

In the doctor's surgery where Chloe had gone with a bump on the head.
'Chloe, let me shine this light in your eye.'
'What's your name?'
'I'm Doctor McLean.'
'No silly, your real name?'
'Mike.'
'Well Mike McLean, why should I do what you say? After all, you're **only** a doctor.'

With hands on hips after a disagreement with me. 'Hmmm, you just don't understand, Grandad.'

Heading off a scolding after doing something wrong. She sidles up to me and flutters her eyelids. 'I'm very, very sorry Grandad.'

In a restaurant and tucking into sausage and chips. Watching a lady clearing tables and moving in her direction. 'I'm not finished yet! You can't take my plate, go away!'

Watching a nurse approach with a hypodermic syringe for her pre-school jab. 'You're not sticking that in me!'

Madge and I see a lot of Chloe and she frequently stays overnight in our house. Madge in particular has a very close relationship with her and gives her a great deal of 'one to one' attention.

* * *

Lauren:
We had a bit of a shock when one day Richard informed us his girlfriend Sharon was pregnant. It wasn't something we were expecting even though the two were living together; and from what I understand they weren't expecting it either. However, such blessings are often bestowed unexpectedly and some months later and about 10 weeks after our first granddaughter, Lauren was born. She developed into a gorgeous little girl. All blond curls and a lovely smile, with a placid temperament that was a contrast to the more fiery Chloe.

She loved to come to our house and play in the garden or conservatory. She particularly liked to watch the 'babbits' as she liked to call the rabbits, Dolly and Fudge. After a while we let her feed them but despite being shown how to gently offer the food to the bunnies her version was to hurl it in their general direction. At least this it gave the babbits a bit of exercise dodging and weaving to avoid the missiles raining down.

On one occasion, Richard decided to play with Lauren 'who do you love best, daddy or 'X''. After beating 'X = chips' he thought he was onto a winner, only to lose out to X = cats, dogs, Barbie and crumpets.

Like the other grandchildren Lauren got spoiled rotten by her parents, grandparents and other relatives on both sides of the family. Something we enjoy doing enormously. At the time of writing Madge and I collect Lauren from playschool on Mondays to spend some time with us and we also look after her all day on some Fridays. We generally see her on Saturdays as well.

She is almost 4 years old and everything a little girl of that age should be. She also has the distinction of being the first (and currently only) member of her generation with the rather special surname of Bicheno.

*   *   *

Lewis:
Lewis was Emma's second child; he was sizable at birth and grew rapidly. Everyone thought he would take after his dad Wayne who is a strapping 6-footer and a semi-professional footballer. All went well until he approached his first birthday. He was on the brink of walking when he seemed to reach a plateau and not progress any further. We were also somewhat concerned his head appeared larger than normal and a little misshapen. Emma took him to the doctor but he said there was basically nothing to worry about.

Time passed and Lewis no longer thrived and started to lose weight. He was always grizzling and not an easy child to take care of. Madge and I looked after him for 4 afternoons a week and it was always difficult. He required constant attention, moaned all the time and was never still. He also showed no inclination to walk although now approaching 18 months.

Madge was concerned for him and both she and Emma made return visits to the doctor with no real problem being identified but simply being told some children were like that. Things then reached a critical point when Lewis appeared to be losing his balance and toppling over even when just crawling. The doctor said it was an ear infection and prescribed antibiotics.

After the course of medication had been completed Lewis still had his balance problem. Emma returned him to the same doctor who said there was nothing to worry about but he would make an appointment for Lewis at the children's ward of St Mary's Hospital, a date that turned out to be 3 weeks later.

Shortly afterwards, Madge and I had been away for a few days and it was our turn to have Lewis on the following day. I don't know whether it was down to us not seeing him a for a while (when you see someone every day you tend not to notice gradual changes) or whether his condition had deteriorated but the second we clapped eyes on him we whisked him to the doctor, insisting on seeing a lady doctor who we knew had children of her own. She took a couple of minutes examining Lewis before she left us and made a phone call. She then returned and said we were to take Lewis to St Mary's Hospital children's ward for assessment immediately.

We phoned Emma who met us at the Hospital. Lewis was examined and given a head scan. The doctors took Emma and Wayne (who had arrived by then) into a side room and told them they believed Lewis had a brain tumour. They were to take him immediately to the specialist Neurological Ward at Southampton Hospital, 20 miles away.

Madge and I undertook to look after Chloe for what turned out to be some time while Emma lived at the Hospital with Lewis and Wayne supported her when he was able to. A brain scan showed the worst. A large tumour was living inside the 3rd ventricle, which is a reservoir area for brain fluid between the two hemispheres of the brain. He would probably have died had we waited for the 3 weeks before he saw a paediatrician, which was the arrangement made by the original GP. His swollen head was due to the growing tumour and the excessive brain fluid that had built up.

Lewis underwent major brain surgery in a 7-hour operation and then spent 2 days in intensive care. Afterwards, he was moved to a regular ward. Emma remained by his bedside watching over him, except for one occasion when Madge relieved her overnight. Madge was equally vigilant, remaining awake all the time but come the morning when she picked Lewis up, she was distraught and horrified to discover his face had swollen up dramatically.

It appears he should have had his head propped up to assist the brain fluid draining away and as he was lying flat and face downwards, the fluid had instead collected around his facial features. Emma turned up and went hysterical but fortunately once the problem was understood and Lewis sat up, the symptoms quickly subsided. It's just a pity Madge (or Emma) weren't warned beforehand about the sleeping posture being important.

The surgeon (Mr Sparrow), doctors and nurses were all simply superb. That Lewis came through this ordeal alive was due to them; together with the lady GP who realised there was a severe problem; the St Mary's Hospital doctors who diagnosed it and moved with such speed; and the Southampton Hospital doctors who detailed the extent of the problem, carried out the operation and post operative follow-ups.

Incidentally, Madge caused hysterics from the nurses on the ward when she one day innocently but mistakenly greeted Mr Sparrow, the highly eminent surgeon, with 'Hello, Mr Crow'. She said afterwards in her defence that she knew it was a bird's name of some kind. I suppose we ought to be grateful that 'vulture', 'magpie' or 'tit' didn't pop into her mind.

You can imagine our opinion of the original GP who totally misdiagnosed the situation. Yes, Lewis had an extremely rare condition but if a couple of experienced parents can tell there is something fundamentally wrong then a trained GP should have done better.

We were visiting Lewis as often as possible, which was most days and taking Chloe along when Emma said it was OK, but Wayne's mum and dad also attended which we thought good of them. Then a bombshell was dropped. We knew Wayne's mum had tragically lost 3 babies at birth. Wayne had told Emma about it and she had told us but there was no detailed information supplied and Wayne's mum always refused to discuss it. Which is not altogether surprising and nobody felt they could pursue such a delicate subject with either her or her husband.

Then, with Lewis still recovering from the operation and all of us waiting for the results of the test on the tumour that was removed, Wayne's mum revealed all 3 of her babies (all boys) that died had suffered from a genetic problem which had resulted in symptoms close to what Lewis had been experiencing.

You can imagine how everyone close to the situation felt about such news suddenly being imparted. You have to feel sympathy for anyone who has lost infants at, or close to, the time of birth but where a problem might be hereditary then she had a responsibility to warn the two boys that lived (Wayne and his younger brother) and also to say something to their wives. As it is, today we are unsure as to the origins of Lewis's illness and it might have been 'one of those things' rather than be inherited and even if it was, may be unrelated to Wayne's ancestry.

Related or not, Wayne's mum had actually seen Lewis's symptoms, including his swollen head (a possible sign of hydrocephalous – water on the brain) and said absolutely nothing to warn her own son and his wife. Emma was deeply upset, as Lewis's condition was close to fatal when he had been operated on and if this information had been revealed earlier it might have resulted in a more timely intervention rather than taking things to the wire.

It may, or may not, have been related to a similar genetic problem but a warning would still have resulted in earlier action being taken. It was so close Lewis could easily have died. Emma refused to receive visits from Wayne's parents and would not even talk to Wayne's mother for months. For Wayne's parents' part, it appeared they were oblivious to the whole situation and could not fathom why Emma was so upset.

The problem was eventually diagnosed as 'Dandy Walker Syndrome', where part of the base of the brain is missing. This in addition to having the brain tumour that may or may not have been related. Both these conditions can be accompanied by hydrocephalus.

Lewis spent several months shuttling to and from Southampton Hospital for examinations and scans. Problems occurring very soon after the original brain operation were relieved by the fitting of a 'shunt', which drains excess brain fluid through a valve and tube arrangement into another part of his body. This was another significant operation and one likely to be repeated throughout Lewis's lifespan, as 'shunts' are usually life-long arrangements.

Lewis bounced back rapidly from each operation and soon started walking for the first time. He gradually put on weight and started to talk. All good news but we are always in constant terror of a relapse or him falling over and banging his head or knocking his 'shunt', plainly visible just under the skin on the right side of his head.

Then at Christmas 2002 Lewis became very wobbly when walking and at times even resumed crawling. His head also started to get bigger again. It seemed the hydrocephalus was back, but what about the tumour? Emma took him back to Southampton but as he seemed well in himself they did not want to make him endure further anaesthetic / scans as he was due for a check 3 weeks hence anyway.

So in early January Emma was back again and Lewis had his scan. It showed Lewis was clear from any tumour but his shunt had become blocked, allowing the hydrocephalus to return in large volume. He underwent further surgery, not only replacing his shunt with one that drained faster but also relocating it into the centre of the brain rather than on the periphery.

Throughout his ordeal Lewis remained a cheerful, loving little chap. He is also bright; the only major damage the syndrome seems to have done is in terms of his balance. He needs constant and total supervision to ensure that he does not accidentally injure himself. Barring such an injury, his outlook is now good, although he will have to desist from some sports and activities, such as rugby and boxing (obviously) and he will need to be careful regarding things such as scuba diving that bring pressure to bear on the skull.

That aside, and allowing for occasional shunt replacement for various reasons we are now hopeful he can lead a reasonably normal life. And of course Emma will ensure not only Lewis is fully aware of the implications of his condition but also any future partner is similarly advised.

To round things off, a précis of Lewis's story was published in the Portsmouth News edition of 9th April 2003 and a short story about him appeared in the magazine 'Chat' on 9th July 2003.

*   *   *

Jessica:
Jessica was a 'honeymoon baby' and after the experiences with Lewis the family was deeply concerned as to whether or not the new infant would be OK. However the pregnancy went well and although doctors were unable to give a definite reassurance, the baby being a girl gave everyone (rightly or wrongly) a degree of optimism, as all the babies we knew about with a similar problem were boys.

At birth, all seemed normal and there were no indications of hydrocephalus. However after a few weeks Emma noticed Jessica sometimes turned blue. Emma took her to the G.P. who immediately referred her to St Mary's Hospital. A round of checks followed as they tested for a heart irregularity. After all the tests had been done, they concluded Jessica had narrow arteries, prone to circulation problems, hence the blueness. Hopefully in time this will disappear, as she grows bigger. So at the time of writing there have been no further problems of this type and we are optimistic but have our fingers crossed.

Jessica still has to have tests conducted to see if she has Lewis's problems as she is considered 'at risk' but full brain scans necessitate her being older than she is at present. Again we are all just carrying on as normal and trying not to worry about it until the time comes.

Jessica remains a small baby and has been a little slow to put on weight, although she is healthy. She is very bright and can sit up by herself and even crawl at just 6 months of age. At the time of writing she is chubbying up nicely, smiling constantly, gnawing at everything and giving Emma and Wayne all the usual sleep deprivation parents come to expect.

Chapter 9

Pets

Earlier on in the book I described how my parents had acquired Fred the rabbit from their friend Albert. This was in 1960 when I was in my early teens and my younger sister Frances was about 7 years old. Fred was a 'Dutch' rabbit, gray in colour with a white band around his neck, white underside and paws.

My mum decided as a family pet he would not live out his existence in a confined hutch but would be given the run of the house and garden. That was fine, except he was only a baby and there were lots of cats living in close proximity. Much to my mother's amusement, whenever she let Fred run around the garden I would patrol the perimeter with a broom in my hands to repel any aggressive moggies.

People who know me are aware I go around with a slight stoop, looking at my feet. Fred is the original reason for this tendency. When you've got a rabbit charging around the house and you know it's likely to be fatal if you tread on him you tend to walk around looking down. After several years I became stuck with the habit. Even with Fred gone I had Sid the rabbit and then latterly 3 dogs all of which reinforced the lack of posture. Not that you would wipe Daisy out by treading on her; it happens regularly and she just shakes herself and ambles off.

Back to Fred. One day in the garden an amazing thing happened. There was a sheet of newspaper lying around and I suddenly became aware it was moving rapidly down the garden path. Then it veered off to the side and started going around in circles. I realised Fred was underneath it and at first thought he was just caught up in the folds. Nope, Fred was grasping the paper in his mouth from underneath and running along. I tore a piece of the newspaper off and offered it to him. He grabbed it from me and started to dance. Spinning in circles, running to and fro and all the time uttering a humming sound as if he was singing to himself.

From that day on Fred played with pieces of paper all the time. We lived in a corner property and the back garden was on view to anyone walking past. People would come from all around the local area to see that mad rabbit waltz around the garden with his paper. He didn't stop there though. He would jump up a series of boxes onto the top of the coalbunker adjacent to the perimeter trellis fence, where he would survey all that walked past the house. When he felt daring he would use the coalbunker to out flank the trellis that ran along the wall, all around the back garden and he would walk along the top of the wall on the outside of the trellis. He was also known to stick his head through the trellis and rub noses with any dog willing to put their paws up on the side of the wall and offer their snout.

Unfortunately Fred was not house-trained, nor was he well behaved in that (or in fact any) respect. We put trays of earth on the floor to encourage him to use them as a toilet and occasionally he did, but he was just as likely to go into a corner of the room, turn around with his bottom in the corner and leave a puddle and some currents. If you tried to admonish him he would fly at you, spitting and grunting and bite your leg.

Visitors would sit in an armchair and marvel at this rabbit scampering about like a dog or cat and they would smile and laugh. Then they would get up to leave and find this furry little bundle had devoured their shoelaces while they were sitting there.

Fred didn't stop at shoelaces. We often dried clothes on a clotheshorse or a chair in front of the open coal fire. If you didn't hang them high enough you might well find teeth marks along the material. My sister Frances used to play on the floor with paper cut-put dolls, dressing them with cut-out paper clothes from magazines. If Fred was about, the air would be full of shrieks as Frances tried to wrest her cuttings away from his chomping jaws.

One thing you didn't do was to buy each other slippers for Christmas that were in the slightest bit fluffy. If you did, Fred would have an instant attachment to the furry objects in more ways than one. He would do what rabbits do best, immediately and with zest. Try and walk past him wearing furry slippers and you would immediately have the weight of a copulating bunny on your foot.

His foulest trick of all was not dissimilar to what skunks do to those who provoke them. With his back to you he could somehow raise his bottom in the air and shake it, at the same time emitting a stream of urine that somehow travelled backwards and from side to side. He did it when he got very annoyed which was most of the time.

I recall on one occasion he went under a low corner unit and started to burrow into the carpet. My dad got down on all fours and stretched out his arm along the floor and under the unit to try and grab him. Fred let him have a salvo that caught him full in the face. We very nearly had rabbit pie that evening.

Fred lived to a ripe old age (11) and loved every minute of it. He was a law unto himself and provided huge entertainment for the family and entire neighbourhood. The family was distraught when he finally popped his clogs and made for the great paper factory in the sky.

*　　*　　*

After being married for a few months I suggested to Madge we buy a rabbit, partly because of my memories of Fred and partly because I thought family pets were good for children and therapeutic for the parents.

We went to the local per shop and selected a pure white rabbit with pink eyes. I named him 'Sid' as I thought it a suitable earthy name as had been 'Fred.' Sid had a hutch by the shed but we gave him the run of the entire back garden and also the back room of the house in Chichester Road.

He had a whale of a time, especially when I started growing our own vegetables in a small plot. It was only about 8 feet by 4 feet but I crammed it with all sorts. I realised Sid might be tempted to the area so surrounded it with a 3-foot fence. I shouldn't have wasted my time. Every time I went into the garden Sid was sitting in the vegetable patch munching away. I kept hoiking him out but 5 minutes later he was back again. I was amazed as I knew he couldn't jump a fence that high but what he did was to take a run up the adjacent wall and then hurl himself across the top of the fence. Rabbit 1, human 0.

Unfortunately Sid died at a fairly young age before the children were old enough to get the benefit of seeing him and helping to look after his needs but other pets fulfilled this intention. We went through the usual goldfish routine and then bought another rabbit. This one was vicious and no way could we let the kids near it, which rather defeated the object of having a pet, to learn about animals and to care for them. The rabbit actually disappeared under mysterious circumstances only Madge knows about but refuses to discuss.

We then had a longhaired guinea pig called 'Gizmo.' He was a cute little thing resembling a brown broom head. Being long haired his fur grew over his face so he couldn't see where he was going half the time. The children even tried to feed the wrong end of him on more than one occasion, as all you could see was a mass of fur. He wasn't too appreciative of having a carrot stuck up his bum and would run off grunting.

On the other hand he would run around squeaking with excitement if the kids chased him around the garden. The problem was his fur became matted and it was a lot of work to keep his coat in good condition. The kids of course didn't help at all and so with me working all hours, it inevitably fell to Madge to take care of him. Eventually the effort became too much. She threatened we would get rid of him if the children didn't help out more, but it made no difference.

In the end we decided to give him away to an animal sanctuary, along with his hutch and run, to show the kids if they were not going to contribute then there would be consequences. We took him to the appointed place and he seemed delighted to meet others of his kind. The sanctuary was equally delighted to get a good quality hutch and run so everyone was happy with the arrangements.

However it wasn't long before the younger kids started hankering for a pet again. Bearing in mind the lesson they learned in not looking after Gizmo, we decided to scale things back and so it seemed appropriate and safe to move to hamsters. We bought a beautiful golden hamster, the children called Bertha, as she looked big and chubby. The usual happened of course. The kids played with her for half an hour then got bored. They cleaned out her cage for the first week and then decided it was not a pleasant task and they would rather delegate it to mum.

However, once her cage had been cleaned out for the week, Bertha once again became very popular for a few hours, if intermittently so. She lived to a ripe old age (for a hamster) but one day in her dotage became very poorly.

We phoned the vet that evening and described her symptoms. He didn't sound too hopeful but he suggested we might try to give her some children's 'Calpol' painkiller medicine and then take her to see him the next day, if she was still around. It sounded a bit 'kill or cure' but we wanted to do anything we could for the old girl.

The problem was how to administer the pink, syrupy fluid. She would not drink it and so I decided to cover the end of my little finger in it and offer it to her, the assumption being she would lick it off. Like hell. Bertha decided my finger must be a honey stick and honey sticks got crunched up. I offered my finger, only to see her give it a sniff and then try and amputate it with her very large main fangs. Having finally and with some difficulty extricated my pinkie from her jaws, I spent the next hour clutching it in agony while the rest of the family and Madge in particular rolled around in helpless laughter.

Unfortunately, even the Calpol and my finger couldn't save Bertha. She joined the growing pet cemetery in the garden, with appropriate tears and ceremony. The boys decided as a replacement they would get a pair of Russian hamsters. I agreed, thinking they would be similar to Bertha. No way. They were half the size of Bertha but vicious. You could cuddle Bertha but not these brutes.

They would bite anything moving within range, a trait that was not helpful to a friendly relationship. I best remember them for the way they tackled the wheel in their cage. They would run inside it for hours at a time. Sometimes side-by-side, they even changed places as it whizzed round. If I'd have thought of it I could have connected the wheel up to a generator and run a couple of light bulbs off them.

They were not particularly long living creatures and I wasn't wholly upset to see them eventually depart. Not letting me off the hook for a moment the kids decided to revert back to the 'Bertha' type of hamster for their next sojourn into the world of pet ownership and they duly picked a large white and very fluffy one they christened 'Flossie'. She was very much in the Bertha mould and was well loved by all of us. Unfortunately she didn't live as long as the old girl and passed away after a couple of years.

*   *   *

I don't know if it was as a direct response to this episode but after a pet-less period the boys, in particular Mike, decided in 1996 to get into exotic pets. There was a bit of a false start when Madge opened his bedroom chest of drawers and found a small Chilean Rose tarantula spider sitting there in a bound but transparent box. After the screaming subsided Mike explained it was all he could afford at the time and hid it because he knew it would upset us. Too right.

Later, when he was a little older and had a bit of money he started out again, partially nudged towards this by his friend who happened to work in a reptile shop at Emsworth, a few miles away. He was able to extol the virtues of such pets and also give lots of good advice. Mike told us of his plans and both Madge and I said OK as long as he took care of everything himself from providing the correct environment to feeding and generally looking after the creatures. Mike was more grown up than the younger kids and so I was confident we wouldn't get them dumped on Madge and I to look after, as the furry pets had been. Not that I could see Madge taking care of these particular species.

We weren't expecting more spiders but we got two more Tarantulas; the difference being they were full size this time. Another Chilean Rose and a Mexican Red-Rump. Snakes and lizards I can handle, quite literally, but spiders give me the heebie-jeebies. Madge also dislikes creepy crawlies but to a much lesser extent than me. She can actually bring herself to kill house spiders but I'm packed and out the front door when faced with a big one.

The only aspect Madge and I fall out over is when she kills spiders and insects in general, she splatters them all over walls, ceilings etc and I have to come along and clean up and redecorate afterwards. If only she would be more selective in her weaponry, amount of force used and location of execution, it would save me a lot of work. However I am very grateful she takes care of them for me.

Mike used to sit and look at his Tarantulas for ages, sometimes dropping large house spiders into their glass tanks to see what would happen. The invariable and inevitable result being - Tarantula 1 House Spider a messy 0. Eventually Mike got a handful of flicked hairs from the Red-Rump which caused a rash on his skin and this gave us the excuse to demand he got rid of them. Mike then moved on to reptiles.

To give him credit Mike set about building a reptile vivarium with great gusto. He used some spare wood from an old discarded cupboard and wired it up with help from his elder brother Stephen. He then bought glass and turned the panes into sliding panels. We took him to a couple of reptile fairs, one of which was some distance away.

I must say it was quite fascinating just browsing around. Even Madge was intrigued seeing men walking around with large iguanas draped across their shoulders. Mike bought heat mats, controllers and specially prepared wood branches for climbing along with other bits and pieces. The only thing he didn't have was something living to put in the vivarium.

I was slightly disconcerted when I came home one day to find he had selected 2 scorpions. It sounded good but in fact they were a terrible disappointment. They barely ever moved at all and eventually when one died nobody even realised. Mike reviewed the situation and told me he would sell the surviving scorpion and move on to lizards.

He was after a 'bearded dragon', a slightly fearsome looking creature, but quite tame and easy to handle. They were quite expensive but one day Mike's friend told him the pet shop had been given a young adult bearded dragon that was defective and therefore going cheap. In what way defective? Well he'd had one of his back legs bitten off just below the knee joint by an aggressive male when he was but a youngster. He had got used to the absence of half a leg and scampered around quite happily. Madge of course went along with it, as she was automatically drawn and supportive to any living being which seemed to need help.

So Mike bought the little creature and settled him in to his new abode. The name he chose was I suppose inevitable; he called him 'Stumpy'. Stumpy was a great success. Mike often got him out of the vivarium and played with him in his bedroom.

I was quite fascinated to watch Stumpy feed. He ate live crickets for his diet and would chase them around. Until they stopped that is. Lizards are attracted by movement and you could have a silly situation where there was a large juicy cricket an inch from his nose and Stumpy couldn't see it because it wasn't moving. There would then follow a long period when both hunter and victim stayed completely motionless. Eventually the cricket would forget why it wasn't moving and start to walk off. At which point there would be a blindingly fast dart of the tongue and Stumpy would munch away happily.

If he missed, which wasn't often, he would end up with a mouthful of the wood chippings that littered the floor of his home and being completely stupid he would munch on those for a couple of minutes before it dawned on him he was chewing wood and not insect.

Mike would buy live crickets from the reptile shop in large numbers held in small transparent boxes. When it was time to be fed and Mike approached the vivarium, holding the box with a couple of dozen crickets leaping about and banging themselves against the insides, Stumpy would get really excited. If you slid the glass door back to get the box of crickets inside the vivarium then Stumpy would dart at the plastic container and try to eat it.

If you managed to get the container open then mayhem ensued. Stumpy would be trying to leap into the box while all the crickets would be trying to jump out. Lizards are incredibly stupid creatures and very single minded. On one occasion Stumpy ripped the lid off the box and virtually the entire contents of crickets hopped out. To stop them escaping into the room Mike closed the sliding door which left Stumpy with a weeks worth of food inside the vivarium, jumping about around him.

I can understand Stumpy going potty and stuffing his face with insects but I can't fathom why he didn't stop. He just kept on eating them. Even when his stomach was full and then when his mouth was full and he couldn't swallow them any longer, he kept on hunting them down. In the end Stumpy could no longer breath and collapsed. Mike hauled him out and used tweezers to remove sufficient crickets from his mouth and throat to give him an airway. He quickly recovered and immediately went hunting again.

To avoid such chaos the best way to feed Stumpy was to set up a diversion. You first attracted his attention to one end of the vivarium by showing him some crickets and then opened the other end and shook a few crickets from the container. Unfortunately with so many lively crickets it was inevitable not all of them ended up as Stumpy's dinner. Some leaped into the bedroom instead.

If Mike saw the escape take place he would grab Stumpy and use him like a vacuum cleaner. Holding him around the body, he would dip Stumpy's head forward and make horizontal passes a couple of inches above the carpet. As Stumpy encountered a cricket the tongue would flick out and return with a juicy titbit. Of course a few crickets didn't wait around long enough for this and disappeared into nooks and crannies.

You know those films set in the jungle when you get the chirping sound effects at night. Well there were times when I lay in bed at night thinking I was in the jungle with several crickets chirping away somewhere out on the landing and every now and then others chirping back in reply at some other location. One even took up residence behind the gas boiler in the kitchen and I couldn't get the damn thing out. It drove us mad for several days before it went quiet. I presume it either died of natural causes or cooked itself.

The success of Stumpy gave Alan ideas. He bought a lizard, a StarAgama he called 'Pleb'. A small, slow moving and slow growing type. We put it in with the much larger Stumpy and the two would sit on a rock together side by side, basking under the heat lamps. If one of them wanted to move and the other was in the way then the one would march straight over the top of the other who in turn wouldn't even flinch. That's how dumb the pair of them were. At least there was no competition for food as, unlike Stumpy, Pleb was vegetarian and ate leafy greens and cucumber.

The arrangement worked well until one fateful day Stumpy became poorly. We could tell from his loose bowels and general attitude things were not as they should be. Mike phoned the vet who suggested

Stumpy had just eaten someone that disagreed with him and if we starved him for a couple of days then his tummy would settle and all would be well. It sounded a good idea and not unlike what we humans would do in similar circumstances, so we carried on feeding Pleb with vegetables but stopped Stumpy's crickets.

With hindsight, the mistake was to assume Stumpy had lost his appetite for food, as humans might well do, but unfortunately this was not the case. After more than a day without food Stumpy must have been very peckish but we didn't realise just how peckish at the time. Then somebody noticed Pleb was no longer inside the glass tank. We searched everywhere for him until somebody said.

'Do you think Stumpy looks a bit on the plump side?'

It was only then the full horror hit us. Stumpy had eaten Pleb! Even then we couldn't quite accept it and kept looking around for the missing lizard. It wasn't until a couple of days later when Stumpy did a giant poo it settled matters. There, in the middle of the dump, sticking out, was a clawed hand. I would like to say it had two fingers thrusting upwards in a last defiant 'V sign' but it didn't. Pleb had become the lizard equivalent of a cowpat. At least one good thing came out of the episode. It may not have done Pleb much good but it certainly cured Stumpy's galloping trots. A rather expensive meal though. Pleb cost Alan £15. After getting over the shock, everyone (except Pleb) could see the funny side and everybody we told about the misfortune simply curled up with laughter.

Life moved on as not only Mike but also both Alan and now Marie wanted further lizards. A Uromastyx lizard called Harold appeared, another bearded dragon called Naz that Alan reared from a baby and the ultimate creature was Tyson the Bosc Monitor who was a baby but capable of growing into a pretty formidable animal about 3 feet long and big enough to challenge a small dog. We insisted on separate living quarters this time and so Alan also built a vivarium, with Mike's help and Mike built a couple more for himself.

Apart from Stumpy my favourites were 2 green Water Dragons each of which bore a remarkable resemblance to the Muppet 'Kermit the Frog' but with very long tails. They were kept in Marie's bedroom and the family used to sit on the bedroom floor and then let the lizards loose.

They were very fast, running mainly on their two large stick-like hind legs. They would climb everything, particularly the humans and happily perch on shoulders, heads and anything else they fancied. The only problem was when they disappeared you had to be very careful you didn't accidentally hurt them while conducting a search.

Mike began to get more ambitious. Stumpy was now fully grown and a bit too big for his vivarium, so Mike built a much larger one from a discarded MFI wardrobe. He also built other vivariums he started to populate with snakes, although nothing poisonous or particularly large. There was a Californian King snake for Mike, a Carolina Corn Snake for Alan, a Milk Snake, a Boa Constrictor and finally a Royal Python. They all started small and grew up to about 4 feet in length in the time we had them. Like the lizards, snakes sizes are curtailed by their diet and the size of the living accommodation.

The snakes were less entertaining than the lizards as they spent most of the time curled up in corners but when Mike fed them, which initially was on 'pinkies' (dead baby mice) going through to 'fluffs' (full size dead adult mice) it was quite amazing to see them dislocate their jaws and take the entire prey down whole.

The royal python escaped from its home on two occasions. Mike's vivarium wasn't built quite true and when the glass door was shut there was a small gap at the top. It was only about a quarter of an inch but it was enough for the python to start with and use his extremely muscular body to work the opening larger, so he could get through it.

On the first occasion he got out we didn't realise the faulty build and thought Mike had accidentally left the door panel open and so did nothing about it. The second time we twigged and re-designed the sliding door. The python didn't realise how lucky he was. The first escape only went as far as the nearby airing cupboard where he snuggled up to a nice warm boiler pipe. However the second time he actually made it down the stairs and was found by the front door. Fortunately found by us and not the 3 terriers that surely would have made short work of it.

The event that put a stop to the exotic pet experiments was the arrival of the electricity bill. After some estimated accounts, the previous quarterly bill had been very high but being a winter month I let it pass. This time however we had been blessed with excellent weather but the electricity bill was astronomic. The high cost had undoubtedly been caused by the numerous heating mats and sun lamps. There was only one thing for it; the reptiles had to go.

Alan and Marie had by then got over the novelty and were happy about the situation. We agreed with Mike, Stumpy could stay and he would find good homes for all the remainder, assisted by his friend from the pet shop.

To my surprise and to be honest, slight disappointment, Mike also decided to sell Stumpy. It seems he got the urge to be a Herpetologist out of his system and so by early 2001 the exotic pet chapter in our lives came to an end.

*   *   *

Madge decided the next household pets would be less of the exotic species and more of the traditional furry type. So a bunny it was but this time she decided we would get two. ('They'll be company for each other'). Actually as it turned out they were to be very much company for one another. Madge selected a baby Dutch rabbit, white and light brown in colour. The second was white with black blotches. Both were females (we're not that stupid!) and were named 'Dolly' and 'Fudge' respectively.

They actually got on extremely well and were often seen nestling up together. They were both very young and small but as they grew it became apparent Fudge was a much larger rabbit than Dolly but this difference in size did not affect their relationship at all. They lived for many years together and provided us and the kids and the grandchildren with much affection and entertainment.

The grandchildren would feed the 'babbits' as they called them. Their method of feeding being to walk up to them holding a carrot and then hurling the carrot in their general direction and running off screaming, as soon as the rabbit made a move towards them. Handfuls of rabbit food rained down the same way.

I suppose it was inevitable we would have an emergency one day. Following an incident I describe in more detail in the next Chapter, Dolly was nowhere to be seen. We looked in the hutch and in all the nooks we provided for hiding in. Nothing. Could she possibly have jumped the four-foot fence? Unlikely, as she was a very small rabbit. So small she might just be able to squeeze into an impossible space. I squinted down the tiny gap between the shed and the fence. There was Dolly, half way along with her back to me. I went around the other side of the shed and pulled off some boarding so I could see her face. Her eyes were staring in fright and her nose twitching and quivering at the same time.

Madge took over, as Dolly knew her best and would be less frightened of her involvement. Despite furious rows, the kids had quickly abandoned the rabbits soon after they arrived when they realised dirty hutches had to be cleaned out. Madge had taken them over as she did with any human or animal needing looking after. Clucking around and making them her 'babies.' Madge tried cooing and calling and making a noise like a carrot but all to no avail. I fetched a stick, suitably blunt at the end and tried to gently nudge Dollies rear. She appeared to be stuck fast and very, very frightened.

We carefully considered all the alternatives like waiting for a couple of days until she starved down to a size that might slip out or going next door and demolishing the neighbours flower beds while dismantling the fence.

We finally came down to the plan of getting at her by making a hole in the shed from the inside. The problem was how to do this close enough to reach her but without hurting her or scaring her to death. Rabbits were well known to be susceptible to 'death by shock.' We could not afford to be too long about it because of Dolly's state and also the light was beginning to fail.

A measure of the distance to the bunny copied on the inside of the shed quickly gave the point of access which I marked high to be above her ears. I gathered all the cutting tools I could find that didn't make a lot of noise and set to the task. Madge constantly monitored Dolly while I hacked and sliced away.

After a few minutes I had a bit of a hole, which I could get fingers into and lever the wooden slats back a little. I kept going until the access seemed big enough and then, being unable to see her, groped down gently with my hand. Dolly flinched but stayed put. I managed to get my other hand through and with a hand at each 'end' tested the distressed bunny for 'give.' There didn't seem to be anything digging in her and so I cautiously lifted. Seconds later we had Dolly back with us. Madge took her and after a reassuring cuddle put her in the hutch where she quickly recovered with Fudge and some food.

Unfortunately we were not to be so lucky a year or so later. Dolly had been badly scared by an incident and although completely unharmed physically, died of shock in my arms. Both Madge and I were distraught and the kids were in tears.

After this event Fudge was left on her own and we moved her hutch out into the main garden. There was still a fenced off area adjacent but we thought if she had the entire garden to explore and run about in all day it would take the edge off the loss of her companion.

She liked this arrangement hugely, in fact a bit too much. The problem was we couldn't get her to go back into her hutch at night. Madge and the kids were in hysterics as they watched me chasing her about across the lawn and from bush to bush, with a broom in my hand, trying to 'steer' her in the right direction. To her it was a great game.

For months Fudge lived an ideal life and then one day it all came to an abrupt end. I heard Madge shrieking from the kitchen and I looked out of the window. There in the centre of the lawn was a large fox. There could be no doubt as to what it was after and for all we knew it might have already succeeded. I rushed out and chased the animal, which ran back to the end of the garden and cleared the 6-foot barrier with some ease. Fudge was nowhere to be seen but neither were any tell-tale pieces of fur about.

Madge and I scoured the garden, looking under all the bushes but still no sign. Finally I looked in the shed. The door had been open and there were lots of nooks between the benches, racking and miscellaneous contents that would have aided a scared rabbit to hide. I looked under the workbench and there in the corner was Fudge. She was perfectly still. I lifted her out. There wasn't a mark upon her but she had died from the shock of being chased by the fox. We buried her in the garden alongside her friend Dolly.

It was after the exotic pets had gone and well before the loss of the rabbits that part of the family (led by Marie) decided they wanted to acquire a pet that would see out a decent number of days and not pop their clogs in a matter of weeks or months. This was heavy stuff and the alarm bells rang loudly.

They were asking for a major commitment here to a significant animal of some kind and the brunt of looking after it would come in my and Madge's direction. I was still fairly confident of fighting off any extreme suggestions from the kids, like a dog. However I wasn't prepared for some unexpected support for their cause and for what happened next.

Chapter 10

Dogs

(Notice 'dogs' are not included in the 'Pets' chapter for the simple reason our dogs are not pets but fully-fledged members of the family). For the record, the official pedigree names of our dogs, Monty, Tasha and Daisy are 'Hampshire Laddy', 'Westscott Ideal Girl' and 'Top Lass' respectively.

10.1 Monty, Tasha and Daisy

The reader will have seen at the beginning of this book I was very anti-dog. As a father I was ready for the children's initial assaults of 'I want a dog.' I had an impressive defence. A list of good reasons for not yielding, forged from many encounters over the years. It was easy to rattle them off.

1.   Dogs have big teeth and bite.
No dog can be fully trusted not to bite. There are always circumstances which can trigger an attack and which are not always easy to predict.

2.   Dogs are very noisy.
They bark loudly leading to disputes with the neighbours. Often they bark without warning and from just behind you, thus leading to nervous dispositions, heart attacks and head shaped dents in the ceiling.

3.   Dogs are expensive to keep.
They eat lots and need supporting equipment such as lead, basket, bowls, coat, etc. They run up large vet bills and need constant treatment for worms, fleas etc. Their chewing of innocent objects during moments of boredom can cost the replacement of such things as furniture, carpets and neighbours.

4.   Dogs defecate.
That's only natural. What's not so natural is picking it up in a bag and walking around with it until a suitable receptacle can be found. Ghastly!

5.   Dogs are a health hazard.
They collect fleas they bring into the house and deposit on furniture and your lap. They also carry a variety of worms internally. (Do you feel itchy reading this?)

6.   Dogs are a tie.
You can't easily take them abroad with you because of the strict anti-rabies quarantine laws governing re-entry into the country. You have to organise someone to look after them. Even a day trip or short notice break away becomes a headache. Kennels cost a fortune and I'm sure the dogs are unhappy there as they miss their normal surroundings.

7.   Dogs are smelly.
They are always getting dirty and at worst actually roll in things that defy thinking about. The smell then invades your house, furniture and carpets. They then have to be cleaned!

8.   Dogs are anti-social.
They put off friends, relatives and neighbours from visiting by means of several of the items listed above. Although I have heard some people arguing this point is actually an advantage when it comes to certain relatives.

9.   Dogs and children don't mix.
A child might easily but unintentionally provoke a dog that may then retaliate. Accidents happen very easily with children or dogs about and to have both more than doubles the chances of such an occurrence.

10.   Dogs try and fight each other.
A simple dog walk could turn out like World War 3 if you encountered another canine with at worst, resultant physical damage to all involved and potential law suits or at the very least, much embarrassment.

   So that's it. A pretty solid case against 'man's best friend.' I didn't like dogs and felt confident the very last thing I would ever become was a dog owner.

Over the years I'd fended off several attempts to acquire the nasty beasts both with the above list and also by buying off the kids with other less intrusive pets (see earlier Chapter on Pets). However I wasn't prepared for what happened next.

Madge had always been keen on having a large family and I had become used to recognising the signs when she was thinking about another baby. Over 13 years we'd had 6, the last being 7 years ago.

She had been clucking about for some time and I'd encouraged her to think towards future grandchildren as a way of assuaging her strong maternal instincts. However, none of the kids looked like producing a grandchild and to be honest we wouldn't want them to, until it was in the context of a strong relationship with a sound financial base. So Madge was becoming increasingly broody and looking to me to do something about it.

About that time Marie, who was seven years old, started giving me the big-eyed treatment and pleading with her lovely daddy to provide a smelly animal called a dog. I was about to say a resounding 'No' when I suddenly had a thought. Suddenly a solution presented itself.

Perhaps, rather than bringing another child into the family, a dog might be a more reasonable substitute. A dog would give say 12 years of torment as opposed to a lifetime from the human equivalent. It would be less expensive to bring up and if the worst came to the worst you could always sell it on, unlike a child. So perhaps a dog was a viable proposition after all.

As soon as I gave the smallest hint I might be amenable, Madge saw the prospect of getting her hands on a baby, albeit with 4 legs and big teeth, and jumped on the dog bandwagon. Finally I acquiesced.

Having allowed myself to be persuaded by a combination of Madge and Marie to acquire the beast, I managed to get in one condition I regarded as damage limitation. I insisted I personally picked the breed.

I had very little idea regarding such things but I was vaguely aware there were several types. Although they all shared the common attributes of being noisy, smelly, had sharp teeth and crapped a lot, I might just be able to achieve a few redeeming features.

I bought a book on dog breeds and scanned it closely. It quickly became apparent dogs came in 2 types and 4 sizes. The 2 types being male and female and the 4 sizes being 'toy,' 'small,' 'large' and 'buy a bigger house.' I parked the male/female debate, as this seemed the lesser priority.

Although I did not see eye to eye with Madge about 'size is important' in all things, in this particular case it was. I wanted to feel I could take on this brute if necessary with a better than even chance of coming out on top. A somewhat smaller animal also implied it would be less intrusive in the house and easier to haul about in public.

The 'very large' dogs like the St Bernard and Irish Wolfhound went out the window pretty sharpish. The next size down I dwelt on, as it included Labradors and Retrievers, which I had come across and found 'so so' but they were still a bit on the big side for my comfort. So it went down to the 'small' and 'toy' dogs that were actually quite close in size and in my terms 'manageable'.

After looking at the pictures of the 'toys' I decided I would feel pretty foolish being seen out walking with most of them, they would take a good deal of looking after (like finding them for a start as some of them were small enough to disappear into nooks, crannies and cats stomachs) and basically they really didn't do a lot for me. So it was settled. It had to be a 'small' dog. The question was, which one? And what about pedigrees and cross breeds?

I thumbed through the pictures and closely examined the characteristics. What came out of this was it had to be a pedigree pooch. It was the only way you could be fairly sure of what you were getting, as with a mongrel the genes would be so mixed that anything could be the outcome and knowing my luck, probably would.

I could end up with one that had looked like a sweet bundle of fluff and behaved like a Rottweiller. (Which is extremely ironic, as with Tasha, that's exactly what we ended up with – see later).

I needed to be certain about what to expect so it had to be a pedigree animal where the genes would be true to the breed. I ploughed on.

What I was looking for was a dog that was physically robust, as it had to be to survive in our household. (Being trodden on would be a regular hazard). It also had to be good with children and especially with grown up adults like me who didn't particularly like them and were likely to give them a hard time. Bags of personality would help as this might make me forget what a nuisance they really were.

It came down to just the one breed. It was called the 'West Highland White Terrier.' It seemed to be about the right size and with the Scottish breeding, likely to be sturdy and healthy, as well as hairy. The book claimed it was amiable, affectionate and reasonably easy to train. (Well, speaking from hindsight it got 2 out of 3 correct. You want to try training the little blighters). So that was it. The next question was 'where do we get one from?'

I had been warned to avoid places called 'puppy farms' that churned out dogs just for the money with scant regard for the health of both the breeding mums and the offspring. Such places I regarded (and still do) with contempt for the owners, tempered by pity for the poor dogs. The 'rescue' centre was a possibility and indeed we visited the local one. However, nobody could be sure as to how the treatment from the prior owner might have affected the animal psychologically and we needed to be certain about the temperament to protect the kids.

In any event, as most of the dogs at the centre were fully grown and having experienced taking on an adult rabbit that was not used to us (talk about not being able to teach an old **dog** new tricks, you want to try it with a bunny) and having a difficult time, I decided we needed to take on a pup.

According to the books, puppies had to stay with their mums until fully weaned, which in practice meant about 9 weeks, after which they could be separated without mum or puppy having a traumatic time.

So where would we find a 'Westie' pup? The local 'free-ad' paper carried advertisements for a wide variety of puppies but they tended to be 'home bred.' Although in time I came to regard this as perfectly OK, especially if you could meet the parents (the doggie ones of course), at the time we felt we needed to play safe and go for a 'professional' breeder.

I wasn't sure how to go about this but then by chance came across an advert for a breeder's society in the 'Exchange and Mart' paper. For a few pounds they sent us a list of dog breeders that had litters available or due shortly. That was the good news. The not so good news was they were fairly sparse with none of them near to where we lived.

Another complication was we hadn't decided between a male and a female. Here I must say I don't like the official term 'bitch' for the female dog. The word has been abused by association with somewhat undesirable human females who tend to populate the 'Gerry Springer Show' and as far as I'm concerned have given the dog a bad name. So I stick with 'boy' and 'girl' dogs.

The books gave pros and cons as to sex, going on about males wandering off to seek females 'on heat' and females producing messy blood on their 6-monthly cycles. They didn't tell us males would want to cock their legs up trees and bushes with quite the frequency Monty has demonstrated a need for, or females would lick you to death as a puppy substitute.

Of the two traits the latter is a bit easier to put up with but perhaps not when you're all dolled up and about to go out, as my wife has found out. So we decided to leave the gender to chance. The nearest place was over 100 miles away, which was a test of both our commitment and car.

We contacted the breeder and registered our interest. The puppies were due shortly and would become available to take away from their mum at about 9 weeks of age. We could however view them earlier than that date and make our selection. The next few weeks became tense as we waited on the phone call from the breeders. It was almost like awaiting the birth of your own child.

Finally the call came, mum had given birth to 3 strapping boys. That at least resolved the 'gender' issue. We had no choice but to take a male. But the tension was barely released as we were dying to see them. We passed the time thinking of a name. As part of the agreed deal, I got to choose the name as well as the breed. I wanted a name that had a formal, rather ostentations long form but a very usable and 'chummy' sounding short form. I suppose it shows a total lack of imagination on my part I selected 'Monty,' it being short for 'Montgomery', the famous WWII Field Marshall.

Although we couldn't take the puppy home until it had been weaned we were allowed to go about a month before to select one from the litter. Everyone wanted to go and view the puppies but Madge and I took just the two youngest children on the appointed day. We made our way to the kennels located on the very edge of Dover, with a large house and a number of outbuildings in several acres of grounds.

The breeders were very friendly and helpful. We were shown to a small shed where the mother Westie sat with her pups milling around her. The mum was very amiable and we spent some time making friends with her before moving to her brood. My first surprise was the puppies were meowing, almost like kittens. The second surprise was all three looked identical. What was the point in choosing?

It seemed as if you might as well do a 'dip, dip' selection. 'Not so', we were assured. The 3 had individual and very different personalities that showed through even at this very early age and for identification purposes the tip of each puppy's tail had been painted with a different colour of nail varnish.

We were left alone with mum and pups, with the parting advice of 'pick them up by all means but please don't drop them!' Each puppy was about 10 inches long, chunky and resembled a Labrador more than a Westie. There was none of the shaggy white coat to be seen and the ears were turned down. The mother didn't seem to mind the total strangers at all, not even when they started to touch her young. This all boded well as far as I was concerned. This was just the sort of temperament we needed.

We sat on the floor, playing with the puppies. The breeder was right about the different personalities. One of the pups was clearly more adventurous than the others and was dashing about, full of energy. A second was very quiet and stayed close to mum. The third was a bit of a mixture of both the other two.

I suppose it was inevitable we would all pick a different pup. Madge went for the quiet one, as she felt sorry for it. The kids preferred the boisterous one and I just couldn't decide. I knew there was a danger we would end up with all 3 if we didn't have a clear decision. 'I know,' I said 'we won't pick the puppy, we'll let the puppy pick us.' This seemed to go down well.

We all sat down a short distance away from the puppies and waited quietly. At first, nothing happened. Then one of the pups walked over to us and meowed, trying to clamber up on an outstretched knee. We'd been chosen by the 'middle' one of the three, who immediately became 'Monty.'

We told the breeder, who noted Monty's identifying nail varnish colour, and eventually dragged ourselves away. Before we left we were introduced to Monty's dad. He looked a really beautiful Westie, carrying himself almost regally and bounding around. There were 2 champions in Monty's pedigree and you could see why when you saw the dad. Madge took his lead, about 20 feet long, and let him run about, which he did with great gusto.

It had been our first experience of the Westie breed and we were all very impressed. The adult dogs were everything the breed description said they were and the puppies had been gorgeous. We had taken a video camera with us and filmed everything I have described. It enabled us to see our dog in the few weeks we still had to wait for him and the video still gives us pleasure even today when we view it.

The next thing was to get all the necessary bits and pieces. Like feeding and water bowls, bed, lead etc. It reminded me of getting stuff together when our first baby came home from the maternity ward. A few weeks later we made the trip again to collect Monty. We had left a cash deposit and now paid off the balance of the £250 due.

We were given some dried dog food to get us started; the registration documents and some advice sheets. Then we met Monty again and we didn't recognise him! He had grown so much. He was much bigger, had the start of his white coat and posed a somewhat quizzical figure with one ear up and one still down.

He was the first of the litter to be collected but the others were due to go within the next 48 hours. I felt a bit sorry for his mum, losing her babies so quickly. 'Don't mind about her,' I was told 'she's fed up with them under her feet the whole time.' Nevertheless I had pangs of guilt as we took Monty and left.

It had all happened so quickly and we had not really been re-acquainted before we set off. It was also going to be a long trip for the pup. We drove a couple of miles and stopped in the car park of a supermarket. We had an estate car and now put the rear seats down to make a large, flat area and spent the next half an hour getting to know each other again. We offered Monty food and water, talked to the pup and generally made a fuss of him. We then resumed the journey home.

Over the next couple of weeks Monty settled in and his floppy ear straightened up so he looked just like the pictures of the pups we had pored over in the books. He was still too young to take out but the kids played with him to stop him getting bored.

The favourite game was to walk about in front of him with no shoes or socks on. Marie had found out accidentally Monty liked to pounce on bare toes. From then on the kids would walk barefoot until he attacked and then leap onto a chair to escape. The screams of excitement occasionally turned to screams of pain when Monty was quicker than they were but with his baby teeth he couldn't do any real damage.

Alongside all this we were trying to house train him. Dogs are naturally very clean and will avoid fouling their own immediate living area but in a big house, that still gave him plenty of scope for 'accidents.' We put newspaper down on the places he was inclined to perform and he soon learned he was expected use the paper as a toilet.

At that young age the male dog doesn't cock his leg up but just squats like the female and so everything went into the paper. We then put newspaper outside the back door and placed him on it every time we thought he needed the loo. It didn't take long at all before he always went outside. Finally we removed the paper and Monty used the small grass patch outside the door for his ablutions.

Unfortunately we trained him too well and he was too conscientious.

Marking what he regarded as his territory with squirts of urine came naturally to him and he would happily do this when he went for a walk but when it came to 'big jobs' he refused to do it anywhere other than his patch of grass outside the back door. If we were out and he wanted to go to poo, he would whine like crazy and paw at us desperately. We would whisk him home and he would trot outside and do what he had to.

After a while the situation became ridiculous; we could only go the places with him that left us within a few minutes travelling time of his bit of ground in the back garden. Finally we'd had enough and the next time he started whining we ignored him but walked him onto some nearby waste ground. He became increasingly desperate until he could hold on no longer and made a full deposit. We made a big fuss of him and told him how clever he was. That immediately broke the dependency on the back garden but on the down side was the beginning of carrying poop scoops. My least favourite bit of dog ownership.

The back garden of our home after the conservatory was added is about 70 feet long and 40 feet wide but before we could let Monty loose in it, I had to carefully go around the entire perimeter and check for gaps in and under the fences. I carried out a few repairs and blocked off some likely exits.

We also have a narrow sideway running on both sides of the house which he could escape down. One of these led into the side area we already let him run around in and was deemed 'safe' and the other had no function and so I just blocked it with a piece of fence panel. Monty still confounded us all. His activities hidden by trees and bushes, he dug an escape tunnel under the fence and got into next doors garden. Fortunately there was no way out from theirs onto the road and we were able to retrieve him with the neighbour's cooperation.

When we had collected Monty, the breeder had given us a small amount of dry dog food and recommended we keep him on this diet for life. However not only did this seem a bit boring for him but it proved impossible to prevent everyone (including myself) offering him titbits from their plates at mealtimes. Monty loved being fed like this and would move from person to person, sitting quietly next to their chair, not making a sound but staring at them intently. It took a strong person to resist this level of intimidation and ignore him but if it happened he would just move on to the next chair until somebody capitulated and gave him something to eat.

Although he'd had his inoculations, we weren't allowed to take him out until he was 12 weeks old. It was therefore a big moment when we took him for his first walk. Madge took his lead and he trotted along, constantly looking up at her for direction and reassurance.

From the early days Madge carried Monty around like a baby. He loved it as he was much higher off the ground and could therefore see far more. When she took him to Havant on her own she would not tie him up outside a shop but instead carried him inside. Most shops were very good about this and in fact he was so small, cute and fluffy he regularly attracted a throng of children and quite a few adults as well.

As he got older Madge stopped this practice of going into shops with him but still carried him about at times and he loved every minute of it. The result of all this attention was Monty has always had a very strong bond with Madge. There have been times when he point blank refused to go for a walk with me but as soon as Madge took up his lead, off he would trot, ears and tail erect.

One day when out for a walk with Monty we passed by a building that had a low stone wall bordering the pavement. To our astonishment Monty hopped up onto the narrow wall and walked along it. From that time on, whenever Monty came across a wall low enough for him to jump onto, then up he would go and he would walk the length of it before jumping down again.

When he was young, Monty was always on the lookout to escape from the house. If anyone left the front door open then he would be off in a flash. We had to run up the road after him a few times. Fortunately he would head for peoples' gardens rather than run across a narrow but busy main road but we had hearts in our mouths every time it happened. It eventually prompted us into having a porch built onto the front of the house, which Madge wanted anyway. We then had an extra door for him to negotiate and in practice this put a stop to his wanderings.

The early days of letting Monty off the lead in a park were a disaster. We were never really sure whether or not we would get him back again. I recall an episode where a park was adjacent to a large island of bushes and trees and Monty headed straight for the middle of it. Madge and I were both there but we couldn't see across to the other side of the bushes and had no idea where or when he would emerge. No amount of calling him brought any results and he took great delight in scampering off on those occasions we almost got within reach of him. It was only when he got bored and tired he voluntarily gave himself up.

What was particularly worrying was there were so many exits from that park onto busy roads and so we stopped going there and instead went to a larger park fully open to view and which had an almost completely enclosed perimeter. Even there we had problems getting him to come back after we let him off the lead.

As his trick was to let you come close before running off I carried an umbrella with me so that, when opened behind him, it would scoop him up or at least prevent him from escaping; at least that was the theory. Madge was treated to the sight of me running around the park, waving an umbrella in headlong pursuit of a young Westie enjoying every moment of the chase.

We decided what Monty needed was a bit of obedience training. He already knew his name and sometimes came when called, which was a good start, so we confidently booked him into a local dog obedience class. We went along at the appointed time and found a hall full of about 20 dogs of different breeds, which had one thing in common. They all behaved impeccably and seemed to naturally understand every word and gesture from their owners.

I thought we had inadvertently stumbled into the 'advanced training' evening instead of the 'beginners' class but apparently not. When we were told to let our dogs off the lead, the others stood or sat quietly while Monty just ran around like a nutter and caused such chaos we were politely asked to leave. Was it possible all dogs were born into this world with the instincts of instant obedience, except for ours?

Forced to deal with the matter ourselves, we managed to get him to 'sit' by pushing his bottom down to the sitting position when we said the word and then rewarding him with titbits afterwards. He got that one quite well but we had no success at all with such things as 'stay,' 'come' and 'stop chewing the furniture.' It clearly needed more thought.

I sat Monty on my lap, facing me. 'Monty,' I said, 'I've been meaning to talk to you for some time and now I feel it can't wait any longer.' His deep brown eyes focused on me and his ears were up. 'You see, if we are to have an ongoing relationship, then there's something you need to understand.' His head cocked to one side. 'Believe me it's for the best I say this and I don't want you to think it in any way diminishes my opinion of you.' He studied me carefully, 'You see, I'm a human and you're a dog!'

Monty of course knew better. Our relationship was not 'human to dog' but based upon the principle of the 'pack.' All humans and dogs in the household were members of the family pack. All relationships therein were negotiable and there was nothing a good strong set of sharp teeth couldn't sort out in terms of the pecking order.

*   *   *

We'd had Monty for almost a year and had all become very attached to him, when Madge came up with an idea. 'Wouldn't it be interesting to get another Westie, a female this time, so we could experience having both a male and a female?' The idea was actually quite appealing.

If a relationship with one Westie was fun to have then having two Westies should be twice the fun. In fact more so, because as well as having separate human relationships with each dog there was also the relationship they had with each other to appreciate. We started looking around again and I must admit for my part, it was with genuine eagerness rather than the grudging commitment I had previously displayed.

We used the same source for available puppies and again found there were few litters about, all of which were a considerable distance away. The best bet was a litter in Bedford. We phoned the kennels and was told just one puppy, a female, remained from the litter all the rest already having been sold or committed.

Madge is always attracted to waifs and strays and being the last one she imagined the pup had been rejected by everyone else and was therefore in need of a bit of 'tlc'. So it was a forgone conclusion. We arranged to visit the kennels on the next available weekend.

It was a long trip to Bedford and I became puzzled as we got closer to the location we had been directed to. Monty's kennels had been in the countryside with open fields around but this time we were in a heavily built up area.

When we found the address it was just a semi-detached house in a long row of urban dwellings. We knocked on the door and were directed up the sideway into a back entrance. There was a tiny back garden and very small conservatory. No dogs in sight. A woman appeared and introduced herself. She said all of the litter except for our pup had been collected and the dad wasn't there but we could see the puppy and her mother.

She went in the house while we waited outside and soon reappeared carrying a beautiful little Westie pup about 10 weeks old. I got the camcorder out and took some footage of the pup's first look at us. The Westie mother looked fine and allowed both herself and her pup to be fondled by us. The woman said the litter was full pedigree and had been registered already with the Kennel Club but she had no paperwork to show us.

Madge was already smitten with the puppy but I had a few misgivings about the situation. The house didn't present itself as a proper kennels and the woman's explanation regarding the litter, the father and the paperwork didn't entirely ring true. However, we had come a long way, the puppy seemed healthy, bright and alert and there was no way I would be able to prise Madge away from the fluffy bundle.

So we paid the money and left with a female Westie we immediately christened 'Tasha'. The name came from the 'Star Trek - Next Generation' TV series on at the time and related to a female character that was both strong willed and independent, which certainly described the puppy in question.

Madge sat in the back of the car with the puppy cupped in her hands, cooing to her all the way home. The big concern was what would Monty make of the new arrival. He was a year old and quite sizable whereas Tasha was tiny and vulnerable. We had come prepared and before we went into our own home we popped Tasha into a dog carrier for her own protection, just in case.

I took the carrier into the house and placed it gingerly on the floor while Madge brought Monty into the room in her arms. Monty immediately realised what was going on and struggled to get down. Madge put him onto the floor and he flew to the carrier, sniffing furiously all around it. To our amazement, Tasha didn't flinch at all but seemed totally unconcerned at having this large adult dog in a very excited state with only a metal grill between them.

We let them spend a few minutes sniffing each other through the grill and when Monty had settled down a bit, we opened the door. Tasha just strolled out and investigated the room, totally ignoring Monty; he just trotted along behind her. Immediately the pecking order was firmly established and despite the relative sizes, Tasha's strong personality already put her firmly in charge.

We waited for the Pedigree papers to turn up and I had to phone several times before they arrived. I still felt something wasn't quite right and later got hold of a copy of the full set of Kennel Club registrations for that year. I found the record of the litter Tasha was supposed to be part of but her registration was separate from the rest of the litter and gave her a different name to the others.

Pedigree dog names are a bit odd but they follow a pattern so dogs in the same litter might be called something like 'saucy Monty of Bedhampton' and a sister might be 'happy Tasha of Bedhampton.' In this case all Tasha's brothers and sisters had similar 'family' names but Tasha's pedigree name was totally different. I couldn't understand then and still can't fathom why this should have been so.

Not only did the dogs have to adjust to one another but we had to recognise the nature of their relationship as well. We learned the pecking order was very important. If I attempted to give Monty some food without first offering some to Tasha she would fly at him growling and nip his feet or ears until he backed off. I was unsure whether the reason was wholly the pecking order or whether there was an element of the male never making an aggressive move towards the female but for whatever reason I have never seen Monty make any kind of attacking move towards Tasha. He will sometimes use a defensive posture, duck and weave, even occasionally make mock attacks but never, ever actually attack her, despite his size advantage.

Having established the pecking order, Monty and Tasha got on like a house on fire. They often lay down together, occasionally sharing a sleeping basket. She would lick the inside of his ear as a token of affection, just as she would lick our legs and arms when we petted her.

There were many differences in the behaviour of the two dogs, whether it was down to gender or personality I simply don't know but it was fascinating to observe it. Tasha didn't share Monty's love of walking on walls but on the other hand she would show great pleasure by crawling along the ground with her front paws and dragging or pushing the rear legs while the whole of her legs and body remained in close contact with the ground. I called it her 'commando crawl' as it was very similar to the movement carried out by soldiers.

One day when Tasha was still very young we were walking through Bedhampton and the level crossing gates came down just before we reached the railway lines. Rather than wait several minutes we decided to take the two dogs up the footbridge alongside, even though Tasha had never done anything similar before; not even up the stairs at home.

Monty walked confidently up and down the other side. Tasha, still a young puppy, was reluctant to climb up. She could see the ground some distance below between the wooden steps and this seemed to make her nervous.

With a lot of coaxing she went all the way up and then down again. As soon as her feet touched the ground on the other side she started to leap up and down very excitedly. It was as if she knew she had conquered her fear and accomplished something special. We made a big fuss of her.

Monty and Tasha were frequently seen together. Every morning they would wake us up by their barking. I used to stagger out of bed and look over the landing rail. The two of them would be sitting side by side on the telephone seat at the foot of the stairs, looking upwards expectantly.

Another interesting thing was they shared their responsibilities for looking after the family and our property. When we were at home it was Monty's job to patrol the garden, bark at pigeons, squirrels and any other interlopers but when we were in the street Tasha took over and guarded us from anything she deemed threatening.

Not only did Monty and Tasha differ in temperament but even when Tasha was fully grown they differed physically as well. Monty was the classic Westie and looked similar to those dogs of the breed you see in books. Tasha was much shorter and stubbier and seemed to be of a different sub type. Also, it wasn't so apparent when Tasha was a puppy but their fur coats were completely different.

West Highland Terriers actually have 2 coats of fur. There is a very short, fluffy and slow-growing inner fur they have from puppyhood and then growing through this there is the long, coarse fur that's the one most visible on the outside. The combination of the 2 layers is the Westie secret for survival in the rigours of the Scottish Highlands.

Tasha only had the inner fur layer with no sign of the long coarse coat. This meant she was comparatively fluffy but if there was a problem with her fur it took forever to grow out. I wondered whether this 'defect' was the reason for Tasha not being selected earlier from her litter and also for the slightly odd attitude of her breeder. Both Monty and Tasha had champions in their pedigrees within the 3 previous generations and maybe only 'perfection' in meeting their breed specification was good enough for some people. Seeing Tasha's fur problem made us look more closely at Monty.

To our astonishment we realised he didn't have any inner fur lining, just the top coat. So between the pair we had a complete set of inner and outer coats but neither had the full combination. It made no difference at all to our attitude towards them, if anything it made Madge and I feel more protective of them, being even more 'special' than we thought.

The big question for us was what would happen when Tasha matured and came into her first season. Given their furry coat problems I imagined any offspring from those two could have anything from a complete set of furs to being completely bald. Knowing our luck I bet I know which way it would go. Even so, we were quite keen on the idea of them mating but we wouldn't want it to happen too quickly as we thought Tasha might be a bit too young to handle a pregnancy.

We had also been warned when a girl dog had a period it could be a bit messy but as it turned out we never had any problem of that kind at all. In fact, we would not have even realised Tasha had come into season if it were not for the impact it had on Monty.

Clearly she must have started emitting some kind of odour which was undetectable to we humans but Monty noticed it. Boy did he notice it. He started barking at Tasha, who totally ignored him. He whimpered at her and still got no reaction. The barking went on. We tried putting him in another room but the barking went on.

It lasted 2 days and nights until his voice gave out and he just croaked. Poor Monty, we were quite concerned for him and certainly didn't appreciate how distressing the whole episode would be for him.

We would probably have had them both 'done' immediately but we quite fancied a litter of Westies. I saw it as a way of offsetting some of the expenditure our furry friends had cost us but I just couldn't see Madge agreeing to part with any of the pups.

Once when walking the dogs over Hayling Island we had met a woman who was walking 12 small 'Yorkies' together. It was utter mayhem. She explained two of them were the parents of a large litter and she didn't have the heart to part with any of the pups.

I could see I would have exactly the same problem with Madge if we too ended up with puppies. Despite my reservations regarding the impact on Monty and the future of any potential litter, we agreed Tasha deserved another chance at becoming a mum.

So 6 months later, when she came into season once more, we went through the same traumatic episode of Monty in increasing distress, barking and whimpering and Tasha not moved in the slightest. We came to the conclusion Tasha was simply not the maternal type and she didn't want to know. I empathised with Monty and there was no way I would allow him to go through that again in another 6 months time, so we took both to the vet and had them 'done.'

It was goodbye to our dreams of a litter of Westie pups but with some relief we wouldn't be up to our ears in them either. Monty sailed through his operation, which after all was quite minor. Tasha's operation and anesthetic was that much greater and she was very groggy when she was returned to us. She lay in her basket looking very tired and forlorn for several hours. Then the anesthetic, if not the pain seemed to clear away and she tried to resume normal activity.

The problem is dogs don't seem to realise when they are incapacitated or ill, they try to carry on as if nothing was the matter. Unlike some humans who just need a stray sneeze to convince them they have flu and need to dive into bed straight away, dogs seem to be made of sterner stuff.

In Tasha's case we were concerned she might try and do too much too quickly and hurt herself or tear her stitches in the process. We took it in turns to sit with her and keep her relatively quiet. We brought food and drink to her and kept Monty away, just in case she saw him do something she disapproved of and wanted to get up and box his ears.

*   *   *

When Monty was approaching 2 years of age and Tasha was one, Madge started getting twitchy again. She had now completed the transformation from babies to puppies and in the continuing absence of grandchildren; the need to have another puppy was back in evidence. This time, though, it needed more thought.

Getting Tasha when we had Monty was one thing but introducing a third dog, male or female, could upset what to date had been a very stable relationship. Two males might fight over a female or two females just fall out with each other. Tasha was very strong willed but physically very small; if she met an equally strong willed but larger dog, then she could end up getting badly hurt. I had many misgivings but as usual Madge's mind was made up.

What was it with Madge? She always went over the top on everything. Multiple kids, multiple jobs, multiple caravans (see later). The only thing she ever had one of (to date!) was husbands, so I suppose I should be grateful for small mercies.

Anyway, I thought the lesser risk would be to go for a female. Monty at least would respect a girl dog even if Tasha took umbrage, whereas if we were to select a male dog then both incumbent dogs might go to war with him. We hoped a puppy might appeal to Tasha's maternal instincts but had some reservations about this.

Although I had been converted to Westies I was still not a fully-fledged 'dog' person by any means so I insisted if we had to have another puppy then it was the same breed again. We carried out what was becoming a familiar routine to search for a litter. We thought we had struck lucky when we found a litter would be due very soon at a breeder in the Midlands.

Madge rang them and found they had just been born and there were 6 puppies in the litter, split equally between boys and girls. The only problem was, all six were spoken for. Ouch. Madge was distraught. She'd set her mind on a puppy and having done so, wanted one quickly. Madge has never been renown for her patience. I scoured the press but was not able to find another Westie litter that would be ready in the near future.

Then our luck changed. We had left our phone number with the breeder just in case a potential buyer pulled out. They rang up to say an elderly couple that had booked a girl dog had cancelled as the husband had been admitted to hospital. We didn't like the idea of our benefiting from someone else's misfortune but we were assured the gentleman would be OK. It was just the period of convalescence he would have to take meant they had put their acquisition of a puppy on hold for a few months.

So fate had been kind to us and the matter was settled. We could pick the puppy up in a few weeks and the time passed with the sort of growing excitement and anticipation one normally associates with the birth of your own child.

Madge had insisted on having the right to name the puppy as I'd named the first two. She picked 'Daisy,' which was met with universal approval from both the children and myself. Finally the day arrived to collect her. It was a long drive but we arrived at the appointed time. The breeder's house was on a housing estate and the normality in appearance of the detached house at the end of a 'close' gave no hint dogs were bred there.

I did wonder if we had the correct address. We rang the doorbell and were ushered in by a middle-aged man, along a hallway and into a living room. As we passed the kitchen I saw several tiers of cages, housing a variety of animals. Yes, there was a smell. 'Who in their right minds keeps a lot of animal cages in a kitchen', I wondered to myself.

Both the puppy, already named Daisy, and her mum were in the living room waiting for us. As with the other puppies it was love at first sight. She was such a beautiful fluffy bundle. There was one difference however in comparison with our memory of Tasha and Monty. Daisy appeared to be far bigger. I double checked with the breeder on her age. Yes she was 10 weeks old, a fact supported by her pedigree certificate and her ears were not yet being upright.

I asked if we might take some video footage of Daisy on our first meeting with her, just as we had done with the other two. To my surprise the man seemed very reluctant and started to question us as to why exactly we wanted the pictures. I thought for a moment the situation might turn nasty and jeopardize our acquisition of the puppy but fortunately his wife intervened and calmed him down. I hastily concluded my filming and paid the money (£350). Madge had quietly picked up Daisy for the video and was now making a beeline for the exit. I joined her and we practically fell out of the front door.

We jumped in the car with Madge in the back holding Daisy and drove off. Then as we got to the end of the close a man dressed in overalls ran out into the road and waved us down. Having just escaped a slightly dodgy situation I wondered what on earth was up this time and wound down the window. The man asked how we had come by the puppy cuddled up on Madge's lap.

'What's it to you?' I ventured.

He explained he was from the Local Authority and suspected the couple we had just met of using their premises for commercial trading purposes without proper licensing. He was effectively carrying out a covert operation and staking out their house. Hells bells, I'd never imagined working for a local council could be like a James Bond undercover operation.

As he clearly had no intention of trying to take Daisy off us I relaxed a bit and took my foot off of the accelerator. If he had threatened to take Daisy he might just have ended up decorating the radiator as we disappeared in a cloud of dust.

I answered his questions about how we had come to be there and where we had seen the advertisement. I didn't volunteer details of what we had seen in the house and he didn't ask. We finally got away, leaving the man to continue masquerading as a window cleaner. If he had been there on his 'stakeout' as long as it appeared then the houses in that 'close' must have had the cleanest windows in the area. We had a good laugh on the way home about the whole situation and I wonder to this day as to whether the undercover window cleaner finally got his man.

When we got home, we put Daisy into the dog carrier and took her into the back garden where Monty and Tasha were sniffing around. Both came bounding over as we placed the carrier on the ground. Monty gave some interested sniffs and wagged his tail. Tasha went ape. She barked and snarled at the tiny pup. Daisy was petrified. She rolled onto her back in a gesture of total submission. A tendency incidentally she has retained even today in adulthood if anyone speaks to her sharply.

Madge put Tasha on a lead and backed her away while we undid the carrier door. Daisy emerged very cautiously and as Tasha took a frenzied lunge towards her she again rolled onto her back. Tasha seemed to calm down slightly and Madge eased her a bit closer so she was well within sniffing range but not so close she could snap at her. We spent several minutes trying to get the girls used to one another. Monty was no trouble at all; he just lay down next to Daisy. Finally we took the puppy back indoors.

'What have we done?' asked Madge rhetorically. 'If we leave them to it, then Tasha could kill her.' I agreed. I desperately hoped the situation would calm down and, in the meantime, we would have to segregate Tasha and Daisy. We still had a couple of child safety gates and I fitted one across the open cloakroom door. We put Daisy inside the cloakroom with some food, water and a comfy bed. Neither of us wanted to isolate her in this way but we would take turns to sit with her to make her feel wanted.

I settled the puppy and then stepped through the gate into the hallway, closing it behind me. I heard a noise and half turned back and suddenly there was Daisy next to me! Being tiny, she had squeezed between the bars of the gate to be with us. Madge gently returned her to the cloakroom and cuddled her there while I fetched some plastic chain link fencing and cut a section to fit across the gate to block the gaps. She could still see through it and keep up with 'goings on' in the house and hopefully make distant contact with the other dogs. For the moment Daisy would be safe. I sat in the living room and Madge joined me a few minutes later.

We were discussing what we would do when we heard a slight bump come from the hallway and a few seconds later Daisy walked into the room. We couldn't believe it. I thought at first, even with baby teeth,

Daisy had managed somehow to chew enough of the plastic fence away to clear an exit but as I looked at the gate it was clearly intact. She must have used the links in the fence as a ladder and simply climbed to the top and then just hurled herself onto the floor, hence the bump we heard. We were both staggered a tiny puppy could have achieved this as well as highly relieved she hadn't hurt herself.

Madge made a big fuss of her while I found a large piece of cardboard and fastened it to the inside of the gate. Daisy would now be faced with a smooth wall on her side, impossible to climb. Then, with a premonition that defied logic I put a couple of cushions on the floor next to the gate on the hallway side. A few minutes later Madge and I were back in the lounge continuing our discussions when Daisy walked in the room again. I looked at Madge.

'I think Houdini has come back as a dog,' I said.

Madge cuddled Daisy while I inspected the gate. Everything was in place but there were puncture holes all the way up the cardboard. She had managed to use her claws as climbing pitons all the way to the top and again throw herself over the other side. I popped her back into the cloakroom and we both hid around the corner. A couple of minutes later a furry nose appeared and Daisy clambered onto the top of the gate. I rushed forward and grabbed her before she plummeted down. She might not escape injury indefinitely the way she was carrying on.

We were staggered. Only 10 weeks old and she was climbing like an expert. Apart from Monty and his wall hopping there was nothing from the others to compare to this. Despite some reservations over Tasha we were delighted. Every dog had brought something new and different to the pack and Daisy was only just beginning. If only Tasha would accept her more readily.

Finally, our prayers seemed to be answered. After only a few days Tasha stopped her aggressive moves towards Daisy, although Daisy herself continued to roll onto her back whenever Tasha approached. It seemed Tasha had just been marking her card and showing her from the outset who was leader. Now she felt the message had been rammed home, things started to quiet down. However, we still had to be very careful to respect the pecking order so we didn't inadvertently spark something off.

Talking about pecking order, what about Monty and Daisy? We seemed to have a confused situation here with each seeming to have precedence at certain times. I sort of worked it out, I think. Monty was the number two and Daisy was at three. However, in certain things

Monty gave way to Daisy, although it appeared more on the basis of a male displaying a degree of gallantry and letting the lady go first. This particularly applied to feeding when Monty would refuse food until first Tasha and then Daisy had been given something.

The relationship Daisy developed with the other two was much more distant than the close bond between Monty and Tasha. Daisy was simply petrified of Tasha. Even when she grew to be twice the leader's size, Tasha's personality continued to dominate her. Daisy would rarely go ahead of Tasha when we took the dogs for a walk; if Tasha stopped then Daisy stopped to stay behind her and any tugging of the lead on our part was met with a digging in of all four feet. Daisy spent her time in the house staying as far away from her as possible, which meant she was also usually away from Monty, given he tended to stay close to Tasha.

So did we make a mistake in getting a third dog? Probably yes. Daisy is a beautiful dog with a great temperament, but her fear of Tasha tends to dominate her life detrimentally and it's been unfair on her. The only time Daisy will hold her own against Tasha is when we are preparing to go for a walk and Daisy joins in the general hurly burly trying to get their leads on first or when the dogs are welcoming Madge or myself home after an absence of one or more nights. All three dogs will pile in together and swamp us with love and affection.

Daisy has a slightly alarming habit of greeting you on such occasions. She grabs your hand in her very large jaws and holds it gently while her tongue licks all over your hand and fingers. If you are not expecting it you might well think you are about to get your fingers ripped off. Don't let the size of a Westie mislead you. They are small because of short legs, many of them have heads as large as much bigger dogs and larger heads generally mean larger teeth. Monty and Daisy in particular have very sizeable fangs.

We decided to re-visit the subject of obedience training. Having tried and given up with Monty at formal obedience classes we decided not to take either Tasha or Daisy along after we acquired them. So the entire dog training was down to us and I'm afraid Madge and I were disastrous failures in this respect. Westies, at least our ones, like to do their own thing and although they want to please us, their enthusiasm takes the form of displays of affection rather than obedience.

We tried throwing a ball and seeing what they would do. They all responded the same way. They would rush after it, give it a good sniff and then come back to us without it, wagging their tails like mad. At least Monty and Tasha waved their bushy tails back and forth while Tasha just whirled her little furry stick about.

As they've got older and well set into a routine and pattern of behaviour the dogs basically do what we want, when we want them to, without any formal words of command. The only problem is if a cat, hedgehog, squirrel, supermarket trolley, piece of paper blowing in the wind or anything else suddenly appears. In which case all semblance of obedience goes flying out of the window in the general melee that follows and as far as I'm concerned it's too far embedded within their breed to prevent it from happening. All we can do is try and contain the situation when it occurs.

The size and shape of the dogs was very relevant when we had to consider the question of 'dog flaps'. During the summer months we had been happy to keep doors open or at least ajar for the dogs to go in and out. As the weather turned colder we started to shut the doors and relied on the dogs 'asking' to go out. They did this either by barking for attention or just sitting next to the door and looking pleadingly at anyone within range of their brown-eyed stare.

After a bit of debate we decided to get dog flaps for both back and side doors. I bought the 'medium', size and for ease of fitting located each of them in the lower door panel about 9 inches off the ground. To aid access I fitted a 'step' to ascend and descend on either side of the door. Then I stood back and motioned to the dogs to jump through. They just stood and looked at me. They had no idea as to what I was going on about.

Madge and I spent the next hour trying to show the dogs how they could pass through the dog flap but either they were exceptionally thick or playing a game with us. Just waiting for one of the family to try and actually demonstrate the technique and get stuck. Finally, showing her usual level of patience, Madge just picked the dogs up one at a time and threw them through. That did the trick.

* * *

Although we had 3 fully grown dogs, at the time we still had the 2 rabbits, Dolly and Fudge. We took great care to keep dogs and rabbits apart and even laughed when we saw the dogs digging to get under the fence into the rabbit enclosure while at the same time just inches away the rabbits would be digging at the other end of the same tunnel, presumably to escape. We stopped the excavations before they met up but we were unable to stop them meeting up with dramatic consequences, some time later.

The rabbit enclosure incorporated a low wooden gate into the garden where the dogs roamed free. I secured the gate and piled wood up against it to raise the height so the dogs would be unable to jump it. We reckoned without Daisy's proven abilities as a climber. One day a piece of wood was added; a length of trellis, which sloped down across the gate and into the garden. It may have been a trellis to us but to Daisy it was a handy ladder. A while later there was a commotion. Monty was barking and Tasha was going hysterical. Not totally unusual but the tone of the noise said something far from usual was going on.

Rushing outside we saw Daisy in the Rabbit's enclosing chasing Fudge around. Daisy thought it was a great game but somehow Fudge didn't see the amusing side. Fudge disappeared behind some boarding, which we put there as a protection against foxes, just like matadors run behind a protective screen to escape the fond attentions of the bull. (Talk about cheating, it's not like the poor old bull has much of a chance anyway). Although Daisy might have carried off some kind of comparison with a bull the way she charged about, Fudge was no Matador and simply quaked behind her screen.

I scooped Daisy up and chucked her over the gate into the garden as gently as I could manage under the circumstances, where Tasha immediately disciplined her for daring to go after the rabbits without her leader.

Dolly was nowhere to be seen. What happened to her has already been described in a previous Chapter and involved me demolishing part of the shed to retrieve her. Suffice to say everything ended well. Daisy hid with her ears down for a while, knowing she had been naughty but she was only following the instincts of her breed, and was quickly forgiven.

The dog's personalities were fascinating to see develop, with Tasha, physically inferior, but very much in charge of what she regards as her pack. She always stays very close to us when off the lead in the park and always reinforces any stern tones by us in addressing one of the others with a quick snarl and nipping of the feet or neck fur. Tasha is like a bomb waiting to explode should anything cross her path to which she takes offence. Like roller skaters, trailers and half the local population minding their own business.

Monty with his quiet personality always gives way to her. He regards it as his job to patrol and protect the property just as Tasha sees herself as protector of her people. Daisy is different. She has learned to growl at things to support Tasha but really, apart from being by far the largest physically of the 3 dogs, her aggressiveness rates a little lower than that of a very large and fluffy chicken.

The dogs don't have an outside kennel, as they are more than happy highjacking our home. Why is it the dogs are always curled up in comfy chairs and I end up either standing or sitting on the floor? ('Don't disturb the poor dears, they're asleep.') Perhaps I should take up residence in the dog basket?

My eventual salvation was the arrival of the grandchildren. A young child does not appreciate what a dog is and might well treat it as they do their toys. Like trying to winkle the eyes out with a finger or attempting to pull the legs off. Some dogs will put up with a lot (not Tasha) but every dog has a limit. They can walk away when things get rough but if cornered by a toddler bent on havoc then incidents can happen.

There was also the matter of the garden. The dogs fouled the grass on occasion when they hadn't had a walk, which meant we couldn't let the children play there. So, not wishing to take risks, we decided to segregate the species. We scratched our heads over how to achieve this. We decided the dogs would be excluded from the main garden and I erected a piece of fence and a home made gate between the conservatory and shed to achieve this.

The dogs then had the small paved area to the side of the house with entry into the side porch where we placed their food and drink bowls. A dog flap led into the kitchen and then a door led out of the kitchen and into the hallway. As the hallway lead to other rooms we needed to partition it off in some way but we racked our brains as to how we could achieve this.

We took the drastic action of commissioning a local wrought iron manufacturer to make up a specially measured piece of wrought iron fencing and gate to be fitted halfway along the hall. The only problem was the kitchen and downstairs cloakroom were on the dog's side of the gate and the children would need to use them on occasion. We decided they would only do so when escorted by an adult.

The children had the closed off back garden, the large conservatory on the back of the house, leading into the dining room and lounge and then into the hall. We closed off the dining room door leading to the dogs' part of the house and placed a child gate across the lounge door into the hallway.

*   *   *

So much for security but it's nigh on impossible to prevent an inquisitive and resourceful Westie from escaping from your protection and control every so often. While out for a walk or running free around the park Tasha will never run off, unless she was in hot pursuit of a cat or similar target (like kids on skateboards).

Monty or Daisy however are the first to explore a gap in a fence and trot into a garden adjoining the park and have a sniff around. If the garden has an exit route elsewhere then we would be in trouble. Luckily they won't stray far and when Tasha barks then they return, albeit with some reluctance. With all 3 on leads and out for a walk they're reasonably well behaved, except when we meet anyone else with a dog, when some kind of skirmish sometimes occurs. For some reason a dog on a lead is more aggressive than when roaming free.

We tried not only socialising them in the park but also took them to places where there would be a lot of people. One thing we found out was Westies do not mix well with Car Boot sales. The events tend to be held in the summer months when the weather is hot and the dogs are slowly cooking and hence very edgy. There are usually other dogs there too, which means an inevitable confrontation (where Tasha is concerned). Nothing serious of course. Just a lot of frantic barking and tugging of leads with a lot of people giving you the old 'can't you keep your noisy dogs under control then' looks.

If you're in luck and there are no other dogs around then our three will generally just sit quietly in the shade. That is, until some well-meaning person comes up exclaiming 'Oh, what lovely dogs.' Is this 'Mum, Dad and Baby then?' I suppose Monty with his dogly, almost regal stature does look like a 'Dad' and Daisy could pass for 'Mum,' in fact, given her size, she could pass for several mums all rolled into one.

However, despite her diminutive stature, there is no way Tasha will put up with being 'babied.' She's the leader and she doesn't mind pointing this out to anyone who isn't fully cognisant of the fact. She will certainly not be belittled in front of the others and a soft cooing will generally be met with a deep rumbling growl. 'It's alright,' we usually explain. 'she's just being protective of her parents.' The explanation being reinforced with a toe up Tasha's bottom.

There was just one occasion I took Monty to a Car Boot sale on his own. Being cautious, I waited until just before the allotted finish time then marched towards the church car park where the event was being held. I was met with dozens of people leaving the event and coming towards me. At this very moment Monty decided to answer a call of nature. Big ones! Right then and there, on the pavement outside of the priest's house. And I didn't have a 'poo bag' with me! I don't want to write about it any more. I get choked with embarrassment just thinking about it. Thanks for the mini cowpat Monty!

Control over the dogs in all these situations is only as good as the lead and collar constraining them and this sometimes gives a problem. A collar too tight and you'll choke them or at the least they will be very uncomfortable; too loose and with enough pulling and wriggling the dog can shed the collar.

The usual advice about the tightness of a dog's collar is to be able to put 2 fingers only inside it when fitted. We often allow a little more slack as the dogs seem to be a bit more comfortable like that but they have occasionally pulled their heads from their collars when being walked and run off into a garden. The problem is they have no id badge when that happens as you're left clutching it on the end of the lead. Luckily, we usually know where they have run off to and a knock on someone's door is usually enough to retrieve the miscreant.

There was one occasion we thought we might lose Daisy when she was off the lead in the Park and was picked on by a couple of Labradors who frightened her; she took off in a mad panic, flying right out of the gate. Fortunately, both Madge and I were present and I left her with the other two while I took a lead and went in search of Daisy.

I was desperately hoping she wouldn't get lost or have an accident with a car. She left the park at some speed and I thought she would instinctively try to make her way home, about 400 metres away.

I hurried along praying she was OK. I reached our drive and there she was, lying under a car near the closed front porch door, panting heavily. I walked quietly up to her and clipped her lead on; breathing a deep sigh of relief.

While writing this book we had the biggest scare of all. I have described elsewhere when we had to make a hole in the side of the shed to rescue the rabbit. The dogs eventually had access to this shed and started to widen the original hole. I wasn't too bothered as the only thing beyond the shed wall was the garden boundary fence. I reckoned without a team of enthusiastic Westies. I suspect it was Daisy, as resident escapologist, leading the 'work' but they managed to crash through the fence panel and into the next-door neighbours garden.

We were oblivious to this until the lady who lived 3 houses up knocked on our door to ask if we were missing a dog as she had one sniffing around her back garden. 'Not us' said Madge confidently and then looked around and saw no trace of any dog. She rushed outside and saw the matching holes in the shed and the fence and panic stations set in.

I rushed off with a lead, following the woman back to her garden where I found a remorseful Daisy trapped up a blind alley by her garage. On the way back I encountered Madge who had Tasha in tow, retrieved from the garden next door but of Monty there was no sign.

For the next 2 hours we searched high and low for Monty but to no avail. Marie, Alan and Mike all joined the hunt but drew a blank. We had all the neighbours checking their gardens but no clue as to how far he might have wandered. When Monty is absorbed in having a sniff around he can be oblivious as to where he's going.

By now the evening had closed in and darkness fallen. I had come back home to pick up a torch and had set out again to further the search. With the extra quiet you seem to get when night falls, Madge went out into the back garden to call out Monty's name and listen for any sign of a response from him. After several shouts of 'Monty', she thought she heard something. After more urgent calls his bark could be clearly heard and from not too far away. The next-door neighbour emerged with a torch as he also recognised the bark.

Our gardens backed onto the rear of a long garage block serving the people living at the back of us. Our son Mike climbed over the wall and joined the neighbour at the bottom of his garden. The garage block split in two where he was and there was a small gap of a few inches, tapering away to nothing towards the front end of the block. The gap had filled over time with rubbish of various kinds.

You've guessed it. Monty was wedged into that gap. He couldn't go forward because as I said the gap narrowed as it went forward and the rubbish was preventing him from backing up. It was pitch black by now and he could barely find enough space to fill his lungs to bark. There was also a danger of some wood and rubble coming down on top of him.

Mike pushed himself as far into the gap as he could while the neighbour held the torch to guide him. At full stretch Mike could just about get his hand under Monty's body and lift him firstly upwards and then back towards him. Finally Monty was free and to everyone's relief reunited with the rest of the family of both the human and canine type.

It could all have ended so differently if Madge hadn't tried the desperate calling of his name and Monty hadn't picked up on his mum's voice and answered back. He might not have survived such difficult circumstances through a long night. As it was, even Tasha was so happy that on his return she didn't even tell him off.

10.2   A Day in the Life

I thought describing a typical day would be a good way of explaining our dog's personalities and the relationship between each other and with the human part of the pack.

You'll remember mid way along our hallway there is a wrought iron gate and fence that serves to contain the dogs and keep them and the grandchildren apart. Typically when I come downstairs in the morning, Tasha is sitting just inside the gate whining piteously. As soon as I open it she starts to bounce up and down on her back legs, with front legs pawing the air and twisting her torso in mid air in a body swerve. She obviously wants something. In the hall there are 2 empty dog baskets, one of which was recently occupied by Tasha.

We always put out more sleeping areas than we really need as the dogs don't have set pitches but often play 'musical dog baskets ' during the night, which usually translates into Tasha changing her mind about where she wants to sleep and the others moving around to accommodate her. There is also an old chair Monty is now curled up on. It makes it more difficult for Tasha to disturb him there 'Good morning Mont' I venture. Monty ignores me and gently snoozes on.

As I walk through to the kitchen Tasha follows me, hoping for a tit bit. There is another dog basket in here within which Daisy is crashed out. She is a sizeable dog with a very dense and very white coat, like a polar bear cub. As I approach she rolls onto her back in the classic 'give up' posture and invites me to tickle her tummy, which I do.

I go out the far side of the kitchen and through the door to the side porch where the washing machine is. The 2 food bowls are empty by now and the 2 water bowls are pretty low. There is 1 empty dog basket next to the washing machine and by the exit door to the sideway where the dogs can run about is a small puddle of wee. Although they were walked at 22:00 the previous evening, for one of them it seems the night was a bit too long.

I turn to them and in a scolding voice show my disapproval of the act. Tasha immediately follows up my tone of voice by growling at Daisy (who is the only one of the others in range) and nipping her in her neck fur. I grab the mop and bucket and clean things up. I empty and re-fill the water bowls and put food into the other 2 bowls, one with dry food and one with soft meaty chunks. Tasha pays no attention to the dog food; she's after   tastier stuff and knows I always go to the fridge to get the milk out for breakfast.

After washing my hands, I open the fridge door and she looks expectantly at me with those big brown eyes. I toss her a couple of slices of lean ham. Tasha ignores it and still looks at me. I give in; pick the meat up, tearing it into small strips and offering it to her. She takes it daintily from my fingers. Daisy just looks at me. I chuck her a couple of slices as well, having another slice ready for Tasha, otherwise she will take Daisy's food off of her.

Monty is still asleep but his nose is twitching and his ears are up so I know he's aware of what's going on.

'No more, go and eat your own food' I instruct Tasha. I return through the gate and look back. Both Tasha and Daisy are looking at me through the fence bars. Westies are good at just looking, with their big brown eyes. Especially when they think it's time for food or a walk, which is just about any time they are not asleep. They fix their gaze on you and track you as you move about, just waiting for a bit of eye contact you must avoid at all costs, as doing so brings on feelings of guilt that you are not attending to them.

For the next couple of hours the household busies itself while Monty and Tasha stay in their baskets, watching and listening to everything happening around them. Daisy has gone outside to avoid upsetting Tasha.

Come 09:30 the 3 dogs know they are due for a walk and assemble by the hallway gate. They sit in the upright position with large brown eyes firmly fixed on whoever approaches, waiting for the 'w' word. After a while Daisy gets bored and goes outside. Finally Madge goes through the gate to them. 'Walkies!' she calls out. Monty and Tasha are already there, tumbling about under her feet. There's a crash from the dog flap as Daisy takes it at speed and joins them. They continue to mill about while Madge fixes the leads and takes them outside.

They decide to have a sniff about in the front drive. There's obviously been a cat invasion overnight; attacking one of the bin bags and boy do they know. Madge doesn't stand any nonsense, shortens their leads and hauls them out the drive and up the road. They pick up the pace until the corner, where the postman is emptying the letterbox. Daisy plonks herself down onto her plump posterior to watch him. Trying to move a stationary Daisy is like trying to drag a concrete block about, so Madge pauses. The postman finishes, jumps on his bicycle and peddles past. Tasha barks like mad at the bike and Madge moves them off, dragging Daisy who is still looking over her shoulder at the man peddling into the distance.

Round the corner Monty stops dead. He has spotted a post he wants to wee up. It's about 10 feet in front of him but Monty likes to give notice he is going to stop by stopping in advance then walking slowly forward to the object in question. He tries lifting the right leg but isn't happy with that; he re-addresses the post with the left leg but the goes back to the right leg again. Madge hauls him up the road.

A man is cleaning his windows so Daisy plonks herself down to watch him. Madge's patience is starting to wear thin so she scolds Daisy. Tasha recognises this and darts at Daisy, nipping her in the neck fur. Off they go again. The weather is good and they can go to the park today. It's about 400 metres away but once the dogs know they're heading in that direction they pick up speed.

Once inside the park, Madge removes their leads and they scamper off, working their way along the edge, constantly sniffing. All the dogs do their numbers 1 and 2 that Madge picks up in her poo bags.

Part way round the dogs meet their friends coming the other way. Taz, a big dog that looks like a cross between a boxer and a Great Dane, a couple of Labradors and two Dalmatians. They all mill about wagging their tails and sniffing each other. Madge chats to the other owners who she knows well. Walking dogs is a good way of socialising oneself as well as the dogs.

Of they go again. Tasha does a 'commando crawl' (body flat on the ground and paws out in front, pulling the body forward) indicating she is very happy. The other two run off but Tasha always stays close to Madge. Just before they go out of the far side of the park Madge pulls out their titbits and calls the dogs by name. They rush to her and devour the goodies while Madge puts their leads on. Out of the park and around the corner for the walk home.

A lady is doing some gardening as they walk past. Daisy plonks herself down to watch, only to get hauled off. It's getting a bit warm now and the dogs have chased about quite a bit. Their little pink tongues emerge as their means of sweating and they pant as they move erratically forward, taking turns to stop and sniff. Madge drags them up the road and finally reaches home. The dogs head for the water bowls and drink their fill, then retire to their beds for a rest.

Midway through the afternoon somebody leaves the hallway gate open by accident. Now if Tasha is there she will never attempt to go through the gate unless she has her lead on and is going out for a walk. Daisy will sometimes run through the gate, depending on whether or not Tasha is present. If she is then Daisy will not incur her wrath by going through it.

Monty on the other hand always has one eye on the gate and can often be seen 'testing' its security by prodding it with a paw. Given the opportunity he will always charge through the open gate and head up the stairs at a rate of knots. He then disappears into our bedroom and hides out under our bed. Any attempt to extricate him is met with growling and threatening teeth.

In this case only Monty shoots out and up the stairs. I follow with his lead. I've found a frontal approach doesn't work as he just moves away; an attempt to grab his collar will guarantee being nipped; an oblique approach aimed at clipping a lead to his collar rather than grabbing his person, however, works a treat. Monty is led back downstairs where the 2 females are ready to box his ears as soon as he gets back through the gate. I protect him as best I can and calm the situation down.

Evening comes and with it dusk and darkness. The dogs are alert now for visitors, including cats and foxes diving into our rubbish bins. Don't ask me how they know but they do. Monty's barking announces the arrival of Marie's friends several seconds before the door bell rings. They are admitted and start up the stairs to Marie's room, to a tempest of barking from all 3 dogs. The upstairs is a hallowed place and if they are not allowed up there, they don't see why complete strangers should be given access.

By mid evening the 3 dogs think it's time for their late walk and start to congregate around the hallway gate. Every look in their direction meets with the silent stares I know so well. However, they also know I only walk them wearing a certain coat and shoes and are watching out for these. As soon as they see me decked out thus there is a bustle of anticipation. I go through the gate and say 'Walkies!'

Immediately Daisy runs outside and starts to feed from the shared food bowl. Monty just runs away and hides. Why the two of them behave like that to me is a mystery. They don't muck Madge about but always play 'hard to get' when I'm doing the drag around the block. Tasha hasn't moved and waits patiently for her lead to be clipped on.

Eventually the others return. I kneel down and Monty puts his paws up my chest to be tickled underneath. Not to be ignored, Daisy taps my arm with her paw. I have to tickle her as well. After a few minutes of close attention we finally set out. Progress is slow. They are all having a jolly good sniff and Daisy has noticed somebody walking down the road about 200 yards away and insists on waiting and letting them walk past before she will move off.

Suddenly we move from a stuttering drag to a headlong charge as they get wind of something and race off with me just about hanging on. Tasha is going hysterical; when she barks in her high pitched yelp she sounds like a dog in pain and you can see all the curtains twitching as people look out to see what's going on.

I finally reel them in and things calm down. I'm always reluctant to strong-arm them when they get excited, as I don't want to hurt their necks and throats by pulling the leads back too sharply. It's quite common for them to breath hoarsely for a while after one of their mad dashes.

By now the leads have platted themselves together rather like when dancing around a Maypole. I spend a minute untangling them while they keep sniffing. Monty starts to do one of his 'shuffles'. Whereas the girls do their 'number 2s' in a pile, Monty insists on doing his on the move, which has certain practical problems when it comes to picking it up, especially in the dark. I take out my bag and put my hand inside, pulling the bag back over the hand and proceed to carry out a task which doesn't bear think about. At this point I just want the walk to end or at least to reach a disposal bin.

We press on until I can just see in the distance a fox walking along the middle of the road and clearly oblivious to everything. The dogs have not yet spotted it. Their vision is not that good and the wind must be carrying the noise and scent off in another direction. I hastily re-direct the walk down a side road.

Finally after a good deal of tugging we get back home. The dogs each get a titbit, scarcely merited, but they have come to expect, feeding Tasha first of course. The water bowls are re-filled and the dogs adjourn to their beds, waiting for Tasha to make the first pick as to where she will sleep tonight.

Peace descends until about 02:00 when Tasha can be heard whining pitifully. She has gone out through the dog flap and now can't get back in again. The flap is several inches off the ground with a step up to help the dogs negotiate it. Unfortunately when Tasha is a bit tired she can't always climb up, especially on the return trip when the jump up is a bit higher than on the way out. I go downstairs and open the door; she marches in wagging her tail. I go back to bed, only to be woken at 04:00 am with exactly the same thing. I make a mental note to saw the bottom of the door off the next day, dispensing with the steps and I finally return to bed. Madge complains about my cold feet.

Having dealt with a representative day, I would now like to move on to describe what we have learned about our Westies behaviour and needs, set out in a number of dedicated sections.

10.3 Looking after Dogs

There are 2 key things in a dog's daily life (or 3 if they haven't been 'done'). Feeding and 'walkies.' But other things are important as well, if only to the dogs owner. This is where I get a bit boring and talk about certain aspects of dog ownership. So here are a few things to be considered and what we did when we found out about them. I'm not saying for one moment we are necessarily correct; but the newish doggie people out there can just add this to the pool of knowledge that helps to create true, practical experience.

Feeding:
1. Do you stick to just one food all the time for the dog?
   If you don't want your puppy to 'decorate' your carpet, it's best to select a good quality puppy food and stick to it while they are very young and their stomachs can't cope so well with change. Later on I see no reason why the diet cannot be varied, although it's best to introduce any change on a gradual basis. It seems to be acceptable to the dogs and more interesting for them too.

2. What about 'hard, dry food' as opposed to 'moist chunks'?
   I believe both are fine. The only practical point is the dry food keeps for a long time whereas the moist food will 'go off' or attract flies if it is not eaten quickly. So in my opinion there is a higher risk of 'food poisoning' arising with the latter. I also believe crunching up the dried food is better for a dog's teeth and gums than the softer varieties.

3. What about human food for the dog?
   Members of our family often offer the dogs food from their plates or some leftovers after they finish. I see it as a 'bonding' thing. There is also occasionally surprise pickings for the dog when there is an accident in the kitchen and foodstuffs drop on the floor.
   Interestingly, not all food is equally appealing to all our dogs. For example, Monty simply loves cheese but Tasha hates it. Tasha loves yogurts but Monty is indifferent to them. Daisy on the other hand will eat absolutely anything offered to her, unless it has a de-worming tablet secreted within it. In which case she

separates the tablet in her mouth, spits it out and eats the remainder.

4. What about 'titbits' and treats?
We started to introduce titbits to Monty when we trained him to 'sit' and in the dog training programmes I have watched on TV this seems to be the recognised way of rewarding a dog for doing the correct thing. The only problem we had was it appeared Monty also watched the same programmes on the box and was ready for us. After the success of 'sit' we couldn't get him to obey any other instruction and he became impervious to the treats.

However the giving of 'titbits' in the park at the end of the run-around session proved a remarkably successful way of getting the dogs to come back to us so we could put them back on their leads for the walk home.

The only type of treat we stopped giving were pigs ears and the like which the dogs tended not to eat in full immediately but have a bit of a chew and then 'bury' them for later. This led to fights when Monty or Daisy innocently sat in a dog basket Tasha had 'buried' her treat in earlier.

5. What about drink for the dog?
On this one we are much stricter than on the food. We have only ever given water to the dogs to drink. (Having said that I have a deep suspicion Stephen once emptied a can of beer into Monty's bowl when he was our only dog). The water needs to be very fresh and cool, especially in the warmer months.

6. What about sharing food when there is more than one dog?
This is a very tricky one as not only does each individual dog's whims and degree of hunger come into play here but also the 'pecking order' within the pack. If segregation is important (e.g. if tablets are to be given) then food or 'treats' can be handed to the individual dogs. Most importantly to Tasha first as she is the leader, then Daisy and lastly Monty.

Notice although the sequence of feeding is vital, the quantity of food given goes largely unnoticed by the dogs. So, for example, as Tasha is a smaller dog than the other two then although we feed her first it will be with a lesser quantity than we offer the others. Tasha is oblivious to this fact; as long as we offer food to her first then she's quite happy.

The dogs are surprisingly gentle when taking food from our hands and only Daisy when she is ravenously hungry gets a bit careless and poses even a slight threat of an accidental nip. Quite often after a hand feeding session the females will reward the giver with some licks of delight. Monty doesn't 'kiss', he's a male after all and above such sloppy things.

Dogs in their nature, being pack animals, want to do whatever the leader (the owner) wants and so they are naturally obedient. However they don't speak English and only react to tone of voice or very obvious body language. If you want them to obey commands then you are into 'training' where over time and with rewards the dog learns to associate an action with a command (verbal or gesture). Well that's the theory of how to have an obedient dog. The problem with Westies is their natural inquisitiveness and powerful terrier instinct make training comparatively difficult. To see how we got on, please see the next section.

*   *   *

Obedience:
I am the very last person to claim to be an expert in achieving dog obedience. Come to think of it, that also applies to wifely obedience. Despite having on many occasions reminded Madge she promised to 'obey' as part of her wedding service vows, she has steadfastly refused to accept the situation. Instead, claiming she felt a bit poorly standing at the altar and so couldn't be held to anything she said at the time and besides which, she had her fingers crossed.

Generally speaking, one word from me and the dogs do exactly as they please (and that goes for Madge as well). When we bought Monty we actually started off with the best of intentions and took him to dog obedience classes when about 6 months old, as I described in an earlier Chapter.

Since then I have found Westies seem to be at the extreme in terms of 'doing their own thing.' Monty has learned to 'sit' but that's just about it. Unless of course you issue commands to do things he'll do anyway. Like 'Eat!' 'Sleep!' or 'Go and pee up the leg of that woman standing over there with her back to you!'

There were 2 breakthroughs that salvaged the situation. One was to take treats to present to him when he came back to us when we were about to leave the park. This worked most of the time but when he was in one of his particularly playful moods then he still wouldn't return. The clincher was when we got Tasha. She always stayed close to us even when off the lead and one look from her, let alone a bark in his direction, was always enough to bring him quietly to heel whenever we wanted.

*   *   *

Health, Hygiene and Grooming:
The problem with dogs is they can't talk or at least they don't speak English. They do, however, communicate through their doggie language and through their behaviour. If your dog is behaving in a languid manner, sleeping a lot, eating grass, off their food or not responding to your presence with their usual enthusiasm, then there is a possibility they are unwell in some way. Other signs may be constantly licking their paw, scratching, nibbling a part of their body, dragging their bottom along the floor, unusual faeces or making strange noises. In other words, a bit like teenage boys.

Westies as a breed are prone to skin problems but only Monty has shown any sign of this. He actually had quite a bad time of it until we were recommended a medicated shampoo that did the trick. For a while he had to suffer the indignity of wearing a protective cone collar to stop him chewing at himself.

The kids called him 'satellite dish head', 'cone head' and various other rude titles, not that he seemed to mind; he was too busy trying to get it off. After a while he got used to it and didn't seem to mind at all. The only problem was the day when Tasha spotted a squirrel in the garden and started to bark like crazy. Daisy shot through the dog flap and into the garden with Monty in hot pursuit. Unfortunately the cone collar was larger than the dog flap opening and there was an enormous crash as something gave way. Fortunately it was the dog flap, rather than Monty.

Dogs are infamous for having fleas but for us they have never been a problem because we have always used the Frontline spray. It's expensive but well worth it. The dogs absolutely hate being sprayed and rubbed down with the foul smelling stuff but we always take them for a walk immediately after being done so they are not breathing in the worst of it and they have something to take their minds off of the aroma.

The walks in the park, and particularly the areas of long grass, have gained a few 'ticks' on odd occasions and it's not always obvious that they've been picked up. They can be removed by various means but the only very difficult one we had was on Daisy's face right next to her lip and the dog was unwilling to have us monkey about with her in that location. Working an inch away from the fairly sizable fangs of a panicking dog tends to focus the mind but Madge managed it. (I've got more sense than to try, which is a nice way of saying I'm a coward).

The only operations (bar one) the dogs have had is when they were all 'done'. Monty's operation was a snip (pardon the pun) but for Daisy and Tasha it was significant surgery. The upsetting thing was to see them trying to behave normally when they came round from the anesthetic but being in pain and unable to move freely.

The only additional operation was when Tasha had a nasty lump growing in her chest. We knew she had developed a problem as she squealed if we picked her up with our hands in a particular place. Over the weeks a large red lump appeared which didn't respond to the usual creams and ointments. The vet eventually operated to remove it and tests showed it was potentially lethal. However, they seem to have done a good job in removing it all and there has been no recurrence to date.

Grass seeds are occasionally a problem when the dogs get them trapped between their toes. You spot them gnawing at their feet and have to make an examination and remove them promptly before they start to cause infection.

The most serious potential problem is of course 'worms'. It's essential to give the dogs a de-worming tablet or the equivalent injection on a regular basis. In our case such a simple activity is far easier said than done. The tablets are very expensive and seem to have been made as unpalatable as possible to the canine taste or at least to the taste of our three dogs. None of them will take a tablet willingly.

For Tasha and Monty, Madge has adopted a technique of grabbing the dog's jaws, opening them and then putting the tablet as far down the throat as possible before letting them go. I think she's mad and inviting a nasty bite. However, not even she will risk Daisy's jaws with that trick so every 6 months we have a battle of wits with her.

Daisy's Achilles heel is her enormous appetite and so we usually bury the tablet deep inside her favourite food and offer it to her. She sniffs it carefully and takes the food; after a bit of rolling it around inside her mouth she spits out the tablet then swallows the food. Then we start all over again with a different food and the same tablet. By the time we finish we have a rapidly disintegrating tablet, a couple of fraught dog owners and a very well fed dog. After years of this I finally think I've found the right food to put the tablet in. Lambs liver. The dogs are potty for it and gulp it down without the slightest sniff.

While I was completing this book we noticed Tasha was eating and drinking very heavily but steadily losing weight. A visit to the vet confirmed what we suspected. She had diabetes. Now she has a daily insulin injection, just like humans suffering from the same condition. This has proved difficult to administer in practice, as she seldom stays still long enough for the insulin to be injected. It has also curtailed Madge's and my social activities as, to date, the kids are afraid to do the injections in our absence.

Largely because of her illness, Tasha has become weakened so that she can no longer manage the walk to and from the park, although she still loves to sniff her way across the grass and mix with other dogs. Madge has solved this problem in typical style. Every day plopping Tasha into a children's pushchair and carting her off to the park with the other 2 dogs trotting alongside. Much to the amusement of all passers by who look into the pushchair expecting to see a baby but are met by the big, brown-eyed gaze of a white fluffy dog thoroughly enjoying the trip.

Westies have a particularly long growing outer coat that is prone to getting matted and tangled if not regularly attended to. Their short legs don't help keep their bodies clear of wet grass etc and so they tend to get dirty fairly easily. We pop ours in the downstairs shower cubicle when they are a bit on the mucky side. It's something you can overdo however as frequent washing prevents their natural oils doing their own work on the coat. The dogs respond very differently to this treatment. Daisy quite likes it, Tasha will tolerate it under protest and Monty has to be dragged into the cubicle, alternating between quaking with fear and snarling with rage.

We also give their coats a brush every now and then. Tasha doesn't really need it as she has no topcoat and the undercoat is very short and fluffy. Monty and Daisy however require regular attention and their undersides tend to get matted as they are relatively close to the ground. The problem is Monty will roll onto his back when required but won't have his fur touched and Daisy obstinately refuses to cooperate in any way at all. Madge usually just shouts at them until they do what they're told, probably because they fear the loud voice will attract Tasha's attention.

Dog's nails can be a problem as they can grow over long. We used to have Monty's claws trimmed back but after the vet made a misjudgment and sent a jet of blood across the room and Monty howling in pain we decided not to do it that way again unless absolutely necessary. Instead we walk them frequently on hard surfaces that tend to wear the nails down naturally.

* * *

Travel:
Although all 3 dogs had spent long journeys in the car when we first bought them as puppies, only Monty had followed up the experience with regular car journeys and hence he is by far the happiest about travelling about. Tasha is OK, mainly because few things faze her but she is too small to easily see out of the windows when sitting on the seats and so gets less out of the experience.

This is probably for the best as on those occasions she puts her front feet onto the window to look out, she invariably goes into hysterics watching other dogs being walked along and the equally threatening sight of little old ladies towing shopping bags on wheels. Daisy hates car journeys and usually whimpers from the moment we start to the moment we halt, when she scrabbles furiously at the door to get out.

As a puppy we often took Monty to Havant in the car, with me driving and he sitting on Madge's lap in the front passenger seat, struggling to look out the window as he was a little on the short side. This became his favoured position and even now he's fully grown he sits there scanning the world as we go past. The problem is his claws are a bit sharp at times if Madge doesn't have jeans on, so we keep a blanket around to use as a buffer.

If Madge drives and I'm not in the car he is a bit too short to see out of the window easily when sitting directly on the front passenger seat, so his second favourite position is spread out on the parcel shelf at the back. He was lying there one day when Madge pulled up rather quickly and he found himself flying through the air and plastered over the front windscreen, like one of those stick-on Garfield's.

When we acquired Tasha, I continued to drive into Havant with Madge in the passenger seat and with the 2 dogs. However, both of them wanted to sit on Madge's lap. The funny thing was although in just about everything else Monty is willing to give way to Tasha, when it comes to Madge, he stands his ground. It isn't so much he prevents Tasha from assuming the favoured position on the front seat, it's more he doesn't actually get off to make room for her. So Madge ends up trying to balance two Westies on her lap at the same time.

As Tasha grew there was even less room and sometimes Monty would lean forward placing his paws on the dashboard. It meant he gave up some room on the lap but got a better view through the windscreen. Tasha was too short to try this manoeuvre, as she couldn't reach the dashboard without the risk of falling off Madge's lap.

Because the others aren't so keen, Madge sometimes smuggles Monty out and drives around with him on the seat next to her. He loves it but has to put up with the 2 girls having a go at him when he eventually gets back.

Nowadays if I open the car door then the dogs will automatically jump in and sit on the back seat. Monty will try and move onto the front seat if you don't stop him and Daisy will start to hyperventilate. If we take a route leading anywhere near the vet's building Tasha will cry and Monty will shake. Other than that they're fine!

So having gone on at length about pedigree Westies. Here's a little tongue in cheek quiz to test your knowledge of Westie cross breeds, or at least to test what you've found out in this book about their nature.

10.4 Mixed Dog Breed Quiz

Although I have lauded the pedigree Westie, you occasionally meet a cross breed which has inherited some of the Westie characteristics. Test your knowledge of such things with this tongue-in-cheek quiz.

Question: Which breed is well known for rescuing people trapped in snowdrifts? Searching them out by investigating every tree, ski-lodge, chocolate bar wrapping and snowflake until the dog trips over the victims and after administering a good licking, asks for a titbit.
Answer: The St Westie.

Question: Which breed is used by police and armed forces to detect drugs, explosives, illegal immigrants, dead frogs and unmentionable deposits left by other animals?
Answer: The German Westie.

Question: Which breed is used extensively as a ferocious guard dog to defend property and access, snarling at anyone who approaches and licking them to death if they come any closer?
Answer: The Rottwestie

Question: Which breed makes an ideal guide dog for a blind person? Leading them safely across the road whenever the pelican-crossing symbol shows green or across the same road at very high speed and directly in the path of on-coming traffic if a cat of any colour appears on the other side.
Answer: The Labrawestie.

Question: Which breed looks good when sporting parts of it's tail and body as bare with occasional 'pom poms' of fur along the way? The overall picture contrasting with the nasty scratches and bite marks up the owner's arms.
Answer: The Westieoodle.

Question: Which breed is used as a gundog, rushing off when a flying bird is felled, unerringly locating it, giving it a good sniff and returning to the gun bearer without it?
Answer: The Retriwestie.

10.5 Canine Conclusions

Having cast abuse upon our canine friends in an earlier Chapter, where I did my best to give sound reasons for not having them, I suppose it's only fair I review that list in the light of my practical experiences. So here is the list again with revised comments.

1.	Dogs have big teeth and bite.
A dog never bites unless it is given reason to do so. To ensure such reasons do not include being abused by small children we have placed an internal barrier inside the house to keep the children and dogs separated, except when they are under adult supervision.

2.	Dogs are very noisy.
Dogs only bark when there is just cause, usually when something has disturbed the status quo, like a stranger entering the house. It has been very useful to have the dogs alert us to people entering our front drive or back garden for nefarious purposes.

3.	* Dogs are expensive to keep.
Dogs can be expensive but pet insurance will keep the really big bills at bay and who counts the cost of a loved one anyway?

4.	Dogs defecate.
True and picking it up is not a pleasant action that comes easily, especially when you are being keenly observed by the local neighbourhood watch. I don't use a poop scoop but my hand in a carrier bag turned inside out. All I can say in mitigation is, like babies poos, somehow it's different when they belong to you.

5.	Dogs are a health hazard.
Our dogs were regularly de-wormed and treated with Frontline flea spray and we experienced no real hazards to the family health.

6.	Dogs are a tie.
True and we would never contemplate putting them in a kennels but the family rally round and help look after them when Madge and I are away.

7.   Dogs are smelly.

Perhaps it's because I'm acclimatised to it but I rarely smell dog odour. Ours are bathed in the cloakroom shower every so often or when they've got a bit mucky. The only odour we've had a problem with is when the dogs have done a wee on the carpet at night because they've been bursting and the back door was closed. We have replaced the carpet with laminate flooring and mats that can be cleaned or disposed of.

8.   Dogs are anti-social.

The dogs are generally very friendly once they've been introduced to somebody by one of us (i.e. a leader from their pack).

9.   Dogs and children don't mix.

They do mix when under supervision and as I said above we have taken steps to ensure they are separated unless supervised.

10.   Dogs try and fight each other.

This is happily a very rare occurrence but quite frightening when it happens. The dogs have lots of friends they meet in the park and get on well together. The 'difficult' dogs are known and the owners usually keep them at a distance. Tasha has her moments but only when on a lead anyway.

So, I suppose you can say I'm a convert to dogs but mainly it's only my own. Others' dogs I can still take or leave but I am much more tolerant towards them now and recognise half the problem previously was down to me judging them by human standards and behaviour, instead of allowing them to behave like dogs.

One sometimes comes across a useful little table in dog books, which gives a clue as to dog age compared with human ages. 'Table 1' below gives my assessment, based on the observations of our own dogs. The general pattern is of rapid growth followed by a relative levelling out. (The numbers are in years). What you do is to look up the dog's actual age in the first column and the number against it in the second column gives the human equivalent. Note this doesn't work for all breeds as, generally speaking, the larger the dog the shorter the overall life span.

Table 1 (Dogs)		Table 2 (Boys)	
Dog Age	Equates to Human Age	Actual Human Age	Equates to Behavioural Age
0.5	9	1 - 9	1 - 9
1	15	10	10 - 14
2	24	11	15
3	28	12	16
4	32	13	18
5	36	14	17
6	40	15	15
7	44	16	14 - 11
8	48	17	12 - 8
9	52	18	11 - 7
10	56	19	10 - 6
11	60	20	12 - 10
12	64	21	15 - 13
13	68	22	18 - 16
14	72	23	22 - 20
15	76	24	24

For comparison, you can use the same idea to express the age of human male adolescents against 'normal' human beings. Again I can confirm this by personal observation. The pattern here is initial regular development, followed by deterioration into a 'Neanderthal' state and intermittent hibernation while adopting strange nocturnal habits and reverting to a language based on primeval grunts. Again you use the first column to look up the youth's age and the value against it in the second column is an assessment of his behavioural age.

Having dealt with the flesh and blood monsters, I shall now go on and describe my relationships with the metal variety.

Chapter 11

Vehicles

You might reasonably ask why I have included a separate Chapter in this book on the subject of 'vehicles'. It's just they have played a significant part in our lives and deserve to be recognised as such. We have had and relied upon a number of different cars over the years. Some more reliable than others in terms of getting about and in varying degrees of comfort. Some purchased entirely for the benefit of the children, either learning to drive or providing them with their first form of independent transport.

But I'm racing ahead of myself because before the cars came the motorcycles, at least for some of us. In the midst of the cars came the caravans, a means of cheap holidays and of upsetting all the other motorists sharing the same single carriageway.

11.1   Motorcycles and Scooters

I can't really tell you why I bought one but I did. Motorcycles are the single most dangerous things on the road (except for my wife's friend Josephine). And I bought one!

My excuse is in 1969 it provided a cheap means of travelling from my home in central Portsmouth with my parents, to my place of work at the SEB Computer Centre in Havant. The other excuse is I couldn't drive at the time and anything was better than the bus, which had been my mode of travel until then and took forever to get me to work and back.

Anyway, my kids will tell you it was not really a motorcycle. In their world anything less than a 250cc machine is a mere toy and only deserves to be laughed at. This was a Honda 90. 90ccs of mean acceleration and arse tightening speed – not!

I bought it from the Honda dealer in New Road (now gone) along with all the gear. It took an age to get the heavily oiled clothing on and off and the helmet was so tight my head felt it been down the birth canal and re-born every time I took it off. I had panniers and a windscreen fitted to the bike and really felt I had arrived. After all, it was much more powerful than the Honda 50's prevalent at the time. (Stop laughing, kids).

In those days there was no compulsory CBT training and with 'L' plates fitted you were on your own. You could then spend the next 2 years causing carnage to others, if not yourself, until you were forced to take a test. I never got that far. After a few months of horrendously over revving the engine when trying to change gear, accidentally driving up pavements and cleaning flies off my face, I'd had enough of that particular game.

I started taking driving lessons with the Selborne School of Motoring that had offices along the side of Fratton Bridge in Portsmouth. After about 20 lessons I took my test and passed first time. All this without a word to my parents who guessed I was up to something and were quite worried about where I kept sneaking off to and refused to talk about. They were fairly relieved when they found out I wasn't sneaking off to have a relationship with a married woman but merely to acquire a license to kill or maim anyone who got in my way.

After that brief but off-putting experience of motorcycles I opposed any and every proposal by Madge and the boys to acquire any vehicle with less than 4 wheels. However Madge wanted some cheap transport to help her travel quickly from home to the 2 schools where she was working and Madge, being Madge, was not put off by the small fact I was implacably opposed.

Unbeknown to me she had seen an advertisement for a Honda Melody (a bright yellow 50cc scooter) at an address in Waterlooville. One day she walked the 3 miles there, bought the scooter and rode it home, despite never having been on anything like it in her life before. She then hid it in the alley at the side of the house so I didn't know it was there.

I knew something was going on because Madge had adopted one of her innocent expressions and over the next few days the kids kept sniggering. Eventually I found the scooter and went ballistic. Talk about unsafe. It was a death trap. I suppose the only justification for having rubbish brakes was the engine couldn't get up enough speed to make it too much of a problem. But the only way I could wean Madge off it was to give my blessing to her getting something more of a 'proper' motorcycle.

So off she went and bought a secondhand 100cc Suzuki RSX that was, at least, in very good condition. She passed her CBT test and after she practiced on the bike for a few months, took her motorcycle riding test – and failed. She was bitterly disappointed. Apparently she had to wear some sort of radio communicator with the examiner who was on his own bike and travelling just behind her. He would give the direction of travel over the link and conduct the test by that means.

Unfortunately when she had put her helmet on it had dislodged the communicator and as she rode around it had gradually worked loose and then disintegrated. She couldn't hear him give directions and had just gone her own sweet way. Other people might have stopped and adjusted the thing but Madge reckoned she rode a lot better without him talking in her ear and putting her off.

After much consoling she put in for another test and to her eternal credit and delight, she passed. Madge always said passing the motorcycle test was one of the few things she had actually achieved in her life, although I pointed out she already had a car license, a certificate for swimming a mile, had overcome dyslexia and raising 6 kids wasn't a bad achievement either.

It was inevitable Madge would want to upgrade the bike. After all, she argued, she had been confined to lower 'cc' because she had been a learner, now she had a full license the world was her oyster. The only constraint was her height and strength. Your feet have to touch the ground on both sides of the bike when stationary to enable you to balance and control the not inconsiderable weight. You also need enough strength to haul it onto it's centre stand when parking and if the worse comes to the worse, pick it up off the floor.

She chose a 250cc Honda Superdream, a sensible choice under the circumstances. I was still worried about her being on motorcycles, which I still regarded as deathtraps, not because I distrusted her riding ability but because car drivers do not always see an approaching motorbike. My point was to be proven only too vividly a couple of years later.

Madge rattled around on her Superdream for a while but the hankering was still there for a 'real' motorbike. She constantly plagued me to upgrade to a monster but I refused to allow it. Finally, I accepted it was something she needed to get out of her system and agreed.

She bought a Suzuki GSX600 costing £2000. In doing so she broke the cardinal rules. When seated she could barely put her toes to the ground at the same time and there was no way she could manage the dead weight of the bike. Nevertheless she rode it and got a tremendous buzz out of doing so.

When she opened it up she just had to hang on for dear life and stay with it, hoping the momentum would keep her upright. For the first time she got 'nods' from other 'bikers'. This is an acknowledgement given within the biking fraternity to other true bikers. That is, people who ride the real bikes and not the toys Madge had managed with up until then.

Eventually after a few months, having got it out of her system, Madge admitted the bike was too much for her and agreed to sell it and go back to the Superdream. Although she had put the smaller bikes down a couple of times when stationery, she had not had an accident on the giant bike but ironically she was to have a couple now she was back on a smaller machine.

The first occasion was when 2 lanes of traffic were waiting at traffic lights in Havant town centre. Madge was moving up on the outside when heard a noise and looked down. With her concentration disturbed she went straight into the central reservation railings and got her arm caught in them. Fortunately she was unhurt, apart from a loose arm but her pride was definitely dented. A short while later something much more serious occurred.

A little old lady who lived just a hundred yards away gave Madge some unwanted flying lessons. Madge had ridden from our drive along the main road on her motorcycle where the little old lady was waiting in her own drive to emerge onto the Queen's highway. Unfortunately either she didn't see Madge or her right foot must have developed a twitch because without warning and just before Madge reached her, she careered across the road and up onto the opposite pavement, into a hedge.

Madge was left trying to occupy the same position in space and time as this moving lump of metal and so collided with the side of the car and made her attempt on the world high jump record. She might have made it too had she not attempted to take the bike with her, gripped between her legs. 'Purely an instinctive reaction,' she explained later.

Madge cleared the car with ease and described a graceful arc in the air before, fortunately, landing on her head, which meant the damage was minimised. The little old lady got out of her car and without stopping to enquire as to Madge's injuries, rushed back into her house and hid. Not the way to behave after you crash into and injure someone.

The old lady was handed a lot of penalty points and told to re-take her driving test but I understand she never again drove a car. Just as well, in my opinion but to this day, despite living only a few doors up the road, she has never apologised to Madge or asked her how her injuries were.

Fortunately, a passing postman witnessed Madge's bike-less journey down the road and rushed to her assistance. Other witnesses and residents hurried to her aid and an ambulance was summoned. It whisked Madge to the Queen Alexandra A&E where, to everyone's astonishment, it was discovered she had broken no bones, although a few of them seemed to have bent a bit.

I was away at the time on business, and was passed a message when I returned to my hotel. After a quick phone call to establish the severity of her condition, which was said to be non-life threatening, I checked out of the hotel and rushed back to the hospital. When I arrived Madge was tucked up in bed and doing everything in slow motion, accompanied by groans and grimaces.

'Have they given you any pain killers?' I enquired.

'Yes,' she said, 'Lots.' and pointed to a small heap of tablets by her pillow.

'You're supposed to swallow them, not collect them,' I ventured but 'she who is as tough as nails' didn't want to know.

'I don't believe in taking tablets, you know that.'

'It's a good job you weren't Moses in a previous incarnation then,' I retorted but Madge didn't seem to get the joke for some reason. The Superdream was a write-off even if Madge wasn't and so the motorbike riding for her came to an enforced conclusion. I didn't give her the chance to resurrect it. Three years later, Madge was finally awarded £4,000 compensation.

* * *

In tandem with Madge's escapades, the children of the family had been bitten by the motorcycling bug to varying degrees. As a teenager, Stephen wanted some cheap transport and we bought a Honda Runaway 50cc machine for him to learn to ride on. He not only proved to be a very competent rider but also was also very keen on the maintenance side. This proved to be the basis of his leaning towards working with mechanical things as a career.

He passed his test first time and after a period of riding a Honda CJ250, eventually went the whole hog and bought a large machine, a Yamaha XJ600. He looked and behaved as a true biker although his youthful enthusiasm took over on one or two occasions when he either went much too fast or put the bike down (fortunately while going at a relatively slow speed). He once took Madge on the back and then did a speed I wouldn't admit to here; Madge came back with a new hairstyle under her safety helmet.

Eventually Stephen saw how Richard had abandoned the motorcycles for cars and did likewise, to my great relief. The XJ600 stayed in our garage for a couple of years until Stephen was forced to bring it back into use. He had to travel about 15 miles to and from work every day and very restricted car parking facilities made having a motorcycle almost obligatory.

Richard had initially followed in Stephen's footsteps, albeit with slightly less enthusiasm for the both the speed and the maintenance side. He bought a 250cc Superdream after passing his test but didn't progress up to the huge bikes but migrated across to cars instead.

In the meantime, Emma had a go on the Honda Melody that was still knocking around but after she frightened herself to death on it trying to negotiate the Havant Hypermarket roundabout, she was put off motorcycles for life and never rode on 2 wheels again.

Mike followed his elder brothers. He learned to ride on a 50cc Yamaha DT50 machine, migrated upwards to a Honda CB125 and after passing his test borrowed a lot of money from us and bought a second hand Kowazaki ZXR 400 sports machine. He rode it for a while but hadn't the dedication of a true biker and had little interest in the maintenance side. Like the others, he moved off onto cars.

To my great relief neither Alan nor Marie had any inclination at all towards 2-wheeled transport and although we had up to 4 machines around for some time afterwards they didn't inspire any move towards using them. Alan was very definitely a car person and saw them as an end in their own right whereas Marie, although enthusiastic for cars saw them solely as a means of getting to college, nightclubs or the shops.

Although Madge has resurrected Richard's Superdream recently as she felt sorry for it rusting away in our front drive, at the moment she can't justify the cost of insurance and road tax so I'm keeping my fingers crossed the mad moment will pass. Richard intends to use the machine during summer months to reduce the cost of travel to his place of work, which is 30 miles distant.

Madge then started to feel sorry for the 2 other decaying machines and first had Mike's old Honda CB125T brought up to spec and then the 24 year old Honda CJ250. Common sense says to sell them to recover some of our investment but Madge doesn't think along those lines. So I think my car will have some company in the garage for a while to come.

So after a look at the motorcycles, lets see how we fared with 4 wheels.

11.2   Cars

Before we get onto the metal objects themselves, I would like to get off my chest a few things about drivers. They say the major safety weakness in any car is the nut behind the steering wheel. I just wonder if the nut has a gender.

I have never for a moment suggested I actually understand women. In fact even after 30 years of marriage to one of them I don't pretend to know what makes them tick. I just know Madge comes from a different planet (and yes I know about the 'Men are from Mars and women from Venus' contention and fully agree with what the book says).

Groucho Marx once stated 'Anyone who says he can see through women is missing a lot'. Well said, but the statement ignores the fundamental point that men just can't see through women anyway. Men can't understand women and women (except for those reading this book, as I don't want to upset you) can't read maps. These are simply basic rules of the universe.

I sometimes read of hot debates as to whether some famous celebrity is 'gay' or not and argument rages about it for months and even years. It's easy to resolve. Just give him a map of London and request a route from the British Museum to Earls Court in the rush hour and you'll soon see if they are of fundamentally male or female orientation.

An extension to the map reading bit is, as every man knows, women can't drive cars. This opinion comes not from a deep prejudice on my part or general male chauvinism but from simple observation over many years from behind a steering wheel. I acknowledge almost all men drive to so-called **excess** (* see below) but I contend women are simply drivers in varying levels of medium to low competence (** see note below). Not that I blame them.

I have come to the conclusion women are lacking a basic gene in their make up. This leads to them being vulnerable to medical conditions with long Latin names affecting driving concentration, such as 'passenger gabblitis' and 'parkus reversi neverinamillionyearsum.'

* like too fast (simply enjoying the exhilaration of speed); or driving too close to the vehicle in front (I just want to take a look at that sticker on the back window); or driving aggressively (my wife will be upset if I don't get home on time).
** like never checking the instrument panel (I don't like the colours anyway); or never checking lights/tyres etc before journey (but I've just

done my nail varnish); or signalling one way and turning the opposite (it's the dyslexic indicator stalk to blame).

Men and women have differing priorities when it comes to driving. A man's priority is to demonstrate his driving competence and to prove his superiority over everything else on the road. A perfectly valid attitude; however a woman's priorities are communication and appearance. A woman won't be able to tell you the colour of the traffic lights she's just driven through but she'll give the person next to her chapter and verse on the colours and style of the dresses in the adjacent shop window.

What about the technical side of driving?
Madge has friends mentioned in an earlier Chapter, named Jennifer Lawson and Josephine Carpenter, although I am tempted to refer to the latter as Mrs X, to blur things from a legal standpoint, given some of the things I shall be revealing about her. Don't get me wrong, both are very nice ladies who I like and welcome into my house but that's got nothing to do with my opinion of women drivers.

One day Madge and Josephine got into the car with Jennifer behind the (steering) wheel when she drove off, turned into a main road and started to drive up the wrong side of it. After a bit of blind panic when reality set in, the situation was corrected but afterwards Jen claimed it wasn't her fault because there were 2 other women drivers in the car and they didn't notice either.

One day when Madge went to the school to do her job she saw her friend Josephine trying to reverse into a parking bay between a saloon car and a brand new, electric blue, 4x4 vehicle. It took Jo five attempts, moving back and forth, before she finally managed to scrape all the way down the side of the 4x4.

Madge walked over to her and suggested she move her vehicle before the owner returned, as there was a slight chance of him being upset his brand new car had been demolished. Jo tried to drive forward out of the bay with the side of her car locked against the 4x4. After a bit of manoeuvring, she ended up still inside the bay, parked diagonally and wedged between the two adjacent cars. Now that's what I call talent!

Madge won't attempt to reverse into a car parking space unless there is sufficient room to park a dozen London buses. I once knew a woman who refused to drive anywhere unless she could get there by only making turns to the left.

What about the following conversation that Jo had late one evening with a police officer that had pulled her over for driving erratically (i.e. her normal style).

'Tell me madam, where have you been?'
'I've been to see my best friends wedding.'
'And did you drink any alcohol there?'
'No officer, they didn't have any.'
'What, no alcohol at a wedding reception?'
'It wasn't a wedding reception, it was a cinema'
'A cinema?'
'Yes, I've bee to see the film 'My Best Friend's Wedding'.'

Exit confused police officer with colleague stuffing hanky into mouth to stop laughing.

Madge planned to have Jennifer and Josephine round for coffee one morning and I cleared out of the way to give the girls freedom to chat. When Jo turned up, she said to Madge.

'Just my luck to arrive when your husband was leaving.'
'Why was that?' asked Madge.
'Because I was doing a 'U' turn in the road and was up on the pavement when he drove past me. He just looked across and sadly shook his head.'

Q.E.D.

And then there's Madge herself. She once came home and told me a police car had waved her down and a policeman had got out and shouted at her for doing something dangerous. When I asked her what it was, she said she didn't have a clue. God help us!

Still, Madge at least realises the reality of these things. We were driving home late one night when a car went by on the other side of the road with no lights showing at all. 'Look at that stupid woman, driving without lights' Madge said.

'Hang on' I responded, 'It's dark, how did you know it was a women driving?'

'Because the car didn't have any lights on,' came the irrefutable reply.

Then there's common road courtesy. Trying to get out from a side turning onto a busy main rode is often made easier by a kind person letting you out but how many times is it a women driver? In my experience, virtually never.

Mind you the same can also be said about nearly all BMW drivers, irrespective of gender. For me, BMW drivers are almost universally arrogant and rude and deserve to live out their lives making left handed widgets in a Skoda factory.

So much for my tongue in cheek opinions on women drivers that are likely to get me short shrift from Madge, her friends and all the other females reading this book. Let's take a safer look the vehicles themselves I've been associated with over the years.

* * *

The first family car I can recall is my dad's old Austin 10, complete with running boards. It was in this car the family made the trip to Scotland and back, when my dad was posted to Lossiemouth in 1954. We had dad, mum and 3 kids crammed into the car with the luggage and all sorts strapped onto the roof. Given there were no motorways then, it did pretty well to make the trip. So did we.

My father was keen on large cars and later the family wallowed around in a Vauxhall Wyvern, followed by a Humber Super Snipe, complete with pullout wooden trays in the back. As money became tighter he moved onto Russian built Lada's, the butt of jokes in those days, but were still a notch up from the Skodas and provided reliable and cheap transport if you could put up with a lower level of comfort.

Like shouting above the noise of the engine (I assume was a scaled down version out of a tractor). They even came complete with starting handle most people found hilarious until they couldn't get their cars started in the dead of winter and suddenly decided it was a good idea after all.

* * *

I described earlier how I passed my driving test in 1970. Shortly afterwards I sought my first car. I had my heart set on a Ford Escort that had come highly recommended to me as a first car and of which I'd read glowing reports in the motoring press. Obviously, I could not afford a new one, but my budget could stretch to one about 2 years old.

With my dad's help I bought a vehicle for £525 and away I went. Although the car drove well it was notoriously unreliable and proved to be a rust bucket. Like the house we were living in at the time (in Chichester Road – see earlier Chapter) the Escort gave me plenty of opportunity to develop my car maintenance and diagnostic skills.

It also gave me an insight into the insurance industry after the car was struck twice when left parked outside of our house. I eventually got fed up with worrying about it and started to park 2 side streets away for safety, only to have it hit there by a passing milk float. I truly believe that car was fated to jump in cowpats as well.

One day my dad told me he was getting a new car and would be trading in his Lada (for a brand new Lada!) for £1000 part exchange. I offered to buy the old Lada off him to make his deal easier and for cash. He agreed if we, in turn, passed my Ford Escort on to my sister Frances and her then husband. I wasn't sure what he had against them to make this part of the deal but it all happened and we started to drive around in my dad's old Lada. It actually served us well for several years and in it we had several family holiday trips to Butlins at Minehead.

We did a lot of things as a family in those days. Like going boating on Petersfield pond. This was a roughly circular pool of water, maybe 600 yards in circumference, about 10 miles north of where we lived. Although I had hardly ever rowed before and certainly not with a boat full of boisterously active kids, off we went.

Madge tried to stop the younger ones jumping overboard while I wrestled with the oars. I kept to the edge of the pond as best I could to avoid ramming other craft. Then I heard a series of 'pinging' sounds and some shouts from the bank. Fishing from the pond side was a popular pastime and it seems I had inadvertently ploughed straight across a row of fishing lines, severing the lot. I don't think I was very popular and kept an anxious eye out for irate anglers when we finally disembarked.

Getting back to the green Lada. The only negative aspect was when Madge was out one day, shopping in Park Parade with the kids and left the Lada in the car park. When she returned she found a man had broken into the car and was still there rummaging around, stealing things. Madge flew at him and made him empty his pockets out then and there. She then ordered him to jump in the car so she could drive him to the police station. The man ran off.

Madge has always attributed this happening to the car being green. Madge is very superstitious about the colour and firmly believes green attracts bad luck. I can only agree and would link it to my very first cowpat experience (Chapter 1) because Ireland is well known as a green country and the fields where cowpats reside are invariably green. However to make the colour superstition water tight with cowpats, there would have to be a bit of brown mixed in as well somewhere. The Lada had a brown vinyl roof, so there you go.

The green Lada still remains a significant car because this was the vehicle in which I taught Madge to drive and she passed her test at the second attempt. We used to conduct her practice sessions initially around the Airport Service Road in Portsmouth and then the roads of Gosport, with 3 screaming kids fighting in the back seat. Not easy to maintain concentration!

We still had the same car when we moved to The Keep and later took on my dad's next cast off, which was a white Lada. This one wasn't so good and soon clapped out. So what did I do? I bought a red Lada costing just £350. We ran it for a while then passed it on to Madge's dad Ted. I wish it had been in better condition and served him better than in fact it did.

By then I'd got Ladas out of my system and could afford a little more luxury, as well as needing far more space for a growing family. My dad put me onto a brown Datsun Bluebird Estate, up for sale some distance away. We went to look at it and it seemed just the job and became a much-loved workhorse for several years.

I started to get real car problems when Madge decided she needed her own transport and was finally forced off of bicycles, tricycles and motorcycles. She didn't exactly tell me this. I arrived home one day and flipped up the garage door. There looking at me was a car I didn't know we had.

It was a very small, old and tatty, Fiat 126, brown in colour. The colouring was fortunate as it tended to mask the rust holding the body tremulously together. It was only missing a large key mounted on the rear engine to give the impression of a clockwork car that had somehow escaped onto the road.

Madge emerged from the house, 'I bought it from a student. I managed to negotiate him to £200.'

'What from, 4 pounds 50p?' I replied.

'It's a bargain,' she insisted. 'it even has a sun roof.'

I looked at the top of the car. A large hole was badly covered by a leather/cloth combination that appeared to be held in place solely by the weight of the grime and moths.

I noticed Madge had left the keys in the ignition. A handy habit if she repeated it in public places, although it was unlikely anyone in their right mind would want to steal such an eyesore. I gingerly turned the key and the engine in the boot coughed into life with all the delicacy of a demented lawnmower.

'Just one thing,' I said, 'there's this red warning light on the dashboard which isn't going out. It looks like the oil pressure. Did it go out when you drove it round here?' It was a foolish question. Madge never bothers to look at her instrument panel.

She is not alone in this tendency as far as women drivers are concerned. Her friend Josephine had recently passed her test (I assume when the examiner's judgment had the day off) and bought a car. She reported back after her first journey the car was pulling poorly and a lorry driver had shouted at her, although she couldn't make out what it was as the smoke was putting her off.

It seemed she had driven for 5 miles with the hand brake on, despite the warning light screaming at her from the dashboard. I expect the lorry driver wanted to cook his breakfast on her hubcaps. It could of course happen to anyone, but usually only for a few feet.

Incidentally Jo carried on in this vein and in the next few trips she drove into the back of a car at a set of traffic lights, later reversed into another one and then removed her bumper on a lamp post while turning left. I banned Madge from travelling with Josephine, at least until I could take out some more accident insurance on her.

Some people might think I'm being a bit unkind in my comments about Jo (who incidentally is a very nice lady) but how many other people do you know have had their driving test stopped and were then driven back to the test centre by the examiner.

OK, I can hear the 'holier than thou' accusations flying at this point, so I'll hold up my hand and admit yes, I did once reverse into somebody. It was in a car park and I was about to reverse out of my bay when a truck pulled up behind me. I contend it had no business stopping there and that my attention was momentarily distracted by this young lady who happened to be walking in front of my car at the time and by the time my gaze had reverted to where it should have been it was too late. Bang!

I'm sure the entire male driving population can identify with this and find me totally blameless. My simple philosophy in life leading to this incident is whatever a lady is willing to show, then a gentleman should be willing to look at. And when she reads this bit, Madge will send me to the doghouse again. Move over Monty!

Picking up the tale. The brown Fiat had some pretty amazing controls but I couldn't find the winder for the elastic band in the engine. However, it did have two small levers near the hand brake for the choke and something else. Nobody knew what the 'something else' lever actually did but it was essential to pull it up when trying to start the car or the engine wouldn't burst into life.

My theory was the lever when raised, automatically sent a prayer to the patron saint of difficult cars that won't start – St Basil. Named after that wonderful demonstration by Basil Fawlty of how to deal with a petulant car in an episode of 'Fawlty Towers'.

If your car doesn't have such a magic lever then the incantation can be made orally. It goes something like: 'Oh God, Oh God. Please start. Why don't you start you utter b*****d. If you don't start you're going to the scrap yard on Monday'.

The Fiat 126 of course didn't last long but Madge was so taken with it ('It's got real character, you know') she insisted on another. Reluctantly I bought a much newer Fiat 126, blue and in generally good nick. At least it was until I forgot to top up the radiator water (in my defence I was used to cars having an overflow tank) and Madge drove it around with the red light glowing brightly at her for quite some time.

I keep telling her dashboard lights are not a form of pretty decoration but actually mean something but she just smiles at me and carries on as before. Having cooked the engine we paid out for temporary repairs and sold it on as soon as possible ('caveat emptor' when Madge is about).

By the way, I'm reminded as I mentioned the colour of the car above. Why is it when you ask a bloke what sort of car he would like to have you get an answer giving the make, model, engine size, bhp and the like but when you ask a women she says 'a blue one'?

By now the kids were getting in on the act. Stephen was still on motorcycles but Emma, to my relief wanted a car. This is probably the right time to give Madge a gold star, as it was she (aided by a few formal driving lessons here and there) taught **all** of our 6 children how to drive. She used to come back pretty fraught at times I tell you. If you're wondering why I didn't teach them, I claimed I had done my bit in teaching Madge and my nerves and stress levels couldn't take any more, which was basically true.

Madge can be like a mouse in some situations but as a driving instructor you just don't get in her way. During the sessions when she has taught our children to drive, Madge was about as docile as a bunny with a machine gun.

Like on one occasion when Emma stalled at traffic lights and the lights changed 3 times before she got it started again. The cars behind hooted their disapproval and so Madge got out and gave them all a V sign before getting back in and driving away.

On another occasion when Emma stalled, Madge got out of car, pointed at 'L' plates on the back and shouted 'Look at that; what is it? Have a bit of bloody patience will you!' On a further similar occasion, Madge got out of the car and was about to impress the driver behind with her best Anglo-Saxon when she noticed the 'L' plate had fallen off our vehicle. She waved an apology and quietly got back into the car.

Mind you when Emma spun the car when doing her emergency stop on the real driving test, the examiner was speechless. I bet Madge would have thought of something to say though.

Of course it's not just a matter of the car itself being significant but also the environment you are driving in. I'm thinking here about driving abroad on the 'wrong' side of the road. The first experience I had of this was on my first visit to the USA in 1990. It was a bit of a baptism of fire in that I was on my own and so had no co-driver/navigator to help and I flew in at about 5am, according to my body clock, having had no sleep at all for almost 24 hours.

I had to drive about 50 miles to my hotel but the good thing was having got out of the airport, it was mainly 'freeway' all the way. It gave me a chance to get used to sitting on the wrong side of the car and changing gear with the wrong hand. I rarely used the car when I was there, my business activities being in walking distance (having said that, throughout my 20 minute walk each way, I never encountered another pedestrian). So I just had to manage the return trip to the airport and that was about it.

Emboldened by the above experience, when Madge and I took the 2 youngest to Majorca for a week's holiday, I booked a hire car to help us explore the island. Things didn't get off to too good a start. We arrived at our hotel in Alcudia in the early hours and our room wasn't ready, so had to stay in makeshift accommodation for the first night. The next morning, rather bleary eyed, I was in the apartment/hotel reception when I was paged.

A bloke beckoned me outside and when I went with him he urged me to get into the back of his car where two other people already sat. Despite not knowing him from Adam and his English being very poor, he managed to convey he was from the car hire company. I tried to tell him I needed to go back into the hotel to collect the relevant booking documents and to let my family know what was going on but either he didn't understand me, or chose not to, because I got the distinct impression this was my one and only chance to meet up with my car, and if I didn't go there and then, was on my own regarding the arrangements.

I reluctantly cooperated and got in the car only to find my fellow travellers were not from my hotel and didn't speak English either. Guessing the situation awaiting me, I desperately noted some landmarks as we went along. We drove for about 3 miles and then pulled in to some offices where after some difficulty, as I didn't have the documentation on me, I was given the keys to a car and pointed at a green Opel.

So there I was, sitting in a left hand drive car in a town I had only seen part of in pitch darkness a few hours before, staying at a hotel about 3 miles distant in the general direction of 'over there'. I blundered my way back and by some miracle found the hotel and parked.

Madge had been running around anxiously looking for me. She explained she'd ascertained from reception I'd been seen going off with some bloke in a car but didn't know whether I'd been kidnapped or just arrested. I'd been gone a little less than an hour but it was a heart stopping time for her not realising what was going on.

The story has a happier ending however. We were recompensed for our makeshift room on the first night by having several free breakfasts and dinners in the restaurant (we were supposed to be fully self-catering). We also liked the car so much when the time came to get Madge her own car, I bought the English equivalent of the holiday vehicle, which was a Vauxhall Corsa.

The only other time I have driven abroad (so far) was when Madge and I decided to take a short and inexpensive break to Bruges (Brugge) and I decided to keep the cost down by making our own way. The Channel Tunnel had not been built so we drove to Dover and took a ferry across (actually a hover-ferry) and then we were on our own with just a map from the travel company to guide us. The map was misleading and in terms of the exit we needed to take off of the motorway to Bruges, downright wrong.

However, we managed to find our way onto the outer ring road and could see at a distance the famous bell tower in the central market square we knew to be very close to our hotel. Unfortunately, I reckoned without the town's one-way system. Bruges in a very ancient (medieval) town, not built for vehicles and actively discourages their presence. There are very few car parks and lots of restricted access but fortunately our hotel had it's own parking facilities, or so I had been advised. Try as I might, I could not find a road that led to our hotel next to the tower. Every time I got close, the one-way system diverted me in another direction.

I finally ended up on one side of the large central market square with the tower on the other and our hotel just behind it. The only problem was the 'no entry' sign looking at me. I was desperate. Quickly checking for policemen, I sped through the 'no-entry' sign and ended up where I wanted to be. I drove round behind the hotel to the underground car park and promptly found it was closed. Ouch!

A notice told me about a public car park not too far away but there was no way I was going to haul the luggage even a couple of hundred yards. In those days our suitcases didn't have wheels fitted. I carried on around to the front of the hotel where there were some drop-off parking bays. We parked there and took our suitcases into the hotel. The idea was we would check in and I would leave Madge in the room with the cases, settling in, while I found the public car park.

It shouldn't take long and I knew I would have to move my car quickly before I got clamped. I reckoned without Madge and her fear of lifts. She will always use hotel stairs and I will go with her except when I'm burdened by luggage, as was the case on this occasion.

After checking in, it was a bit of a hike to the lift. I looked around for the staircase (normally adjacent) and found nothing. Nobody else was about to ask where the stairs were. Being pressed for time I didn't want to haul back to reception to find the staircase so I asked Madge to come up in the lift with me. She refused. There then followed a pantomime of me trying to push, pull and drag Madge, along with 2 large suitcases into a lift. It didn't work. She wouldn't come with me and she wouldn't let me go without her (in case I didn't manage to find my way back).

I searched further and found what seemed to be an internal fire escape going upwards. That would do. We climbed the stairs to our floor and found the door at the top locked. Some fire escape! We went back down, going a different way this time and found ourselves at the foot of the steps but outside the hotel. Back around to the entrance; the people in reception gave us a very funny look as I struggled in with the luggage. It must have been like 'Groundhog Day' for them, except I was a bit redder in the face this time around.

I plonked Madge down in reception while I took the lift up to our room and left the suitcases and then we went together to re-park the car. On our return I ascertained the location of the proper stairwell and from then on Madge was happy. I just collapsed in a heap. I needed the holiday to recover from that lot.

*   *   *

I had always wanted a Company car and continually plagued my boss at work (David Mengham) to get me one, however he always turned the request down as being 'not appropriate'. I thought the wording was an outrageous cop out as a stated reason but worth remembering for the future, in case I had to use it myself in rejecting a staff request otherwise fully justified.

Eventually I was granted a car and chose an Austin Montego, 2-litre, because it had 2 folding child seats in the boot area. It proved highly practical with our large family as we could seat 7 quite easily and when 3 years later it came up for renewal I chose the same model again but opting for a 'red' colour rather than the bland 'stone grey' I had chosen the first time around.

The Ford Mondeo was my next choice and the 2-litre model in dark blue was the one that took Madge and I to Bruges and the family tour of Scotland in 1998. We all had a great deal of affection for that particular car that served us so well and so reliably over the 3 years. I actually got it back temporarily after Madge pranged up its successor (a silver 2.0 Mondeo this time) while it was being repaired. I was quite upset to see it hadn't been looked after and was in a bit of a state. The silver Mondeo was the car in my possession in 2001 when I was offered and accepted the early retirement package.

As was customary, I was offered my current car as part of the retirement deal but it was at a ridiculously high price, especially as Madge had already backed that one into a tree at Oakland School and completely stove the back in. (She swears the tree upped and moved towards her).

I turned down the car offer and shortly after I left, started to look for a new vehicle of my own selection. Armed with a retirement lump sum I had plenty of choice but for some reason started looking at people carriers. I was so used to having family orientated vehicles I automatically gravitated towards them. My kids knew better. 'Get yourself something swish,' they commanded, 'you only live once!'

They were quite right but I couldn't quite force myself to seriously consider a 2-seater sports job, just in case Madge and I needed to give someone a lift.

Then one day we were returning from a trip to Littlehampton when on the outskirts of Bognor Regis we went past a car showroom that had a row of Coupes out front in a range of different colours. They looked pretty sensational as I glanced across and I couldn't help stopping and walking back to have a nose. They turned out to be Hyundai cars. I spoke to a young fellow in the showroom who gave me some leaflets including the information another branch of the same dealership was actually quite close to where we lived.

A few days later I took my sons Mike and Alan with me and went to the local car showroom. We went for a test drive without anyone accompanying us and took the car back home to show Madge. She was very impressed with it but said it was up to me. The boys thought it was great.

We went back to the showroom and after a bit of negotiation I signed up on the spot for a 2-litre Coupe in silver. I also had it 'Teflon coated' at a very cheap price to help keep it in pristine condition.

What put the icing on the cake was when Alan spotted a cherished car number in a magazine that read B1 CHS. It virtually said BICH'S and so I just had to have it. It cost me £2,500 plus VAT and I thought it good value. Madge reckons it could also stand for a short form of BIcheno CHriS. Either way round I was tickled pink with it.

The adoption of the cherished number also set Madge off. She reckons her little Corsa's reg of KTR was worth a lot of money to someone called Katy with a surname beginning with R and if M4DGE ever comes on the market she'll probably sell the house and kids to get enough money to compete with Madonna for it. In the meantime I secretly acquired M22DGE to give to Madge as a 50th birthday present, being the nearest thing to her Christian name I could find and afford.

I mentioned, in passing, I bought Madge a Vauxhall Corsa. Until then Madge had made do with old bangers and it was the occasion of our 25th wedding anniversary. So I decided to push the boat out and buy a new car for her. It was a pretty basic model and didn't even have 'power assisted steering' but we both became quite fond of it as it took over as our workhorse after my retirement.

So much for my and Madge's cars. We have also had a legion of cars pass through our hands as we have provided a vehicle for each of the kids after they passed their driving tests. As an aside here I must reiterate Madge taught each and every one of our kids to drive. Well, OK, they all had a few formal lessons, some more than others but it was basically her helping them along that enabled all of the children to obtain their driving license within a few weeks or months of their reaching the qualifying age.

The cars for the kids were usually old bangers costing about £500, except for the first car we got for Emma that was a very presentable Ford Fiesta we acquired off of an ex-colleague of mine and cost £1800. Unfortunately those were the days when Emma was going through her relationship with 'the bouncer' and he frequently borrowed the car from her and delighted in driving it into the ground.

We actually replaced this car with another Fiesta of much lesser value but ended up almost making up the difference in helping Emma out with various repair and maintenance costs.

Stephen had been on motorcycles but when he cut over to cars we helped him acquire his Fiesta XR2, after which he bought a Nova. After he pranged that, he took over a Ford Mondeo from Mike.

Richard was also on motorbikes for a time after which we helped him get a Fiat Uno from a friend of my dad that did him until he could afford to buy his own vehicle. Mike had an old Fiesta, again until he could afford to buy his own car.

Alan was the exception. He was the moneybags of the kids, not earning huge amounts but squirreling away almost every penny. He bought a Ford Escort in very good condition out of his own funds; I just helped him check it out and bring it back from London for him.

Marie was the last one. We bought her a VW Golf from a supposed friend of the family that gave us no end of trouble with the engine overheating. One of the boys' mates kindly fitted a manual switch so the driver could turn the fan on by hand, rather than rely on an internal switch that worked only erratically.

I sincerely hope I have come to the end of buying and selling cars; at times I've done in such volume I thought I was becoming a second hand car salesman.

So much for cars and matters associated but a Chapter on 'vehicles' would not be complete without considering our adventures with the caravans we towed behind them occasionally.

11.3   Caravans

Although we'd had several holidays in large static caravans on holiday parks, I had no inclination towards 'real' caravanning in a touring caravan, as I was too fond of life's luxuries. Madge was mad keen to try camping under canvas but as far as I was concerned that was an even bigger step towards a primitive lifestyle than living in a touring caravan. However circumstances developed which affected the debate and effectively resolved it.

Stephen, as we have seen, had some educational issues caused by his dyslexia and frustration in dealing with it. We were offered a place at a special school that handled such situations and had a good reputation. It was called 'Brickwall House School' and was located about 10 miles north of Eastbourne in East Sussex, about 90 miles from where we lived. Stephen had to board there but we were very keen to keep in regular and close touch with him. Every 2 or 3 weekends at least. We knew logistical arrangements would be difficult but it was important to us Stephen didn't feel we had abandoned him. He was only 13 years old and had never been away from home on his own.

Madge and I considered the situation. I was willing to collect him from school late on a Friday and deliver him back on a Sunday evening. It meant 2 round trips of 180 miles but I could see how concerned Madge was about his well-being. The car (a Nissan Bluebird estate) would take a bashing with so much mileage and it wasn't a young vehicle but I was confident it could handle it. However, it was a lot to do on a regular basis.

Madge did a deal with me. If I obtained a touring caravan so we could take it down to the Eastbourne area and be more local for Stephen at weekends, she would drop her nagging to go on holidays in tents. What could I do but go along with the proposal?

I did, however, insist we tackled it 'properly.' The first thing was to join the Caravan Club. This gave me access to all sorts of information and advice. The next thing I did was to book myself on a Caravan course run a few miles away at Caravan Club hired premises in Fareham. It covered all the basics regarding equipment, hitching up, loading, towing and the dreaded reversing with a caravan connected. The last bit especially gave me huge respect for those HGV drivers who tow the enormous trailers and reverse the things back into narrow openings.

I hadn't realised there was so much to caravanning. I had a tow-bar and electrics fitted to the Bluebird and Madge and I started to scour the local area for a caravan to buy. A new van was financially out of the question but there were several places in a 20-mile radius selling second-hand ones. We worked out what we were looking for.

It had to be fairly large to accommodate the whole family, as all the children were too young to leave behind. It also needed to be in reasonable condition and not too heavy for my car to tow. The relative weights of car and van are a vital safety consideration when towing. The loaded van must not exceed 80% of the kerb weight of the empty car. You can tell the vans too heavy for their tow cars or have been badly loaded; the rig is usually found on its side in the road causing traffic chaos. What else were we looking for? Well, I wanted the 'kitchen' to be over the wheel axle rather than at one end as it gave more stability. I also wanted a 'loo,' however small.

Our search for a van went on. It was amazing how much choice there was. Finally we settled on a Swift Dannette we found on a sales site near Chichester. It was about 10 years old but in good nick. It had a gas hob and grill, a small gas heater and a tiny loo compartment with a minute sink but no w.c. built in.

It could sleep 2 at one end, 2 at the other and a bunk bed could be set up for a fifth. It had an awning within which several more people could sleep in sleeping bags or in a small pitched tent. It cost £2000, which was at the top end of our budget, but it was important we had it. I went on my own to hand over a building society cheque and collect the caravan. The bloke simply handed me the keys and wished me goodbye. No offer of assistance at all.

Boy, was I glad I had been on the caravanning course or I would not have had a clue how to hitch up the rig. It's easy once you know how but if you don't get it right then either the caravan nose will hit the deck with a sickening thud or it may go 'walkies' off the back of your car when you are driving along. Such an occurrence would be a terrifying thing to happen, even if you managed to connect up the emergency brake. I managed to hitch up, connected a safety stabiliser and then very gingerly drove home, a distance of about 15 miles.

Even when I safely arrived, negotiating the drive entrance from a narrow approach road was another challenge. There was just enough length to the drive for me to get the car in without the caravan on the back sticking out into the road and causing an obstruction. I got out and chocked the van wheels as we were on a slight slope. I managed to disengage the car and dropped the van's jockey wheel. I drove the car forward into the garage to give some manoeuvring room and then the whole family turned out to manhandle the van into its designated position in the drive.

We were now caravaners. I already had some gear like the extended wing mirrors and wheel chocks but I needed even more items before we were ready. A portaloo with chemicals, battery to power the internal lights and a few other bits and pieces.

A couple of weeks later the whole family set off in the car with the caravan on the back to visit Stephen. We even took the pet hamsters with us as we would not be home to look after them for a couple of days and we didn't like to impose on anyone to do it on our behalf. I had the address of a campsite from the Caravan Club that had all the basic amenities if no actual entertainment.

It took me several trips in the following months before I found the optimum route for towing a caravan through Brighton and negotiating some pretty hairy steep hills en route to our destination but on this first occasion I was glad I was wearing brown trousers and had packed a couple of spare pairs.

We reached the site, registered and were able to pick from several plots. I chose the one that seemed the flattest. By this time it was quite late on the Friday evening and so Madge and I decided we wouldn't do battle with the awning in the dark, trying to set it up, but would all sleep in the caravan.

I went in the car to pick Stephen up while Madge organised the kids. Eight of us piled into the 5-berth van. Not forgetting 2 hamster cages and 3 hamsters. Every bit of space had a sleeping bag in it. The next day, after we got the kinks in our bodies sorted out we decided to put up the awning. We'd had it out of the bag at home but this was the first time we'd assembled it in anger, as it were. It was also the first time we realised such an activity was great fun for non-participants and provided entertainment for everyone in viewing distance.

Putting up an awning, especially for occasional users or in a high wind is a great spectator sport. Also, as it is usually carried out immediately after a fraught journey and before the holiday proper has begun, it sets the tone for the entire time away. Poles never seem to fit in the right place, the awning won't thread through the channel which runs around the edge of the van, the tension of the cloth is all wrong and when you're finished it's lop sided.

Throughout the setting-up process, the air gets steadily bluer, voices become higher pitched and louder and invariably at the end the participants aren't talking to each other. In our case we took it quite slowly but got it right first time. No, actually I've just lied. We took it very slowly and made a complete hash of it.

Still in the end it was sort of up, was stable and would keep any rain off. What more could you ask for. Well actually you could ask for it to be securely pegged down all the way round so when zipped up it was proof against animals wandering in, in the middle of the night.

There were also occasions, like heavy rain leading to moving water, when sleeping in the awning was not a comfortable option, even if raised on a camp bed. It's bit disconcerting to peek over the edge of your camp bed and see your shoes float by.

Madge elected to spend the second night in the awning and finished up in the car after an episode with a hedgehog. I snored on blissfully unaware until I copped an ear bashing the next morning. So passed our first expedition. Completely undaunted, Madge declared the touring caravan would form the basis of our holidays from now on, although she kept her options open regarding sleeping inside the awning.

* * *

We spent a couple of summer holidays travelling between touring parks around the New Forest area. Village Holidays at Oakdene and Bashley Park at New Milton being our favourites, especially the latter. At Oakdene we had a potentially nasty incident when we arrived onto our pitch and I was going through the process of unhitching.

Normally I would chock the caravan wheels as a precaution but on this occasion I didn't as I thought the pitch was flat and even. Wrong! As soon as I disengaged from the car the caravan started to run backwards. I pulled on the handbrake and tried to stand firm but a laden caravan was too much for me. Fortunately my anxious shouts brought a couple of neighbouring caravaners running to my assistance. I don't know if they were good Samaritans or had visions of my runaway van crashing into theirs but for whatever reason I was most grateful for their intervention and we got the van back under control.

After a few such holidays, the kids were all getting bigger but none of them was yet old enough to make their own separate holiday arrangements, so we still had the full set along with us. Madge was complaining about needing an oven as well but we'd already invested in a fridge for the caravan and the central kitchen housing was full.

Madge came up with the answer, typically without consulting or involving me. I arrived home from work one day to find a small 10-foot Alpine Sprite caravan blocking the drive. Madge had bought it for £400 and towed it home with the Bluebird. She'd never towed before, I hadn't showed her how to hitch up and she basically didn't know what she was doing but she upped and did it anyway.

The man at the caravan sales place in Cowplain had hitched up for her and she had gingerly driven about 4 miles home. She left the van attached to the car in the drive, as she didn't know how to unhitch it. The Sprite, despite its small size could sleep 4 and was equipped with an oven, the main criteria that had driven Madge to buy it.

The solution to both our accommodation problem and the absence of an oven had been obvious to Madge; we just go on holiday with two caravans. What was less obvious to me was how we were going to go on holiday with two vans, when we only had one car capable of towing. Presumably 'muggins' would have to make two trips. (The South of France was in that case firmly out of the question).

Fortunately there was an excellent caravan park with great entertainment facilities at Selsey, about 20 miles away. A double caravan run to there and back was just about viable. We tried it out. I took the main van over with some of the kids in the Bluebird while Madge followed on in her Fiat 126 with the rest of the brood.

We set up camp in a field without marked plots and I returned for the small van that I could manage on my own. Back to the field where Madge was getting things ship-shape. We placed the vans close together, initially without the awning up so we could just step out of one van and into the other. It worked well; so well we bought an awning for the small van as well. We also invested in a couple of windbreaks.

The overall effect we ended up with, when we holidayed in that field in Selsey, was to have a parked car, next to a caravan, next to an awning, next to a wind-break, next to another wind-break, next to another awning, next to another caravan, next to another car. The whole thing ate up about 60 feet of the perimeter of the field.

We had a great time going on like this until one year, tragedy struck. By then I had acquired a company car and fitted it with a tow bar, which meant Madge could use the Bluebird. I was towing the main van with Madge following on a few miles behind with the Sprite. We were half way along the bypass between Havant and Chichester when there was a bang from behind me and I was overtaken by a wheel. I looked in the mirror and saw the caravan swaying violently and a shower of sparks coming up from the nearside wheel hub.

I managed to pull up in a controlled manner and onto the hard shoulder. The wheel had come off the hub completely and there were no wheel bolts to be seen. They must have either unwound themselves over several miles or sheered off in one explosive happening. I told the kids to stay in the car and walked up the road to recover the wheel. A few minutes later Madge caught us up. She told me afterwards she saw a caravan heeled over on the hard shoulder ahead and was just feeling sorry for the people involved when she realised it was me. I called the AA.

There was very little wrong with the caravan itself, which seemed to have taken the impact very well indeed. There also appeared to be no reason for all the bolts to have 'gone' at the same time. At this point I found out something about my caravan wheel bolts. They were completely non-standard both with cars and with other caravans. The AA man phoned a couple of major caravan dealers close by but they both said we would have to send away to get wheel bolts that fitted my van and it would take maybe 10 days.

The AA man and I consulted. We decided if I took 2 of the 4 wheel bolts from the good side and fitted them to the loose wheel in a diagonal fashion, I might just be able to tow safely. I would have to keep the speed well down. The only problem was the bypass had no turn off. I would have to follow it all the way to the end, around the roundabout and back the other way. It seemed like one of the longest trips I ever made but I got the rig back home in one piece.

We booked it in for repair at a small caravan repair shop not too far away and went back on holiday. We made do with the small van, the awning and the two cars, using the cars for storage and living in the small van and its tiny awning. Some holiday that was.

With a repaired van we carried on with our regular touring holidays but as the children grew up and went off with their own friends we found we had no further use for the small van's additional capacity. By then we'd had electrics fitted to the Danette so could link up to the camp electrical points and run all sorts of gadgets so we didn't even miss the oven.

We sold the Sprite but were a bit sorry to see it go. But this was tinged with some relief as it meant Madge wouldn't be called upon to tow again. She had nodded off at the wheel on one occasion when moving in a queue and if Emma hadn't screamed at her she would have ploughed into the back of the vehicle in front, which happened to be me. Madge is famous for falling asleep in a moving vehicle, which I why I now don't allow her to drive long distances.

The next significant change was when we had Monty. We were a bit apprehensive about taking a dog on holiday with us. Madge stoutly refused to have him put in a kennels and I agreed with her. He was part of the family and so should go on holiday with us. We discussed security, as we were concerned that with the caravan door being constantly opened he might just nip out and run off. Given he would be in a totally different area to that which he knew, he would be completely lost.

I bought a large corkscrew device that could be driven into the ground and he would not be able to pull out. We would attach his lead to this and all would be well. So off we went and everything was fine to begin with. Monty spent most of his time on a very long lead attached to the big corkscrew and he was free to snuffle around the outside of the van and awning. At night we would bring him inside of the caravan.

However, on the second day our nightmare scenario came about. Monty was quite happy until he saw the rabbit. There were lots of rabbits on the site and they scampered about during the day as well as the evening. Monty's reaction when he spied the bunny was to pull on the lead until it was tight against the big screw. He then shook his head and backed out of his collar. It all happened so fast I couldn't intervene. One moment he was there and the next he was streaking off in pursuit of the rabbit. He was quickly out of sight.

Madge was already off after him. I shouted at kids to join in the hunt and we all ran off to find him. The next hour was one of the longest of my life. Then Mike appeared carrying Monty. He'd found him trapped at the bottom of a dried out ditch, unable to climb the sides. Thank goodness there was no water at the bottom. We couldn't risk anything like that happening again. Especially as in the next couple of years we acquired 2 more dogs.

It turned out to be our last touring caravan holiday, although to the time of writing we have still retained the Danette caravan and use it for storage. It's become a bit dilapidated but we might just do it up and sell it on. Our current cars are my Hyundai Coupe, totally unsuitable as a towing vehicle, and Madge's Vauxhall Corsa that could barely pull the skin off a rice pudding. So I see no caravanning future other than possibly staying in the large static caravans in holiday parks.

I have no regrets about finishing our caravan adventures. Towing a 'van was not the most pleasurable of experiences in my book and I always found living in it a bit uncomfortable. Probably the best holiday I had in the 'tourer' was when I tore a hamstring trying to play football with the kids on the first day and was laid up for the remainder of the vacation, totally immobilised and with a large bag of frozen peas strapped to my leg.

Having said all that, I expect Madge will come up with some kind of camping plan one day; or I'll come home and find she's parked a new caravan in the drive again.

* * *

Well I think that about wraps up the story of myself, my family and our way of life. I've described our ancestors and other, more recent family members, together with our parents, brothers and sisters.

I talked about how Madge and I met and were married; how we lived our lives together and how we brought up our children. Then more recently our role with the grandchildren.

I described both my and Madge's careers over the years; the many pets we have owned and of course the dogs.

Finally I included sections on the fraught time we've had with the various form of vehicles we've owned.

I trust, overall, it has conveyed a reasonably accurate picture of myself, my wife and family and our lives together. I hope I have managed to do it in a way that has kept the reader amused and informed. I also hope that I haven't upset too many relatives or lost friends in the process.

Epilogue

Well that's about it. They say every person has one book in them and this has been mine. It's been a bit of a mission to write it, sometimes working with competing priorities on my time and energies but I am dearly glad to have done it, as it forms part of my legacy to my family and descendants.

I acknowledge the help given to me by relatives providing background information on themselves, other people and what it was like to live in other eras, all of which have enriched the contents. A few family skeletons have had to remain unrevealed in their closets, as they are still a little too hot for the present generations to handle.

At times Madge has helped and supported me in writing the book and at other times she has understandably resented the time and effort it has taken to develop and finally push it over the line. For whatever reason we will both be happy the task has been completed.

I've unburdened myself onto paper some of the events from past years and hopefully given you a little entertainment at the same time, kind reader. If you are actually mentioned in this book then I trust I have done so fairly and with reasonable accuracy and you have my apology for any errors or omissions. If you are a relative or descendent reading this book, perhaps many years ahead in the future, then I hope this has given you a small insight into the life and times of your family and ancestors.

If you've actually stomped up a few quid for this book then thanks very much. If you got it from an Oxfam shop then go back and give them a few pence more and if you are perusing it at a Car Boot sale, look very carefully at the seller. If he's a short chubby bloke with spectacles and a beard, stooped with the pressures of life and a bunch of Westies under his feet, offer him a sympathetic word and ask him if he spends most of his time jumping in cowpats. Then give him a good price for the book. Many Thanks.

Timeline

1220   Earliest recorded mention of probable ancestor as 'Birchenhoe' regarding property in Whittlewood Forest.

1520   Ancestors confirmed as living in the village of Over in Cambridgeshire.

1527   Birth of John Byccenho, my great, great, great, great, great, great, great, great, great, great, grandfather.

1550   Birth of Richard Bicheno, my great, great, great, great, great, great, great, great, great, grandfather and the first to have the surname spelled as such.

1582   Birth of Edward Bicheno, my great, great, great, great, great, great, great, great, grandfather.

1616   Birth of Edward (2) Bicheno, my great, great, great, great, great, great, great, grandfather.

1650   Birth of James Bicheno, my great, great, great, great, great, great, grandfather.

1704   Birth of James (2) Bicheno, my great, great, great, great, great, grandfather.

1723   Birth of William Bicheno, my great, great, great, great, grandfather.

1782   Birth of Joseph Bicheno, my great, great, great, grandfather.

1785   Birth of James Ebenezer Bicheno, who gave his name to the town called 'Bicheno' in Tasmania.

1819   Birth of Hemington Bicheno, my great, great, grandfather.

1852 Birth of Warren Bicheno, my great grandfather.

1856 Birth of Richard Lenton, Madge's paternal great grandfather.
Birth of Frederick George Colbourne, Madge's maternal great grandfather.

1877 (approx) Richard Lenton moves from Salisbury to Portsmouth.

1887 Birth of Frederick Arthur Lenton, Madge's grandfather.

1891 Birth of Percy Bicheno (Poppy), my grandfather.

1895 Birth of Beatrice Martha Colbourne, Madge's grandmother.

1901 Warren Bicheno moves family to Portsmouth.

1915 Birth of Percy (2) Bicheno, my father.
Birth of Norah Emily Crowley, my mother.

1916 Birth of Rose Jones, Madge's mother.

1921 Birth of Edward ('Ted') Richard Lenton, Madge's father.

1940 My parents, Percy and Norah are married

1945 Madge's parents Ted and Rose are married.

1947 Birth of Christopher Bicheno. (i.e. me!)
Bicheno family moves to No 1 Daulston Road.

1953 Birth of Madge Elizabeth Lenton, my wife.

1958 I go to school at St John's College, Southsea.

1964 I leave school and start work at the Southern Electricity Board.

1968 I join the Computer Department at the SEB.

1972 Madge and I meet for the first time at the Mecca dancehall.
Madge and I become engaged.

1972 I purchase 291 Chichester Road in Portsmouth.

1973 Madge and I are married.
      Madge and I move into 291 Chichester Road.

1975 Birth of Stephen, our first child.

1977 Birth of Emma, our second child.

1978 Madge and I move to 61 The Keep in Portchester.

1979 Birth of Richard, our third child.

1981 Birth of Michael, our fourth child.

1983 Birth of Alan, our fifth child.
      Madge and I move to 91B Hulbert Road in Havant

1986 Birth of Marie, our sixth child.

1993 Monty born, our first dog.

1994 Tasha born, our second dog.

1996 Daisy born, our third dog.

1999 Birth of Chloe, our first grandchild.
      Birth of Lauren, our second grandchild.

2001 Birth of Lewis, our third grandchild.
      I retire from work at Scottish and Southern Energy.

2003 Birth of Jessica, our fourth grandchild.
      My Book 'Jumping in Cowpats' is published.

INDEX

Abercrombie Street, 95
Aboyeur, 14
Adams, Sarah, 8
Adrigole, 1, 37
Aitchison, Alex, 176
Albion Street, 89
Alpine Sprite, 340
Anaheim, 187
Andy, 43, 68, 70
Arthur, 210
Ashbourne, 96, 97, 99
Austin 10, 325
Austin Montego, 333
Baffins Pond, 18, 29, 44, 107
Bansal, Gurmel, 190, 191, 193
Bashley Park, 339
Baynes, Edith, 7
BCS, 180
Bechinoe, 5
Bedford, 280
Bedhampton, 37, 145, 211, 281, 282
Beecheno, 5
Beechenow, 4, 5
Bellinger, Ron, 177, 178, 184
Bennett, Betty, 40
Bernadette, 42
Berney, John, 201, 202, 203, 204, 207
Bernie, 210
Bertha, 259, 260
Bicheno, Alan, iii, 22, 143, 144, 145, 148, 149, 151, 176, 234, 241, 244, 245, 247, 263, 264, 265, 295, 321, 334, 335, 347
Bicheno, Alf, 10, 15, 16, 38
Bicheno, Alfie, 19
Bicheno, Arthur, ix, 13, 14, 28, 29, 32, 90, 346
Bicheno, Betty (Barton), 26, 27, 28, 40
Bicheno, Bill, 15
Bicheno, Bill (b1923), v, 15, 16, 17, 20, 21, 22, 32, 38, 50, 174
Bicheno, Brenda (Tomkinson), v, 24, 28, 32
Bicheno, Charles, 19
Bicheno, Charlie (b1894), 12, 15
Bicheno, Christopher, 4, 346
Bicheno, Dennis, 28
Bicheno, Edward (b1582), 6
Bicheno, Edward (b1616), 7
Bicheno, Elsie (b1927), 23, 24, 32

Bicheno, Emma (Hine), iii, 135, 136, 137, 141, 142, 143, 144, 150, 151, 152, 162, 163, 169, 171, 213, 214, 236, 237, 238, 239, 241, 243, 245, 249, 251, 252, 253, 254, 255, 320, 329, 330, 334, 335, 341, 347
Bicheno, Frances (Weighell), 36, 42, 43, 44, 45, 54, 68, 79, 240, 256, 257, 326
Bicheno, James (b1650), 7
Bicheno, James (b1693), 7
Bicheno, James (b1752), 9
Bicheno, James (b1886), 14
Bicheno, James Ebenezer (b1785), 9, 10, 345
Bicheno, Jim, v, 12, 19, 20, 21, 22, 29, 30, 32, 194, 206
Bicheno, John (b1525), 6
Bicheno, Joseph (b1782), 9, 11
Bicheno, Liz (Hardman), 20
Bicheno, Mabel (b1926), 14, 17, 23, 32, 113
Bicheno, Madge (Lenton), iii, v, vii, ix, xi, 17, 23, 30, 31, 40, 42, 43, 47, 57, 59, 60, 61, 62, 63, 64, 65, 67, 68, 69, 72, 73, 75, 76, 78, 79, 80, 81, 82, 83, 84, 88, 89, 90, 92, 95, 97, 98, 99, 100, 101, 103, 104, 105, 106, 107, 108, 109, 110, 111, 112, 113, 114, 115, 116, 133, 134, 135, 136, 137, 138, 139, 140, 141, 142, 143, 144, 145, 146, 147, 148, 149, 150, 151, 152, 153, 154, 155, 156, 157, 158, 159, 160, 161, 162, 167, 169, 170, 171, 172, 173, 181, 186, 187, 198, 204, 205, 206, 208, 209, 210, 211, 212, 213, 214, 232, 234, 235, 236, 237, 238, 239, 240, 241, 242, 243, 245, 246, 247, 248, 250, 251, 252, 258, 259, 260, 261, 262, 266, 267, 268, 271, 272, 274, 275, 277, 278, 279, 280, 281, 283, 284, 285, 286, 287, 288, 289, 290, 291, 295, 296, 298, 299, 300, 305, 307, 308, 309, 310, 312, 316, 317, 318, 319, 320, 321, 322, 323, 324, 325, 326, 327, 328, 329, 330, 331, 332, 333, 334, 336, 337, 338, 339, 340, 341, 342, 343, 344, 346, 347
Bicheno, Margaret, v, 2, 33, 35, 39, 40, 41, 42, 43, 44, 45, 46, 50, 54, 63, 76, 79

Bicheno, Marie, iii, 35, 99, 144, 152, 156, 208, 210, 211, 245, 246, 247, 248, 264, 265, 268, 271, 276, 295, 300, 321, 335, 347
Bicheno, Marlene (Browne), 22
Bicheno, Mary (Castle), 22
Bicheno, Mary Theresa, 35
Bicheno, Mike, 79, 80, 88, 97, 102, 103, 104, 107, 110, 142, 143, 148, 149, 151, 240, 241, 242, 243, 244, 245, 247, 249, 260, 261, 262, 263, 264, 265, 295, 296, 320, 321, 334, 335, 342
Bicheno, Norah (Mum) (Crowley), 31, 33, 34, 35, 36, 37, 38, 39, 40, 42, 346
Bicheno, Richard, iii, 5, 6, 7, 51, 60, 83, 88, 89, 91, 101, 104, 105, 106, 141, 142, 144, 155, 157, 171, 172, 234, 239, 240, 241, 244, 247, 250, 320, 321, 335, 345, 346, 347
Bicheno, Richard (b1550), 6
Bicheno, Rita, 18
Bicheno, Stephen, iii, 134, 135, 136, 141, 142, 144, 145, 148, 156, 181, 208, 234, 235, 236, 237, 240, 241, 261, 304, 320, 329, 335, 336, 338, 347
Bicheno, Wally, 15
Bicheno, William (b1723), 8
Biddlesden Abbey, 5
Billy Line, 95
BIM (CMI), 188
Birchenhoe, 5, 345
Bishopmill, 46, 47
Blackley, Dorothy, 7
Blenheim Palace, 27
Bloxham, John, 58, 59, 60, 61, 62
BMC Software, 200
Bognor Regis, 333
Booth, Paul, 195, 196, 206
Bottisham, 7
Bowen, Jill, 191, 193, 196, 197, 206
Bowie, Adam, 196, 202
Bradshaw, Pat, 198
Bransbury Park, 22, 24
Brean, 79, 82
Bremner, Iain, 199
Brent Knoll, 81
Brichener, 5, 6
Bricheno, 5
Brickwall, 234, 235, 336
Bridgwood, Mary, 97
Bristol, 194
British Empire Medal, 36
British Expeditionary Force, 96, 100

Brother Charles, 51
Bruges, 331, 333
Brunel, Isambard Kingdom, 86
Buckland, 31, 35, 37, 85
Buddy Holly, 50
BUPA, 163, 165, 169, 170
Burgess, Sharon, 171, 240
Butlins, 41, 143, 326
Byccenho, 5, 6, 345
Byrchenor, 5
Cade, Cheryl, 243
California, 187, 192
Cambridge, 4, 7, 8, 11
Can Alley Station Street, 97
Caravan Club, 336, 338
Carpenter, Josephine, v, 316, 323, 324, 328
Carroll Levis, 38
Castle Street, 140, 141
Castle, Fred, 22
Chicago, 192
Chichester, 26, 236, 337, 340
Chichester Road, 66, 81, 133, 140, 145, 152, 239, 258, 325, 346, 347
Christchurch, 23, 24, 32
Cleverly, Steve, 198
Clokes Menswear, 210
Clough, Neville, 191, 193
Coat-of-Arms, 15
Cockerills, 210
Colbourne, Beatrice Martha, 84, 89, 90, 346
Colbourne, Frazie, 93, 96, 97, 100, 101
Colbourne, Fred, 90, 91
Colbourne, George Kervell, 89
Colbourne, Martha, 90
Colbourne, Martha Beatrice, 83
Coleman, Archie, 18
Collings, Richard, 193
Colosseum, 161
Columbo, 176
Colwell Road, 93
Copnor, 31, 42, 66, 79
Corpus Christi, 41, 43, 51
Corsa, 161, 331, 334, 342
Cosham, 15, 16, 33, 38, 87, 93, 94, 101, 102, 211
Count, 4, 162
Countess, 162
Cowplain, 19, 340
Cox, Elayne, 186
Critchett, 35
Crookhorn, 43, 211

350

Cross Street, 92
Crowe, Russell, 161
Crowley, Ada, 37, 38, 39, 40
Crowley, Dorothy (Dilly), 7, 37, 38, 40, 174
Crowley, Math, 37
Crowley, Matthew, 37, 38, 39, 40, 42
Crowley, Vera (Seager), 37, 38, 40
Dad (Percy), 19, 23, 29, 31, 33, 41, 45, 46, 47, 48, 49, 73, 240, 257, 325, 326, 327
Daisy, iii, vii, 97, 256, 269, 286, 287, 288, 289, 290, 291, 292, 293, 294, 295, 297, 298, 299, 300, 301, 303, 304, 305, 306, 307, 308, 309, 310, 347
Daley, Dave, 177
Datsun Bluebird, 235, 327, 336, 337, 340
Daulston Road, 35, 36, 39, 40, 43, 44, 45, 346
Davidson, Emily, 14
D-Day, 22, 35
Dean, Jenny, 183, 185, 196, 207
Des O'Connor, 154
Devereux, Matt, 190, 192, 193, 194, 195, 197, 198, 199, 200, 201, 202, 205
Dilley, Bill, 174
Disneyland, 78, 187
Dockyard, 14, 15, 17, 20, 34, 45, 85, 86, 87, 88, 91, 92, 93, 95, 96
Dolly, 250, 266, 267, 268, 291, 292
Dorset Dairy, 31
Dover, 17, 78, 274, 331
Dover Road, 17
Druids Lodge, 14
Dunton, Dave, 185
Earley, Trevor, 102
Eastern Road, 18
Eastney, 19, 24, 31
Eaton, Mike, 198
Edgar, Pete, 198
Edney, Paul, 197
EDP, 179
El Alamein, 34
Elayne, Cox, 186
Elgin, 46, 47
Emsworth, 157, 260
Epsom Derby, 14
Evans, 20
Evans, John, 199
Eye and Ear Hospital, 209
Falk, Peter, 176
Fareham, 110, 139, 336
Fareham House, 110
Farmer, Carol, 197

Farmer, Neil, 185, 197
Farmer, Rodney, 182, 197
Fawlty, Basil, 329
Fearn, Annie, 96
Fiat 126, 327, 329, 340
Fiat Uno, 335
Finch, Terry, 203
Flossie, 260
Flower, Elinor, 7
Forbes, Alistair, 200
Ford Escort, 111, 115, 325, 326, 335
Ford Fiesta, 335
Ford Mondeo, 333, 335
Foster, Amos, 16, 17, 29
France, 8, 95, 100, 158, 237, 340
Fred (Rabbit), 49, 256, 257, 258
Frederick Street, 89
Freemantle House, 110
Freeston, Roger, 191, 193
Fryer, Percy, 14
Fudge, 250, 266, 267, 268, 291
Gartshore, Dr Philip, 191
Gary, 192
Gerry Springer, 72, 273
Gibraltar, 12, 13
Gizmo, 258, 259
Glenda, 111
Glover Street, 8, 12
Gosport, 35, 87, 91, 327
Green, Richard, 197, 206
Groucho Marx, 322
Groundhog Day, 332
Grover, Lisa, 202, 206
Guards, 209, 210
Gunwharf, 17
Haddenham, 8
Hall, Liz, 198, 205
Hambledon House, 110, 208
Hampshire County Council, 214
Hampshire Street, 35, 38, 45, 50, 88
Hampshire Telegraph, 86, 90, 92
Hanley, Elizabeth, 7
Hanover Street, 88, 90
Hard, The, 86
Harding, Steve, 199, 200, 202, 203, 207
Hatfield Road, 17, 18
Hatton Garden, 161
Havant, 151, 154, 157, 176, 177, 178, 193, 194, 200, 234, 236, 238, 278, 309, 316, 318, 320, 340, 347
Hawke Street, 90
Hayling Island, 95, 284
Hemington (b1819), 10, 11, 12, 345

Herstmonceux, 41
Hillary, Sir Edmund, 45
Hillman, Christine, 20, 59, 60, 61, 62, 111, 209, 210
Hills, Alice, 11
Hindry, Mark, 190, 191, 196
Hine, Chloe, 171, 213, 239, 249, 250, 252, 253, 347
Hine, Jessica, 171, 238, 255, 347
Hine, Lewis, 14, 171, 214, 238, 239, 251, 252, 253, 254, 255, 347
Hine, Wayne, 137, 171, 239, 251, 252, 253, 255
HMS Bulwark, 35
HMS Eagle, 35
HMS Formidable, 34
HMS Illustrious, 35
Hobart, 10
Honda CJ250, 320, 321
Honda Melody, 317, 320
Honda Superdream, 318, 319, 320, 321
Horndean, 44
Houdini, 288
Hulbert Road, 145, 153, 188, 347
Hurford, Eddie, 174
Hursley, 194, 240
Hyundai Coupe, 334
I.T, 179, 184, 186, 188, 189, 190, 191, 192, 193, 195, 196, 197, 198, 199, 200, 201, 202, 203, 204, 207, 238
IBM, 190, 192, 193, 194, 195, 199, 200, 239, 240
ICL, 183
Indiana, 192
Ireland, 1, 37, 70, 326
Jamieson, Alan, 185
Jonathan, 42
Jones, Charles, 96
Jones, Frances, 96
Jones, Lilly, 96
Jones, Madge, 96
Jones, Phil, 42, 191, 193, 196, 197, 204, 206
Jones, William, 97
Kay, Stan, 188, 189, 190
Kensington Road, 37, 39, 42
Kilmiston Street, 88
Knight, Mark, 194
Kniveton, 96
Kowazaki ZXR 400, 320
Lada, 325, 326, 327
Landguard Road, 16, 17, 32
Lawson, Jennifer, 105, 106, 323

Lenton, Annette (Orriss), 101
Lenton, Beatrice Martha, 83, 84, 89, 90, 91, 92, 93, 94, 95, 101, 346
Lenton, Blidge, 94, 101
Lenton, Clara, 89
Lenton, Ellen Louisa, 89
Lenton, Ernie, 94, 101
Lenton, Francis, 89
Lenton, Frederick Arthur, 89, 93
Lenton, George, 89
Lenton, Hendy, 88
Lenton, Lyn (Earley), 79, 101, 102, 211
Lenton, Mike, 79, 97, 101, 102
Lenton, Richard, 97, 101, 108
Lenton, Richard (b1856), 88, 91, 346
Lenton, Rose (Jones), 79, 95, 96, 97, 98, 99, 100, 102, 103, 104, 105, 107, 108, 111, 260, 346
Lenton, Rose Letitia, 89
Lenton, Steve, 58, 97, 99, 102, 103, 104, 110
Lenton, Ted, 25, 80, 91, 94, 95, 96, 97, 98, 99, 100, 101, 102, 111, 327, 346
Littlehampton, 333
London, 9, 11, 12, 15, 27, 32, 53, 54, 56, 66, 95, 155, 156, 161, 177, 178, 185, 240, 322, 323, 335
Long, Sue, 198, 205
Lord Strathcona, 36
Los Angeles, 187
Lossiemouth, 41, 46, 325
Louise, 42, 102
Marble Mountain, 12
Matapan, 34
Maundy Money, 36
McClure, Jim, 194, 195
McGee, Jim, 199
Mecca, The, 58, 60, 62, 63, 111, 209, 346
Mengham, David, 186, 188, 189, 190, 194, 203, 333
Mensa, 53
Merwood, Dave, 177, 199, 200, 203, 205
Merwood, Tim, 182
Michelle, 42
Midul, 101
Milton, 5, 17, 22, 23, 60, 99, 100
Minehead, 143, 326
Monty, iii, vii, 55, 269, 273, 274, 275, 276, 277, 278, 279, 280, 281, 282, 283, 284, 285, 286, 287, 288, 289, 290, 291, 292, 293, 294, 295, 296, 297, 298, 299, 300, 301, 303, 304, 305, 306, 307, 308, 309, 310, 328, 342, 347

Moorfields, 155
Mudlark, 88
Munday, Albert, 49
Murphy, Sue, 197
Nancy Road, 16
Nanny, Nellie Bicheno (Foster), 14, 16, 17, 18, 19, 21, 22, 23, 24, 25, 26, 28, 29, 30, 32, 33, 49, 109, 134
Naz, 264
Nelson, Jean, v, 4, 9, 11
New Forest, 20, 198, 339
New Milton, 339
New Road, 316
NIPSCO, 192
Norland Road, 16
North Street, 92, 177, 197
Nova Scotia, 12
O'Toole, Paula, 202, 206
Oakdene, 339
Oaklands, 43, 211, 212, 246
Over, 4, 5, 6, 7, 8, 9, 10, 11, 12, 27, 44, 101, 109, 145, 172, 210, 276, 307, 345
Oxfam, 344
Park Grove, 33
Passalls, Mr, 174
Pearl, 111
Perth, 199
Petersfield, 21, 147, 326
Pleb, 263, 264
Plessey, 20
Pond's Cream, 139
Pond's People, 139
Poppy (Percy Bicheno (b1891)), 14, 15, 16, 17, 18, 21, 22, 23, 25, 28, 29, 30, 32, 33, 49, 346
Portchester, 18, 140, 234, 347
Portsea, 83, 84, 85, 86, 87, 88, 90, 91, 92, 93, 94, 95, 96, 106, 111
Portsmouth, x, 12, 13, 16, 17, 18, 19, 21, 22, 23, 25, 26, 29, 31, 33, 35, 36, 37, 39, 40, 41, 42, 43, 44, 45, 51, 52, 58, 60, 66, 79, 83, 84, 85, 88, 89, 91, 93, 94, 95, 96, 97, 99, 101, 102, 104, 105, 107, 136, 138, 139, 140, 143, 157, 184, 238, 240, 243, 244, 245, 255, 316, 327, 346
Pratt, Ged, 139, 197
Purchase, Alan, 176, 177
Queen Alexandra Hospital, 103, 137, 168, 319
Queen Elizabeth II, 36, 45, 105
Queen Street, 45, 85, 86, 88, 91, 92, 93, 95
Queen Victoria, 23

Radio Victory, 143
Railway View, 105, 110
Ray, 210
Reginald Road, 19, 23
Rex, Jane, 89
Rockley Sands, 50
Rogers, Gordon, 177, 178, 181, 182, 183
Rome, 158, 161
Ron (b1930), v, 23, 24, 25, 26, 27, 28, 180
Royal Yacht, 14
Salisbury, 14, 84, 88, 91, 346
Saville, Jimmy, 22
Scotland, 41, 43, 46, 47, 48, 51, 200, 325, 333
Scottish Hydro-Electric, 198
Scutt, John, 16
SEB, 173, 174, 176, 316, 346
SEC, 245
Selborne, 316
Selsey, 340
SESA, 138
Shana, 101
Sharon, 59, 60, 111
Sherlock Holmes, 13, 149
Silverstone, 5
Simpson Road, 33, 35, 45
Simpson, Homer, 110
Snow, Louisa Palmer, 88
Southampton Hospital, 252, 254
Southern Electric, 190, 192, 193, 197, 212, 238, 243, 245
Southern Electricity Board, 55, 139, 173, 346
Southsea, 16, 17, 22, 25, 36, 42, 44, 51, 80, 92, 100, 101, 103, 209, 210, 346
Sparrow, Mr, 252
Spurgin, Steve, 185
St John's College, 42, 51, 346
St Joseph's, 31, 41, 78, 79, 154
St Mary's Hospital, 99, 134, 135, 164, 165, 249, 251, 252, 255
St Paul's Road, 96, 97
St Peter's, 159
St Swithun's, 51
St Sylvester's, 41, 46
St Thomas More's, 149, 211, 212, 213, 214, 238, 246
St Trinian's, 107
Stone Street, 16
Stumpy, 262, 263, 264, 265
Suzuki GSX600, 318
Suzuki RSX, 317
SWALEC, 192

353

Swayne, Martha, 90
SWEB, 192
Swift Danette, 341, 342
Swift Dannette, 337
Syresham, 5
Tangier Road, 18, 44
Tarzan, 154
Tasha, iii, vii, 168, 269, 272, 281, 282, 283, 284, 285, 286, 287, 288, 289, 290, 291, 292, 293, 294, 295, 296, 297, 298, 299, 300, 301, 303, 304, 306, 307, 308, 309, 310, 313, 347
Tasmania, 10, 345
Taylor, Mark, 185
Tee, Brian, 185
The Keep, 140, 142, 146, 152, 239, 327, 347
Thomson, Isobel, 189, 203
Tibbles, 48
Tickner, Jim, 162, 193, 194, 206
Tilman, Elizabeth, 7
Titanic, 14
Titchfield House, 110
Tomkinson, Bob, 28
Tovary, Mr, 174
Trafalgar, 9
Trixie, 49
Twyford Avenue, 210
Tyson, 264
Universal Studios, 187
Vatican, 161
Vauxhall Nova, 11, 12, 335
Vauxhall Wyvern, 325

Vince, John, 197, 206
Vorderman, Carol, 53
VW Golf, 335
Wakeland, Julian, 196, 206
Warren (b1852), 11, 12, 13, 14, 16, 22, 345, 346
Warren, Jim, 197, 206
Waterlooville, 42, 43, 139, 317
Webster, Eileen, v, 4, 9, 11
Webster, Fred, 178, 184
Weighell, Ron, 44
Weld, Tony, 23
West Highland White Terrier, 272
Westie, 113, 147, 148, 273, 274, 275, 279, 280, 281, 283, 284, 285, 286, 290, 293, 294, 295, 298, 302, 305, 306, 308, 309, 310, 311, 344
We-Used-to-be-Good, 139
White's Row, 86, 89
Whittlewood, 5, 345
Wilkinson, Sarah, 7
Williams, John, 203
Williamson, Ellen, 15
Wood, Mr, 174
Woodhart, Peter, 159, 176, 184, 185, 186, 188, 198, 201, 202
Woolas, Mr, 163, 169, 170
Wrights Newsagents, 208
Yamaha XJ600, 320
Yates, Eric, 180, 181, 182, 183, 185
Youngs, William, 14
Zeppelin, 15

Printed in the United Kingdom
by Lightning Source UK Ltd.
117828UK00001B/4